EAST
OF ECSTASY

A HEARTS OF THE ANEMOI NOVEL

EAST

OF ECSTASY

A HEARTS OF THE ANEMOI NOVEL

LAURA KAYE

Entangled Publishing, LLC
2614 South Timberline Road
Suite 109
Fort Collins, CO 80525
Visit our website at www.entangledpublishing.com.

Edited by Heather Howland
Cover design by Heather Howland

Ebook ISBN   978-1-62266-128-2
Print ISBN   978-1-62266-127-5

Manufactured in the United States of America

First Edition April 2014

You are good.

You are worthy.

You are beautiful.

You are lovable.

Never doubt it for even a single second.

CHAPTER ONE

Devlin Eston paced the length of the dark space wondering what the fuck he was supposed to do now. No allies. No plan. And precious little hope.

The world had no idea it was standing on the precipice of disaster. Nor that Devlin was the main thing that stood between humanity and a madman bent on power and destruction. And that was probably a good thing. The idea that Devlin was *anyone's* best hope for salvation was almost laughable—his own brothers could testify to that. Which was why he'd been camped out in an abandoned building in the middle of nowhere Maryland for the past twenty-four hours trying to get his emotions under control.

Devlin had an anger management problem of divine proportions. Literally. When he got mad, things caught on fire, blew up, or got fried by electricity. You'd think the fact that he was a rain god would provide a counterbalance to his pyrotechnics, but having the power to put the fire out didn't negate the damage he caused in the first place. He'd already firebombed one hideout, which was why he was here now.

Trying to get his shit together. His heart raced like he was in the middle of a fight, his muscles braced for attack or defense, and his hands burned with preternatural energy just waiting to be called forth.

Problem was, he didn't have good control over himself and he couldn't just calm down because he wanted to.

Not since his grandfather Aeolus, the god of storms and ruler of the winds, conducted what amounted to a divine science experiment on him—with Devlin's full cooperation—a few weeks before. Without question, drinking of the infernal rivers Styx and Phlegethon had given Devlin destructive powers—powers they needed to have a shot at taking out Devlin's evil father, Eurus, who in recent months had earned the top spot on Olympus's number one most-wanted list for a string of crimes against both gods and man. Even worse, since Eurus had stolen Aeolus's Firestone ring six months before—the one that had allowed the storm god to rule and control the Anemoi for most of their existence—Eurus had become too damn strong for the others to successfully fight.

Which was why Devlin had agreed to drink a cocktail of the Underworld variety. After all, of any of them, he had nothing to lose and the most to gain. Namely, freedom for himself and his youngest brother.

And it'd seemed he and his grandfather had been on to something. In those rare moments when Devlin could harness the new gifts the magical waters had given him, he was as powerful as his grandfather. In training to control and master the fire and lightning storms inside him, Devlin had occasionally even bested Aeolus, the strongest storm god of them all. But imbibing the hatred of the Styx and the fire of the Phlegethon had made him volatile. Unstable. Dangerous.

Even more than a lifetime of paternal abuse had already made him.

Now, the foreign energy inside him felt like a car that would suddenly jolt from zero to eighty without Devlin having ever stepped on the gas. And, once the energy spiked, the brakes failed every damn time.

Devlin's emotions were so out of control right now because he'd been outed as a traitor to his father, putting his remaining brother in even greater danger, and yet the rest of his family continued to mistrust and suspect him of secret loyalty to his father. Well, all except his grandfather. But, for the most part, Devlin was damned any way he sliced it.

It had all come to a head two nights ago, when he'd tried to warn his grandfather and his Anemoi uncles that his father, Eurus, Supreme God of the East Wind and Autumn, was preparing to attack them. Animosity had always separated Eurus from his brothers in the north, south, and west, but in the past year, the fraternal feuds among the Anemoi gods had escalated into actual attacks. First, this past spring when Eurus abducted and nearly killed Ella, mate of the West Wind's Zephyros, and second, just days ago when Eurus employed the screeching birdlike Harpies to ambush all the Anemoi after what was supposed to have been a secret meeting deep inside the Rock of Gibraltar. The North Wind's Boreas and the South Wind's Chrysander had both been injured that time, while Devlin had been chained helplessly to the mountaintop by his father's invisible but inescapable will. A forced witness to Eurus's evil. Again. So maybe Devlin shouldn't have been surprised that, instead of a little damned gratitude for taking the risk to warn them before Eurus's third attack, he'd gotten a big steaming pile of suspicion and accusation.

Suspicion that no doubt grew after one of his uncles was killed in the battle that followed his warning. Boreas, Supreme God of the North Wind and Winter, had died in a fight that had raged so furiously Devlin could still feel it in the air around him. Devlin didn't know exactly how Boreas had died except that, without question, it had been his father's fault. Which meant it would be a very cold day in Hades before the Anemoi would ever be willing to fight beside Devlin, guilty by the accident of his birth.

Devlin would have to figure it out on his own. Just like always. Somehow.

Blowing out a long breath, he braced his hands on a dusty counter and let his head hang on his shoulders. Rain fell in a steady metallic *shh* on the barn's old roof, and Devlin tried to concentrate on the clean white noise and nothing else. Over the past few weeks, Aeolus had been secretly training him in various focus and visualization techniques to help him develop the discipline he needed to master the unnatural powers now flowing through him. They'd done it in secret to protect Devlin from his father, maintain the element of surprise in their new weapon—meaning him, and because Aeolus feared that his Anemoi sons wouldn't trust Devlin enough to give him the chance to help. Given Devlin's reception before the battle, it looked as if Aeolus had been right.

Which really pissed Devlin off.

Sparks of electricity sizzled in the air around him.

Focus, damnit. Right. *Breathe. Push everything else aside.* The sound of the autumn rainstorm—a storm he'd unleashed to release some of the overflowing energy inside him—calmed him, slowly but surely easing the tension from his shoulders and jaw. Devlin closed his eyes and began the mental warfare necessary to clear his mind of thought, of image, of emotion.

And it *was* warfare. Because Devlin bore the weight of so much guilt, sometimes he could barely stand on his own two feet. An image flashed into his mind's eye. His middle brother, Farren, begging for his life. Devlin flinched and pushed the sounds and pictures away. Farren's blood running freely down his back, from where a dagger had been buried into his heart from behind. A strangled groan as Devlin fought to clear that one away, too. Sweat beaded on his brow and the counter squeaked and cracked under the pressure of his hands. A field of black opened up on the insides of his eyelids, a little at a time, and a little more, until he was staring at blessed, empty nothingness.

The rain on the roof. The in/out of his breathing. The blackness.

Light and color edged into his visual field. *No! Hold it!* Devlin pushed it back, shaking and grunting as though he fought against a physical thing.

The image won. Alastor. His youngest brother. His *only* brother, now. In solitude. In danger. Imprisoned. His torture was punishment for Devlin's challenging Eurus's authority and insurance that it wouldn't happen again, just as Farren's death had been.

And now Eurus knew Devlin was working against him…

Fire flashed out of Devlin's hands, singeing and melting the Formica counter in front of him.

Devlin jumped back and unleashed a damp wind that smothered the fire before it truly caught, and then a harder gust to disperse the smoke altogether. "Fuck!" he roared, knotting his fingers in the hair on the top of his head, pulling on the length to make it hurt. Just at the point that his scalp stung so bad Devlin half expected clumps of hair to come free in his hands, some of the stress and tension melted out of him. What kind of twisted did you have to be to find pain calming? Problem was, he hadn't found anything else that came close to focusing him and calming the chaos of his mind.

When he was mostly sure he'd driven the fire back, he dropped his hands. The fingers on his left hand brushed the denim over the spiked band of the cilice he'd worn on his thigh since Farren's death. It was a small sacrifice to mourn someone whose death he'd caused, though unlike the saints and clerics of old, Devlin had no expectation that the physical mortification would lead to redemption. Not for someone like him.

Damnit! His lethal powers were of no use to anyone if he couldn't master them.

Devlin needed a way to center himself, to set aside the soul-deep desire for vengeance and eons of rage—both his own innate rage and that amplified by the infernal rivers—so he could focus, concentrate, and do the job that needed done. The job that, since Aeolus had lost the Firestone ring that allowed him to control the winds, only Devlin could do.

Kill Eurus. Kill his own father.

Doing so would solve so many problems. Save so many lives. And free him and his brother once and for all.

Headlights swung across the curtained front windows of his refuge and the soft rumble of a car engine moved down one side of the building. Devlin cursed as the sound came to a halt around back and a car door slammed. Sparks of electricity sizzled in the air around him. As keys jingled at the rear door, Devlin dematerialized, hoping the intrusion would be brief. He'd thought this place was abandoned when he chose it, but if he'd been wrong, he'd have to relocate. He couldn't take the risk of—

A small hooded figure rushed in from the rain, spilling a stream of gray light across the concrete floor before securing the door behind her. On a counter by the door, she dumped keys, a bag, and the hooded jacket, then turned, revealing a woman who appeared his opposite in every way. Petite where he was tall. Soft where he was hard. Nearly white hair where his was jet black. In fact, she was so pale that only a flush on her cheeks and a bit of makeup around her eyes gave her any color.

The woman froze and looked around, her nose wrinkling as if she smelled something bad. The fire. Directing his energy behind her, the door she'd just come through whipped open, and as the woman gasped and turned, Devlin cycled a gust of air through the space to cleanse it of the last of the smell.

In a lithe movement, she dashed to the opening and grasped the handle, tugging it against the wind. "Damn wind," she muttered when she finally secured it again.

The curse was almost amusing. He was damned, all right.

In his invisible wind form, he moved closer, close enough to see that her eyes were as pale as her hair. An unusual light gray.

Devlin flinched. For a moment her coloring so reminded him of Boreas, with the Northern god's white hair and silver eyes, that he thought she must be some sort of wraith sent here to exact vengeance against all those associated with the East Wind. Though Devlin hadn't been present when Eurus killed Boreas, he wouldn't be surprised to learn his Anemoi brethren were hunting him now as they were his father.

Just once in his life he'd like to not have to be looking over his shoulder in preparation for attack from those who *ought* to be on his side.

Whatthefuckever. Electricity rippled over his being.

The woman yelped and pressed herself back into the counter behind her. For a long moment, her gaze zeroed in on the exact spot where Devlin's energy coalesced...as if she could see him in his elemental form. Even more shocking than that possibility was the fact that her gaze shifted from fear to wonder. She slowly reached out her hand toward him.

Devlin bolted. Instantly, he removed himself to the loft above her, wondering what the hell had just happened. He was about to flee the place altogether when the woman spoke.

"I must be going crazy," the woman muttered. "Okay, deep breaths, Anna," she said.

Anna. The name was pure and innocent and *normal*, but her words seemed to indicate she had in fact seen *something*. And that made Devlin curious...suspicious...intent on finding out how the hell a human could perceive him in his elemental form.

Downstairs, a door opened and lights flickered on, spilling a yellow glow into the dark main room below and pulling him from his thoughts. Small sounds reached his ears. Footsteps, the movement of objects, Anna talking to herself. Suddenly, music blared, flooding the near-silence with a driving rock song, and ratcheting up Devlin's curiosity about the woman's activities.

He shouldn't waste the time to see what she was doing. But a part of him needed confirmation that she hadn't seen him, needed to *see* that she was normal with his own two eyes, needed to know she wasn't yet another threat. So, in his elemental form, he found himself returning to the first floor and peering in the room into which she'd gone—

Devlin didn't know what to look at first. The beautiful woman, the racks of art, or the paintings lined up along the floor?

The woman drew his attention first. She'd removed her button-down shirt and now stood in a pair of cutoff shorts and a lacy white tank top that highlighted every one of her curves. She'd also kicked off her sandals and secured the length of her hair in a messy knot held in place by two thin paintbrushes. With her bared neck, arms, and legs, she was showing a dizzying amount of skin, making Devlin notice just how delicate and feminine she was. Pretty. Ethereal, even. Normal and human, to be sure, but still remarkable.

Too good for him. Then again, who wasn't?

Not that he was interested.

He dragged his gaze away to the paintings that filled every space in the room, their bright colors clamoring for his attention. They covered the floor, the walls, large metal racks. A series featuring autumn trees in full color against an urban backdrop caught his eye. She'd depicted the death of his season with such grandeur…

Then he noticed the *other* paintings.

Despite his lack of corporeality, tension shot through him as he moved around a table full of paints Anna stood preparing to the far side of the large rectangular room. These paintings were nothing like the others. Chaotic, violent, almost apocalyptic in color and dynamic and tone.

Six in all. Some broad panoramas. Some narrow studies. All featuring a dark being—a man—wielding immense power over nature at their center.

A very familiar man. Exactly *how* familiar was the only thing he couldn't tell.

Ice-cold foreboding crawled up Devlin's spine.

He turned and approached Anna. Slowly. His instincts back to assessing who she was. *What* she was. What kind of a threat she posed.

Should he investigate her and her strange paintings? Because he didn't have time for anything unrelated to defeating his father. The autumn equinox was in just eight sunrises and marked the day upon which Eurus would come into his full seasonal powers. If somebody didn't take him out before then, he'd be nearly invincible until the new Supreme God of the North Wind, Boreas's adoptive son, Owen, came to power in late December.

By then, it would probably be too late. No, given Eurus's evil and ambition, it would *definitely* be too late.

So Devlin couldn't afford to miss this window of opportunity. Hades, *the world*, couldn't afford for him to miss it. He needed to get his head out of his ass and get himself under control. Like, yesterday.

With intense focus and a fast hand, she added a few details to a rough sketch of a scene on the canvas. Her new painting was to be like the others, then, with the dark man at the center once more.

Devlin studied the woman's face, his mind a whirl of questions and anger.

Were the images of him or his father? What exactly was it that the images depicted? And why in the name of the gods would this human be painting either of them?

Devlin glared. Like he needed another mystery to solve when his own head, his own emotions, his own body, felt like a foreign country.

All he knew was the bone-deep certainty that he had to stay. Had to see what this image became. Had to see how it fit in with the others she'd already done.

From his position behind her, Devlin watched as Anna stood back from the canvas and stared at it, tilting her head as if assessing it. For a long moment, she was perfectly still, the only sounds in the room the loud, angsty rock music against the even drumming of the rain on the roof. Then she selected a paintbrush from a rack holding dozens in all shapes and sizes and leaned in over a palette with maybe a dozen globs of thick paint.

Was it possible she'd met his father? Heat ripped through Devlin's essence, but he fought against yet another knee-jerk response. No, couldn't be. Eurus viewed humans as little better than the mud on the bottom of his shoe. Then how—

The question died in his throat as Anna hovered her brush over the palette and the paints began to glow. With a shaking hand, Anna dipped her brush in the dark-blue paint, stepped to the canvas, and began to add color to the expanse of white. And the glow of the blue followed her like a sheer ribbon, streaking through the air, emanating from the brush, washing across the canvas. Darker, even, than the blue had appeared on the palette.

What in the name of Hades?

She worked painstakingly slow at first, and then faster. Precise strokes sometimes gave way to slashes of the brush against the canvas. The red, the orange, the teal blue, the white, the yellow. Each glowed darkly as if she were painting with light. Devlin watched, stunned and awed and suspicious as all hell as the image came together—the image of a man hovering in the sky in front of a massive dark and roiling supercell thunderstorm. The painting itself appeared nearly three-dimensional, the colors were so dynamic and vibrant upon the canvas.

There is nothing normal about this woman.

The thought immediately snapped him out of the stupor the human's unexpected capacity for magic had caused and opened his senses. Divine energy. Subtle but unquestionably there. And coming from *her*. From Anna.

But it wasn't his father's. Eurus hadn't been here, hadn't been around her, hadn't marked her with his malicious unluckiness.

Devlin moved closer, poised for attack or defense as circumstances warranted. *Who are you, little human? And exactly who are you related to?*

Because this changed everything. Knowing this woman had a god swimming around somewhere in her gene pool meant there was *no way* these paintings were coincidence. Which meant he had to get answers to the questions ricocheting through his mind. Why was she painting these? Who gave her the information on him or his father? To what end? And what did she intend to do with the paintings?

As he watched, Anna used a thin knife to carve texture into the thick paint. Her concentration was absolute and made her even more beautiful, paint smudges on her cheeks and all. And the fact that he devoted even an ounce of energy to appreciating her appearance only escalated the agitation clawing through his gut. Because he didn't fucking have time for another mystery, even if it came wrapped up in such a cute, tight little package.

Part of him wanted to materialize and confront her now.

But another part argued that he should let her finish the painting first. The image she was bringing to life could be useful. His gaze drifted to the collection of finished paintings lining the far wall.

In one, either he or his father pinned two glowing beings against the front of a building engulfed in flames. In another, one of them marshaled ocean waves that grew bigger and bigger. The third stirred nausea in Devlin's gut—it depicted one of them badly burned and unconscious, or dead, in the middle of a burned-out field. Another had him or his father facing a trio of tornadoes as trees and debris whirled around the funnels. Devlin tilted his head to make sense of the next one. He wasn't sure if it depicted a crumbling wall or ceiling, but through it he could see a sky filled with beings—some glowing, some deathly black streaks. A battle? The last one was small and depicted the man in profile, his black hair plastered against the side of his face as if he were turning into a hard wind. Was this him or his father? Devlin stared at what he could make out of the face looking for clues, because, of course, he was just lucky enough to physically resemble the man he hated most in the world. Then he noticed the man's hand, raised as if shielding himself. And on one finger was a large golden ring with a red stone flanked by wings.

Aeolus's Firestone ring, the one Eurus had stolen.

So *this* painting was definitely of his father.

Devlin studied each of the images again, seeking out small details such as the ring, but on only one other—the man over the ocean—did he find a similar clue. He'd missed it the first time, but the dark man in that image clearly wore a long black cloak, similar enough to the long leather duster his father favored. That one was probably Eurus, too.

But what of the others?

Frustration roared through him.

The only thing Devlin knew was that none of these images were familiar to him. That is, none of them depicted events about which he had any knowledge. For the sake of argument, if none of the scenes in these paintings had ever happened before, then that meant...maybe nothing. Or, just maybe, it meant they were things *yet* to happen.

Which was way the hell out there.

"Not right," Anna muttered, frowning and shaking her head. Devlin's attention flashed back to her just as she raised her left hand and waved over the painting. Shock vibrated through Devlin as darkly shadowed striations appeared in the swirling clouds and the light underneath and behind the supercell took on a sickly green hue.

At the wave of her hand.

He came closer and peered at her face. Did she realize what she'd just done?

Anna shivered, but otherwise went to work again with the thin knife as if nothing unusual had happened. As if her paints weren't glowing and she hadn't just willed the light and shadow in her painting to do precisely what she wanted. As she resumed with the same frenetic intensity, it occurred to Devlin that she painted the way the music sounded — fast, loud, driving, intense.

All his attention focused on her, the comparison stirred something dark and needy deep inside him. He shut the urges down fast. Even if he allowed himself pleasure, which he didn't, now wasn't the time. Besides, magical and attractive or not, she was human. Mortal. Weak.

Over the next hour, Anna added depth and detail with layers of paint and occasional waves of her hand. The end result was spectacular in its realness and its horror as the threatening monstrosity of a cloud approached a small town, the lowest levels of the cloud jagged and craggy, like a giant fanged mouth swooping down from the heavens. Barely leashed power slithered through Devlin's energy as his concern and suspicion ratcheted higher.

When she finally finished, Anna shuddered and retreated from the painting. "What the hell?" she asked, her tone full of disbelief and fear.

Tension whirled through Devlin's being, now even more confused by the reaction to her own creation. There were too many unknowns here to let this situation go unresolved. And he had no more time to let it play out by itself.

He was going to have to confront her.

Chapter Two

Exhausted and strung out, Annalise Fallston stared at the painting, abject horror curdling her belly and crawling into her chest.

She'd painted a horrible, deadly storm right over Jarrettsville. Her hometown. Anna recognized the houses, the curve of the road, the Baptist church spire.

All of a sudden, nausea washed over Anna and the floor went wavy under her bare feet. She swayed and went down, catching herself on her hands and knees. Dread made it hard to breathe, and she sat the rest of the way on the floor, hugged her legs to her chest, and buried her face against her knees.

Why does this keep happening to me? Why won't these images leave me alone?

Painting had always been Anna's outlet, her refuge, her release. And her studio was *the* place where, in the safety of solitude, she could open up the well of creativity inside her mind and heart and let her truest self out. The one who, while painting, could see color despite her lifelong color blindness. The one who could bend color and light to her will with just a thought or a wave of her hand. Anna didn't understand why or how she could do these things, only that she never felt more alive than when she was painting. As a child, she'd quickly learned that no one believed she possessed these abilities, and it often left her feeling as if no one in the whole world truly knew who she was.

Which was why these new paintings bothered her so much.

Normally, painting gave her such joy and a much-needed jolt of energy and contentment.

These paintings did just the opposite.

The image for the first of the Dark Man paintings had come to her six days ago. Now, similar images were all she could see. When they came to her, they felt foreign, as if they'd been forced into her consciousness rather than from her own muse offering up an idea for inspiration. Also strange, nothing about the experience of painting *The Dark Man Amid Chaos* series felt natural to her—not the subject, not the way the paints talked to her while she painted, not the tone or feel of the finished image. Nor had she ever painted so fast. In the past week, she'd churned out six paintings, a small portrait and five larger scenes, going as far as pulling an all-nighter, which she never did—both because her father needed her and because it screwed with her health. Which, given how much her chronic fatigue syndrome had worsened lately, wasn't something she should be doing.

Even when she wasn't painting, Anna felt restless and distracted, as if the images were calling to her to attend to them. And when she painted, she felt almost manic with the need to commit the images to acrylic and canvas as fast as she could.

It had become a compulsion she didn't want, couldn't control, and had no idea how to end. Nothing about these paintings was normal. Not for her.

They left her feeling so drained, so hollow, so alone. Even more than her secrecy and CFS usually caused.

God, she was tired.

On a long sigh, she turned her head, still resting on her knees, and peered up at the painting. Technically, it was good, even if the subject was terrifying. Fantastic plays of light and shadow, and the clouds looked like they could come right out of the canvas. Her gaze settled on the dark man hovering in the sky. "Who are you?" she said. "And why do I keep seeing you?"

Suddenly, her scalp and neck prickled, the kind of sensation you got when someone stood too close to you in an elevator or seemed to be following you in a parking lot. Anna looked over her shoulder, but there was no one there.

Of course there wasn't.

"Stop freaking yourself out," she said out loud. But as much as she tried to dismiss the sensation, her mind resurrected the weird thing she'd seen right after she'd run into the studio from the rain. For less than an instant, she could've sworn swirls of light hovered in the air in front of her. When she'd first caught a glimpse of it from the corner of her eye, it had scared her so bad she couldn't breathe. But then the beauty of it filled her with awe. Just as quickly, it was gone again. If the whole incident had lasted four seconds, she'd be surprised.

Which meant it hadn't been real. Obviously a result of her eyes adjusting from the glaring light outside to the darkness inside. Or something.

Anger and resentment welled up inside her. *I refuse to be ruled by this anymore. Damnit.*

Hauling herself off the floor, she marched to the painting. With less care than she normally handled them, she lifted the canvas from the easel and carried it across the room. She leaned the back of it unceremoniously against one of the others in the series, grabbed a small clean canvas, and returned to her easel. Then she changed the music. Linkin Park could go to hell for all she cared. No more angry, angst-filled music about betrayal and loss and heartache. She cued up Cyndi Lauper's "Girls Just Want to Have Fun" with a *take that!* smile, then put it on repeat for good measure.

Despite her weariness, she forced her mind to focus on nothing but the mechanics of cleaning her brushes and changing palettes and paints for her new piece. Something bright and vibrant and full of the splendor of fall, perhaps. After all, depictions of nature were her favorite and the thing for which she'd garnered the most acclaim. She selected a brush and waited. The shades of brightness she normally saw to represent color transitioned into *actual* color and, as it always did, the change stole her breath in gratitude and awe.

This exact thing had been happening since the very first time she'd ever picked up a paintbrush as a child. At first it had bothered her that no one believed her, but soon she'd realized that hardly mattered when an otherwise colorless world came to life before her eyes. Now, all that mattered was the *color*. Because when you had monochromacy, the rarest form of color blindness, your world was black and white and gray. Most people with colorblindness struggled with the colors red and green, their vision differing from non-colorblindness because their brains interpreted the colors they couldn't see as others—red-blind people saw red as black, for example, and were unable to distinguish between blue and purple, and generally had difficulty distinguishing colors on the red-through-green spectrum.

But when she painted, Anna got the whole ROYGBIV spectrum and then some, and sometimes saw an even greater array of colors than she could find represented in paints.

And not only could she *see* the colors, but they'd talk to her, too, telling her which to use, how to use it, how to blend. Like now, when the gray and brown and sunburnt orange demanded to be blended. Suddenly she saw the subject of her painting. And it was gloriously refreshing.

The image that came to her was as if she were lying on a forest floor at the height of fall color. All around her, tree trunks soared to great heights like the columns of an ancient cathedral, and above her, leaves in every color formed a great domed ceiling, one made of nature's own stained glass. One spring break in college, she'd been lucky enough to go on a study tour of Paris, and as she pictured the color of the leaves against the bright sunlit sky, she was reminded of Sainte-Chappelle, a medieval Gothic church renowned for its towering stained-glass windows set amid narrow columns that looked too dainty to hold up the great ceiling.

What lovely inspiration. Nothing at all like the— No. She

wouldn't even let herself think about anything else.

Anna tilted her head back and closed her eyes, and for a long moment she imagined looking up at the treetops. When she had an image good and set in her mind's eye, she dipped her brush into the light sky blue and stepped to the canvas.

She started with the bright blues and warm yellows of the sky, putting that on as a base against which the trees would stand. Then, using the brown she'd mixed, she painted the tree trunks, working slowly to get their proportions as they got taller and taller just right. Once she got the leaves in, she'd come back and adjust the light to reflect the sunlight. Next, she used the edges of a medium brush to dab in the red-orange leaves, leaving gaps where the sun and the sky shone through.

All the while, Cyndi Lauper kept her company and her toes tapping.

Once she got the leaves filled in, it was time to start playing with the light. Some white and yellow on the leaf tips to show the light dappling the canopy. A light-gray edging to some of the tree trunks, and a thin line of white where the sun shone through. The effect was charming, but still not the vibrancy she saw in her mind's eye.

She worked at it again and again, layering, shading, highlighting, until she got it just right.

And then, she had it. It was beautiful and spirit-lifting and looked so damn real she wanted to stretch out on a carpet of needles and leaves and stare up at it while a fall breeze blew over her face. And, damn, she felt so much better than she had an hour ago. *This* was who she was. *This* was what she did.

It wasn't a masterpiece by any means, but the painting made Anna so happy she wanted to hug it. She wasn't gone, then. At least this part of her was still here.

And maybe, just maybe, that other part of her was done now. Maybe that was out of her system once and for all.

Still smiling, she turned to her worktable to clean her palette and brushes.

A man stood on the other side of the table.

No. Not a man. Not just any man. *The Dark Man*.

For a split second, Anna's throat locked down, leaving her unable to breathe or scream.

And then the scream pushed through and ripped out of her. She stumbled backward, her mind reeling, her heart pounding. Black eyes followed her progress, and he looked so damn real Anna thought she was going to have a heart attack.

"No, no, no," she cried. His mouth moved as if he planned to speak. "No!" she screamed. The room plunged into darkness, unleashing a moan from her throat and sending Anna's pulse into a wild sprint. Especially since what remained in the darkness was a pair of glowing eyes.

Anna turned and fled. Thankful that she'd always had better-than-average night vision, she managed to snag her purse and keys before she exploded out the back door and nearly dove into her Jeep. Her hands shook so bad it took her three tries to get the key in the ignition. The Jeep lurched into reverse, then she shifted gears and jammed her foot on the pedal.

The Dark Man appeared right in front of her hood. Anna screamed and veered, instinct guiding her to avoid hitting him. She clipped the corner of the building in a loud screech of metal against brick. She hit the brakes so hard she fishtailed in the gravel. Teeth chattering with adrenaline and fear, Anna looked in her rearview mirror, then over her shoulder, expecting to see a body laid out in the gravel. Nothing. She hopped out and peeked behind the Jeep, but there was nothing there. A gust of wind whipped her hair around her face.

How could there be nothing?

She jogged to the front of the Jeep and groaned. A dent and a series of deep white scratches ran for almost a foot along the side panel from the headlight, which was cracked but still lit.

Holy shit. What the hell just happened?

Anna had no clue, and she wasn't sticking around to find out. She got back in the Jeep and got the hell out of there.

At the first subdivision, Anna pulled off the road and came to rest under a streetlamp. She needed a minute to calm down and get her wits about her.

"Okay, Anna, what just happened?" she asked, looking at herself in the rearview mirror. "Be rational."

Right, rational. Well. She'd been painting the forest scene and been overjoyed at the idea that she'd painted something so normal. She'd hoped that meant she was done painting the Dark Man. And then she'd seen him right in front of her own eyes. Despite the fact that the air in the Jeep wasn't that cool, she shivered. The lights had gone out and she'd seen a pair of floating glowing eyes, like something right out of a spooky movie. And then the man had somehow made it outside and she'd driven through him but then he hadn't been there when she'd looked.

That about summed it up.

Still staring at herself, Anna yawned until her eyes watered. Her gaze dropped to the clock on the console. Nearly one in the morning.

Given the long nights painting, how drained she felt after wrenching these images out of her head and onto the canvas, and the all-nighter she'd pulled on Thursday, she was exhausted. And strung out. Plus, she really hadn't eaten much of the chili she'd made for dinner.

Chuckles bubbled up Anna's throat. The stupid Dark Man wasn't in her studio or her driveway. He was in her head. And she'd just totally spooked herself when the lights went out. That's all.

She felt ridiculous, like a young kid who'd watched a horror movie all alone and then couldn't go anywhere in the house without turning every light on and checking every closet.

Shaking her head, Anna pulled a U-ey and came to a rest at the stop sign. A left took her back to the studio where, she realized, she'd left her phone in the stereo dock. A right took her home.

Anna looked both ways, debating. One of the reasons she hated scary movies was because some female character always went searching through a dark house investigating a weird noise while you screamed at the television for her not to be an idiot because the serial killer was hiding behind the door. Annnd that thought did it. The irrational scaredy-cat inside her gave an *aw, hell no!* and said she could come back for her phone in the morning. With one last glance to the left, Anna turned right and headed home. She clearly needed a very good night of sleep.

CHAPTER THREE

Anna sat on the front porch swing, nursing a cup of coffee and listening to the sound of the rain that had been parked over Jarrettsville for the past two days. Despite getting seven hours of sleep, she didn't feel the least bit refreshed. Instead, she'd woken up with a headache and with a fogginess in her brain she couldn't quite make go away. Her CFS, no doubt, which the late nights of painting were clearly not helping.

The constant exhaustion had set in about six months before. She'd come back from running one morning and had suddenly felt as if someone had laid a lead blanket over her head. After a whole day in bed, she'd dragged herself to the doctor certain she'd come down with the flu. But the exhaustion, muscle and joint achiness, headaches, and feeling of fogginess never went away. After several more doctors' visits, they'd diagnosed her with chronic fatigue syndrome. Now here she was, twenty-nine years old, solely responsible for the care of her sick father, and so tired she could let herself fall over on the swing and sleep all day.

Instead, she sipped her coffee and scanned the street, her gaze going from Mr. Hendrick's house next door to the empty house for sale across the street to the Nolans' house on the other side. Everything was quiet and still. Yet she had the strangest feeling she wasn't alone.

Knock, knock. "Tessa, what are you doing out there?" came a muffled voice that startled her. Coffee almost sloshed out of her cup she'd jumped so badly. But it was just her father, Garrett, confusing her once again with her mother, who'd died eight years earlier, the year before his dementia had set in and Anna had boxed up her life in New York City to move home and take care of him.

She peered over her shoulder to the window, where her father had pulled the living room curtain aside and was staring out at her. "I'll be right there, Dad," she said, loud enough for him to hear through the glass.

Anna's shoulders sagged. Alzheimer's had stolen from her father twice over—first in making him forget what he'd lost, and second in rendering him incapable of even knowing he'd forgotten. Yet he could still recite case law and play the piano beautifully without ever needing a sheet of music. Tears pricked at the back of Anna's eyes. Alzheimer's didn't only steal from its victim. As much as love and loyalty had led her to put her dreams on hold and return home to care for her dad, the pain of knowing he wasn't really there anymore made it damn hard not to wish the disease—or something—would set them both free once and for all. She really hated herself for those thoughts. She'd lost her big brother, Michael, when she was fourteen and her mother when she was twenty-two, so her dad was all she had left.

Two more knocks sounded against the windowpane. "Tessa, I think you should come in now," Garrett said louder, discomfort slipping into his voice and pulling her from her thoughts. In the past few months, he'd become anxious about venturing from the house. His anxiety extended to her leaving, too, so much so that she was now reduced to sneaking out of the house like a teenager.

Blinking away the tears, she got up and heaved a deep breath. Staring at her reflection in the storm door, she practiced smiling. Everything stressed her father out these days, so her illness was yet another secret she carried. Putting on a chipper face, she stepped inside, closed the door, and leaned against the arch that led into the living room, still decorated the way her mother had remodeled it years before she'd died. "I'm here, Dad."

"What were you doing?" he asked, staring up at her from his recliner. He'd slept there last night, which meant he'd had a bad night, too. Even though he'd be sixty-eight next month, his hair remained mostly brown and he didn't appear much older than he'd ever looked to her. For the millionth time, she wished the father she'd admired her whole life were actually here with her. Once, he'd been able to deduce whether she was happy or sad in just one glance. Now, he often didn't know who she was.

"Just listening to the rain."

He frowned. "What day is it?" he asked, the question part of their morning routine.

"Sunday, September fifteenth." She glanced at the clock over the mantel. "And it's nine o'clock," she added. For some reason, repeating the date and time seemed to help him grapple with his increased confusion. "Are you ready for breakfast?"

His shoulders relaxed and he settled against the backrest. "What are you making?"

"Omelets?" she asked.

"No veggies. I don't like omelets with veggies."

She sighed and walked toward the door to the kitchen. "Nope, no veggies. Sausage and cheese."

Her dad's smile was instant, like the reaction you got if you told a kid he could have a piece of candy. This man had been an intellectual giant in the field of corporate law, and now forgot to get up from his chair during the day. At all. If she asked him to do it or tried to help him do it, he'd get angry and refuse. But if she dangled a carrot in front of him—or, in this case, a sausage and cheese omelet—he'd often manage it.

Anna rounded the doorway and got to work. She'd browned and diced the sausage before her dad had awakened, so all she needed to do now was throw everything together in the skillet and make some toast. As the savory smells wafted through the kitchen, Anna nearly held her breath to see if it would be enough to tempt him out of his chair. The moment he became immobile—whether it was because his body or his mind stopped working didn't really matter—would be when she finally had to confront the question of putting him in a home, something he'd once made her promise never to do. She busied herself with setting the table.

A creaking sound came from the living room, and Anna let out a long breath. Her dad entered the kitchen and paused at the end of the counter, watching as she slid his omelet onto a plate. "Smells good," he said.

She smiled up at him, struck again that there was one thing dementia hadn't managed to steal—his commanding height that had always left her feeling small and safe and protected. "Come sit down." He took his seat at the old kitchen table as she brought their plates over and refilled their coffee.

Her dad dug in immediately, his *lack* of commentary expressing his approval of the food. When something displeased him these days, he let her know it. Once, Garrett Fallston had been a master storyteller, barely allowing others a word in edgewise. Not that anyone had ever minded, because her dad had always had the ability to keep a crowded table in stitches so that you hardly knew where the night had gone. Now, even if she told him about her day or asked him questions, he rarely said a word when they ate together.

She took a big forkful, and as the spice of the sausage warmed her mouth, a suffocating sadness flooded into her chest. Sometimes life took and took and took, even from good people who deserved every happiness. Anna looked across the table at the man she'd idolized her entire life, the man who'd always been her biggest source of encouragement and support, the man who'd taught her by example that following dreams and taking risks and swinging for the fence were how you got the most out of life. *This* man deserved happiness and dignity if anyone did. Her emotions darkened, and rage had the edge of the metal fork cutting into her fingers.

On the heels of the anger, a hazy image flashed into her mind, a variation on a stream of similar images she'd been seeing lately. The Dark Man standing in front of bars. For a moment, she clenched her eyes against the onslaught even as she felt the claws of compulsion slinking around her brain. "Want more?" Anna said, forcing herself out of her head and into the here and now.

Her father finished the last of his toast and brushed his fingers off over the plate. "Nope. You did good, Tess. Just the way I like it."

Anna took a deep breath and faked a smile. She didn't even look like her mother, who had had brown hair to Anna's own pale blond. "I'm glad."

He wiped his mouth and left the table for the living room, where he'd settle in with the Sunday newspapers and some morning talk shows. She brought him more coffee, a bottle of water, and a bowl of his favorite snack—popcorn, which she knew was all he needed to be content for the next few hours. Anna employed a home health aide during the week so she could paint and teach occasional art classes at the community center, but on the weekend, she could sneak out only after her dad had gone to bed or while he was deep in the midst of routine. Like now. The one positive consequence of her father's forgetfulness about getting up and his anxiety about going outside was that she could often leave him long enough to run errands without his even noticing. Luckily, his Alzheimer's hadn't resulted in any wandering problems. So far, at least. And since they lived in such a small town, everyone he passed would know who he was and call her right away even if he did.

Her dad all squared away, Anna resolved to return to her studio in the light of day to retrieve her phone and, more importantly, prove to herself nothing was amiss. She grabbed her keys and purse, sneaked out the back door, and tiptoed down the wooden steps that led to the driveway. Her gaze landed on the dent and scratches. Man, she'd really done a number on it, hadn't she?

In the Jeep, she met her own gaze in the rearview mirror and rolled her eyes. Good thing no one had seen how she'd behaved last night, because she felt so stupid about having freaked out and fled just because she *thought* she saw something.

In less than fifteen minutes she was turning into the lot that surrounded her studio. An old barn that had once served as a general store, it was red with a metal gambrel roof. A wide porch jutted off the front, and she remembered from when she was younger eating farm-fresh ice cream at the tables with umbrellas that had then filled the space. Puddles splashed and gravel crunched under her tires as she pulled around to the rear.

Anna absolutely hated that a flicker of anxiety—or maybe it was just anticipation?—ran through her belly.

She'd been to this place a thousand times to paint, always alone, and she'd never once freaked herself out as she had last night. No way she'd let getting a little spooked take away from the refuge she'd found here.

Without painting, she just might go stark raving mad.

Right. So. Anna gave the back door a hard stare and then hopped out of the Jeep and into the never-ending rain.

Frustration roared through her when she paused with her hand on the knob. Finally, she yanked open the door and stepped out of the wet morning and into the cool darkness of the main room. Except, when she secured the door behind her, she noticed that it wasn't dark. The light in the room she used as her studio was on. The one that had been off when she'd left the night before.

"Okay, Anna, that's easy enough to explain. The power went out and when it came back on, the light was still on from last night," she said out loud, just to add sound to the quiet stillness surrounding her. Quiet…because her music wasn't playing. Obviously, the battery had run out on her phone overnight. "See? Everything's fine," she said. "Stop being stupid."

Anna settled her purse and keys on the counter, one of the many counters, display cases, and shelves that had been left all over the main room, and stepped to the door of her studio, which had probably been a storeroom in another lifetime.

Everything was just as she'd left it. And no one else was here.

Tension melted out of her shoulders and she released a long breath. This new subject had her so out of sorts that she was seeing things.

"Damnit," she muttered as she walked up to her worktable. Her idiocy last night prevented her from cleaning her brushes or sealing her palette. Now her brushes were stiff as a board and the paint in the tray was hard. She collected everything and went back out to the main room. Tucked against the closest wall was a counter with a sink in it, where the ice cream display had once been. She let the water run until it turned hot, pulled the plug so the sink would fill, and added a lot of dish soap. Soaking the palette and brushes would make them usable again.

Just as the brushes submerged beneath the bubbles, an image slammed into Anna's brain.

The Dark Man standing in front of bars, this time with someone on the far side.

Not again. Not so soon.

Anna grasped the edge of the sink and bowed her head as the image continued to form and sharpen in her mind's eye. Prison bars, and the person on the other side was a prisoner. And, oh God, he was shackled to the wall.

Compulsion roared through her like a drug.

She whimpered as the force of the feeling seized her, overtook her, possessed her.

"No. I'm not doing it right now," she said, hearing the weakness in her own voice. But even as she turned and walked back to the studio, her mind was already deciding which canvas to use and seeing the colors she'd need for the painting.

She grabbed a new palette and pulled a thin sponge layer from the bottom that helped keep the quick-drying acrylic paints moist. Back out at the sink, Anna dampened and wrung out the sponge, then returned to her easel. The image growing in strength and intensity in her mind made her stomach squeeze and her heart hurt. Never in a million years would she come up with such a thing on her own.

Then where are these images coming from?

The question stopped her cold, a tube of paint in her hands. She couldn't begin to answer that. All she knew was the need to get the image *out* of her head. And there was only one way to do that.

Soon, she had her paints prepared, new brushes and knives ready, and her canvas selected. As she stared at the paints, they took on their colors. But as with every other time she'd done one of these paintings, they weren't vibrant, but dull. Not bright, but dark. Like some sort of filter had been placed between her eyes and the world.

The thought sent a shudder down her spine.

Forcing the chaos in her mind away, Anna dipped her paint into the gray and stepped to the canvas. Motion captured her attention from the corner of her eye.

The Dark Man stood in the doorway and leaned against the jamb.

Anna jumped and her pulse raced, but this time, anger flooded in instead of fear. "I will deal with you on my own damn terms," she said, taking a perverse amount of pleasure from putting a figment of her imagination in its place. Because that's all he was.

He didn't move or speak. Not that he could, since, you know. Figment. Of. Imagination.

Anna rolled her eyes, done with being scared and so pissed to have to do this again that she was nearly out of her mind. "I'm doing your damn painting already. So just leave me alone." She cut her gaze back to the expanse of white, but the desire to see if his image would still be there if she looked again drove her to distraction.

Finally, she gave in and…he was still there.

Completely still. Blatantly scowling. Totally unfathomable.

Was this a vision? Another image she'd have to paint?

Her heart tripped into a sprint, and she couldn't look away from him. Like the compulsion that forced her to paint these images, Anna couldn't help but return his stare and memorize his masculine features. The sharp angles of his face, the harsh set of his mouth, the dark shadows around his even darker eyes. Black eyes. Blades of black hair hung low over his forehead and just touched the hooded shirt he wore under his short, scuffed leather jacket. He'd crossed his arms over his chest, and the position caused his biceps to bunch up under the worn leather. In fact, everything about him appeared worn—the coat, the threadbare jeans, the scuffed boots. None of it struck her as the kind of shabby chic you could buy in some upscale store for a small fortune, either. The whole effect was rough. Dangerous. Deprived.

Deprived? What a strange way of describing him. But as Anna's gaze swept over him again, the thought stuck. For his height, he seemed thin, with his lean hips, clad in old black jeans, a trim waist, and pronounced cheekbones. Her fingers twitched around the nearly forgotten paintbrush. What would it feel like to cup that harsh face in her hand?

Anna gasped and tore her gaze away. She had to blink to pull herself out of the haze of thoughts. Frustration surged through her and tensed the muscles of her shoulders and neck. She didn't want to be working on another of these paintings as it was, so the last thing she needed was to lose a bunch of time daydreaming. Or would it be daynightmaring?

As she stared at the blank canvas, the image of the shackled man behind the prison bars filled her mind's eye.

Definitely the latter.

Curiosity pulled her eyes to the left again. The doorway was empty.

"Just paint the damn thing already, Anna," she whispered to herself.

And then the painting took over. The colors. The darkness. The brushwork. Layer by layer, the heart-wrenching image came to life. The shackled man appeared thin and weak, so weak that he sat in a heap on the floor, his legs stretched on the stone floor in front of him, his arms suspended above his head by iron cuffs chained to the wall. Dried blood streaked down his arms from his wrists, the skin long abused by the heavy iron. His eyes were open, but only a little, as if lifting his eyelids required more effort than he could make.

When she had the prisoner just right, she turned to the other figure in the painting. The Dark Man had his hands on the bars, as if he were looking in on the prisoner. His back to the viewer, it was impossible to tell exactly what he was doing, but as he took form on the canvas, she felt a sort of urgency emanating from him with every stroke of the brush.

As she worked on the details and the lighting, her arms grew heavy and her body felt sluggish. A good session of painting always made her tired, but it was different with these paintings. They left her feeling drained, as if she'd poured her soul out with the images, leaving herself an empty shell.

Prickles ran over her scalp and neck. Everything about these paintings just made her feel…violated and used.

Finally, Anna lowered her brush. She'd been gripping the wooden handle so tightly her fingertips had gone numb. But she was done.

Her shoulders slumped and she slipped the brush into the cup of water, massaging her right hand with her left.

She stared at the painting for a long moment. How…*horrible.* Grief and anger became a red-hot pressure in her chest and choked off her throat. She burst out crying.

Despair ripped through her so hard and so suddenly that she couldn't breathe, couldn't stand. Grasping her stomach, she folded in on herself until her head and shoulders lay on the worktable. Her mind was such a whirl of distress that she couldn't think it through, couldn't reason this reaction, couldn't make it stop.

Anna had no idea how long she cried, but by the time she managed to push herself up from the table her throat felt raw and her muscles ached from the emotional outpouring.

She scrubbed her face with the front of her T-shirt, then mechanically removed the new painting from the easel and carried it across the room. Gently, she settled it against the others to dry, then stepped back.

Pouring rain pattered on the roof like drumsticks on a snare.

Hugging herself, Anna stared at the evil and horror and torment gazing back at her. "I hate you," she said, her voice a dry scrape.

"Join the club," said a deep voice from behind her.

CHAPTER FOUR

Owen Winters sat at his grandfather's large mahogany dining table and tried to remain focused on the conversation his uncles—er, rather, brothers—were having. After millennia of calling them *uncle*, it was going to take some time to get used to thinking of them in a new way. But now he was one of them. He was a Cardinal Anemoi. Supreme God of the North Wind and Guardian of Winter. The other Anemois' brother in name and spirit.

He had known the day would come when he would be asked to ascend to this position. He just never thought it would be so soon. Or arise out of such tragedy.

Boreas.

His father. Gone. Murdered in front of his eyes. His life lost protecting Owen's.

Owen fingered the leather lanyard at his throat, the one that held an ancient iron pendant Megan had given him last Christmas. It had been his father's—his birth father's, not Boreas's. Though, his real father had died before Owen had been old enough to remember him, so Boreas had truly been his father in every way that mattered.

Now he'd lost both of them.

As if the wrenching grief wasn't enough, guilt weighed down on Owen's shoulders as if he were still wearing the heavy ceremonial fur robes from the installation rites. Layered on top of this was the soul-deep concern for Megan and Teddy. She was a human, and divine law dictated she could not live in the Realm of the Gods. Hades, she shouldn't be here at all. Only the chaos of the battle two nights ago and her premature labor pains had convinced Aeolus to allow the humans caught in the crossfire of the battle to travel with them to the heavens. Everything Owen had gone through two years ago to be with Megan, only for their togetherness to be threatened so soon, and while she was pregnant with their second child.

"It appears they've both gone to ground," Aeolus said from his seat at the head of the table. "But I will keep looking."

His grandfather seemed to have aged in the past few days. Though he appeared as regal as ever with his mane of wavy brown hair, highlighted with gold and bronze, dark circles marred his eyes and frown lines cut into the skin around his mouth. He'd even discarded his usual ceremonial tunic and robe for human-style black fighting gear. Clearly, Boreas's loss hadn't affected only Owen.

"No doubt they've returned to the Eastern Realm," the West Wind's Zeph said, blue eyes flashing. "Only place we can't easily search for them." He squeezed Ella's hand, and she smiled at him. Owen watched them for a long moment, and then his gaze cut across the table to where the South Wind's Chrysander and Laney sat side by side, their hands also entwined. He was glad that his Anemoi brethren had their mates with them here at Aeolus's compound. He couldn't care less whether Olympic law technically permitted the humans' presence or not. Right now, family had to be held close. None of them could weather another loss like Boreas's.

Without meaning to, Owen looked at the empty chair beside him. Megan's chair. Though her labor pains had stopped, she was tired and understandably upset. She'd just lost her father-in-law and had no idea what her husband's becoming a Cardinal Anemoi meant for their lives. And, really, neither did he.

A hot, hollow ache throbbed at the center of Owen's chest. He pushed the remains of his lunch away.

"I doubt that," Aeolus said. "Devlin would return there only if he'd been captured. Eurus's attack with the Harpies at Gibraltar clearly revealed he knew Devlin was working with me, with all of us."

Zephyros sat forward and jabbed his finger into the table. "Or Devlin led him there. Remember how he just stood on the rock and watched the attack happen while Boreas was nearly ripped to shreds and Chrysander nearly died of hypothermia? I'd say his loyalties are pretty clear."

Aeolus's hand fisted around his napkin. "I swear to Hades, Zephyros. If I say he's trustworthy, why will you not take me at my word?"

"Oh, I don't know," Zeph said, throwing up his hands. "Maybe because you have a long track record of secrecy and selective truth-telling? Most recently in failing to admit Eurus had stolen your ring, which left Chrysander to get beaten all to hell all summer, and in keeping this whole thing with Devlin secret from us."

Owen flinched at Zeph's brutal honesty, but in truth the relationship between the Anemoi and their storm-god father had long been a strained one. After all, back in ancient times Aeolus had once locked the four winds inside the Rock of Gibraltar and forcibly taken their blood so he could ever after control them. Which was why the loss of that Firestone ring was such a big problem—its wearer controlled the Anemoi, and right now, that wearer was Eurus.

Tension hung thick as cobwebs in the air around them.

Chrysander sighed. "I don't know what to make of what happened at Gibraltar either, Z, but Devlin did come to Owen's to warn us about Eurus the other night," he said, raking the fingers of his free hand through his wavy blond hair. "He didn't have to do that. In fact, he gained nothing by doing it."

"True," Aeolus said, his expression a dark storm, "and if Devlin was guilty of betraying me after weeks of our working together and training, I doubt he would've come within striking distance. His powers aren't honed enough to guarantee he could best me. Yet. It argues to his innocence."

Zeph scoffed. "Nothing innocent about that boy or any of the gods of the East." Owen shifted in his chair. Of all of them, the tension and rivalry had always been the worst between Zephyros and Eurus, and Zeph had suffered much at Eurus's hands as a result. He'd come by his mistrust honestly, so it wasn't likely Aeolus was going to change his mind.

"Zephyros," Aeolus said, ice sliding into his tone. "You'd do well to remember that a god of the East will become your successor."

Tossing his napkin onto his plate, Zeph shook his head. "Like I could ever forget. I told you before I'm going to live forever so I can stay in this position for the rest of eternity just to spite this decision."

Owen could hardly blame Zeph for his outrage over having Eurus's son Alastor, an offspring of the eastern god and a goddess of spring, appointed his heir since Zephyros had none of his own. And even now that he'd married, the agreement Zeph had made to save Ella's life and turn her into a goddess had required him to yield on this question of a successor forever. So much of divine politics was defined by quid quo pro—you had to give something to get something. Always.

Chrys chuckled under his breath, earning a cutting glare from Aeolus.

Laney gasped, and her bright-blue eyes went distant.

"What is it?" Chrys asked, leaning closer to her and tucking a thick strand of her nearly black hair behind her ear. "Laney?" Mere seconds lapsed and she sucked in a breath and blinked her eyes, her fair skin paling. Chrys cupped her cheek in his hand and turned her face toward him. "Another vision?" he asked.

She nodded and whispered, "Yeah." Over the past two weeks, Laney had captured the attention of Hephaestus, Zeus's son and the master craftsman of the gods who had long ago been outcast because of his gnarled hands and feet and bent back. He'd apparently admired Laney's protectiveness and selflessness in several times saving Chrys's life, despite her being nearly blind. Hephaestus's interest in Chrys and Laney had earned them all an important ally in the battle against Eurus, first in providing Chrys with several pieces of infernal iron, which could neutralize or harm a god when little else could, and second in providing Laney with the gift of prophetic sight. "I'm…I'm not sure…"

"Just try to describe it," Chrys said as the other men traded glances. Laney's ability was still very new and untested, but given their situation with Eurus and how little time they had until he ascended to his season, they were open to any help they could get.

Laney slowly pulled her face out of Chrys's hand and looked across the table. At Zeph. The disease that had taken her sight had left her a tiny sliver of central vision, but she could also identify the gods because she could perceive an aura of light emanating from their bodies.

"It involved me?" Zephyros asked, his voice carefully casual.

A quick nod, then Laney said, "Yes. I think…someone will be installed as your successor."

Dread slid down Owen's spine, and the tension in the air proved he wasn't the only one. "Why do you think so, Laney?" Owen finally said.

"I see another tall, thin man standing on the big *W* in a ceremony in the compass rose room," she rushed out. Ella made a small sound of distress. "I'm sorry," Laney said. "I could totally be wrong."

Zephyros put an arm around Ella and hugged her against him. "Don't worry. Okay?" he said to her. "We don't know what it means. Or when it might even be taking place."

Given his mindset, Owen's brain went right to the worst-case scenario—Zephyros having died and his heir coming to power. And soon, if Laney's track record was any indication. Good gods, none of them could handle that. Would their losses never end?

Two of Aeolus's underlings began to clear the table, bringing the conversation to a halt. Owen nodded to the lesser god who removed his dish, then waved him off of the plate holding a salad, some fruit, a fresh roll, and a piece of chocolate cake for Megan.

When the servants departed, Zeph looked at Owen and picked

the conversation right back up. "What do you think about this question of Devlin's loyalty?"

Part of Owen was surprised he'd asked because they'd been tiptoeing around him for the last day and a half. Which meant it was time he got his head in the game and did everything he personally could to make sure Laney's vision—whether it was about Zeph or anyone else at this table—never came true. "Seems to me that if the guy risked training with Aeolus, let himself be experimented on, and came to warn not only of Eurus's imminent attack but of Apheliotes's death, that's a lot of evidence on the side of him being exactly what Aeolus has been saying he is. It's worth nailing down one way or the other at the very least."

"Ah, finally, a voice of reason just like your father always was," Aeolus said, giving him a nod as he rose. The comment poured pride and sadness through Owen in equal amounts. If he could be half the god Boreas was he'd be doing good. "I'm going back out to search for him. Problem is, drinking from the infernal rivers has masked his natural divine energy signature, so unless he uses his powers in the open, looking for him amounts to searching for a needle in a haystack."

"Then I'll come, too," Zeph said, brushing his hands over his jeans. Aeolus was usually a stickler for formal dress and protocol, but not since they'd returned from the battle. Not since Boreas's death. "Because I won't be able to trust Devlin until he does something to earn it right in front of my face."

"You have to go?" Ella said, coming to her feet beside him.

Threading his fingers into her brown hair, Zeph nodded. "Yes, love. But I'll be back."

Chrys stood up next. "Count me in."

"No, Chrysander," Aeolus said. "You stay here."

"But—"

"We have a compound full of humans. We need protection here."

"Owen's here," Chrys said, unleashing a flood of gratitude in Owen's chest at the other god's easy confidence in his abilities, new as they were.

"Yes, and he has a pregnant wife and a two-year-old to take care of. Stay, please."

Chrys sat heavily in his seat, discontent rolling off him.

"I can help next time, too," Owen managed. "Megan has Tabitha's company—"

"And mine," Ella said.

"Me too," Laney added.

Owen nodded. "So I can go out, too."

Aeolus gave a single nod. "Very good," he said, though Owen noticed he hadn't actually responded to the offer. But Owen meant it. Every word. He'd do whatever it took to end this once and for all.

"Oh, if I'm not going out, then take this." Chrys pulled something from his back pocket and handed it across the table to Zephyros. The infernal dagger Hephaestus had given him. "Just in case."

"Thanks," Zeph said with a dark smile. "Nice little piece of insurance here."

"Fuckin' A," Chrys said. "I imagine between Eurus's hand and shoulder, he's feeling a tad under the weather right now." The hits Chrys had managed to get in on Eurus during the battle had proven the strength of the infernal iron. As Owen had faced Eurus's lightning lance in the moment before Boreas threw his body between them, Owen had seen the desiccation of the skin on Eurus's hand with his own eyes.

With an exchange of glances and nods, Aeolus and Zephyros shifted into the elements and disappeared.

After a moment, Owen rose with the plate of food in his hand. "I'm going to take this to Megan. Grab me if you need me." He met Chrys's gaze and almost wished he hadn't, because the sympathy he saw in the other god's eyes threatened to pierce right through him.

"You got it," Chrys said.

"I'll come by and visit Megan later," Laney added.

"She'll love that, I'm sure." An awkward moment passed, and Owen finally thumbed over his shoulder. "I should go." He left without giving them a chance to respond.

He passed through long splendorous corridors he barely saw. Muraled ceilings arched over gilded walls and marble floors, but none of it meant a thing to Owen. He didn't want to be in his grandfather's most beautiful estate in the Realm of the Gods. He wanted to be back on his little .37-acre lot in his homey Cape Cod in Fairfax, Virginia, with Megan and Teddy.

Owen came to such a sudden halt that the contents of the plate almost slid off. Their house. It was gone. Burned to the ground in the battle with Eurus. Holy Zeus, but they didn't even have a home for Megan to go back to. Not to mention the little problem of what the human authorities were making of the disaster the battle had left behind.

For a moment, Owen couldn't breathe.

But then he forced a deep breath. And another. They'd figure it out. It would all work out. They'd be fine.

He'd just keep repeating that until he believed it.

Because no way could he give Megan the impression he was worried. She and the baby couldn't stand anymore stress than they'd gone through the past forty-eight hours.

As bad as it would be to lose one of his brothers—and it would be horrible beyond imagination—Owen would be destroyed if anything happened to Megan and the kids. They were his heart, his life, his very soul.

With one more deep breath under his belt, Owen forced himself to move again and made his way to the suite of rooms Aeolus had provided for them. Inside the apartment, the spacious living room was formally furnished and luxurious in finish, and except for giving them some floor space for Teddy to play, they hadn't spent much time in it. His boots thudded against the white marble as he entered a hallway with several bedrooms.

Owen pushed into the room he shared with his wife. "Hey, Angel," he said, forcing normalcy into his voice. "I brought some food back."

Megan lay curled on the bed staring out the picture window

that overlooked lush gardens. Pillows propped up her big belly and supported her back. She was so beautiful it made Owen's heart hurt. How had he ever been so lucky to find and keep someone like Megan?

"Hey," she said, pushing herself into a sitting position.

Owen settled the plate on the side table, then sat on the edge of the bed next to her. He grasped Megan's hand, unable to keep from touching her, proving to himself that she was here and she was safe. "Did you get some sleep?"

"Yeah. I'm okay." She tucked wavy blond hair behind her ears.

Owen smiled and winked. "You're better than okay."

That eked a smile out of her. "I'm going a little stir-crazy, though."

"I know. Laney said she'd come visit later," he added. "How are you feeling?"

"No more contractions," she said. "It'd be great to see Laney. Tabitha and Teddy were here for a while, but she took him so he could take a nap." Funny that their neighbor who sometimes watched Teddy for them was now here in the Realm of the Gods doing the very same thing. The thought beckoned a memory from Owen's mind, the image of Boreas kissing Tabitha before the battle had begun. With his newly shorn hair, new modern wardrobe, and interest in their neighbor, it was as though Boreas had been coming back to life. And now he was dead.

The memory nearly sucker punched him.

Megan's small, cool hand cupped his jaw. "Thinking of Boreas?" How had she known? Owen's gaze cut to hers, and she gave a small, sad smile. "You're not the only one who can read emotions, you know," she said, her thumb rubbing his cheekbone just under his eye. "And your eyes flared."

"I love you, you know that?" Owen said, turning his head to press a kiss into her palm. From across the room, his gaze caught sight of the decorative glass jar into which they'd placed the last gift Boreas had ever given them—three crystal snowflakes infused with his divine energy. He'd apparently made them on Owen's wedding day to Megan, though Owen had learned of their existence only after Boreas's death. Owen sighed. "I miss him," he managed, dragging his gaze back to Megan.

"Me, too," she rasped, her eyes going glassy. "So much." Megan reached forward as if to hug him, but stopped and frowned at her belly. "You have to come hug me. My belly's in the way."

With a chuckle, Owen reached for Megan and wrapped an arm around her shoulders. He drew her scent into himself, using it to find a bit of solace. Love for her nearly overwhelmed him, which was a far better feeling than the avalanche of guilt and grief he'd been shouldering the past few days.

"What did you bring me to eat?" she whispered into his ear. "I'm hungry."

Now that's what he liked to hear. He sat back. "Yeah?"

Megan smiled. "Yeah." Owen handed the plate to Megan, who used her belly as a shelf. "I'm going to miss being able to do this," she said, situating the plate and drawing more laughter from him. Only she could possibly bring him a small spot of joy in the midst of all this grief and chaos. Just another reason—among many—that he loved her. "Now, I know you want to feed me, so don't even pretend like you're all nonchalant over there."

Owen grinned and picked up a strawberry. "You know me too well."

"No such thing," she said, then she bit into the strawberry he held in his fingers. As her tongue swiped a bit of juice from her lip, he tracked it with his gaze. This gorgeous, arousing woman was all his.

And he would do anything to make sure she stayed happy and safe.

CHAPTER FIVE

A scream stuck in Anna's throat as she whipped around. The Dark Man. Again. A strangled whimper managed to wrest free.

Except this time, he'd spoken.

As she stood trembling and staring at her imagination come to life, he tilted his head and narrowed his eyes at her.

And also moved.

Though he radiated a general aura of menace, he took no overt actions to threaten her.

Hoping against hope, Anna clenched her eyes closed, counted to ten, and with a small, silent plea, opened them again.

"I'm still here," he said in a low voice.

"But, I painted you," she finally managed to say. "I did what you demanded. You shouldn't be here."

He cocked his head to the opposite side in a slow gesture that seemed full of languid casualness. Butterflies whipped through her stomach, telling her it was a false impression. "And yet"—he held out his arms—"here I am."

Anna felt her mouth open, but as her brain couldn't make sense of the moment, she couldn't find the right words to say. She pressed her fingers to her lips and shook her head. The exhaustion these paintings brought on, the overwrought grief she'd felt as she'd finished… A nearly euphoric rush of relief flowed through her. That explained this. That explained *him*. "You're not real." Intent on proving it, she barreled forward, dead certain he'd disappear or fade away. Just as he'd done last night when she'd driven through him.

She crashed full-on into a mountain of rock-hard male. Her face against the unyielding planes of his lean pecs, her hands coming up against the ribs she had no difficulty feeling, her bare feet nearly tangling with his boots.

He hissed and reared back as if she'd burned him. As if *he* were the aggrieved party here. The quickness of his movement threw her further off-kilter, making her stumble forward into him.

"Don't touch me, human," he growled.

That was the moment her brain finally accepted the impossible. The subject of her paintings was a living, breathing, rankly pissed-off man standing in front of her.

Terror whipped through her, breaking out goose bumps over her flesh and setting her teeth to chattering. *Run! Get away! Hide!* The instincts whipped through her. The windowless room plunged into darkness.

Time seemed to slow to a crawl. Instead of fearing the unusual timing of the power outage, Anna silently cheered at the advantage of surprise it gave her. After a split second of adjustment, the outlines of everything in the room became clear, and she bolted hard to the left, intending to skirt around the far side of her worktable and then make a dead run for the door.

With a terrified shriek, she crashed into something warm and recoiled just as quickly. *No. Nonono. Not possible. He couldn't have moved that fast, that silently. And how had she not seen him?* She whipped back around the table. "Oomph!" she uttered disbelievingly when she crashed into him again. *Oh, God, he's everywhere!* The basest kind of fear flooded through her, erasing all traces of Annalise Fallston and leaving only a human being in a basic fight for survival.

Her body was already flinging itself away from him. Steely grips settled around her biceps. "Stop," he bit out. A dim light flared, reminding her of the eyes she'd thought she'd imagined the night before. Except here they were again, just inches from her face, directed at her as though he was looking at her, despite the pitch black. She twisted and pushed and kicked. He gripped her tighter and tugged her nearly against his chest to make it harder to effectively fight with her hands and knees. "Stop *now*," he commanded, icy impatience sliding into his tone.

"Let me go!" she rasped. "Please!"

"I'll tell you one last time. Stop fighting me," he growled. But the veiled threat only ratcheted up her fight-or-flight response. Her nails were useless against his leather jacket, her bare feet not strong enough to impact the toes his boots protected. But that didn't stop her from trying. When he let go of her right arm, triumph surged through her. Then his hand pressed to her forehead.

A breeze seemed to unfurl around her. Soft. Lulling. Immediately sedating.

"Please don't hurt me," she managed to force out, despite the sluggishness making her limbs heavy and her senses dull. She wasn't in pain, but she was clearly dying, though her mind rejected that this was how and when her life would end. Grief and regret surged through her. "Daddy," she mouthed, so, so sorry to leave him when he needed her so much. Her eyelids sagged closed. Sound faded away, and then all feeling. Until she was floating. Until she was nothing at all.

೮೦೦೮

Devlin stared down at the woman he'd finally had to force into unconsciousness, frustrated yet amazed that she'd struggled against even that. And, gods be damned, she'd fought as if for her life. Not that it was in danger—yet. And, anyway, the fighting would've been fruitless even if he'd meant her harm. The darkness had been no impediment to his sight, and in fact had allowed him to easily shift between his elemental and corporeal forms as he prevented her escape from the room. Just as he should've done last night.

At last, his will bested hers and she sagged completely into his arms. Even separated as it was by his clothing, her heat against him was foreign and strange. He couldn't recall the last time he'd been touched in anything other than anger and humiliation, which was why the sudden impact of her body against his had caught him so off guard.

Light flooded the room.

Devlin frowned and glared up at the fixture above his head. And then looked back to the human he held. This was the second time the lights had gone out in her presence. Instinct flared and Devlin ran his gaze over her face. If anyone understood the connection between emotions and the manifestation of power, it was him. Both times the lights had gone out, he'd scared her badly. And both times she'd vacated the room—through flight or loss of consciousness—the light had returned.

No way was that a coincidence.

As if he needed another mystery to add to the growing list where she was concerned.

Devlin lifted her into the cradle of his arms, and he was immediately in sensory overload. Her warmth against his abdomen and arms, her scent—all vanilla and woman—surrounding him. She was a slight little thing, small as she was, and it unleashed a wave of protectiveness he had no business feeling. But it couldn't be helped. Black-souled he might be, but the loss of one brother and the torture of another had ingrained that particular instinct deeply.

Not that he'd actually ever been any good at protecting those he should.

He crossed the room, his gaze fixed on a single tear that had leaked from the corner of her eye and slowly rolled down her temple, and settled her onto an old blue couch near the door. Retreating a few paces, Devlin studied her. Small and young as she appeared, she seemed even more so in sleep. And every bit as alluring. Angelic in the purity of her coloring. Devilish in the magnetism of her feminine curves.

And fierce, too.

What must it be like to hold your own life so dear that you would fight tooth and nail to protect it? Devlin wouldn't know. After all, how could he believe he deserved to live when he'd caused the death of another? And not just anyone, but a brother.

He clenched and unclenched his hands. He could still feel the weight of her in his arms, her softness on his fingers. The sensation agitated him even as part of him missed holding her close. It had been so long, he didn't realize he'd forgotten how good touch could feel until now.

With a growl of annoyance, Devlin turned and marched to the door, where he firmly planted his body to ensure she couldn't leave unless he permitted it. Which he wouldn't. Not until he had answers. Leaning against the wood, he crossed his arms and settled in. He wasn't in the habit of interacting with humans, and he had little sense of whether he'd given her a small or large dose of his command to sleep.

Just one more power he had to hone. Take a number.

Staring across the room, his gaze settled on the painting she'd just finished. The one that showed him—and the short leather jacket proved it was him and not his father—clutching at the bars to Alastor's cell. Devlin knew for sure that scene hadn't happened, because damn it all to Hades but he'd never seen Alastor shackled that way—which made it imperative he find out what it meant and when it took place. One of his major objectives in taking a stand against his father was freeing his youngest brother. Eurus had imprisoned him years ago to force Devlin's obedience to his authority, so it was on Devlin to make it right by freeing him once and for all. At least, from his shackles and cell. Whether the younger god could free himself from whatever damage Eurus's torture and deprivation had caused remained to be seen.

And that would be on Devlin, too.

If the open eyes could be trusted, at least the painting depicted

Alastor still alive. But Devlin felt each passing minute like a collar tightening around his throat. Soon, Eurus's patience would run out and his rage would overflow. And, given his imprisonment, his brother would undoubtedly get caught in the eye of the storm.

"Hang on, Alastor. I'm coming for you," he said, projecting the words in a way his brother should be able to hear—assuming he was lucid. But it had been months since Devlin had heard Alastor's voice in reply.

Quiet minutes passed, and Devlin allowed his eyelids to fall shut.

Complete blackness. Total silence.

The peace so startled him that his eyes popped open and Devlin pushed off the door, heart suddenly a jackrabbit in the chest. How the hell had he managed that? No concentration, no breathing techniques, no battles against the past. Just…peace.

Raking his fingers through his hair, Devlin shook his head and paced a few steps, mentally backtracking the past few minutes to see what he'd done differently. What he'd done *at all* to clear his mind.

But as he replayed the moments between speaking to Anna for the first time and closing his eyes seconds before, not a single thing stood out to him.

Dumb luck? What other kind did he have?

Utter mental exhaustion? More likely. Usually, his mind was such a battlefield that sleep eluded him. Some nights he never even bothered to try. Trying and failing to sleep actually left him more strung out and pissed off than never lying down in the first place.

Devlin, where are you?

For a moment, the sound startled him with the possibility that Alastor had finally managed a reply. But the voice was all wrong—too deep, too robust, too commanding. Aeolus. It wasn't the first time in the past forty-eight hours he'd heard his grandfather's summons, nor the first time Devlin had ignored it. He didn't know whether to feel reassured or threatened that Aeolus searched for him.

Settling in against the door again, Devlin peered down at the woman sprawled in long, lean lines over the worn blue denim of the couch. He needed to figure *this* situation out first. Because his chest hummed with the certainty that these paintings were significant. And if his gut was right that she was painting freeze-frames of the future, the next thing that emerged from the tip of her paintbrush might reveal whether Devlin could trust Aeolus or whether, even now, the Anemoi intended to give him a one-way escort to the deepest, blackest pits of Tartarus.

Thirty minutes passed. An hour. Devlin spent the time struggling to hold onto that quiet blackness, but with every passing second it got more and more difficult, and the horrors of the past crept back in on him, like a slowly rising sea that brought with it the inevitable finality of drowning. Of death.

Finally, he gave up. And in that acquiescence his ears tuned in to the fact that Anna's breathing had changed. From slow and shallow, it was now deeper, faster, louder.

Eyes still closed, her brow furrowed and she licked at her lips. Her hands twitched and dragged up her body to settle on her stomach, pulling the hem of her T-shirt up and exposing a sliver of porcelain skin above her jean shorts.

Her smooth perfection sucker punched him with a totally unexpected, foreign jolt of lust. He wasn't a virgin, but for the amount of time that had lapsed since he'd last allowed himself the pleasure and ecstasy of a woman's body, he might as well have been. Abstinence was hardly a sufficient sacrifice for Farren's death and Alastor's torment. Even if it had lasted more than a century.

Blink of an eye in the life of a god.

Or so he told himself.

Besides, from his ruined skin to his battered psyche, he felt dirty down to his very soul.

Anna's eyelids fluttered, not yet focusing, not yet seeing, not yet aware of what happened around her.

He couldn't imagine laying himself bare to…to someone like her.

She made a small noise of sleepy confusion and pushed up onto her elbows. "What— Oh, God!" On hands and feet, she scrambled backward into the farthest corner of the couch.

Since he'd earlier popped out of thin air and sneaked up behind her, he supposed he shouldn't take it personally that a single look at him sent her into a terror. But how was he supposed to know that she wouldn't believe she was actually seeing him all those earlier times he'd manifested in front of her. He'd had to take it up a notch or he'd have ended up wasting time convincing her he was real.

It wasn't the first time he'd encountered the human propensity to deny what was right in front of their faces.

"You're still here," she said, gaze raking over him, body braced for fight or flight. Again.

How could he reassure her? Keeping his feet and body planted in front of the door, he slowly raised his hands. "I'm not here to hurt you. But I do require answers."

"Oh, well, then." She scoffed, but he could see through the false bravado to the fear underneath. It showed in the jumping vein on the side of her neck and the hands she knotted to hide their trembling. "About what?"

"What you are and why you paint those images," he said, nodding toward the far side of the room.

"What I am? You mean, a painter?"

"Don't play dumb, human. It's clear you wield magic."

She frowned with her whole face and pulled her legs tighter against herself. "What? I don't know what you're talking about," she said, shaking her head and glancing sideways. No doubt evaluating her options for escape.

Might as well put that one to rest right now. "You cannot escape. And you cannot harm me. So save your energy." He arched an eyebrow and dared her to challenge him. Color rose into her cheeks and anger made her gray eyes almost sparkle, but she held her tongue. "Who are you working for?"

"I hear that the words you're speaking are English, but you might as well be speaking Chinese for as much as you're making sense to me."

Though her fear was obvious, he sensed no subterfuge from her. Still… "Who are you related to, then?"

She frowned. "You mean, like, my father?" Devlin gave a single, sharp nod. "His name is Garrett Fallston. Why? What does he have to do with this?" She bolted off the couch but stopped short of coming within arm's reach. Like that mattered. "You better not have hurt him!"

Devlin towered over her. In neither height nor breadth of shoulder did she begin to compete with him. And her weight in his arms had been next to nothing. Surely she had seen these differences between them, too. But it didn't keep her from standing up for her father, from desiring to protect him, even if their differences gave her no meaningful way of doing so. A grudging respect settled into his gut. "I don't know anything about him. I'm talking about the god that gave you your magic."

"Magic?" she asked in a fear-twisted voice. She blanched and shook her head. "Oh, God, you're crazy."

The accusation was like a blow to the gut, stealing his breath and beckoning a knee-jerk defensiveness. Devlin *knew* crazy. Crazy gleefully killed its offspring. Crazy tortured and tormented those it should care for. Crazy yearned to take over the world and punish it for every perceived slight it had ever experienced.

His *father* was crazy. Certifiably. Maliciously. Incurably.

The last thing Devlin wanted was to be anything like his father, but he was well aware that the maelstrom of rage and grief always swirling inside him set him on the same path of damnation. Question was, had he traveled that path too far already to ever make his way back?

His Anemoi brethren certainly thought so. Preternatural heat whipped through him and crackled over his palms.

"Be that as it may," he seethed, "tell me how you came into your magic. *Now*."

Taking a slow step backward, Anna threw out her hands. "What magic?"

Devlin muscled back his growing irritation, but didn't bother to hide his hands when they started throwing off sparks. "The glowing paint. Your command over light and dark."

Her gaze on the growing fireworks, Anna swallowed, the sound thick and dry. "I…" Retreating another step, she shook her head. "I don't—"

Devlin closed half of the space between them in the blink of an eye. "The truth, human. I saw it with my own eyes. I have neither the time nor the tolerance for lies."

Eyes wide, Anna's gaze jumped from his hands to his face. "Why do you keep calling me that?" she whispered.

He willed himself to move right in front of her, causing her to gasp and stumble into the metal rack behind her. The words came out low and cold as ice. "Because that is what you are. Mostly. Which brings me back to your relations."

"I'm just…a woman," she said, pressing herself back into the skeletal structure of the metal behind her.

Devlin didn't allow her the space, and he leaned into her until their faces nearly touched. "You deny making the colors glow?" He pointed to the paintings. "Creating light and shadow with a wave of your hand as you paint?"

Impossibly, her face paled further. "I…I…I don't know. It just… happens," she said, her voice and body trembling as though she was freezing. A whimper spilled from her throat. The lights flickered.

Devlin pointed toward the ceiling and arched a brow. "And that, too."

Anna's gaze followed his gesture, and in the silence all that sounded was her breathing and the steady drumming of rain on the metal roof. "What? I didn't—"

"Enough! People's lives are on the line!" he roared. Devlin felt the energy congregating in her muscles a breath before she tried to make a run for it. She cried out, and the room went suddenly pitch black. Again. *Not this time, little human.* He stepped so tight against her that his legs surrounded hers, his arms braced on the shelves around her shoulders. His body completely boxed her in until they touched from thigh to forehead.

She fought him, just as she had last time, squirming and kicking and pushing.

Attempting to halt her assault without harming her, Devlin banded his arms around her and hauled her so tightly into his chest that he lifted her from the floor.

Which created another problem. Because her writhing motions were so fucking arousing that his mind fogged, his focus fragmented, his body tensed.

Not because of her fear. Because of her touch.

But if he let her go, he'd just find himself playing cat and mouse with her around the room again until they ended up back where they were right now.

He sucked in a fast breath as her hips shifted against his and her teeth sank into his neck.

Long buried and totally base desire stirred from somewhere down deep.

Instinctively, Devlin flashed into the elements, shielding his body from these physical sensations by becoming the wind. The relief from the pressure of his own neglected needs flowed through him.

Oh my God, what's happening? Anna.

She'd joined him. Of course she had. Touching her as he shifted forms changed hers as well. He'd known this was possible, but had never actually engaged in such a thing himself.

And though the transformation had ended his physical torment and her ability to fight, what *hadn't* gone away was her proximity. In the wind, their essences entwined so completely that he felt as surrounded as she must've moments before.

Mister? Are you still here? Oh my God!

We're in the wind. If you'll stop fighting and answer my damn questions, I will return us.

Despite the terseness of his words, the panic receded from her energy. *I'm trying,* she said, *but I don't know how to answer everything you're asking. But…but I'll try.* The lights strobed, then finally stayed on again, clearing up any remaining doubt he might've had that she was the cause of the outages.

As important, her earnestness reverberated through her essence and into him. The strength of it was so…strange. Gods were a lot of things, but honest and genuine were not among their strong suits. At least, not in Devlin's experience. Farren. *Farren* had been the truest, most honorable god he knew. His middle brother had been good to the core. In the end, that had prevented him from seeing their father's true nature. Not that Devlin blamed him. What he wouldn't give to be able to believe in goodness, to expect something besides treachery.

The memories of his brother forced Devlin to another realization—he hadn't had companionship while in the elements since before Farren died. If he didn't count the many times his father had forced him into the elements against his will to do his bidding, Anna, a slip of a mortal woman, was the first being with whom he'd voluntarily shared the wind in over a century. Desire for companionship roared through him—and he resented the hell out of it. Because it made him face the ache of his loneliness, all while knowing it wouldn't be changing any time soon.

A gasp, and then a surge of a powerful emotion so foreign to him he couldn't immediately identify it. *The colors,* she said.

Are you there? Anna's voice—her very self—became a red flag waving in the face of a charging bull. *She* was the one making him miss things he no longer had and want things he'd never get again.

Suddenly, her proximity was suffocating.

He forced them out of the wind and into the physical world. The moment his molecules slid back into place, Devlin pulled away from Anna, needing to be free of her and everything she unleashed within him.

CHAPTER SIX

Disorientation left Anna feeling like a spinning top twirling at full speed. One second, her body didn't exist, but she could somehow still see the room as though she remained in it. The next second, her feet were on the ground again and her shoulders crashed against the metal shelf behind her. Her vision blurred and warped, and she flung out her hands in an attempt to find something—anything—to which she could anchor herself.

Her right hand caught hold of the corner support of the old store shelving as the world in front of her began to obey physics again. "What the hell just happened?" she rasped, heart racing in her chest.

"I'm…" A throat cleared. "I didn't know it would be like that for you," came a low voice.

Forcing a deep breath, Anna turned and found the Dark Man watching her, full lips frowning, brows slashed downward. Except, no way this guy was a *man*, was there? Not after that little trick. More than that, the way he'd advanced on her as he questioned her before their disappearing act. He moved without moving. Or, rather, without taking steps with his feet as normal people did. Another argument that he wasn't a man. Her brain resurrected the memories of all the times he'd disappeared after she'd seen him, and there was no question.

"Are you a ghost?" she whispered. The hair on her arms raised just giving voice to the suspicion.

"No. I'm a god," he said, totally deadpan, that same dark expression on his harsh face.

A god? Oh, great. A ghost with a sense of humor. "You're making fun of me."

"No."

Feeling that the floor was steady beneath her feet again, Anna let go of the shelf and slowly turned toward him. Between the black and the leather and the scowl, he didn't look like any god she'd ever imagined. Not that she spent much time imagining such things. Still, he'd made her body disappear, and that sure made him *something*.

Needing a break from his intensity, she stepped toward the couch.

The man—or whatever he was—stepped in front of her.

"I was just going to…" She gestured toward the couch.

He didn't move. "You won't try to escape." Not a question.

Still, she answered. "No." She met his eyes, even though the intensity staring back at her was difficult to hold. "You made your point." With a single nod, he stepped aside, but quickly took up the role as her shadow as they crossed to the old sofa. She sat. He didn't. Picking at a bit of dried blue paint on her finger, she appreciated having something to concentrate on that was so mundane, so normal. Because if he was telling the truth… Just wow. Consider her mind blown. She gave him a quick sideways glance.

She dropped her hands into her lap and peered up at him. "So, a god?" she asked, her brain still reeling.

"Yes," he said after a moment.

No hesitation, no awkwardness—her gut said he told the truth, no matter how fantastical it was. Her belly flip-flopped as if her life had just taken a hard right turn at full speed. Could this really be possible? Anna blew out a shaky breath. "Um, do you have a name?"

His gaze narrowed as he tilted his head. "Devlin."

A shiver broke out over her skin despite how normal the name sounded. Then again, the archangels had names like Michael and

Gabriel, assuming they'd actually been real. Which, if Devlin was really a god…

"Um," she said, meeting his eyes. He wore an almost wary expression, which seemed odd given who, or what, he was. Why in the world would a *god* be wary of *her*? "God? God of what?"

Dark eyes narrowed. "I am the god of autumn rain and heir to the East Wind."

Blinking, Anna struggled to make sense of the words. "I, uh… wow." She tucked strands of hair behind her ears. "So, the nonstop rain we've had…" He nodded, then arched a brow she could just make out through the long strands of hair across his forehead. Suddenly, the room went totally silent except for the chaos between Anna's own ears. Because the drumming on the roof had ceased. Completely and instantly. She bolted to her feet. "Did you just—"

"Yes." He stepped closer, unintentionally towering over her. Granted, Anna was short, but Devlin was also unusually tall. The top of her head didn't even reach his shoulders. "Now, have you had enough proof that I am what I say?"

Though she still had a million questions, none doubted his divinity. The man—*god*—could control the weather, for God's sake. *Annnd* now that phrase took on a whole new meaning. Shaking her head from the ridiculous thoughts, she met Devlin's gaze. "I believe you."

Devlin's eyes widened as if she'd surprised him, and light flared from behind his eyes.

Attracted to the strangeness of that light, Anna stepped closer. The movement sent her heart into heavy thuds against her breastbone, because her most primal instincts were jangling with the awareness that Devlin could easily turn his powers on her. Already had. Not that he'd hurt her. Slowly, she reached up a hand, curious to see if the light would reflect on her skin.

He flinched, his head and shoulders jerking back. Without her even seeing the movement, his hand caught her wrist. An odd prickly heat emanated from his palm against her skin. Tension bristled out of him, and the light grew more intense.

"I'm sorry," she said, reeling back from him as much as his hold would let her. *So stupid, Anna.* The sound of his voice yelling at her not to touch him earlier came flooding back to her. "I didn't mean anything. Your eyes are glowing again. I just wanted to…" She bowed her head as blood pounded behind her ears. "I'm sorry."

His grip loosened, then released her altogether. "You are curious," he said.

She nodded, uncertain if there was a correct answer here, one that kept her with all her parts firmly attached where they were right now. Fingers caught her chin and tilted her face upward. Intensity radiated from his gaze, his expression, the hard set of his jaw.

Anna's heart tripped into a sprint. "I'm sorry," she blurted again in a fast, whispered rush. "I'm completely color-blind. Except when I paint, my world is all shades of black and white. But painting in color has allowed me to learn to distinguish shades of gray enough to recognize them as colors. And when your eyes glow, the shade makes me think of the color purple."

"My eyes are black," he said.

She lifted her gaze and shook her head despite the hold of his fingers on her chin. "Doesn't look that way to me."

As his gaze bored into hers, his expression was part curiosity, part wariness. Devlin dropped his hands and raked them through his hair, pushing the longish strands of black out of his face…and giving her a clear view of his eyes. And his harshly handsome face, all sharp angles and dark shadows. Radiating power from the intense stare of his eyes to the hard clench of his jaw. After a moment, his eyebrows lifted as if to say, *Well, what are you waiting for?*

"It's okay," she said in a low voice. She took a small step backward, not wanting to make another mistake. "I don't—"

In a flash of imperceptible motion, Devlin advanced on her, grasped her hand again, and lifted it toward his face.

Anna nearly stumbled forward he'd so surprised her with the movement. Once she recovered, she moved her hand closer, still held in his grip, until she was a few inches from his left eye, almost as if she were going to cup his cheek. Light danced across her palm. She gasped. "Do you see that?" she asked, glancing to his eyes.

Suspicion shaped everything about his expression. His gaze flickered from her body, so close to his, to her face, and finally to her hand. His brows cranked down. "Yes," he said, surprise lightening his tone. A little. "It is a visible manifestation of our power. Happens sometimes. I've seen it in my…in others, but never paid much attention to it in myself."

Anna smiled, enjoying the low rumble of his voice, and curious as she'd maybe ever been in her life about another person. "Something tells me you're not the type to stand around primping in front of mirrors."

His gaze cut to hers, and the corner of his lip *almost* lifted into something that might've eventually become a smile. Then it was gone. And so, apparently, was his patience for their little getting-to-know-you moment. He dropped her hand, crossed his arms, and shuttered all emotion from his eyes. "I need to know about the paintings, Anna. And I need to know right now."

ಶಿಧಿ

Devlin wasn't sure what in Hades had possessed him to encourage Anna, but her closeness, her heat, her wonder worked on his senses in ways that completely frickin' overwhelmed him. He'd *wanted* her smile, her laughter, her touch. Add her easily stated belief in his identity—which was a little thing but, pathetically, way more than he ever got from anyone else—and it all left him feeling a lot as though the earth had started rotating in the wrong direction. Like he needed anything else knocking him off kilter.

And that pissed him the fuck off. Electricity rippled over his palms.

"Well, human?" he asked, hating himself when she flinched at his tone, at the way he'd addressed her when he damn right and well knew her name. But he needed every kind of distance he could get from her right now. Hurt flickered over Anna's expression, making him feel like an even bigger bastard than usual.

"What do you want to know?" she finally asked, not quite meeting his eyes.

"Why did you paint these?" he shot back in a hard tone, forcing his mind to return to what mattered most.

"I don't know," she said in a flat voice. Was she shaking again?

So much for not being afraid of him. *No, you scared her. On purpose. There's a difference.* "You don't know why you paint them?" he asked just as hard, releasing some of the angst crawling through him by letting the rain fall again.

The instant the deluge began hitting the roof, Anna's gaze cut skyward, then flickered to him. She hugged herself. "No, not really."

Impatience flowed through Devlin, spurred in part at the regret slithering through his gut. Watching her right now was like seeing a fully blossomed flower close up and fold in on itself—an apt analogy given that he was a god of the East, responsible for the decay and death of the autumn season. Gods, Anna's withdrawal made him feel like he was Medusa turning someone to stone with his gaze. Devlin's chest filled with an achy pressure. "Damnit, Anna. You must know why—"

"Because I have *no choice*," she yelled in exasperation. She threaded her fingers into her long pale hair and turned away.

Ice-cold foreboding clawed up Devlin's spine. He had way too much up-close-and-personal with being forced to do things against his will to not react to that. "What do you mean?"

Anna whipped around, gesturing with her hands. "Just that. When the images come to me, it's like they take over. I can't think of anything else. I can't focus or concentrate. I can't eat or sleep. Painting is like an exorcism—I don't get myself back until it's out of my head and onto the canvas." The words had poured from her so fast that she gasped for air. "And now it won't stop. And the images…*God*, the images are so horrible. They leave me feeling sick and drained and weak with a grief I don't understand." Glassiness filled her pale eyes, but she barreled on. "So don't come in here asking why I'm doing this. If anyone should know, it's *you*. They're *your* paintings, so *you* tell *me* what the hell this is all about. Because I don't know and I want it to stop," she yelled. A strangled cry spilled out, and Anna pressed her fingers to her lips. Her expression appeared on the verge of shattering, but as Devlin watched she muscled the emotion back. Her expression eased and she heaved a deep breath.

Her tirade stunned Devlin. That she'd stood up to him. That she'd pushed back. That she felt so deeply and could just lay it all out in the open. For what felt like an eternity, Devlin had spent all his time boxing up his emotions and putting on an act of disinterested obedience for his father. And Eurus, *gods*, his father was a master of deception.

As Devlin stood staring at this fierce, beautiful woman, realization hit him like a two-by-four to the forehead—this was the most honest conversation he'd had in eons. "I'm just as surprised as you are," he said, working to gentle his voice. "There is only one thing I know that you don't."

For a long moment, Anna's gaze bored into him. "What's that?" she asked in a tone still full of fight.

"They're not all of me. Some are of my father."

She frowned. "Your father? Is he a god, too?"

A single nod. "Supreme God of the East Wind and Guardian of Autumn." Not that he'd done much guarding lately. Or ever? Eurus was sometimes called the Harbinger of Misfortune, and it was a title he'd earned by intentionally spreading unluckiness in his wake. Just for shits and giggles.

Anna's eyes went wide. "So, when you said you were heir to the East Wind, do you mean to say that…that would be you? Someday?" Her wonder wasn't as apparent on her expression, still reserved after their heated words, but it slipped into her voice.

"Yes." *Hopefully sooner rather than later*. Not that he'd ever coveted the position, or the status or power associated with it. But Devlin's ascending meant that Eurus would be gone once and for all.

And then they'd all be free.

"So, you look alike?" she asked.

Gods, it rankled to admit to even the slightest similarity to the man he despised most in the world, but in this instance it was the undeniable truth. "Yes."

"Can you show me which ones?" she asked. "Maybe that'll help us make more sense of them."

Nodding, Devlin gestured for Anna to lead the way. She skirted around him as though she wanted to make it clear she wasn't going to try to touch him. He appreciated the gesture—after a lifetime of abuse, his body was primed to expect more of the same.

So then why did he find himself leaning toward her as she passed?

He followed her across the room, trying to keep his mind—and eyes—on the question of the paintings rather than on her small, heart-shaped ass shown off to such perfection in those tight jean shorts. Damn.

"Okay," she said, coming up before the group of stacked paintings. "If you'll help me move these, we can lay them out in the order I painted them. Maybe that will mean something to you?" She glanced up at him, and he schooled his expression and nodded.

"Could be. Tell me where you want them."

Anna lifted the one she'd finished a few hours before, the one of Alastor shackled somewhere in the depths of his father's estate in the Realm of the East. "Put this one anywhere and we'll work backward," she said, passing the horizontal canvas to him. Her arm brushed his on the handoff, sending a zing of awareness and warmth through his body despite the clothing that separated her skin from his. When she gasped, he knew that she'd felt something, too. "Sorry," she murmured as she turned away.

When his gaze fell on the tortured depiction of his brother, whatever pleasure he'd enjoyed the moment before turned to dust. Where *exactly* their father had imprisoned Alastor, Devlin didn't know. Under Eurus's dominion, the Eastern Realm had become a living, breathing incarnation of the unluckiness, misfortunate, and malevolence that the ancients had first attributed to autumn—which they'd even refused to recognize in ancient times as its own season. The whole place was a gigantic, booby-trapped house of horrors, except the things that jumped out at you were all too real and even more dangerous. And the impenetrable compound where Devlin grew up was the worst part of it all. Situated on the top of a craggy mount, the ancient fortress extended many floors into the rock. And the doors, hallways, and stairwells that filled the inside were ever-changing. Literally. Long ago, Eurus had performed an incantation over the place meant to confuse and entrap, and ever since then the architecture of the building magically changed itself at random times and in unpredictable ways.

But I will find you, brother, Devlin silently vowed as he placed the painting against a rack on the far side of the room.

"This one's next," Anna said.

"What do you do with all these paintings?" he asked, nodding at the shelves as he accepted the second painting.

"I sell them. I have a few private patrons who commission my work, relationships with galleries in New York, Chicago, D.C., and L.A. that show certain pieces, and an online store where I post photographs of everything."

Devlin wasn't surprised to hear her work had met with such success. The paintings were vibrant and moving and so damn real he felt that he could reach into them. For the next couple minutes, they worked quietly, sorting the paintings into a long line from the first one she had done to the most recent. Oddly, Devlin felt a peace born of companionship that was so strange that it stopped him dead in his tracks when he realized that his brain wasn't flooded with the usual churning river of self-loathing.

"What's the matter?" she asked.

Devlin shook his head, not sure he could explain it if he tried, which he had no intention and even less desire to do. "This all?"

Looking away, she nodded and walked to the beginning of the line. "I painted that one about a week ago," she said, pointing to the one that depicted Eurus—or him—pinning two glowing white beings in front of a building engulfed in flames. "Can you tell if that's you?"

Crouching before the painting, Devlin studied the back of the god floating in the air and finally shook his head. "Why did you paint these two this way?" he asked, looking at the glowing figures.

"It was the way I saw them," she said. "None of these come from my own imagination. The pictures come pretty much fully formed in my head. I can't alter them."

"They are other gods, I'm guessing, but I don't know where this is," he said.

They worked down the line, but in the end Devlin couldn't discern anymore about the identity of the Eastern god or the meaning of the images than he had when he'd surveyed the images himself the night before. Maybe none of them had yet happened? But when they started coming true, perhaps knowing the order of the images would allow them to plan and react—and maybe even change the outcome? Who knew. Devlin crouched in front of the last image, his heart squeezing at Alastor's blank expression, bloodied wrists, and too-thin body.

"This one's you," Anna said. "The jacket…"

"Yes," Devlin said without looking at her.

"What is this?" she asked. "Do you recognize it?"

Devlin rose and turned to her. "To an extent. The man is my brother, Alastor, who my father has imprisoned for years."

Anna gasped. "Why?"

Not going there. Bad enough to cause such misery let alone admit it to another, especially one who looked at him with awe in her eyes. "It doesn't matter," he said, hardness slipping back into his voice. "Beyond that, I don't know. Because this moment has not happened. At least, not yet," he said, admitting his growing suspicion.

Her gaze dropped to the painting. "Yet?" she finally asked.

"Anna," he said.

She looked up, her expression filling with fearful realization.

"I think you've been painting the future."

CHAPTER SEVEN

"The future?" Anna whispered. Among all the revelations the last hour had included, this one most shook the ground beneath her feet. Because it was about her. Believing someone like Devlin existed and that he had special powers was one thing—and *not* a little thing—to wrap your head around. Believing that she was capable of telling the future was…just about impossible to believe. "No," she said, shaking her head.

"Yes," Devlin said, meeting her gaze head-on. "As a god, Anna, I can sense divine energy. And when you paint, it surrounds you. Question is, who did your energy come from?"

Anna shivered. "I'm just a woman. I'm not—"

"You are *not* just a woman!" Devlin roared as he closed the distance between her and grabbed her by the arms. Wind whipped through the room and thunder crashed outside.

Anna froze, surprise and fear making it impossible to think, to react, to breathe. The lights went out and with a strangled cry she shoved against his chest. Hard.

"Anna! Anna, calm down." Devlin's grip eased, though he didn't let go. "I scared you on purpose to make you see. Calm down and concentrate on turning the lights back on. Just as you turned them off."

Confusion and adrenaline whirled through Anna's brain, scrambling the meaning of Devlin's words. All she knew was the need to run, to hide, to get away.

"You can do this, Anna. Do it."

Slowly, his meaning pierced the haze of her fight-or-flight response. Anna fought back her fear and forced a deep breath. Shaking, she focused on Devlin's glowing eyes and the hard angles of his face she could make out in the blackness.

"That's it," he said, voice deep and gritty. "Now restore the light."

Anna blew out a shaky breath and concentrated on his ridiculous demand.

Nothing.

"I can't," she whispered.

"Take another deep breath and concentrate. You are safe. I won't hurt you."

His words were calming, encouraging, almost lulling. She did as he said, forcing her shoulders to relax as she released a long breath. *Restore the light*, she thought, echoing his words.

Light immediately flooded the room.

Anna gasped, her gaze going to the fixture above them and then to him. "Oh my God. Did I really just—"

"Yes," Devlin said, the hint of a smile playing around his lips, all the fierce anger of a moment before completely gone. Jesus, she'd been completely terrified of him. But it had been a ruse, a trick to make her confront his reality.

She stared at him, soul-shaking fear flooding every cell in her body. What in the hell was she that she could use her mind to make the lights turn on and off? *You use your mind to control the light in your painting.* The thought sliced through her growing panic and froze her where she stood. She did do that, and she'd done it all her life. Was this merely more of the same, just on a grander scale? Anna looked at Devlin anew. After all this time, was he someone who had the answers to why she could do these things?

"Anna?" Devlin frowned and concern filled his eyes. "I know this is all a lot—"

"*I* did that. I *did* that." Adrenaline and awe made her feel as if she were filled with jumping beans. She could barely stay still. And *he* was the one who'd helped her make this discovery about herself. "Thank you," she said, jumping up and throwing her arms around his neck.

Devlin went absolutely rigid.

Realization pierced through her joy. *Holy crap, Anna, what are you doing?* Red-hot embarrassment flowed through her and she released her hold, but his significantly greater height forced her to slide down the front of him.

An arm banded around her lower back, freezing her tight against him. Chest to chest, her face just below his.

"Oh, God, I'm sorry," she said. She'd just tackle-hugged a freaking *god*, and now he wouldn't let her go. Despite the fact that she'd apparently committed a major faux pas, Devlin's body felt *damn* good. All hard, lean muscle up against her. Power and strength evident in the fact that he held most of her body weight in the grip of one arm. And, *geez*, he smelled fantastic, like the cool, earthy spice of a beautiful fall day. She had to resist pressing her nose to his throat and drinking him in.

"Look at me," he said, his voice like gravel.

Anna dragged her gaze upward, over the steady pulse beating in his neck, over the hard angle of his jaw, over the dark pink of his full lips. His eyes absolutely blazed back at her.

"I'm s—"

"*Don't.*" His gaze narrowed. After a moment, fingers brushed the side of her face as Devlin slowly tucked a strand of hair behind her ear.

The gesture was so sweet, so tentative, that it made Anna's breath catch and her body warm. Instinctively, she shifted her hands upward from where they'd come to rest on his shoulders to gently cup the back of his neck.

His gaze flashed from where his fingers had been stroking through her hair to her face. And then his eyes zeroed in on her lips.

Anna's heart tripped into a full-out sprint, pounding blood through her everywhere they touched. This couldn't be happening. Could it? Was this man, *this god*, really going to kiss her?

In maddeningly slow motion, Devlin leaned toward her, his lips dropping open, his beautiful dark eyes backlit by a brilliant light, desire softening the angles of his masculine face. Need surged through her body in return.

Devlin shuddered and his brow furrowed. He froze, his face so close to hers that she could feel his breath on her lips. He blinked and shook his head as if dragging himself from a dream. "Don't," he gritted out, his tone nearly a plea. The almost-lost expression on his face made her wonder which of them he spoke to. After a moment of embattled hesitation, he set her down and stepped away. Words in a language she didn't know spilled forth as he roughly yanked his hand through the long strands of jet-black hair.

Anna was at a total loss. She missed his heat. The way he'd brought her body to life with just a touch. The abject need on his face as he'd looked at her. Now, awkwardness rang like a bell between them, and she had no idea how to make any of it better.

Then again, maybe she'd only imagined his desire. In a rush of memory, she recalled how he'd frozen at her touch, the fact that he'd pushed her away. Why in the world would a god want her? That wasn't low self-esteem talking, either. Anna knew she was attractive enough, even if in a sort of unusual way, and she'd never had a problem finding men to date. But Devlin was *a god*.

She peered up at him. *Damn*, she would've thought he was a god even if he hadn't told her he actually was, though just of the usual, incredibly sexy kind.

Without question, this was the craziest day of her life. And the fact that she didn't question the reality of it made it all the crazier.

Clearing his throat, Devlin crossed his arms and stared at a point between them. "Do you believe me now?"

"About what?" He arched a brow in silent reply. "Oh! The lights." She sighed, grateful for something else to obsess about other than the ridiculous topic of their near miss of a kiss and what it did or didn't mean. "Um…I guess." His brow lifted higher. "Yes," she finally said. "But I don't understand how I did it."

His posture eased, as if he, too, were glad for the diversion. "Your ability seems connected to your emotions. Has it always happened?"

The word *no* sat on the tip of her tongue, but then her brain resurrected memories of a different sort. Like the string of power outages that had happened so frequently in her childhood home that her parents had joked about having the unluckiest house on the block, because they'd often lost power during storms when, inexplicably, the rest of the street was lit up like the Las Vegas strip. Like one time during college when she'd been walking along a dark stretch of sidewalk and been absolutely sure she was being followed, and as she'd broken into a run and wished for help, the dark lampposts along her route all had begun to glow. Like the day a few years ago she'd received a personal invitation to apply to be artist-in-residence at a prestigious arts program in New York City, and then screamed into a pillow upon the immediate realization that she had to pass it up because she couldn't leave her father. The power had gone out the minute she'd unleashed her grief and frustration into the plush cotton.

Oh my God. Devlin's right.

Suddenly, her life looked totally different, as if she'd been wearing glasses with the wrong prescription all this time. "Um." She pressed her hands to her face and closed her eyes. "I think it actually has." She'd just never thought to connect the strange stuff that happened when she painted to these other experiences. But, now, because of Devlin, it was as though someone had shone a light on her life. "It's all true," she said. "Everything you've told me."

Her gaze cut to Devlin, watching her with guarded interest. "Yes."

These revelations were more than enough to take in without adding her attraction to him into the mix, so Anna turned away and slowly paced to the other side of the room. As she walked and struggled to make sense of everything she'd learned, she studied the paintings they'd laid out, almost feeling as though she was looking at them for the first time.

When she got to the last one, she turned again, her gaze snagging on the old clock on the wall. It was after noon. *Dad!* "Oh my God. I have to go," she said. She'd missed her father's usual lunchtime. He was probably flipping out by now. "Way to go, Anna," she muttered, darting across the room.

Devlin stepped in front of her, eyebrow raised and expression full of suspicion. When Anna tried to step around him, he shifted, blocking her way. "We're not done here, Anna."

Guilt for forgetting about her father and how overwhelmed she felt combined to make her impatient, agitated. "Maybe you aren't, but I am. I have to go."

"No," he said.

Anna scoffed. "Look, you might be a god, but I answer to a higher power—my father." Something dark flickered within Devlin's gaze, but Anna pushed on. "He's sick and needs my help, and I've totally lost track of time with...all this," she said, waving her hands. When he still didn't move, she planted her hands on her hips. "So, what's the plan here? Just keep me locked up until I'm not useful to you anymore?"

She was being a smart-ass, but her stomach flip-flopped at the possibility. Because she wouldn't be able do anything to stop that, would she?

His gaze narrowed, his cheeks colored with emotion, and the air felt almost electrified between them. For the space of a breath, Anna thought he was going to explode. "Sick how?" he asked, restrained anger making his voice tight.

"He has Alzheimer's." Devlin frowned as though he didn't understand. "Dementia?" she asked.

With a nod, Devlin scrubbed his hand over his face. "You are his caregiver."

"Yes," Anna said, crossing her arms. "Now do you see? I have to go to him."

A series of emotions Anna couldn't read passed over Devlin's face. "Yes," he finally said.

Relief nearly made her sag. "Thank you," she said, stepping around him. He didn't block her this time, allowing the fight to drain out of her. "I'll come back." She stopped in the doorway and looked over her shoulder.

Devlin was *right there*.

"I'm coming with you," he said before she could even ask.

"What?"

"I'm—"

She braced her hands against his chest, refusing to care or question why he flinched as he'd done every other time she'd touched him. "You can't come with me."

"You can't stop me."

Anna sputtered. "Devlin, my father is out of his mind, literally. And all kinds of things set him off—"

"Is he violent with you?" he asked, a storm rolling in behind his black eyes.

"No. Not at all," she said, though sometimes he got very angry, and it broke her heart because the Garrett Fallston she'd known all her life had never even raised his voice. "He gets very upset when anything out of the normal happens. He's all about routines now, and I've missed his lunch. So he's already going to be in a bad place when I get home without bringing a stranger along for the ride." Let alone a man. Anna didn't know why, but the dementia had made her father suspicious of and combative with most men.

"I understand," he said, "but it doesn't change that I can't leave you. Not until I know more about these paintings."

Anna's brain got stuck on the spin cycle as it became clear they were just going to go round and round until she was even more late getting home. "Well, I guess it doesn't matter what I say," she said. She spun on her heel, grabbed her belongings, and marched out to her Jeep.

Devlin was leaning against her car, elbows braced on the hood as though he didn't have a care in the world.

Anna nearly screamed. "Holy shit," she said, pressing her hand to her heart. "That's not cool."

Apparently untroubled by her reaction, he raised his hand and held his thumb and forefinger just millimeters apart. "It's a little cool."

"Oh, so Mr. Tall, Dark, and Angsty has a sense of humor?"

"On rare occasion."

So now *he wants to be charming.* Though, as she recalled his concern and the way he'd touched her face and hair, she knew it wasn't the first time he'd charmed her. Rolling her eyes, Anna stepped to the Jeep's door. "You riding with me or using your invisibility cloak?"

He frowned. "Invisi—"

"Just get in." Not waiting for his reply, she hopped into the seat and closed her door.

"Automobiles have always been one of my favorite human inventions," he said from the seat next to her.

Nearly jumping out of her skin, Anna gripped the steering wheel and forced a deep breath. "I'm surprised you don't just flash yourself to my house," she muttered.

He crossed his arms over that broad chest. "I'd rather stay with you."

The words set off a tingling inside her belly that Anna didn't let herself consider too closely. She started the engine, backed out of her spot, and gripped the steering wheel as if she were holding onto reality itself. As she turned onto the road in front of her studio, the silence filling the Jeep between them felt more and more awkward until Anna couldn't stand it anymore. "Do you have a favorite?" she managed, scrambling for a topic and feeling ridiculous.

"Favorite?"

She threw a sideways glance at him…and holy *wow* did he look good sitting there, one arm's bicep bunched from the way he held onto the ceiling strap, his long legs parted, his other big hand lying on the muscular bulk of his thigh. "Car."

"Hmm." He gazed out the window at the passing scenery. "The

faster they go the more I like them," he said, almost reluctantly. "Bugattis, Koenigseggs, McLarens."

"I've never heard of any of those." Though she loved the way the foreign-sounding words rolled off his tongue, and the hint of pleasure in his tone.

"European models," he said.

"Do you get to drive a lot?" she asked.

Just when she thought he wasn't going to respond, he said, "No. Not as much as I'd like."

Michael would know what to say right now. The thought came out of nowhere, but she immediately knew it was true. Her brother had loved fast cars, too. A guy thing, she guessed. Thinking of her brother gave her an idea… "If you like speed, do you like motorcycles, too?"

His gaze cut back to her. "Yes. Why?"

"I have one." She shrugged, and for a long moment the *thump-thump* of the windshield wipers was the only sound filling the Jeep's cab. Not that she rode the bike enough to justify keeping it, but she couldn't imagine getting rid of it, either. "It's a Daytona 1200," she said, suddenly hearing her brother's excited rambling off of the bike's specs the day he'd bought it. Just six months before he'd died.

Devlin shifted. "That's a damn fast bike."

Glancing at him again, she smiled. Eyes wide, face relaxed, he wore an expression that slipped past interested to almost eager. God, it transformed his entire face. And for some reason filled Anna's belly with giddiness. "What is it with boys and their toys?" She winked. "Yes, it's very fast. I've never pushed it as far as it can go, but my brother took it to a racetrack a few times and said he got it up to a hundred and fifty, easy." Just the thought of riding the Daytona that fast made her stomach flip. "You could ride it sometime, if you want."

"Yeah?"

She smiled at his obvious interest. "Sure."

He nodded. "You have a brother?"

The troubled tone was so different from the enthusiasm of a moment before that it drew Anna's gaze again. The dark shadows and hard angles had returned to Devlin's face. Damn, it was hard to keep up with him. "Had," she said, trying to puzzle out the fast shifts of the god's moods. "Michael died when I was fourteen. Not on the bike. He was changing a flat tire on his car on the side of the road and a guy in a pickup hit him." Anna clamped down on the grief that threatened to well up whenever she talked about what had happened. But the senselessness and wastefulness of Michael's death punched her in the gut every time, and the passage of time never seemed to make a difference.

"I'm sorry," he said in a voice so low she wondered if she'd imagined it. For the rest of the trip, Devlin's gaze remained locked to the window, as if the passing fields and farmhouses were completely enthralling.

Anna didn't push the conversation again until she turned onto her street. "We need to talk about what's going to happen when we get inside."

"You don't want him to see me," Devlin said in a flat tone.

"I don't want to upset him," she replied.

"I won't show myself, then."

"What? Like, you'll stay invisible but you'll still be there?" Devlin nodded, and Anna shivered. "That's…just…that's weird. I'll spend every second looking over my shoulder and wondering where you are." She blew out a long breath as she turned into the driveway and pulled all the way in. "Is it really necessary for you to hang out here? I promise I'll come back to the studio. And now you know where I live so you can find me one way or the other."

Devlin's gaze narrowed. "I need answers, Anna. And I don't have much time."

Their stares locked for a long moment, and Anna scrambled to think of a solution that would satisfy her stubborn god and not agitate her father. Well, not *her* stubborn god. Whatever. Maybe she could sneak him in the back door and hide him? Maybe she'd just have to accept him being there but not visible? If he didn't have much time, how long would it be, anyway?

Suddenly, Devlin's gaze shifted to a point over her shoulder. "Who is that?" he asked in a low voice.

Following his gaze, Anna looked out the driver's-side window to find her dad's home health aide standing on the back porch, hands braced on the railing, watching them and presumably waiting for them to get out of the car. "Oh, hell," she said, dreading finding out how Evan had ended up here. He wasn't supposed to work today. She turned back to Devlin. "Do you think he saw you?"

"Yes," he said, eyeballing Evan.

Anna placed a hand on his arm, ignoring the way his muscles tensed beneath the worn leather. "That's Evan. He's my dad's full-time caregiver and my friend, and he's a good guy. But now that he's seen you, we need a story. Um… Ah, I know. You're an old college friend. We studied art together at the Pennsylvania School of the Arts. You are definitely *not* a god. Got that?"

He nodded, though he hadn't taken his gaze from Evan.

"Devlin, look at me," she said, echoing his command from earlier. "He's a friend."

A flash of light from behind his eyes. "Got it."

"Come on." Wondering how else this day could get derailed, Anna pushed out of the car. "Hey," she said, calling up to Evan. "I'm afraid to ask."

"It's okay now," Evan said, his gaze flickering from Anna to Devlin as he came around the front of the Jeep.

Which meant it hadn't been okay before. Thank God for Evan. With his bald head and light-brown skin, he was the first caregiver her father had fully accepted. For the past four years, Evan had worked for them on a full-time basis as a home health aide, but they'd become more than just employer-employee. Evan had become a friend and confidant—really, Anna's only friend since she was self-employed and otherwise just took care of her dad. She truly didn't know what she'd do without Evan. Anna sighed as she made her way up the steps and onto the small back porch, Devlin right behind her. "Devlin, this is Evan Williams. Evan, this is Devlin—" And…she didn't know his last name. Shit. Shit shit shit.

"Devlin Eston," he said without missing a beat.

Evan extended his hand and smiled. "Hi, Devlin." After a split second of hesitation that had Anna nearly holding her breath, Devlin returned the shake.

"How do you know each other?" Evan asked politely.

"We both went to Penn School of the Arts," Devlin said. Gratitude filled Anna at the easy and completely believable way he'd spoken.

"So you're an artist?" Evan asked.

"How's Dad?" Anna interrupted, not wanting Devlin to get tripped up in details. "How did you get sucked in over here?"

"I was on my way home and dropped off a prescription I forgot to pick up yesterday, saw your Jeep wasn't here, and heard Garrett calling for Tessa over and over. Figured you got held up somewhere so I stayed."

Anna cringed. "Thank God you did, Evan, but I'm really sorry. I lost track of time." Just one more reason why she loved the fact that Evan lived only two blocks away.

"It was no problem, really."

She unleashed a long breath, letting go of some of the stress that hadn't settled into her muscles. "How is he now?"

"Better. Not as agitated as he was. He'll be fine." Evan gave her arm a pat. "But now that you're here, I'm gonna run. Jake's probably waiting for me."

She smiled at the mention of Evan's longtime partner. Jake was as awesome as Evan and they were great together. "Tell him I said hi and sorry I held you up."

Evan gave her a kiss on the cheek. "Will do. See you tomorrow."

Nodding, she stepped to the door. She gave Evan a last wave as he hit the driveway, then she cut her gaze to Devlin, who'd been quietly watching her exchange with Evan. "Come on in," she said. "Just please wait in the kitchen while I check on my dad."

Devlin nodded, and Anna stepped inside, ditched her belongings on the counter, and beelined for the living room. Her father's expression went from surprised to relieved to angry when she walked through the doorway. "Hi, Dad," she said, immediately running her gaze over him to make sure he was okay. He was, at least physically.

"Where the hell have you been?" He sat forward in his chair and gripped the plush armrests.

She knelt beside his recliner and cupped his big hand in hers. "I'm sorry. I lost track of time. Can I do anything for you now? Can I get you anything?"

"No. Evan made a mess of my lunch but I ate enough, I guess." His gaze ran over her face.

"Can I make you some coffee?" she asked, rubbing her thumb against the back of his hand.

He harrumphed and settled back in his chair. "No, but I don't want you going anywhere else today, Tess. I don't like it."

Hard to hide that she'd gone out if she wasn't here in time to keep him on his schedule. *Way to go, Anna.* "Okay," she said with a smile.

"Yeah, yeah," he said, but the relief was evident in how his brow relaxed and his muscles eased beneath her touch. "It's chilly," he said.

Anna tugged the heavy knit blanket she loved from the arm of the couch and spread it over him. "Here. How's that?"

"Better," he said as he kicked out the leg rest. Experience told her he'd be asleep in less than ten minutes, though a glance at the clock revealed she'd held up his daily nap by more than an hour.

"Good," she said, glad he didn't seem intent on holding a grudge. All thanks to Evan's saving the day before things got too bad, no doubt. She crossed to the kitchen.

"I don't like when you're gone, Tessa," he said in a low rumble that made her ache.

I miss her, too, Dad. Hand on the arch between the living room and kitchen, Anna looked over her shoulder. "I know, Dad. But I'm here now." When he didn't pull his gaze from the football game playing on the television, she left the room.

"Sorry 'bout that," she whispered to Devlin when she returned to the kitchen. He stood by the table, out of the line of sight from the living room. His gaze lit on her and something in his face gentled. Devlin looked like every cautionary tale a father might've told a daughter. Black hair, black eyes, black leather. Pure tortured bad boy from the longish hair to the sneak peek of black ink she'd seen on his wrist as they'd laid out her paintings to the ass-kicking boots he wore. Yet that gentling of his expression reached right into her chest and tugged at her heart. She walked to the counter and refolded a towel that was already folded. What the heck was she supposed to do with him here? "Um, would you like something to eat or drink? Some coffee? Oh." Anna froze with her hand on the handle of the coffeepot. "Do you eat and drink?" she whispered.

Devlin smirked. "I do." The humor dropped off his face. "I don't want to cause you any trouble."

She might've thrown some sarcasm back at him if two things hadn't happened—if his expression hadn't gone serious, revealing his sincerity, and if his stomach hadn't growled. Loudly.

It was the best release of tension ever. Anna chuckled. "I think your stomach just answered for you," she said quietly, glad for once that her dad had the television on so loud. Devlin's gaze narrowed, but when she told him to sit down at the table, amazingly, he listened. She opened the fridge and surveyed her options. "Do you like—"

"Anything you offer will be perfect," he said in that same seriousness. The words were almost weighted with a significance Anna didn't understand. And was probably imagining.

Anna made quick work of heating up chili and cornbread from the night before for both of them. Before long, they sat together at the table over their late lunch. They hardly talked—because Devlin ate like a man who'd missed way too many meals and didn't know when he might get his next. There wasn't anything impolite about his table manners, exactly, besides the fact that he ate with an air of desperation that made her heart beat harder and her throat go tight.

The possibility that he really *was* desperate—and for food, of all things… He was a god—how could that even be possible?

Not wanting to make him uncomfortable, Anna dug into her own meal, sneaking a quick peek across the table every so often. "How 'bout some more?" she said when he cleaned his bowl. "There's really only enough for one serving left, anyway. You might as well finish it." She popped a piece of cornbread into her mouth, not wanting to do anything to reveal just how apparent his hunger was.

He tilted his head and studied her before giving a single nod. When she reached for his bowl, she pretended not to notice the slight backward jerk of his body, as if…as if *he* feared *her*.

"Do you have a favorite food?" she asked as she fixed him another helping.

"I'm not picky," he said in a low voice.

"I'm not picky either, but that doesn't mean I wouldn't kill for a plate of lobster ravioli in a rose cream sauce." She smiled over her shoulder and found him watching her intently. Heat lanced through her body—and made her realize he was the only man besides her father or Evan who had sat at that table since she'd come back home to take care of her dad. She didn't date often, and when she did, she didn't bring them home. But, God, it was really nice to be taking care of a man in her own space.

An ironic thought given that her relationship with her father had pretty much devolved entirely into one of caregiving. But this…this was different.

"Well," he said, shifting and crossing his arms in what seemed to her to be a defensive posture he adopted almost reflexively. "Um, there's this thing called shepherd's pie."

Anna smiled. She'd had no idea what kind of a food a god might hold as his favorite, and yet his choice was so simple, so normal, something she liked herself.

"What?" he asked, narrowing his gaze at her good humor.

"Nothing. I like it, too," she said, bringing his refilled bowl back to the table.

"Thank you," he said gruffly.

"When was the last time you had shepherd's pie?" she asked, her mind mentally running through her cupboards to determine if she had everything she'd need to make it. And how perfect that it was something her father would like, too.

Devlin paused with his spoon halfway to his mouth. For a moment, his gaze went distant, and then he shook his head and continued eating.

"Well?" Anna asked.

"You don't want to know."

Bracing her elbows on the table, Anna laced her fingers together and stared at him. "Sure I do." When he didn't answer right away, she took a drink of her water.

"Over a century ago," he murmured around a bite.

Anna choked on her water. Setting the glass down, she pressed a napkin to her mouth until she managed to clear most of the water from her windpipe. With watery eyes, she peered across the table to find Devlin staring at her. *A century?* Holy crap, it shouldn't have surprised her given everything else she'd learned about him, but it did. She grabbed hold of the table's edge to anchor herself to the real world.

"Told you," he said, emptying his second bowl and polishing off his third piece of cornbread.

"You did," she said, drying her eyes. "And, of course, now I'm curious about how old you are."

"How old are you?" he asked.

"Twenty-nine," she said.

"Hmm." Carefully, he collected his dishes into a pile as if he meant to carry them to the sink.

Anna rose. "I'll get that."

"I can help."

"No doubt," she said with a smile. "But you're my guest. Right?"

"Not that I gave you much choice."

Anna shrugged and reached to clear his place at the table slowly, not wanting to startle him as she always seemed to do.

He grasped her hand. "I thank you for the meal."

Such formality. "It was nothing," she said.

His grasp tightened. "Kindness is never nothing, Annalise. Trust me."

The reverence in his tone filled her chest with an aching warmth. She didn't even mind his use of her full name—which had always struck her as an old lady's name—because he pronounced it as if his tongue were caressing each of the syllables. She blinked away the ridiculous thought and replaced it with a far more important one: what kind of an existence did he lead if a simple meal represented extraordinary kindness? "You're welcome," she managed.

Suddenly, she no longer just grudgingly accepted his presence here—even though he was right, he *hadn't* given her a choice. Instead, she was almost surprised to find that she was glad he was here. Because, as head-spinning as everything about him was, how was she going to go forward in a world where she knew he existed but would never see him again? If he didn't have much time to find out what her paintings meant, that meant…she didn't have much time with him, either.

The realization settled on her shoulders like an anvil. Quietly, mechanically, she cleared the table and moved everything to the sink.

As she went to turn on the faucet, Devlin rose. "Wait," he said, cocking his head as if listening to something.

Anna braced her hands against the counter. "What?" she asked, not hearing anything out of the ordinary.

As if tracking the sound, Devlin crossed the kitchen and stepped through the arch to the living room.

"Devlin!" she whispered loudly. *God, please let Dad be asleep.* He was. "My father," she mouthed, waving Devlin back toward the kitchen.

Frowning, Devlin pressed one finger over his lips as if to shush her. Anna would've rolled her eyes, except he wasn't looking at her. Instead, he focused on the television.

Peeking around Devlin at her thankfully sleeping father, she tiptoed closer, nearly holding her breath from the anxiety that he'd wake up and find them standing there. Devlin was a stranger, a man, and with Anna—a trifecta of things sure to make him go ballistic.

"What's the matter?" she whispered when she stood next to Devlin.

He jutted his chin toward the TV.

A weather special report had interrupted the football game. A map of the East Coast flashed onto the screen, showing a red line and a blue line making two alternate paths up the coastline. Both originated from a rotating symbol—a tropical storm on the verge of hurricane force. The blue line had the storm making landfall in the Carolinas. The red line had the storm making landfall at the Chesapeake Bay…pretty much exactly over Jarrettsville.

As this news sank in, Anna became as riveted by the meteorologist's analysis as Devlin, especially as he predicted that storm would be a serious hurricane by the time it hit land toward midweek.

"*As the fifth storm of this year's hurricane season,*" the forecaster explained, "*an 'E' name was selected, but this is the first time Eurus has ever been used in the history of recorded storms. And it's an interesting choice, because Eurus was an Anemoi, a wind god the Greeks believe controlled the east wind. And I'd say they picked an appropriate name given Eurus's definite collision course with the East Coast…*"

Eurus was a Greek wind god… Prickles broke out over Anna's skin. Questions on the tip of her tongue, she turned to Devlin—and her stomach dropped to the floor.

Sparks flickered all around him, his eyes blazed with what she could only call black light, and his body seemed to fade in and out before her eyes.

"Devlin?" she gasped. Clearly, the storm's name wasn't a coincidence. And this wasn't any usual storm.

CHAPTER EIGHT

Devlin was a powder keg ready to blow. His inability to get his shit together had given Eurus a wide-open door to build this storm. And now that it was underway, they'd be hard-pressed to overcome what his father had started. Not as long as he wore that damn ring. Now, more people would die and more of nature would be decimated—and it was all Devlin's fault. Again.

He had just enough presence of mind to hear Anna gasp his name before he shifted into the elements and removed himself to the backyard.

As far as he could make it before he lost all control.

Fire and electricity exploded out all around him, the legacy of the Phlegethon. Steam smoldered off the rain-saturated ground creating a cloud of fire and smoke with its creator at the center.

Fight it, Devlin. Fight it, came Aeolus's voice from deep in his memory—beyond the rage, beyond the hate, beyond the chaos. *Control it.*

But in that moment, there wasn't enough of the god named Devlin present to heed his grandfather's words. Devlin was rage. Devlin embraced the hate. Devlin danced in the destruction of the chaos.

Fucking Eurus.

As if the errant thought had conjured the god himself, Devlin heard another voice, thin and distant.

Give in. Join me. It is your birthright…

The summons spoke to the darkest parts of the rain god's psyche. Taunted. Beckoned. Seduced.

A scream. Another. The sound tugged at Devon's consciousness until he felt nearly ripped down the center.

Devlin suddenly saw himself as if in the middle of a long hall. On one end, darkness and damnation. On the other, light and salvation. The alluring words came from the darkness. The screams from the light.

What sense did that make?

More screams.

His consciousness drifted toward the light, ravaged as it was by fire and smoke.

A woman's voice? Calling his name? But who?

Never knew his mother. Had no sisters. He hadn't even consorted with a female in more than century. Then…

"Devlin!"

The voice was familiar, urgent, important. And he understood none of it.

"Devlin, make it stop! You can do it!"

The command pulled him to the end of the tunnel, just shy of the light.

"If I can do it, you can do it. Now, Devlin! Before the house catches!"

Like a hook around his body, the words yanked him into the human realm and into corporeal form. Fire ravaged the grass in every direction around him, just licking at the porch on the back of the house. Two small trees near him were totally engulfed.

With a great gasp of breath, Devlin regained some semblance of his senses. Heat seared his skin. Thick smoke choked his lungs. The roar of the flames and screams of the woman—

Annalise.

Struggling to focus, Devlin finally found her hiding behind her

Jeep, using the cage of steel and glass as a shield. Against him.

They locked eyes across the fire, and the relief that flooded her strange gray gaze tugged at something inside him. Something that wanted to please, to help, to do the right thing.

"Devlin, please! Whatever this is, you have to control it!" she yelled.

Yes.

Rain.

Before the thought was even fully formed, the heavens ripped open and poured a deluge to the earth, dousing the fires, but having no impact on the bolts of electricity lashing out here and there.

For a moment, he was back inside the bowels of the Rock of Gibraltar, training with his grandfather to master this terrible power. The training exercises. Shaking with exertion both physical and mental, Devlin visualized the power as a great beast he controlled. He focused on the sound of his breathing to clear his mind and recall the beast to the cage inside Devlin's heart.

But it was not the sound of his own breathing that gave him the clarity he needed.

It was Anna's. Her ragged, rasping breaths as she choked on her fear and the smoke. The triple-timing beat of her heart. The repeated whispers of his name from her mouth, like a litany. A prayer. A spell.

The electricity boomeranged back inside him from every angle.

The shock of the impact held him upright for a long moment, and then Devlin hit the ground like a ton of bricks.

On his back in the middle of a great circle of fire-ravaged grass, Devlin stared unblinkingly into the gray sky.

"Devlin?" Crunching footsteps approached him. "Devlin?" came Anna's shaky voice again.

Anna.

"Oh, God," she said, coughing. "Oh, God."

He tried to force a swallow, but his throat was scorched dry. Slowly, he parted his lips, and he would've thought he'd attempted to lift Mount Olympus it took so much effort. The droplets of cool rain that slipped over his lips and onto his tongue were life itself.

Soothing warmth pressed against his fingers. "Devlin?" Anna asked from his side. "Is it over?"

The question echoed in his mind, unleashing waves of desperate foreboding.

No, Anna, he wanted to say. *It's only just beginning*. Eurus's storm proved that. Its name was no coincidence—it was his father's twisted sense of humor at play. *Now* Devlin knew why his father hadn't hunted and found him in the two days since the battle that ended Boreas's life. Because he was already making his next move.

And here Devlin thought he'd hidden well.

But he couldn't say any of this to Anna, because the great explosion of his new powers had drained his divine energy so dangerously low that Devlin's soul struggled to remain attached to his physical form.

Warm, smooth heat moved up his bare arm. Over his biceps. Onto his shoulder. "Devlin?" came a voice filled with shock and grief.

But he couldn't focus on that one, couldn't make sense of it. Because he was fading away.

In his final moment of consciousness, he did something he hated doing. He asked for help. He sent the summons, but had no idea whether anyone would respond to a request from the second-most-reviled god of the entire pantheon of the Anemoi.

§

Anna scrambled closer to Devlin as his eyes rolled back in his head. *Oh, God, oh, God, oh, God!* "Don't be dead," she whispered, her heart pounding so hard and so fast she was almost light-headed.

Or maybe that was from nearly being burned alive.

"Devlin?" she whispered, reaching a shaking hand to touch his rain-spattered face. Though his wet skin was covered in smudges of black soot and his clothing hung in ragged tatters on his lean frame, his temperature felt normal to the touch. She dragged her fingers to his throat and pressed two into the soft spot below his jaw. "Come on," she said. "Please." Nothing.

With a whimper, she grabbed his closest wrist and felt for a— *There!* A heartbeat. *Oh, thank God.*

Jesus, what the hell had just happened?

Anna couldn't begin to imagine, but she had no time to figure it out now anyway. He might be alive, but he wasn't well. And he needed her. He needed help.

"I'll be back," she said, dashing across the puddles already forming here and there on the burned grass and up the charred wood of the back steps. She grabbed the handle on the screen door and hissed. It was hot as hell, something she probably should've guessed given how heat-warped the molded design of the door itself was.

Daddy! Had the fire gotten into the house? As she tugged out the hem of her shirt to wrap her stinging fingers in the soft cotton, her gaze surveyed the back of the house. The white aluminum siding had melted from the heat, but everything about the structure itself appeared intact.

Using her shirt like a hot pad, Anna tried the handle again.

She darted inside, scooped her phone from the charging station on the kitchen counter, and beelined to the living room. She had to choke back the stream of questions and reassurances sitting on the tip of her tongue. Somehow her father had slept through the catastrophe in the backyard.

Thank goodness for small favors. No doubt this would've turned his anxiety about venturing outside into a full-blown phobia.

Quietly backtracking, she debated what to do and settled on dialing 911. Who knew if human doctors could help Devlin, but what other choice did she have? She rushed outside and into the backyard. The scene stole her breath anew. It was like a bomb had exploded and Devlin was ground zero. How the hell was she going to explain this?

"9-1-1, what is your emergency?" answered the operator.

"My friend is unconscious. He…he…" A perfect explanation

clicked into place. "He was struck by lightning and then the yard caught on fire," she said loudly, trying to be heard over the pouring rain. She knelt beside him again as the dispatcher walked her through a series of questions about Devlin's condition, their location, and what kind of help they needed. Anna assured the woman she didn't need to stay on the line now that help was on the way.

Despite her soul-deep yearning for adventure in the big city, Anna had probably never been more grateful in her whole life that she lived in a small town. Mere minutes passed before she heard the distant wail of sirens. "Hang on, Devlin," she said, gently holding his hand. Lying there so still, he appeared younger, more at ease, and a helluva lot more vulnerable. It squeezed Anna's heart. "Don't you dare die," she said as a single stinging tear leaked from each eye and mixed with the rain on her cheeks. He was her sole connection to something so magical, so special, and so much bigger than herself.

She wasn't ready to lose that. She wasn't ready to lose *him*.

Before more chaos erupted here, she had to make another call. She speed-dialed Evan, feeling terrible for needing his help so soon again, and gave him a bare-bones explanation of what'd happened. He offered to come take care of her father before she'd even asked.

When the roar of the big engines was close enough to hear, she pushed from the ground to flag them down. Panic lanced through Anna's chest over whether they'd be able to tell Devlin wasn't one of them. But too late to worry about that now. She jogged out to the front of the house and waved her arms at the bright-red fire truck and ambulance. Rainwater flowed along the curb of the street in a rushing stream. Men in full gear spilled from both vehicles, and she recognized a few of them from around town. "This way," she yelled, guiding them up the driveway to the backyard.

"Sweet Jesus," one of the firefighters said. "This was from lightning?" he asked.

"Yes," she said. "The grass caught fire but the rain put it out before it reached the house."

"The house never caught?" he asked, walking the line from one corner of the building to the other.

"No," she called over the rain. "I was on the back porch for part of it, and then I hid behind the car." Chills erupted on her skin and she shivered at the memory. She'd seen everything except the initial ignition, which she'd heard as a weird, sizzling pop, like one of those firecrackers that sparkled and crackled. By the time she'd come outside, Devlin stood in the middle of a swirling haze of translucent fire that grew and grew around him until she hadn't been able to see him anymore.

The firefighter turned to two others. "Take some of this siding down just to be sure," he said, gesturing to the most melted portion at the far side.

"Anna!" called a voice from behind her, and she whirled to see Evan rounding the corner of the house.

"Oh, God, thank you for coming," she said, falling into his arms and returning his hug.

"Are you okay?" he asked, pulling back and squeezing her shoulders. His gaze swept over her.

"Yes, I'm fine. But Devlin's hurt and Dad has to have heard this commotion by now."

"I'll take care of Garrett, don't you worry." His gaze tracked to the EMTs kneeling in the middle of the field. "Is he okay?"

"I don't know. I better go see," she said before Evan asked her a bunch of questions she wouldn't be able to answer truthfully.

"Go on, now," he said. "I'm here for as long as you need me. Don't give it a thought."

Relief and gratitude making her heart swell, Anna waved and jogged to where Devlin lay in the center of the black circle, an EMT kneeling on either side of his chest.

Black circle.

Dizziness gripped Anna as a wave of déjà vu suddenly made her feel as if she were floating.

Oh my God! The painting! The painting of the man lying prone and injured in the middle of a burned field. This...*this* was *that* painting.

I think you've been painting the future. Devlin's words echoed between her ears. He was right. She'd done that painting four days ago. Which meant somehow, someway, she'd known this was going to happen.

Holy crap, could she have prevented this?

She blew out a shaky breath and sank to her knees near Devlin's feet. His boots were absolutely shredded and charred. Still, she cupped her hand around his ankle. Just to touch him. Just to hold him. Just to let him know she was there.

No, she couldn't have prevented this. Hell, she hadn't even known Devlin was capable of whatever it was he'd done, or had been done to him. But for sure, Devlin was right that the paintings represented the future, and if that was important to helping him in any way, Anna would do whatever it took to figure it out.

Especially if it would keep him from being hurt again. Because he *would* get better. Anna couldn't imagine any other outcome. She couldn't lose him after knowing him only a few days.

As one paramedic worked on Devlin's vitals, the other cut his shirt away. "Christ," he muttered under his breath. He slanted a gaze toward Anna and then leaned closer to his partner. "Look at this."

Anna followed the man's gaze to Devlin's bare, sculpted chest, absolutely covered in scars, some seemingly accidental, others in obviously purposeful shapes. *What the hell had happened to him?*

One of the medics called in Devlin's condition—lightning victim, unconscious, rapid, shallow breathing, thready pulse, cardiac irregularity, likely smoke inhalation. Soon, they were ready to lift him onto the stretcher.

Anna stood up—too fast, apparently, because she stumbled and her knees nearly went out from under her.

"Whoa," said the EMT who caught her with an arm around her shoulders. "I think I need to check you out, miss."

"No, take care of him," she said, letting him guide her to sit on the edge of the stretcher.

"We're taking care of your friend." He examined her eyes, her throat, the burn on her hand.

"Heart rate's slowing. We gotta move, Joe," the other paramedic said to the man working on her.

He gave a nod. "Ride along with us so we can check you out."

"Okay," Anna said, sliding off the bed and moving out of the way. She was glad he'd told her to ride along so she hadn't had to debate it with them. Because something deep inside her didn't want to leave Devlin—and didn't want him to wake up alone.

The ambulance ride was a jostled blur. They'd made her wear an oxygen mask because apparently her breathing was raspy. She hadn't even noticed. Because whatever might've happened to her, it was nothing compared to whatever was going on with Devlin—and *had* gone on with him, given the battered state of his body. If human doctors couldn't help him, who could? Were there others like him? Would they know something had happened to him? God, she was so out of her depth here.

And holy hell, but she'd been *so* right about him being desperately hungry. Because lying on his back shirtless revealed his protruding ribcage, collarbone, and shoulder bones. He was so tall that his feet hung off the end of the stretcher, and his size made his thinness even more pronounced.

Every time her mind conjured the image of him scarfing down her chili, tears stung her eyes. He really had been starving. It took everything Anna had not to crawl up on the stretcher beside him and hold him tight.

The urge felt both strange and fundamentally right.

In the ambulance bay at the hospital, they heaved Devlin's stretcher down from the back of the rig and made Anna ride in a wheelchair. "Please let me stay with him," she said. But her request was lost amid the EMTs firing off Devlin's vital statistics to the triage nurses who met them at the door. "I need to stay with him," she said again.

"It's okay, ma'am. We'll take good care of him," a kind-faced nurse said to her. "What's your name?"

"Anna Fallston," she replied mechanically, stretching to watch where they were taking Devlin. She just saw him being wheeled into a room as the nurse pushed her into a curtained examination area. "Please let me go with him. I'm okay."

"Are you related?" the nurse asked. The hospital ID tag around her neck read Maeve Barnett.

Anna's gaze cut to the woman's face and she didn't miss a beat. "I'm his fiancée."

Maeve smiled. "Okay, well, let's get you checked out and then I'll see what's going on with him."

She blew out a long breath. "All right."

For the next thirty-five minutes, Anna impatiently answered questions, cooperated with her examination, and breathed through a nebulizer treatment for the asthmatic reaction the smoke inhalation had caused.

Finally, the nurse said she'd go check in on Devlin and report back with any news.

Five minutes passed, and nothing. Seven. Ten. The second hand on the big industrial clock moved so tauntingly slow.

Anna couldn't stand another minute of not knowing. She slipped off the exam table and peered around her curtain. No use. A curtain had been pulled across the windows of his room, and all Anna could make out was the shadows of people moving around inside the space.

Glancing right toward the nurse's station, Anna darted left and skirted down the hall to his room. His door was open, but she stopped short of pushing through the gap in the curtain. Instead, she peeked.

An IV needle was taped to the back of his hand, round sensors covered his chest and temples, and an oxygen tube ran under his nose. And if all that wasn't concerning enough, one nurse was telling the other that the equipment was acting up. "Look at this. The readings are all over the place," he said. "This is the second freaking machine."

Dread crawled up Anna's spine and prickled her scalp. Was the problem really the equipment? Or the patient it was monitoring?

"I'll go get another unit," someone said. "Maybe third time'll be a charm."

Anna squeezed herself into the space where the floor-length curtain met the wall and held her breath. A nurse walked right passed her — not expecting someone to be hiding there, of course, she thankfully hadn't noticed Anna.

Just as relief had her sagging against the wall, the curtain whipped back. "What are you doing here?" a male nurse asked. His gaze dropped to her right hand, where a plastic ID bracelet surrounded her wrist and white bandages circled her palm.

"He's my fiancé. Nobody would tell me anything."

Indecision flickered across the man's face before he waved her in and gestured toward a chair. "I'll be right back," he said.

As soon as he was gone, she moved to Devlin's bedside and took his hand again. "I'm here, Devlin." She smoothed her other hand over his forehead, careful not to disturb the sensors. "Open your eyes," she said, longing to see them flash with light again. *God*, she'd have given anything to see that one more time.

Voices sounded from behind her, but given the business of the ER Anna didn't pay any attention to them until she heard the words, "Get him. I'll run interference."

She peered over her shoulder as two of the biggest men she'd ever seen in her life stepped through the curtain. One tightly closed the fabric behind him.

"Who are you?" she asked, turning all the way around and blocking their view of Devlin with her body.

The men looked at her like she had three heads. The slightly taller one had long dark hair with beautiful lighter highlights running through it and the other one appeared younger somehow, and had shorter dark hair and eyes. Neither looked happy.

"Let's just get him," the younger one said, at the same time the older one finally replied, "I'm his grandfather," and nodded toward Devlin. "The more interesting question is, who are you?"

The younger one sighed. "We don't have time for this."

Grandfather. What the older one said finally sank in. If Devlin was a god, and his father was a god, then surely… The room spun and Anna sagged against the edge of Devlin's bed as her heart took off in her chest. The lights above her flickered.

"What are you going to do with him?" she managed in a quiet voice.

The taller man stepped closer and tilted his head, as if appraising her. "He can't stay here."

"Because…because of what he is?" Anna swallowed hard. "Because of what *you* are?"

His grandfather arched an eyebrow—and the expression was so similar to the one Devlin always gave her that she knew their relationship was the truth. "So, he's told you, then?"

Anna nodded.

"Let's figure this out at home," the younger god said. Light flared from behind his eyes.

She gasped. That light hammered the last nail in any doubt she might've had about whether they told the truth. "Can you help him?"

"I can," the older man said. "But not here."

"Wherever you take him, I'm going with him." She crossed her arms and drew herself up to her full height. However, at five foot three inches, she felt like a miniature next to these gods. She doubted they were impressed.

For a long moment, Devlin's grandfather stared at her. "So be it," he finally said. "Zephyros, you take her." Then both of them approached.

"Don't hurt him," she said, her heart beating in her throat as the grandfather moved to the far side of Devlin's bed and began detaching the monitors and IV.

An incredibly gorgeous light-haired man ducked his head and shoulders through the curtain. "Are we ready to rock and roll or what? Oh, hey," he said, smiling at her.

Anna hadn't wrapped her head around how to respond when the one called Zephyros stepped in front of her. "I need to put you to sleep to get where we're going," he said.

Where in the world could they be going that required her to be put to sleep? "Um." She looked over her shoulder to where the older god gathered Devlin in his arms. The image of his prone, limp form would've gutted her except his grandfather had said he could help. Did it really matter where they needed to go? The squeeze of her gut answered that question, and she turned back to meet Zephyros's serious gaze again. "Okay."

"Okay," he said, gentling his tone. He cradled her shoulders in one arm and laid his other palm on her forehead. A warm breeze blew over, just like when Devlin had grabbed her earlier. And that was her last thought before she couldn't think about anything at all.

CHAPTER NINE

Owen sat in the dark on the foot of the bed, elbows braced on his knees, and stared at the contents of the glass jar in his hands. Three crystal snowflakes containing Boreas's divine energy. How could this be all that was left of his father?

Gods, what Owen wouldn't have given to hear Boreas's voice one more time, to watch those silver eyes sparkle with mirth over something Teddy had done. Slowly, Owen turned the jar round and round and watched the snowflakes tumble and slide.

Red-hot anger surged through him until he feared his grip would crush the glass and the treasures within. And then he'd have nothing left of his father at all.

Stretching, Owen returned the jar to the dresser top. It didn't hold the answers he sought anyway. And never would.

Like how to take care of his family when they had no home, his wife legally couldn't live in the Realm of the Gods, and Owen would have to ascend to his season in just over three months, leaving Megan alone to care for their two-year-old boy and newborn baby.

Turning, his gaze settled on his angel, who had finally managed to fall asleep. The baby was so active at night that Megan had been having trouble sleeping, but on the upside his nightly kickboxing routine gave her the peace of mind that everything was okay. At least one of them was getting some rest.

Owen was just about to climb back into bed when he registered several energy signatures approaching the compound. Aeolus, Chrys, and Zeph, but he could've sworn there were others, too.

Everything okay? he asked Aeolus.

Meet us in my chamber.

Frowning, Owen flashed into Aeolus's luxurious bedroom, the walls paneled in carved wood and decorated with lavish tapestries, carpets, and bedding. He arrived just as the three gods did, carrying two others—a man and a woman. His gaze settled on the man, and realization hit like a sucker punch to the gut. "Devlin," he whispered in shock.

Twin reactions warred within him. Vengeful rage at the god whose father had killed his own father. And wary, reluctant concern, for Devlin was unconscious in Aeolus's arms and the little he knew about the Eastern god told him the guy never would've submitted to such a thing if he'd had a choice.

Owen stalked closer, close enough to see that Devlin's chest was a battlefield of scars, which could mean only one thing—the wounds had been inflicted by a superior god. Otherwise, they would've healed.

Chrysander caught Owen by the shoulders and shoved him back a step or two. "Whoa, man."

The temperature of Chrys's superheated touch seared Owen's bare skin, another jarring reminder of his new status. As a demigod, he'd been less sensitive to heat than he was as a full-blown snow god—and he recalled all too well the debilitating consequences of prolonged exposure to heat. Two years ago, he'd nearly died from such a situation, which was one of the reasons he'd gladly accepted the demotion to demigod. Now, as a full Cardinal Anemoi, that sensitivity had returned in spades—and he'd had absolutely no choice in the matter. Not that he ever would've refused the great honor Boreas had bestowed in passing Owen the reins to the North Wind. He'd just expected to be a lot older before it happened.

"I'm fine," Owen said, shrugging Chrys off. As the Northern and

Southern gods, he and Chrys were polar opposites now, and Chrys's touch burned like fire. The movement made Owen realize his fists had been clenched into tight balls.

Holding up his hands as if in surrender, Chrys's palms were bright red from touching Owen's cold. "I know, O. It's just a lot to take in right now. For all of us."

Owen nodded, forcing a deep breath. Gods, he hated the heavy weight that anger had settled on his heart. So unlike him. "Somebody want to explain?" Aeolus crossed the room and laid Devlin on his massive hand-carved bed.

"He's badly depleted. I need to restore his energy," Aeolus said.

From the corner of his eye, Owen saw Chrys and Zeph trade weighted glances, hauling Owen's attention back to the other newcomer—a tiny woman Zeph still cradled in his arms. "Who's that?"

"She said she's Devlin's fiancée," Aeolus said in a low voice. With what almost appeared to be affection, he laid one hand over Devlin's heart and the other on his forehead. "You may as well put her there until she awakens." He nodded at the space beside Devlin, then closed his eyes as if in concentration.

Suddenly, the scene wrenched Owen's memories into the present. His throat squeezed tight and an avalanche of pressure parked on his chest. Nearly two years ago while Owen had courted Megan and a chance at a human life free of the loneliness and solitude of his divinity, he'd badly drained himself of energy. Owen had regained consciousness with Boreas standing over him, having sensed his son's distress and come to the rescue. Boreas had replenished Owen's energy with some of his own.

Owen studied Aeolus's expression—the furrow in his brow and the tightness around his mouth. Had Boreas appeared as concerned, as affectionate, as almost desperate that it would work as Aeolus did now?

It was a question Owen didn't really need to ask. The last two years had cemented the bond between Boreas and Owen. Knowing he'd been so well loved by the god he'd most respected both soothed his grief and worsened it. Because now it was gone.

Blinking away the memory, Owen focused on something else they'd said. "Wait. She's his fiancée?" Owen asked. "Since when?" How did a bad guy on the run find the time to meet a girl?

"Right?" Zeph said, obeying the storm god and grumbling under his breath.

Lying side by side emphasized the woman's petite stature next to Devlin's sprawling length. Not that Devlin was big—at least not compared to the rest of the Anemoi. Owen stepped to the end of the bed. In fact, Devlin's bare chest wasn't just scarred, but lean to the point of deprivation.

"Guy's a sack of bones," Chrys said, echoing Owen's thoughts. "And his skin makes mine look pristine by comparison."

Owen cut his gaze to Chrys's quick enough to catch a flash of dark regret behind the Southern god's eyes. Chrysander had shouldered the brunt of the fight against Eurus over the past six months, and his body bore the scars to prove—scars that hadn't healed because the Firestone ring made the god who should've been the weakest among the four Cardinal Anemoi the very strongest. As strong as the storm god who had controlled the Anemoi since near the beginning of their creation, a power the ring conferred on its wearer.

"Something doesn't make sense here," Chrys said quietly, as if musing out loud.

Zeph crossed his arms. "Such as?"

Raking his fingers through his hair, Chrys nailed Devlin with a stare. "Guy is beat all the hell up, came to Owen's to warn us about Apheliotes's death and Eurus's attack, and has a human fiancée? All that in addition to training with Aeolus and agreeing to down a cocktail of fire and rage?"

Owen nodded, Chrys's words striking a chord inside him even as his embittered anger resisted the idea that Devlin might not share the blame for Eurus's evil deeds. Because Owen needed someone to lash out at as much as he needed the cold, clear air of winter. Still, seemed that Devlin had made a whole lotta choices that would've pissed Eurus off more than earned his favor. Why would Devlin do that if he and Eurus were the allies they'd always assumed the pair to be?

"What happened to him?" Owen asked, watching as Aeolus maintained contact.

"Not sure," Zeph said. "He seems to have taken his new powers for a joyride."

Aeolus's eyes flashed open, dark-green light flaring. "His powers are volatile, Zephyros. And he hasn't had the chance to master them. If he lost control, it's because—"

"It's because he has no business wielding that kind of power," Zeph shot back.

"Enough," Aeolus bit out, closing his eyes again. "I'm not doing this with you now."

Devlin shuddered and sucked in a sharp breath. His eyelids fluttered but didn't stay open. Aeolus dropped his hands on a weary sigh.

"Now what?" Chrys asked.

"Now, we let them rest. When they awaken, we can find out what happened and go from there. Come," Aeolus said, gesturing them to the door.

"We should post guards," Zephyros said.

The storm god placed a firm hand on his son's chest and forced him to a halt. "Leave him be, Zephyros. I don't want to have to say it again."

Owen and Chrys traded glances, and Chrys looked as surprised and mystified as Owen felt. Clearly, there was something more to the relationship between Aeolus and Devlin than any of them understood—which was even more confusing given the lack of affection, attention, and regard Aeolus had given to his son, Devlin's father, when he'd been a younger god. It was part of what had twisted Eurus into the monster he'd become. Though to be fair, who hadn't been screwed over by life at one point or another? No one—not even a god—got through their existence without suffering a broken heart, a bruised ego, or an injustice that was never made right. Everyone suffered, but not everyone took their shit out on the rest of the world.

Ella's near-death attack. The loss of Aeolus's fingers in his fight with Eurus over the ring. The repeated assaults on Chrysander. Alastor's torture. Apheliotes's death. *Boreas's death.*

Eurus had officially exhausted whatever sympathy any of them might've once had for him. Now, all they felt was a shared soul-deep conviction to take him down and put an end to the spread of his evil. Once and for all.

"Fine," Zephyros said. "I hope you know what you're doing."

"I do. Devlin is not his father. And I should know since I made Eurus the way he is," Aeolus said. Zeph stared at him a long minute, the tension from their confrontation and Aeolus's surprise admission turning the air so thick they could've cut it with a knife. Finally, Zeph nodded once and disappeared. Aeolus turned his glare on Owen and Chrys. "Either of you have any grief you want to dish out?"

The internal war over Devlin's trustworthiness and culpability pulled Owen's heart in two. "I'm reserving judgment," Owen managed.

Chrys pointed at Owen, then crossed his arms. "What he said."

"Well, thank Zeus for small favors," Aeolus groused. "Because I'd say we have enough enemies to worry about without fighting one another."

"Agreed," Chrys said. "Well, call me when they wake up. Otherwise, I'm outie." And he disappeared.

With a last look over his shoulder at the couple lying on the bed, Owen turned to leave.

A hand fell on his shoulder. "I know you have every bit as much reason as Zephyros to revile Eurus and, by association, Devlin. I appreciate your open-mindedness."

Owen nodded even as his gut clenched. "I just don't get why it's so important to you."

"You mean, besides the fact that he now possesses the ability to best his father, even while Eurus has the Firestone?" Aeolus's eyebrows lifted, and Owen conceded the point with a nod and a one-shouldered shrug. "Because Devlin is my second chance to heal the rift I caused among the four winds."

Hearing Aeolus make these admissions was like walking into an invisible wall—though Owen was pretty sure he'd have been less shocked at the latter. It just wasn't like the proud storm god to admit his mistakes or seek to atone for them. At least, not like the storm god had before the Anemois' world had become so embattled.

Glancing to the left, Owen's gaze settled on Devlin. If the Eastern god really represented such a thing, then Owen had no choice but to set aside his own needs and personal feelings and do whatever he could to help. It's what Boreas would've done, Owen had no doubt. "Chrys and I will work on Zeph," he said, turning back to Aeolus.

The older god nodded. "Get some rest," he said. "Something tells me we're going to need it."

ဆာလ

Anna gasped awake and lurched onto her elbows. Realized they sank into a velvet duvet. *Where the hell am I?* The dimly lit room could've been a suite at the Ritz it was so luxuriously furnished, all carved mahogany, plush woven carpets, and rich tapestries on the walls.

And she was seeing it all in color. Anna scrunched her eyes closed, counted to three, and opened them again. Color. Everywhere. The blanket beneath her was a deep, rich blue, the carpets were ivory with blues and greens and browns, and the tapestries were golden with bold reds and navy blues and hunter greens. She sat all the way up, her heart racing in her chest, and had absolutely no idea how to explain how this could be happening.

She looked to her right and did a double take. Devlin lay on his back next to her.

Devlin. The accident. His grandfather.

The memories came back in a rush. Those other gods had brought Devlin and Anna…somewhere. Exactly where, she had no idea. Had they helped him as they'd said?

Gingerly, Anna moved closer to Devlin. Soot and mud still smudged his skin here and there, but his breathing sounded more regular than before, slow and shallow in the pattern of deep sleep. "Devlin?" she whispered.

His head turned toward her on the thick pillow and his lips twitched. And that little bit of movement unleashed a tide of relief through every cell in Anna's body. Because it was way more than he'd done while lying in the pouring rain, riding in the ambulance, or being poked and prodded at the hospital.

Not wanting to wake him, Anna slid off the bed and padded across the wide room. The vibrancy of the colors surrounding her overloaded her senses and almost made her dizzy. She turned the door handle as quietly as possible and peeked outside. The dark room beyond appeared to be a formal living room, with a grouping of over-stuffed furniture situated around a massive marble hearth. How cozy that must be with the fire lit…

Though it didn't give her any better of an idea where she was. Or why she was seeing in full color.

The enormity of the individual rooms gave her the sense that the whole house must be massive, probably a big mansion. They were gods, after all. Which meant it might take some searching to find Devlin's grandfather and the others if she went exploring. Anna's gaze reached back across the dim bedroom to where she could just make out Devlin's form on the big bed. As curious as she was, her heart squeezed at the idea of leaving him.

More than that, she felt drawn back to his side.

She secured the door again and returned to the bed. Glancing down at herself, Anna realized she was as dirty as Devlin. Between the fire, rain, and mud, both of them were in desperate need of a hot shower and a change of clothes. But whoever had put them here apparently hadn't worried about that, so Anna crawled onto the sumptuous blue bedding and lay on her side in the middle—close enough to be able to look at Devlin, but not so close that she touched him, though she wanted to. Badly.

God, he was a ruggedly attractive man. Not at all classically handsome, but something about all his rough edges appealed to her heart and her body. Lean as he was, he remained much bigger than her. And lying in a bed with him led her imagination to all sorts of places it probably had no business going. Like, wondering what it would feel like to lie on that broad chest, what it feel like to hold his big body in the cradle of her thighs, what his greater weight and size would feel like covering her.

Heat lanced through Anna's body. Her reaction wasn't just the result of the long dry spell brought about from a schedule that focused on painting and caring for her father. It was about Devlin himself. Maybe it was his incredible power or the vulnerability he tried to hide or the way he'd looked at her with such need and touched her with such gentleness. Maybe it was all of those things. All Anna knew was that she wanted the chance to learn more.

Slowly, she gave into the urge to touch him and smoothed her hand over the soft warmth of the bedding. She laid her right hand on top of his and wished the bandage didn't prevent her palm from feeling him, but at least her fingers were free to slip into the cup of his hand and hold him skin to skin. The touch didn't seem to disturb him, so Anna got comfortable and settled in to wait until Devlin woke up. Unthinkingly, her thumb stroked back and forth and when she focused on the movement, Anna realized she was rubbing over the skin inked with an intricate black band that circled his entire wrist. Earlier, she'd seen a similar marking on his left wrist, which meant he wore one on both. She wondered what they meant.

Before long, the stress of the day, comfort of the bed, and warmth from Devlin's hand made her limbs heavy and her eyelids heavier. Part of her feared falling back to sleep—what if the colors disappeared again when she awoke? But the lure of sleep was stronger, especially as a series of images began to shift and form in her mind's eye. *The Dark Man.* But was it Devlin or his father? That was her last conscious thought before the dream images pulled her under and claimed her for their own.

ജ‌യ‌ഗ‌ര

The first thing he noticed was the warmth, then the softness, then the sweet scent of vanilla. One by one, Devlin's senses came back online, but he was surrounded by such comfort that he didn't want to open his eyes and face the grim reality of his life. Because surely these sensations were holdovers from a dream. His father had always believed that Spartan accommodations built strength and endurance, and so Devlin's bed consisted of a rough canvas cot and an ancient woolen blanket.

Nothing like this.

Devlin burrowed into the warmth, knowing he had to enjoy it while it lasted.

A small, throaty moan.

His eyelids flipped open. He surveyed and cataloged his surroundings...and had absolutely no idea where he was.

That little satisfied moan, again.

Oh, fucking Hades, someone else is in the bed!

Devlin was in the elements before the panic had fully settled in. And then he materialized with his back against a richly paneled wall across the room from the bed. Gods, he'd been lying right up against someone with no idea who it was or how he'd gotten there. His heart thundered, his pulse raced, his breathing rasped as the panic got its claws into him. He scanned the room anew and looked for a threat, but all was seemingly quiet and still.

A shiver ran over his skin and made Devlin realize he was shirtless. *What the fuck?* Except when bathing, he never bared his body, not even to himself. Like he needed the fucking reminder. His jeans remained, but even they hung in tatters, ripped and charred. The wrapping he kept around the cilice to catch his blood peeked through the torn denim.

His gaze continued down his body. And...*sonofabitch*. Where were his boots?

No matter how much he tried, he couldn't resurrect any memory that explained where he was or why he looked this way. He peered across the room. Or who the hell he'd been in bed with.

Slowly, Devlin prowled across the room and came up along the empty side of the bed.

The minute he saw her face it all came back like a wave catching him off guard and knocking him under the rolling, churning water.

Anna.

Eurus's storm.

His loss of control.

In his mind's eye, Devlin saw Anna hiding behind her Jeep, fearful pleading in her wide gray eyes. Gods, had he hurt her? Her father?

"Anna?" he said, not recognizing his own voice as he crawled up on the bed. "Anna?" She looked like she'd been through nearly the same battle as him, her clothes and skin covered in mud and black smudges. And now one hand bore a bandage. Carefully, he cupped the hand wrapped in thick gauze in his. What had he done?

"Hey," came her sleepy voice, then her eyes went wide. "You're awake. Oh, thank God." She pushed up quickly and reached for him. Devlin jerked back, nearly falling off the bed, and she yanked her arms in against her chest. Pressing shaking fingers to her lips, her gaze went glassy as it ran over him.

He crossed his arms over his chest, suddenly really fucking conscious of the fact that he didn't have a shirt. Just as well that she saw the evidence of his shame. Anything to put the brakes on the tension that had sizzled between them when she'd hugged him at her studio. Anything to put a leash on the possessiveness he'd felt when her male friend had kissed her, innocent though it was. And absofuckinglutely anything to suppress the soul-deep gratitude and downright reverence he'd felt as she'd fed him the first real meal he'd had in...days, maybe weeks. Because as much as those others had awakened all sorts of emotions he hadn't flirted with in over a century, it was that last one that most left him feeling exposed and vulnerable and raw. Kindness and satisfaction and basic physical satiation were things he could *not* afford for his body, mind, or heart to get used to or expect. Ever.

Nor was the basic comfort of her touch. Gods, he'd been holding her in his sleep. Touch was such a foreign fucking thing to him, yet *he'd* been the one holding *her*. And now his skin ached for more of that touch as if it were a phantom limb he'd lost and would never stop missing.

"Are you okay?" she finally asked.

Devlin frowned as her question interrupted the churn and burn between his ears. He glared at her bandage, regret of too many damned kinds filling his soul. "Shouldn't I be the one asking that?"

Anna ignored his bark and waved her hand. "This was an accident. God, Devlin, I thought you'd died. And for the record, I really want to hug you right now." She looked at him with such hope and affection and caring.

Disgust and grief flowed through him. He could never accept any of those things from her, and he resented the hell out of her for putting him in the position of having to reject something that tempted him so badly. And besides, why would someone so true and beautiful want to touch someone like him? Especially after what he'd done and what she'd now seen? *Gods*, he was dirty inside and out. Sharp, cutting pressure ballooned inside him. "Are you fucking crazy?"

Her relief-filled expression dropped. Confusion furrowed her brow. "I...I...what are you—"

"Look at me, human," he said, opening his arms wide and forcing his muscles to hold the humiliating, exposing position. "I am a wretched waste of a god. I have earned every one of these marks with my mistakes and sins. I have blood on my hands that will never wash off, and that nearly included yours today."

A quick array of emotions flashed over her face, and then she shook her head. "You didn't, Devlin. Don't you remember? You fought it. You controlled it. I asked you to, and you did. Just like when you made me see that I could turn back on the lights." Tremulous hope crept into her eyes.

Her words resurrected a series of memories. Being caught between the light and the dark. Her voice luring him back to the human realm. Her pleas—no, her *commands*, and the sounds of her lifeblood and breath giving him the focus and discipline he required.

It was a revelation, learning that *finally*—goddamned fucking finally—he was beginning to master his terrible, infernal powers. Gratitude swelled inside his chest *to her*. For reminding him of his accomplishment. And for being the one to help bring it about in the heat of the moment.

But that didn't negate that he'd lost control in the first place. Three seconds of hesitation and he would've lost it standing in the middle of her family's living room.

"You speak of things you do not understand," he said, twisting the knife that he knew he'd planted by calling her "human." As if he didn't know her. As if she hadn't earned far more respect from him. As if he didn't care about her any more or any less than the other seven billion inhabitants of this spinning rock.

Anna sagged back on the bed and hugged her knees to her chest. "Okay," she said in a small voice. "I just thought… Okay." His crushed flower, again.

No, not his at all.

Her presence was like a magnetic force, tugging him to her, sucking him in. He shifted off the bed, yanked at his hair, and paced. "Where are we?"

She glanced at him but didn't make eye contact. "Your grandfather's. Wherever that is. They made me sleep to come here. And I can see—"

His grand— "Good gods. You didn't think to mention this sooner?" The storm. They needed to know about Eurus's storm.

"I—"

"Aeolus!" he shouted. Not because he needed to do so to be

heard, but because he required the physical release.

The lights came up as Aeolus and Devlin's three Anemoi uncles appeared in the room.

Devlin glanced among the gathered men. Family he'd rarely seen and hadn't spent any real time with in centuries. As the tensions and rivalries between Eurus and the other winds had escalated, Eurus had kept him and his brothers more and more secluded from the rest. The animosity was so virulent that his uncles and grandfather had seemed perfectly content with that arrangement. Thus no one else had been around to help when Eurus's abuse of his sons worsened to the point that Devlin had rebelled—and Farren had died for it. And not a single Anemoi had said or done a thing.

Anger surged through him as Aeolus spoke. "Devlin. I'm glad you called for me," he said, not needing to clarify that he meant *before*, when Devlin had been so dangerously drained he wasn't sure he'd ever come back from it.

"My lord," he managed, bowing his head—but not too much. Not with Zephyros throwing off so much hostile energy he could've lit a small city with it. Devlin's muscles braced for attack, but Zephyros only glared. By comparison, Chrysander seemed almost friendly, which surprised him given the fighting between the Southern god and his father for much of the past year.

Devlin's gaze shifted to Owen, the new Supreme God of the North Wind and Guardian of Winter. Except for his strange mismatched eyes—one brown, one blue—he and Owen could've been brothers, they so resembled each other. Though everything he'd ever heard about the quiet god who'd voluntarily allowed himself to be demoted to demigod-dom said that Owen was honorable and true and good-hearted.

So, then, they weren't so much alike after all.

It wasn't their physical resemblance Devlin found most striking, anyway. It was the fact that, despite how his fists clenched and unclenched, nothing about Owen's gaze or expression or posture indicated the kinds of things Devlin expected. There appeared to be no hate, no anger, no vengefulness.

Honestly, it impressed the hell out of Devlin, because he knew what a jagged bitch fresh grief could be, having experienced it himself. He could readily imagine the chaos likely raging behind the calm facade.

Devlin forced himself to meet Owen's gaze, and the god's eyes flared as if he were surprised. Then Devlin took a knee and bowed his head. "I am sorry for the loss of your father and the North Wind's former master. Boreas provided great and honorable service to the North."

The room went rigidly still, but Devlin held his position despite the escalating tension.

"Thank you," Owen finally said, voice quiet and strained. Devlin returned to his feet.

"What about leading Eurus to Gibraltar and then just standing back and watching the show while we were attacked? Aren't you going to apologize for that, too?" Zeph said, his fists clenched.

Devlin shook his head. Of course that's what they thought. "I did not lead him there—"

Zeph scoffed.

"I did not!" Devlin raked his hands through his hair as electricity sparked in the air around him. Breathing hard, Devlin struggled to rein in the fire wanting to burst free. A burning smell reached his nose from the carpet beneath his feet.

"Jesus. He's a bomb waiting to go off," Zeph said, taking a step forward.

"Don't," came Anna's voice. Devlin noted that Zeph halted before all his attention latched onto Anna's words. "Fight it, Devlin. Just like before." The sound of her voice, so filled with belief in him, was like a beacon in the darkness. Everything else fell away. Slowly but surely, the heat drew back inside him. She'd focused him, again.

Swallowing hard, Devlin forced out the rest of what he needed to say to his uncle. "I don't know how he found me. I'd been holed up in the rock for more than a week by then. And I sure as Hades did not stand idly by. I was chained to that fucking rock by Eurus's will. He let me go afterward to make you question my loyalty, which he gleefully said you'd all doubt. Guess he was right, huh?"

A long moment of awkward silence, then Chrysander said, "Uh, Devlin. Maybe you should introduce us to your fiancée?"

"My…what?" Devlin followed the gazes of the other gods to where Anna now stood at the foot of the bed.

The pale skin of her face flushed absolutely scarlet. "I didn't tell them that," she said, waving at the other men. "I don't know how they…" She shook her head. "I lied to the hospital staff so I could stay with you."

"*Hospital?*" What in the name of Zeus and all the Olympians had been going on? It was as if he'd been absent from his own life. "What hospital?"

"You passed out after the—I don't even know what to call it… firestorm, maybe? I could barely find your pulse, so I called an ambulance and they took us to the hospital."

She tried to save my life. Dear gods, despite the fact that I could've killed her, she helped me master the powers and then tried to save my life. And now she's done it again. Awe and confusion filled him until the room spun around him. *No one* had ever tried to save Devlin before. Not even the gods standing in a group on the other side of the room—males who were supposed to be his family.

And because she'd made him feel so deeply, and that was such a foreign, overwhelming thing, of course he acted like a complete bastard. He stalked right up into her space until he towered over her. "Gods, woman, do you know what you might've done? What you might've revealed?" he seethed.

The lights flickered in the room as Anna planted her hands on her hips and narrowed her gaze at him. Color returned to her cheeks again, but this time it wasn't from embarrassment. "Are you done?" she asked, raising her eyebrows in challenge. "Or do you have a little more bullshit you want to dish out at me? Because so far today, you've scared the crap out of me by pulling me into the wind when

I had no idea what was going on. You've appointed yourself my guardian and jailer as long as you think my paintings are useful to you. And you nearly burned my damn house down—with my father in it." The longer she spoke, the brighter the lights in the room flared, as if they were absorbing the energy she was throwing off—energy Devlin could easily perceive now. Which no doubt meant the others could, too. "So, yeah, I'm the *stupid human* who didn't know how else to help what I thought was a *dying* god. I did the best I could under the circumstances."

You could've heard a pin drop as Anna pushed around Devlin and marched up to Aeolus. Her words were like a bucket of ice water over Devlin's head, jarring him into awareness and realization. Clearly he was such an emotional fucking misfit that he didn't even know how to feel and express basic gratitude and respect without losing his shit. He opened his mouth to speak—

"Aeolus, sir? I'm Anna Fallston." She held out her hand and waited. All three of the Anemoi sucked in a breath. You *never* spoke to a god of Aeolus's stature without being spoken to first, let alone touch one. Among the highest gods, such an offense against protocol could warrant death on the spot.

Eyebrow arched, Aeolus slowly slipped his big hand around Anna's little one and returned the greeting. With a tilt of his head, he said, "Well, Miss Fallston. I'd say you've had quite the day." Aeolus's graciousness released the tension in the room.

"I have, which is why I'd like to go home. I have a sick father who had a very bad day, too, and I'm his primary caregiver. I assume I'm not very close to home right now and—just guessing here—that I can't get home by any of the usual ways. So, with all due respect, I'd very much like one of you to help me leave now." She swallowed hard enough that Devlin heard it. "Sir."

Gods be damned, but this woman was fearless. Just another reason she deserved his admiration and respect—and more evidence that he'd failed her in the most basic of ways. Again and again.

And maybe that was for the best. He stuffed down the apology that had been on the tip of his tongue. Let Annalise Fallston hate him. It was far better for *her* that way.

Besides, there was a better-than-average chance that Devlin's shelf life wasn't all that long at this point. Not with everything he had to face in the next few days.

Aeolus appraised Anna for a long moment. "I will consider your request once I understand more what brought the two of you together in the first place. And what happened that landed you in the hospital."

And whose divine energy she possesses, Zeph added telepathically. Chrys and Owen offered subtle nods of agreement.

"The first thing you need to know," Devlin said, stepping closer, "is that Eurus is stirring up a tropical storm in the Caribbean that is headed for the East Coast. It's going to be bad. And as a little calling card, he's somehow influenced the humans to actually name the damn thing after him."

"We know," Chrysander said. "It hit my radar this afternoon. Which explains why we haven't been able to find him for the past forty-eight hours. We weren't looking in the right damn place. We weren't thinking big enough."

Aeolus nodded. "Indeed. At least now we know where he is."

Devlin met each of the gods' gazes. "There is no doubt in my mind this thing is going to be catastrophic when it makes landfall."

"Par for the course with your father," Zephyros said.

Devlin heard the accusation of guilt by association in Zeph's words, and so be it. He wasn't wrong. "I agree. Given where all of you have met your mates, it's almost guaranteed to hit the Chesapeake, just as a way to say, 'Fuck you.'"

Megan, Ella, and Laney were all from the area surrounding the mid-Atlantic bay, a fluke caused by Owen's marrying Megan and becoming a demigod so he could live full-time in the human realm with her. As the other Anemoi visited Owen and spent more time in the human realm with the new family, they had occasion to meet mates of their own.

And now weren't they just one big happy family.

The conversation reminded Devlin of why his frustration had gotten the better of him at Anna's. "Gods, I'd been sitting on my ass trying to get my shit together when I should've been out stopping him from wreaking more devastation and havoc on the human realm. Had I acted, I might've been able to prevent him from summoning this storm." Devlin raked his fingers through his hair. "But, clearly, now that he wears your ring I can no longer sense what he's doing with the East Wind."

Aeolus nodded. "That's because the ring allows him to command *all* the winds, not just the East."

"Don't beat yourself up over it, Devlin," Chrysander said, stepping closer. "We all missed it. He's always going to be one step ahead of us until we get that fucking ring back."

Devlin took the words as an olive branch and nodded, grateful to the Southern god for making the effort.

Chrys held out a shirt and a pair of boots. "Here. Thought you might need these," he said.

Devlin's gaze dropped to the clothing and heat flooded into his face. He quickly tucked his chin to his chest, embarrassment at the offer and the need for it swamping him. He reached forward and grasped the items with a tight "Thanks."

"Don't sweat it, man. Eurus has done a number on my skin, too. Motherfucker," he said, dark amusement in his tone.

The words drew Devlin's gaze back to Chrys's face. The god was clearly trying to do more than offer an olive branch. He was trying to put Devlin at ease. A strange pressure in his chest, Devlin tugged the shirt over his head and stuffed his feet into the unlaced boots.

"Question is," Owen said, joining the loose circle, "how are we going to get the ring?"

Out of nowhere, Anna gasped. "Oh, no. No, no, no." She cupped her palm over her eyes and shook her head. "Not again. No." She whirled on Devlin and shook her hands out like she was suddenly filled with nervous energy. "It's happening again."

Protectiveness surged through Devlin. He hated that these

visions distressed Anna, even as he believed in his gut that what they revealed was vitally important.

The other gods all braced. "What's happening?" Zeph said, suspicion sharpening his words.

"I can't do this again. Not already," Anna said as she hugged herself.

The sadness and despair filling her eyes gutted Devlin. But she didn't have a choice, and they both knew it. "What do you need?" he said.

"I need not to have to do this anymore. Why is this happening to me?" Anna grimaced and grabbed the sides of her head. "I don't want this," she rasped.

Zeph stepped closer. "What the hell is happening to her?"

Devlin angled himself between his uncle and his...and Anna. He met and held Zeph's gaze, making it clear that he wouldn't be cowed by the other god's hatred. "She has powers, as you've already noticed. One of them seems to be receiving visions of the future which she is compelled to paint." Glancing at Aeolus, he continued. "That is how we met. I took shelter in what I thought was an abandoned building. It turned out to be Anna's studio. So far she's painted seven images."

She sees the future, too? Chrys said.

Too? Devlin wasn't sure what the god meant but didn't have time to find out, not with Anna in so much distress.

"One," Anna said, swallowing hard. "One was of you...unconscious in the burned grass of my backyard after the firestorm."

Instantly, he knew which painting she meant. "One down, six to go, then. Or seven to go, after whatever this image is."

"Shit," she said. "I need to paint this, Devlin. You have to take me back. Resisting the urge is getting harder. It's all getting worse. My head is pounding with the pressure." Her eyes went glassy as she peered up at him.

"I think you should all come with us. You're going to want to see the paintings yourselves," Devlin said to the men. "Is that all right with you?" he asked Anna, feeling even worse now for the way he'd treated her. And here she was suffering for him—for all of them.

"It's fine," she said distantly, as if her mind was somewhere else. "We should go."

Aeolus turned to the others. "Chrysander, summon the Ordinal Anemoi to guard the compound while we are gone. With Eurus otherwise occupied right now, it should be safe for all of us to leave, but their presence will give the three of you peace of mind for the women's safety. When they're here, catch up with us."

Chrys nodded and disappeared into the elements.

Aeolus turned to Zephyros. "If you'll take Anna again—"

Possessiveness welled inside Devlin until he was nearly shaking. "I can take her—"

"Not after being so badly drained," Aeolus said. "Your energy has not recovered enough to safely sustain her in the wind."

"Let's just go," Anna said, walking up to Zephyros. "I don't really care how I get there. Do you have to make me sleep again?" she asked him.

"No," he said, drawing Devlin's complete attention. If Zeph took his dislike of Devlin out on Anna, they were all going to have a problem of the Devlin-as-firebomb variety. "You are throwing off enough divine energy right now that you'll be fine to leave the Realm of the Gods fully conscious. Ready?"

Anna scoffed. "No, but let's do it anyway."

CHAPTER TEN

Anna had been so right. No way she could *ever* have been ready for *this*.

Not just a room, but the world…in full color.

They flew through a magical world that at once looked like Earth, and yet didn't. Everything here appeared bolder, more vivid, more vibrant. The flora was fuller and more lush. The architecture grander. The sky, so close as they were to the heavens — or perhaps they were *in* the heavens? — appeared bigger, endless, infinite.

And it wasn't just that she flew in the air. She *was* the air itself. It gave her the most intense and overwhelming sense of being connected to something bigger than herself, or belonging to the world and everything in it in a way she never could've imagined. If this was what it felt like to be a god, how lucky they were.

Anna struggled against the visions coalescing in her mind's eye — not just one this time, but two, and the jumble of visual elements was so confusing it almost made her nauseous. Though as long as she didn't have a body, she supposed she couldn't actually vomit. And at least she had this wondrous scenery to distract her from the pressure building inside her and demanding its release.

As if the view couldn't have gotten more amazing, they left the Realm of the Gods and entered the human realm, far, far above the ground. Even if she hadn't been able to perceive a visible difference between one realm and the next—which she had, she would've known the difference by the tingling ripple of electricity that passed over every inch of her body. As if maybe they'd just passed through an invisible force field of some kind. Not unpleasant, really, just noticeable.

And by the fact that everything went black and white once more. Why had she been able to see color while in the Realm of the Gods? Maybe the place itself had magically cured her condition? Sadness at the loss rippled through her being, but she forced it away. She refused to waste a moment of this amazing, once-in-a-lifetime experience wallowing in what she didn't have.

How are you liking it? Zephyros asked.

They'd explained to her how to communicate once they were in the wind—just will her thoughts to project, and they would, but it was still so strange to be able to communicate from a disembodied consciousness. *It's the most amazing, awe-inspiring thing I've ever experienced.* She felt the pleasure the gods took from her words without them uttering any in reply. And that, too, was astounding. In these moments, she was connected to them in a way she'd never been connected to anyone. The connection wasn't just physical or emotional, but spiritual and sensual. Metaphysical, even.

Or maybe that was just the sensitive artist in her talking. But, she didn't think so.

A ripple of energy seemed to rock through her, and then came a voice. *The compound is well defended. I put Livos in charge until we return.*

Very good, Chrysander, came a deep voice. Aeolus's? Anna wasn't sure and, anyway, had way more important things to think about. Like…what a beautiful, wondrous sight the world truly was. They were so high above the ground that she could see where the sunshine made it daytime behind them and where the darkness meant it was night in front of them. She could *see* both the light and the dark, and it spoke to something so deep inside of her that emotion nearly overwhelmed her.

Oh, how Anna wished she could share this experience with Devlin alone. Though, given the way he'd treated her after he'd awakened, she doubted he'd be interested. Who was she kidding? Somehow she was back to being "the human" to him, so, yeah, there was no question about it. The interest was all on her side. Maybe gods and humans couldn't be together, anyway. What did she know? She'd just really thought there was something happening between them, but—

Um, Anna? Zephyros said.

Yes?

He didn't respond right away, and then she picked up on the slightest sensation of discomfort…

Oh, God! Please, please, please tell me I didn't just—

Yeah, he said. *When you're new at this it's harder to segregate your private thoughts from intentional communication.*

You guys are such…men! I bet a female goddess totally would've thought to mention that!

A wave of good-natured humor washed through her.

Not that she saw any humor in this situation. She'd just confessed her every thought, desire, and insecurity about Devlin to him and his entire family. She couldn't imagine what he must be thinking, and she was totally sure she didn't want to know. And now, she had absolutely no idea how to keep it from happening again.

She needed to occupy her mind somehow, or else she'd either end up over-sharing again or focusing on the images she needed to paint. Only one solution came to mind—she started singing. And, inexplicably, the only song she could think of was the alphabet. Mortification at the choice threatened, but really, how much more could she humiliate herself at this point? Besides, annoying the crap out of them with a rousing rendition of the ABCs—over and over again for as long as it took to return to her studio—served them right. She hoped she ingrained it so far into their consciousness that they found themselves humming it at random moments a month from now.

A, b, c, d, e, f, g…

After maybe the twentieth repetition of the song, Anna realized someone had joined her, but at first she couldn't tell which one of them it was. Definitely not Zephyros, whose voice she recognized now, nor Aeolus, who struck her as *way* too formal to sing a children's song. And, well, she pretty much ruled Devlin out, too, because he did *not* seem the type to break out spontaneously into song. That left the beautiful blond, then. Chrysander.

If Anna had been in her body, she would've been grinning her butt off. She'd barely had the chance to talk to him, but with that one action he'd completely endeared himself to her. Especially when, about fifteen rounds of the song later, he started putting his own spin on it until he was doing something resembling a very bad rap.

Q to the R to the S—

Chrysander! Zephyros yelled suddenly. Thunder rumbled in the distance. *I will seriously hurt you!*

Anna burst out laughing, and then she realized that she hadn't been singing at all but listening to the god make a fool of himself. For her.

Z, dude, don't be a buzzkill, Chrysander said.

They kept Anna laughing as they snarked back and forth at each other, and the next thing Anna realized was that she could perceive the outline of the Chesapeake Bay in the darkness, the moon reflecting off the great moving body of water. The details of the landscape sharpened the lower they went until she could make out the long, snaking length of the Bay Bridge and the congregation of lights that had to be the city of Baltimore. They flew northward over the light-lined ribbon that was Interstate 95 to where the darkness of the suburban countryside took over again.

Before long, they soared in over Jarrettsville, allowing her a too-fast glimpse of her house, and then the roof of her studio came into view. Moonlight glinted off the metal, and even that struck her as beautiful.

Her artist's soul was totally overwhelmed.

But, as evidence of how insidious these *other* images were, she couldn't even think of how she would try to express what she'd seen and how it had made her feel until she expelled this darkness from her mind.

Coast is clear, Zephyros said. Foreboding crept into Anna's being as they slowed and came in along the ground. Clear of what? Or who? They passed through the crack between the door and the jamb to the inside of her studio. *Okay, Anna, I'm going to shift us back into our physical forms. You're going to be disoriented at first, so just hang on. I won't let you fall.*

She wasn't sure how to reply, but it didn't matter because she didn't have the opportunity anyway. Anna slammed back into her body.

Unlike last time, at least she knew what to expect. But, somehow it still felt a lot more jarring than she recalled. She moaned and clutched at something—Zeph, she guessed—as the world spun and warped and slanted around her. Her senses slowly reattached to her body, as if her consciousness was a separate part that needed to be plugged back into her ears and her nose and her fingertips. It was strange and uncomfortable and absolutely fascinating.

"I gotcha, Anna," came a distant-sounding voice. "It'll pass soon."

Finally, the disorientation faded away. Anna chanced opening her eyes and found herself staring at the dark color—the world was still black and white—of Zeph's shirt. Her hands were absolutely fisted in the fabric, pulling it tight across his chest. She looked up at him. "I'm sorry," she said.

He gave a small smile. "Don't worry about it."

A great ball of emotion rolled through Anna's body and she burst into tears. The maelstrom hit her so hard and so unexpectedly that all she could do was bury her face against the god's chest and let it out. "I...I...I don't know why...I'm...crying," she said, trying to speak between racking breaths and sobs.

Commotion and raised voices erupted around her, but Anna couldn't make any sense of it. She wasn't sure how many minutes had passed before the overpowering outpouring of emotion passed.

Finally, she managed to heave a deep breath that calmed the worst of the ridiculous reaction.

"Wow," she rasped. "I don't know what that was, but I'm sorry." Her cheeks heated as she peered up at Zeph from under wet eyelashes.

"Just the physical expression of your emotions catching up to the actual experience of them. The wind thing gets easier the more you do it."

Anna released him and hugged herself. "Okay," she said, shaking her head. The crying jag had taken so much out of her that she didn't have it in her to keep feeling embarrassed about it. "Well, thank you."

"May I?" Zeph asked, gently grabbing her wrists and tugging them toward him.

"Uh, what—"

"You need your hands to paint, right?" he asked, kindness filling his blue eyes.

"Well, yeah…" A swipe of his thumbs over the bandage on her hand made the gauze disappear, revealing the bumpy redness of the burn on her right hand. "Holy…crap. Did you just—"

"Yes. Don't be alarmed. You've been through enough today without trying to paint with your hand like this. Wouldn't you agree, Aeolus?" He threw a cutting glance at the other god.

Anna glanced from where her hand was cradled in his much bigger grip to the oldest god among them who, after just a moment's hesitation, gave a single nod.

"Good." Zeph winked at her. "What do you say we make this better?"

"Uh…" Anna's head spun a little. She'd experienced so many wondrous and unbelievable things today, she'd have thought her brain wouldn't be so shocked with each new revelation. Not so much. "Sure, why not?" In truth, the burn was going to be a bugger to try to paint with, but something told her the dark visions would force her to work through it.

Holding her hand, Zeph laid his other hand atop hers. Golden light shone through the spaces between his fingers. Anna gasped as a warm, tingling sensation spread over her skin—accompanied by a rush of relief as the pain of her cut and burn melted away to nothing.

Zeph removed his hand.

And, even though Anna knew in her gut what she was going to see, she still stared slack-jawed at her completely healed skin. She turned her hand over and fisted it just to prove to herself that what she *thought* had just happened had really happened.

"Thank you," she said, restraining herself from giving him a hug. "That's not enough, but thank you."

He nodded and gave her a small smile. "Now, will you show us your paintings?"

∞

Devlin glared as Anna smiled at Zephyros and nodded him toward her painting room. His ire wasn't directed at *her*, but at the Western god. For so many reasons. First, it had taken every bit of strength he had—not to mention Chrysander's assistance in restraining him and explaining what was happening—to keep Devlin from launching himself across the room and tearing his uncle's head off when Anna started crying.

Devlin had so little experience interacting with humans that he had no idea flying in the wind would impact her so deeply. But, even once he realized Zephyros hadn't somehow hurt her, Chrys's restraint was still necessary—because Devlin wanted to be the one comforting and consoling her, holding her in his arms, feeling her heat and her tears soak through his borrowed shirt into his chest. Then, as if all of that hadn't already made Devlin want to crawl out of his skin, his uncle had healed her. Devlin had never before felt simultaneously grateful and unworthy until that moment—because his association with the decay and death of fall meant he possessed no healing abilities.

Watching Zeph get to be the one to do all that for Anna pretty much made Devlin want to break something with his bare hands.

Repeatedly. Turned out that jealousy added to rage and firepower made a damn volatile cocktail. Imagine that.

"You tight?" Chrys said, standing between Devlin and the rest of the group as they followed Anna into the other room. Devlin met the god's bright-green eyes and nodded. "He's extremely happily married to Ella. Nothing for you to worry about there, you dig?" Another nod. Chrys eyeballed him for another long moment before finally letting him go.

They crossed to the doorway, and Devlin once again found himself not understanding what the hell was happening. Aeolus and Zephyros stood behind Owen, who was crouched in front of the first of the paintings Anna had done, the one where Eurus, presumably, had two beings of light pinned against a burning building. The whole array of Anna's work was still laid out in a line as they'd left it earlier, but it seemed that the gods hadn't yet looked at any of the others.

"Fucking hell," Chrys said.

Devlin followed the Southern god's gaze to the same painting, and then watched as Zeph crouched behind Owen and put a hand on his shoulder. Aeolus and Chrys traded troubled glances.

"What's wrong?" Anna asked from where she'd been preparing her paints at the table. Devlin could've kissed her for being the one to ask so he didn't have to. And wasn't that…an odd as fuck thought?

Aeolus turned to her. "When did you paint this?" he asked, pointing at the first canvas.

"Last weekend," she said. "Why? What is it?"

"It depicts the moment before my oldest son's death, which happened three days ago."

Anna gasped and her face paled. "Oh. Oh, God. I'm so sorry."

The news hit Devlin like a punch to the gut. His gaze cut back to the painting, and as he stared at his father's depiction, arm raised in attack, long lash of lighting gripped in his fist, Devlin knew he'd never hated Eurus more than he did at this very moment.

"It has to stop," he said, not realizing he was going to speak until the words were spilling from his mouth. "How many more must die or be harmed at his hands?"

Zephyros glared up at him, skepticism plain in his eyes and on his face.

"I know you don't trust me, don't like me, probably even blame me. And I get it." One by one, Devlin met the gaze of each of the other gods in the room. "But I vow to do everything in my power to help put an end to this once and for all."

No one spoke. No one moved. Hell, he wasn't sure anyone even breathed.

In a flash, Owen was off the ground and right up in his face. Every one of Devlin's defensive instincts rang out in alarm and his muscles went rigid, expecting the blows to land but of course not sure where.

Silver light flared behind Owen's eyes as he stared straight into Devlin's. And then the Northern god gave a single nod. "Count. Me. In." Owen extended his hand.

Stunned to receive an offer of friendship and alliance—and even acceptance—when he'd been prepared for pain left Devlin dumbfounded. Finally, his brain caught up with the situation, and he placed his hand in Owen's.

Another solemn nod, and Owen stepped away.

"I'm in, man. I've been in all summer," Chrys said, taking Owen's place and shaking his hand.

Aeolus nodded and looked at Devlin with an emotion he wasn't sure he recognized. Pride? Belief? Hope? "And it *is* in your power, Devlin. Especially if we work together."

The others looked at Zeph, drawing Devlin's gaze to where he stood in front of the painting depicting Boreas's death with his arms crossed over his chest. Everything about the god radiated doubt, skepticism, rejection.

"Your father took my wife's human life from her, forcing her to become a goddess without her consent. Had she not retained her memories of me on her own, I would've been forced to have nothing to do with her forever." Zeph stepped closer. "Against my will, he had your brother installed as my successor. And you know why Alastor has the blood of spring flowing through him? Because Eurus kidnapped and raped my first wife, a goddess of spring, and then spread rumors throughout Olympus that I was the one who'd mistreated her." Zephyros came closer still, throwing off Chrys's attempts to hold him back. "And then, three days ago, Eurus drove lightning through my big brother's chest in front of my eyes." He waved out an arm. "In front of *all* of our eyes. And we were forced to watch him die."

Grim-faced, Aeolus made to intercede, but Devlin shook his head. Whatever this was, Devlin would take it if it would clear the air between them and allow them to move on. And he understood Zeph's rage. More than that, given all the ways Eurus had wronged Zephyros, the Western god was completely fucking entitled to it. "I know," Devlin managed, meeting Zeph's roiling blue gaze. "And I'm sorry."

Down deep, it cut to apologize for the wrongs of his father. After all, no one had ever apologized to Devlin, and never would. But should Devlin, by some miracle of Zeus, survive the challenges before him, he would be his father's successor in the East Wind. He would become a Cardinal Anemoi. And that meant he potentially had an eternity in front of him to work with Zeph and all of these gods. So the wound was a sacrifice worth making. Besides, with so many scars, what was one more?

Chrys punched Zeph in the shoulder and glared at him when Zeph whirled. "He's offering a fucking olive branch, man."

Zeph's gaze returned to him and he shook his head. "I'm not there, Devlin. But I'll try."

Better than nothing, he guessed. Devlin nodded.

"Uh, guys?" Owen said, drawing everyone's attention…to where Anna stood furiously painting, her brush flying over the canvas, ribbons of colors waving between her palette, her brush, and the painting itself.

Damnit. They'd been so caught up in their own drama, they hadn't even noticed that she'd been called away from the group and compelled by whatever magic brought these images to start painting.

"Holy shit," Chrys said.

Devlin walked around the group and came up behind Anna.

"You okay?"

"Sure," she said in a low, distant voice.

He leaned to the side to see the painting, his gut filling with equal parts anticipation and dread. It was a close-up on his profile—he was almost sure it was him, not his father. On the canvas, his hand reached out in front of him toward something she hadn't yet painted. But, gods, she'd only been painting a few minutes and had nearly a quarter of the two-by-three-foot canvas already covered.

As the other gods gathered around to watch her work, Devlin stepped to her side so he could see her face. Sweat beaded on her brow and dampened the hair around the edge of her face. "Hey, you don't have to rush," he said.

Her gaze flickered toward him. "I don't have a choice," she said. "Wherever this is, it's some place bad. I have to hurry."

Her words drew his eyes back to the painting, where the background of the image was starting to come to life.

"Christ, I know at least one of the gods in her family tree," Zeph said suddenly, drawing everyone's attention—except Anna's, as if the painting wouldn't allow her the diversion. And if that was true, Devlin hated that for her. He hated that whatever this was didn't give her the choice.

"Who?" Aeolus asked.

"It's been a helluva long time, but since I once courted her, I'm sure of it. Anna is a daughter of Iris," Zeph said. "I'd recognize the energy she's throwing off anywhere."

Devlin's gaze flashed to Anna, who was apparently descended from the personification of the rainbow, a magical creature who also served as the messenger of the gods. Which explained both the color and the visions.

Turning his gaze back to Anna—and to the stream of gold light emanating from her brush—Aeolus said, "Indeed."

"Wait. Aren't the Harpies Iris's sisters?" Chrys asked, eyeing Anna as if he were seeing her for the first time. It made Devlin want to step between them, even as he realized where Chrys's question was coming from—the Harpies had attacked the Anemoi less than a week ago at the Rock of Gibraltar, badly injuring Boreas and Chrys.

Zeph nodded. "Yeah, but there's no lost love there. Never has been. Which—son of a bitch—might be very good news for us."

"How do you figure?" Owen asked, crossing his arms. Thunder rumbled in the distance.

"Because Iris can control the Harpies. And if she's willing to intercede with them on our behalf, we might be able to cost Eurus an important ally." Zeph's smile was the first he'd seen from the god. Maybe ever.

"When we're done here, Zephyros, tell her about Anna and make the request," Aeolus said. "This is damn good news. About time."

"I will. There's another energy here, though. And I don't recognize it." General murmurs of agreement followed Zeph's words.

Devlin agreed. Someone else was responsible for her control over light and dark, but who? "Perhaps Iris can tell us that, too," he said.

Zeph's gaze narrowed, but then he nodded. "Could be." A loud crack of thunder, still some distance from them, punctuated the silence. "With all of us together, this weather's going to escalate. How long will this take?"

In the Realm of the Gods it was a different story, but here on Earth, the longer multiple Cardinal Anemoi congregated in one place, the more the elements from their respective realms competed and collided. While he'd heard that was true, Devlin had never seen the results of such a thing firsthand before, since he and his father never spent any time with the other Anemoi. On Earth or in the heavens. "The one I saw her do earlier today took maybe forty-five minutes."

"Storm will be damn close to catastrophic if we stay together much longer than that," Chrys said, looking at Aeolus. "You might need to rein it in."

Aeolus nodded.

"Devlin?" came Anna's voice, almost breathy now.

He returned to her side. "Yes? Hell, Anna, are you okay?"

Face bright red from exertion, sweat-dampened hair matted to the sides of her face, she looked like she'd been doing manual labor all day. "There's another one. After this. There's more."

Protectiveness surged through him, and he leaned around her to try to make eye contact. "There's another image you have to paint tonight?"

"Yes," she whispered. A tear spilled from her eye.

"How can I help?" he asked, catching the drop on his finger. Her shoulders lifted in the barest of shrugs. His gaze ran over her face as concern filled his gut. At this pace, she was going to run herself right into the ground, especially if the second image was as demanding as this. And, damnit, it had been hours since she'd eaten.

Gods, Devlin hated little more than the feeling of helplessness. There had to be *something* he could do.

A memory flashed into his mind's eye from the first night he'd seen her, the night she'd painted the awful supercell thunderstorm and then the amazingly vivid portrait of the autumn trees. She'd worn her hair up in a knot secured with two paintbrushes.

Devlin glanced at her long hair, flowing down her back and sticking to her face and neck. He hadn't the foggiest idea how to do what she'd done to it. But his hair was just long enough to tug into a short knot on the back of his head when he couldn't stand it in his face anymore, so at the very least he could get it up off her neck.

But with what?

Surveying her worktable, he found two loose rubber bands lying near a pile of brushes. He grabbed one and stepped behind her.

Not caring in the slightest that the other men were staring at him as though he'd suddenly sprouted a second head, he gathered her hair into his hands. Her breath caught as if the touch surprised her. "Just trying to make you more comfortable," he said. As he collected the long strands into a ponytail, he realized how soaked the hair underneath was. In fact, the back of her shirt was damp with her sweat. What the hell were these visions doing to her?

Devlin pressed the back of his hand to her bare neck, and her skin was hot, almost feverish. With a few last movements of his hand, he finished collecting her soft, silky hair and secured the band to hold it up. Then he slipped the length of her hair over her shoulder, leaned in, and blew a cool stream of the East Wind against the long, elegant column of her neck.

The moan of pleasure she unleashed reached inside Devlin's body and grabbed his heart. "Thank you," she said, and then she leaned back enough to press her face to his. The touch jolted him from the inside out, heating his blood and arousing his body. And then she was gone, pulled back to serve the magic.

An ecstatic rush of gratitude and satisfaction flooded through him. He'd been able to help and relieve her, even if only a little. The little reward of affection was maybe the sweetest thing anyone had ever done to him, or for him. And he couldn't believe he'd resisted her earlier efforts to share herself with him. *What a fucking idiot you are.*

"Devlin, do you know where that is?" Aeolus asked, interrupting his thoughts and pointing at the painting.

Anna had finished most of the background now, and it appeared to be a massive, ancient bookshelf filled to the brim with boxes and chests of all different colors and materials. Plain wood, molded silver, cast iron. Something about it beckoned a memory from deep, deep in his past. "It's familiar, but I can't place it," Devlin said.

The closer she got to finishing the painting, the more rapt her work held everyone's attention. And most of all Devlin's—after all, the painting was of his future.

Finally, she had everything done but the very center, the thing his painted alter ego was holding or reaching for. Before all of their eyes, it came to life. An ornate golden skeleton key.

Collective gasps echoed around the room, and realization slammed into Devlin's brain. "Eurus's study. That's his—"

"—lantern key," Aeolus said.

"Sonofabitch. If we could get our hands on that, it would be game over," Chrys said. Every one of the twenty-four total Anemoi—Cardinal, Ordinal, and Inter-Ordinal alike—was represented in a massive compass rose inlaid in the floor of the Hall of the Winds in Aeolus's compound. At each directional point around the compass, a locked lantern containing a glowing ball of the god's divine energy sat installed in the floor. Each of the gods placed his energy there upon ascending to his wind, and upon death, his light automatically extinguished. And each god possessed the single key that could unlock his lantern, because if anyone accessed and consumed the energy within, they would automatically become the new master of that wind, essentially stealing the divine energy from the existing god.

Anna's painting depicted Eurus's key.

The key to the East Wind. A hard gust whipped against the sides of the barn as another, closer clap of thunder rang out.

"The key's hidden in one of the boxes on that shelf," Devlin said, the threads of a childhood memory weaving together. "Of course, pick the wrong box and unleash a variety of booby traps, curses, or unluckiness. I'm meant to retrieve it, then." Which made the trip he'd already planned to the Eastern Realm about a hundred times more important and twice as risky. Because last he knew, the dungeon where Alastor was likely imprisoned was nowhere near Eurus's chambers.

When no one spoke, he glanced over his shoulder. And found a series of grim expressions. Rain poured in a steady drumbeat against the metal roof.

Devlin frowned. "This is good news, isn't it?"

"The general location of the key? Yes," Aeolus said. "That you— or any of us—must go there? Absolutely not."

"It's a fucking death sentence," Chrys said.

"For you, probably. Not for me." At least he hoped. Not that Devlin thought it'd be a cakewalk, either. Eurus now knew he'd been working with Aeolus, so no doubt there were all kinds of special presents waiting for Devlin should he try to go home. But he'd spent an eternity learning some of his own tricks in dealing with his father's incantations, so he had a fighting chance.

Besides, who else could go if not him?

CHAPTER ELEVEN

As Owen watched Anna put the finishing touches on her painting, she dropped her brush to the floor and swayed. Owen dashed toward her, but Devlin was right there and caught her in his arms.

"Whoa, dizzy," she said against a backdrop of rolling thunder and a pounding gust of wind.

"I've got you," Devlin said, holding her against his chest and leaning down to peer in her eyes. And that was the moment Owen knew for sure that Devlin Eston was nothing like his evil father. The god's expression, body language, and careful hold of Anna radiated concern, affection, attraction, protectiveness, and possessiveness. As far as Owen had ever seen, Eurus was only capable of the last of those emotions, and Devlin had been on the receiving end of it, if those scars and tattooed bands on his wrists meant what Owen suspected they meant.

Though some gods bore marks as part of their divinity, tattoos of the human variety were rare because the body would heal the wound created by the needles and thus expel the ink. There was only one exception to this rule—if the tattoo was done by a superior god. Which meant someone more powerful than Devlin had put those black bands around his wrists, not something many superior gods would deign to do without a very special reason—or wanting to make a very particular point.

And hell if those bands didn't look a whole lot like handcuffs.

Given that Eurus was likely already responsible for the death of one son and rumored to torture the other one, it wouldn't surprise Owen at all to learn that Devlin had also been on the receiving end of Eurus's belief that he owned him, and therefore could do whatever in Hades he wanted.

"Just a little hungry," she said, pushing against Devlin's chest.

He held her tighter and stroked her hair. "Just rest a minute," he said, then his gaze scanned the other gods. "She needs food and water. Would, um, one of you—"

"I'll go. Might help calm down the weather, too. You in?" Owen asked, looking at Chrys. While things in their world were so volatile, they'd agreed not to go anywhere solo.

"Always," Chrys said, and they disappeared.

In the elements, they shot several miles down the road they'd soared in over earlier toward a grouping of stores Owen had seen.

Devlin's not like his father, Owen said.

I'm getting the same vibe, man. Not with the way he cares about Anna. Pause. *You okay?* Chrys asked.

Yeah, Owen said, Anna's painting flashing into his mind's eye. Gods be damned but seeing that moment from the outside had been like living through it all over again. Part of the reason Owen had only been too happy to bug out of there for a little while—trying to hold everything in felt as if he'd swallowed crushed glass. But losing his shit wouldn't help anyone either.

A few moments later, they materialized outside a store. "Dude, I could eat, too," Chrys said.

"Well, then," Owen said, opening the door. "Welcome to the human junk food mecca known as the convenience store."

"Ooh, my favorite." Chrys grabbed a handheld basket and wag-gled his eyebrows when Owen arched a brow at it. "What? I don't know what she likes, so we need to get a bunch of stuff."

"Uh-huh."

Five minutes later, chips, pretzels, granola bars, a package of chocolate cupcakes, and several types of soda filled the basket. "Yo, look," Chrys said, pointing at a freezer case full of ice cream.

"I'm good, thanks." Owen couldn't eat right now if he had to.

Chrys's gaze narrowed. "I have never known you to turn down ice cream. Seriously." When Owen didn't respond, Chrys opened the door, sucking in a breath as the cold air blasted him, and grabbed several containers.

"Jesus, Chrys," Owen said, pulling the tubs from his hands and knocking him out of the way. Owen hip-checked the door shut and dumped them in the basket.

"Fuck," Chrys said, blowing on his palms, bright red from how the icy cold had effectively burned him. "How do you eat that shit?"

Owen shook his head. "Same way you eat anything hot. Go stand by the heat lamp, you idiot." He nodded toward where a metal hood emanated golden light onto a tray of plump hot dogs.

"Hey, good idea." Chrys shoved the basket into Owen's hands, crossed the store, and stuck his hands into the light. A minute later, he returned healed and carrying four long aluminum foil bags. "Hot dogs," he said with a grin. "You paying?"

"Naturally," Owen said, drily. Since Owen lived in the human realm, he was probably the only one of them who carried cash.

They returned to Anna's studio, which was really just a big old barn, mere moments later to find her kneeling on the floor painting. This new painting wasn't very far along yet.

"Food's here," Chrys said.

"Where the hell did you go? China?" Zeph said, yanking the plastic bags from Chrys's hand.

"Hey, chill. Us being gone calmed the weather down. And one of those hot dogs is mine."

Zephyros passed the bags to Devlin. "See if you can get her to take a break," he said, tone serious.

Owen frowned and glanced from the dark expression of concern on Devlin's face to Anna. Why was she painting on the floor instead of at her easel as she had before?

"Oh," she said, cupping her hand beneath her face. Droplets of blood spattered her palm, and several had fallen onto a clean part of the canvas on which she painted. Dark red circles bloomed against the white. Anna glanced up, revealing the blood dripping from her nose, the color stark against her fair skin and pale eyes.

Devlin moved instantly, ripping a couple paper towels off a roll on a worktable and kneeling beside her. "Here," he said.

She pressed the towel to her face. "I've never had a nosebleed before."

Aeolus stepped closer. "You're wielding a lot of divine energy for a human, Anna. Do you usually tire when you paint?"

She nodded. "Yes, but I, uh, also have a condition that leaves me fatigued." She slanted a glance at Devlin, whose expression darkened in concern.

"Well, that could be it. Or it could also be that, in our world, special power often comes at a cost. There must be sacrifice for benefit. I fear that's what is happening here."

"Using the magic could be doing this to her?" Devlin asked, glancing to his grandfather.

"That's my best guess," Aeolus said, sympathy coloring his expression.

Owen's gut clenched in regret for both Anna and Devlin, because he knew what it felt like to watch the woman he loved have to suffer because of the fighting and warfare among the Anemoi. Megan had just lost her home, her father-in-law, her whole life as she knew it. All the gods in this room had been through this. Ella had been assaulted and thrown to her human death. And Laney had been whipped with Eurus's lightning, only surviving because of a magical amulet Chrys had given her to wear.

One hand applying pressure to her nose, Anna retrieved her paintbrush in the other and began to paint again. The speed of her brush strokes was several notches beyond manic, and very clearly magical in nature, as was the way colored light flowed and sparkled around her as she worked. Owen had never seen anything like it. The thunder and wind worsened again, the sound loud within the old barn.

Devlin gently dumped out the contents of the grocery bags onto the floor next to Anna's canvas. "You need to take a break and eat something, Anna."

"I can't," she said, not looking away from where she painted lightning shooting from a series of dark clouds.

"You have to," he said. "You're going to hurt yourself." He grabbed her arm, making her smear paint across the canvas.

Her gaze cut toward him. "It already hurts," she said, her gaze part pleading and part steely determination. "My head is killing me. Won't get better 'til I'm done." She tossed the bloodied napkin away and pressed her knuckles to her nose, as if testing to see if the bleeding had stopped. A little red colored her fingers, but nothing like before.

Devlin passed her another paper towel that she held to her nose, then scanned the pile of junk food. He grabbed the bag of pretzels, popped it open, and looked at his hands, smudged from whatever had happened to him earlier. He disappeared. Owen barely had time to throw a questioning glance at the others. A few seconds passed and Devlin returned again, his hands clean and wet. He dried them and dumped a few pretzels in his palm.

"Open," he said, holding the twisted pretzel to her lips. She devoured it instantly. Devlin continued to feed her as she worked, her hunger so pronounced Owen could almost feel it himself. For damn sure, he could see himself in Devlin's actions, because he'd always worried that Megan had enough to eat, especially when she was pregnant. Seeing Devlin behaving similarly gave Owen more proof the god was fundamentally decent.

Devlin gave her food, held water to her mouth so she could drink, and got her clean paper towels as blood continued to leak from her nose. He rubbed her back and wiped sweat from her eyes. There was so much caring in the god's actions, Owen almost felt he was violating their privacy.

But the image forming on Anna's canvas compelled him to stay, to watch, to look. At the center of a great collection of storm clouds were two figures depicted flying in the sky from behind. They weren't in the foreground of the painting, but in the middle, so the details weren't very clear. What *was* clear was that one god—presumably Devlin?—carried another being in his arms, one who appeared unconscious. Or worse.

Thunder exploded overhead and rain spattered against the side of the building, as if the wind were blowing it sideways. "Fuck," Chrysander said, kneeling near the canvas.

"At least we know it's not you," Zeph said, arms crossed, face serious as thunder. Owen nodded. The god being carried had dark hair, while Chrys was the only blond among them. Which meant the painting depicted the injury of either Zeph, Aeolus, or himself. Or the death.

Red-hot dread prickled down Owen's spine. Damn it all to Hades and back, how much more loss could they sustain?

ꝏꝏ

"Done," Anna said, sagging until she had to brace her hands on the floor to hold herself up. She felt like she'd run a marathon, or two. Her muscles ached, her joints throbbed, and her body felt as if she'd aged a whole decade.

"Let me help you up," Devlin said, reaching for her.

She chuffed out half a laugh. "My legs are asleep."

"That's okay. Take my hands," he said from right beside her.

Anna peered up at him from under the lengths of her hair that had fallen loose from her ponytail. Her cheeks warmed. She wouldn't have made it through these paintings without him. God, he'd put her hair up, rubbed her shoulders, and given her food and water. Big and dark and intimidating as he was, he'd been heartbreakingly gentle. A couple of times his fingers had touched her lips as he'd fed her. Under other circumstances, his touch would've made her melt. As it was, she was so moved by the way he'd cared for her that she didn't know whether to cry or jump him. Maybe both.

And damn if she wasn't more confused than ever, too. Because his actions had her feeling a connection between the two of them again. So which was the real Devlin? The one who'd sat at her kitchen table and had all but radiated gratitude? The one who'd jumped down her throat and made her feel unimportant at Aeolus's house? Or the one who had taken care of her as if she was precious and irreplaceable?

Anna slipped her hands into Devlin's.

He pulled her easily to her feet and caught her against his chest when her legs were too numb to hold her weight. And then the blood rushed in. Gritting her teeth against the pins and needles pricking at her skin from toes to knees, Anna fisted her hands in Devlin's dark-gray shirt. All she could do was hold her breath and hang on tight. When the sensation became so intense she couldn't hold back a reaction any longer, her breath exploded from her along with a pained laugh. "I don't know how...something that hurts so much...can almost tickle," she gasped out.

Devlin leaned his face against her hair.

Finally, the discomfort ebbed. Anna's shoulders slumped and her focus landed on her hands clenched around handfuls of cotton. She released Devlin immediately, remembering all too well how he'd flinched away from her time and again.

Except he caught her hands in his and pressed them to his sternum. "Let me help," he said in a voice so low it was almost a whisper. His gaze was both insistent and hesitant.

It needn't have been the latter because just then, Anna needed Devlin's strength to hold her weakness, his heat to ease the chill her bones seemed to have absorbed from sitting on the hard concrete, his magic and power to help her believe in and come to terms with her own.

Thunder clapped so hard from right above them that the building shook.

"I know Anna is not yet recovered, but we need to leave before the storm worsens," Aeolus said.

Resting her cheek against Devlin's chest, Anna watched as Aeolus waved at her paintings. "We'll take these with us lest they fall into the wrong hands."

"Wait, what?" she asked, forcing herself to stand on her own two feet—though the big, warm grip of Devlin's hands remained on her shoulders. It gave her the feeling that he had her back, and she drew strength from that now. "These are my paintings." No way was she just letting the gods waltz out of here with something she'd labored over so intensely—and, more than that, they were the only physical proof of her power.

Stillness settled on the room, as if everyone held their breath.

"Anna?" Devlin said from behind her. He squeezed her shoulder and urged her to face him. "These are unquestionably your paintings. But they tell a story that's vital to every single god in this room. A story that, if it doesn't end the right way, is vital to humanity, too. No one seeks to steal them from you, but for both the story they tell and to keep them safe from our enemies, would you please consider letting Aeolus take them to his home? As a loan?" Devlin's thumbs stroked the side of her neck.

Tingles prickled over her scalp and down her neck. "Vital to humanity?"

He nodded, dark eyes serious and intense. "What Aeolus said earlier about your use of the magic, about benefit requiring sacrifice? The divine realm operates under a principle of balance. Maintained, balance creates natural peace on earth. But I come from…my father is…" Devlin pressed his lips into a thin line, as if he wished to hold in the words he needed to say. His eyes flared and his hands slipped upward to softly grasp her neck. "Evil, Anna. Pure and unadulterated evil. He wishes to destroy every god in this room, take over control of the natural world, and play with humanity like it was no more than a collection of toy soldiers in a sandbox."

A crack of thunder. Then again. Anna jumped at the percussive volume.

Her heart racing, Anna thought of her paintings—the tornadoes, the massive storm over Jarrettsville, the strange beings in the sky through the damaged building. Her gaze dropped to the canvas that still lay drying at their feet. Vague as the image was, one thing was crystal clear—that something bad had happened to the person in the Dark Man's arms. Or, rather, *would* happen, since what she'd painted depicted some moment in the future. Some tragedy waiting to unfurl.

"They're a part of me," she said, looking Devlin in the eye. "As long as you'll take care of them."

"You have my word," he said without hesitation. And then he kissed her on the forehead.

Heat bloomed over Anna's entire body. The day. The magic. *This man*. Every part of her was overwhelmed, and especially by him. Just another way this day had been the most exhilarating, terrifying, and amazing of her entire life.

"Should we take her materials, too, in case another vision comes?" Zephyros asked.

Anna frowned and pulled away from Devlin's grasp. "Why would you…I mean, why would I…" Realization hit her like a ton of bricks and she gaped at Zeph and crossed her arms. "My stuff should stay right here, since that's where *I'll* be."

"It's not safe here," Zeph said. "Our divine energy is all over this place. And so is yours."

"Yeah, Anna," Chrys said, a sympathetic smile on his face. "Sooner or later Eurus will pick up on it. And you don't want to be here when he does."

"No, you're not hearing me," she said, whirling on Devlin and nailing him with a stare. "I can't just leave here. My father needs me. I have work to do."

"Dude, the energy from your explosion hangs over her house like a neon sign on the Vegas strip," Chrys said to Devlin. "When E comes—and you know he will—it'll be like a target is painted on the roof."

Gasping, Anna looked from Devlin's gaze to Chrys's, then to that of the other gods as well. They all wore the same expressions full of regret and certainty. Fear melted every other concern away, leaving only her dad.

"If my house is that unsafe, then I especially can't leave. I need to pack my father up and get him out of there. God," Anna said, pushing wisps of her hair behind her ears. "You have no idea how huge this is going to be for him. He's sick. He needs routine. Change absolutely terrifies him." She dropped her face into her hands. "What have I done?"

Lightning flashed again and again, lighting up the darkness of the adjoining room.

"Devlin," Aeolus urged.

He nodded, but there was no way he was forcing her before she was ready. "We'll figure out a way to make him safe, Anna," Devlin said. "I promise."

Slowly, she raised her eyes to him. "I don't take that word lightly, Devlin."

Light flared from behind his eyes. "Neither do I. Look," he said, turning to the others. "I'll stay with her at her house tonight. Go back to Aeolus's and, if you can spare them, send some of the guards from there to Anna's. If Eurus is guiding the storm, we probably have a day or two window. Enough time to get things straightened out here and then get out of the way."

Devlin...staying with me? And guards? Holy crap, how is this my life?

Aeolus stepped forward, brow drawn, lips tight. "Devlin, if you have any chance at all of retrieving Eurus's key, you must go to the Eastern Realm while he is otherwise occupied with building the storm. That gives you very little time."

Chrys's voice labeling the trip a death sentence rang between Anna's ears. Her belly throbbed with an aching emptiness that had nothing to do with hunger.

Beside her, Devlin gave a single nod. "Understood and agreed. We'll return to your compound tomorrow afternoon, and I'll make the trip by tomorrow night."

"That's cutting it damn close, Devlin," Zephyros said. Anna liked Zeph—despite his initial grumpiness, he'd been kind to her, held her while she cried without making her feel weak or silly, and had healed her. The wonder of that still echoed through her mind. So she was glad to see that the god's face wasn't filled with his typical angry scowl toward Devlin, just deep concern.

Devlin nailed Zeph with a hard stare. "Tell me you would handle this differently." An odd tension rolled through the room, and the expressions on the men's faces made her feel they were having a conversation to which she wasn't privy.

Thunder crashed and punctuated the weighted silence. Finally, Zephyros simply said, "No, I wouldn't."

"Then it's settled," Aeolus said, sending the room into a flurry of action. Chrysander and Owen hurried to gather the paintings into a stack, and Anna was equal parts alarmed at the prospect of their loss and relieved at the gentle way the big gods handled them.

"What do you need from here, Anna?" Devlin pointed to the worktable. "We need to hurry. Our collective presence here is causing this." He pointed to the ceiling.

"Oh. Um," she said, looking at the mess she'd left from the manic way she'd prepped the two paintings. Normally she was so careful and organized with her supplies. That her workspace was in such disarray was a physical representation of what the inside of her head had felt like when the compulsion of the visions took hold. Nothing else had mattered. Not her body, not her hunger, not the conversation going on around her—

She gasped and whirled on Zephyros. "What did you say?" She waved her hands. "Before." His eyebrows drew up in silent question. "About who I am?"

"Oh, uh…just that…" His gaze flickered to Devlin, and Anna's followed.

"You already know you have divine power, Anna. Zephyros was just able to narrow part of it down to a source. A distant ancestor. *Your* distant ancestor. Iris is the personification of the rainbow and a messenger of the gods. He recognized the energy you throw off while you paint."

Leaning back against the table, Anna had to grab hold of the plastic and metal to ground herself against the way her head spun. "Iris," she said, testing the name out on her tongue. "But, if I'm truly descended from a rainbow goddess"—and just saying that made the floor shift and spin—"why am I color-blind? Why am I only able to see color when I paint? *Oh!* And when I was in your realm. I could see color then, too."

"You could?" Devlin asked, then shook his head. "Probably has something to do with whatever other divine ancestry you possess. Or it could be something from your human lines."

"So you think…I have more than one god in my family tree?" Devlin's nod was barely perceptible, almost as if he feared that acknowledging this new reality too boldly would throw her over the edge. And the way she felt right now, maybe it would. Because though knowing this about herself changed nothing fundamentally about her as a person, it still left her feeling a whole lot like she was a stranger in her own life. Had her brother been magical, too? Her parents? And did people in her family suspect anything about themselves, but just never talked about it? *Oh my God! Will my kids be this way?* In that moment, she wasn't sure if that was bad or really, really cool.

"Guys, Owen and I are going to start back so we can dial down this storm," Chrys said.

Anna barely paid attention to what the others were saying, though. She spun and braced her elbows on the table, accidentally planting her righty in the blue paint of her palette. The tangible texture of the cool, thick acrylic grounded her, gave her something real to grasp onto, and pulled her back from the brink of a panic attack. "Okay," she said to herself as she grabbed a paper towel and wiped off the worst of the paint. Wasn't the only place a swipe of color marked her skin. But between the day's earlier crisis and a night spent manically painting, Anna was going to crawl right out of her skin if she didn't get a shower. And soon. "Um, I have a travel set I can take. I just want to add some things to it," she said.

Forcing herself to focus on the mechanics of her body moving and her lungs pulling in air, Anna crossed the room to a shelf by the door. Owen and Chrys had in fact left, she noticed, and her belly flip-flopped for worry of her paintings, most of which were gone. She grabbed the larger of two wooden briefcase-shaped kits that sat there because it included a small, built-in easel that flipped out from the lid. Back at her table, she flicked open the silver clasps and laid the portable paint set open. Quickly, instinctively, she switched out a couple of colors, tucked the tubes of a few others into the blank spaces between the banded-in supplies, and added a few more brushes.

"This should do it, I guess," she said, securing it again.

Devlin held out his hand, accepted the case from her, and then handed it off to Zeph. Stepping in close to her, Devlin leaned down to look directly in her eyes. "Don't worry, okay?"

A million different responses fought for airtime. "Okay."

After a quick round of good-byes and urgings to be safe and stay aware, the rest of the gods disappeared before her eyes. Of all the things that'd happened in the past twenty-four hours, their vanishing act wasn't even by far the strangest. And wasn't that saying something.

"Ready?" Devlin asked.

No. "Sure," she said, completely overwhelmed.

He grabbed her hand and yanked her closer, so close that she had to tilt her head back to meet his eyes. "Now, hold on tight."

His gorgeous face, her body, almost all physical sensation—it all fell away as they shifted into the wind. But Anna knew without a doubt that Devlin was right there beside her, because his energy was so much more intense than Zephyros's had been. Warm, surrounding, reassuringly heavy, like the feeling of a man resting his weight on you after mind-blowing sex.

Heat shot through Anna's psyche, and she almost swore she heard an answering low, masculine groan.

For the record, Devlin said, the tone of his thought almost a growl, *I would've given just about anything for your first time truly flying in the wind to have been with just me.*

CHAPTER TWELVE

Throughout his whole existence, Devlin had probably spent decades' worth of time in the elements as the wind and rain of autumn. But he'd never spent a single moment of that time in the wind with a human.

It made everything about the experience different, new, wondrous. As they flew together through the nighttime world, the storm downgrading by degrees as the Anemoi separated, his power holding her being in this form, Anna's excitement at the experience of flying rocked through him, her curiosity forced him to be present in the moment in a way he rarely ever was, and the intensity of her emotions was almost like being reborn. Because Devlin wasn't sure he'd ever before experienced the kind of ecstatic joy this woman was feeling right now. On some level, he wasn't even aware it was possible to feel this depth of happiness, period.

All that despite the fact that she was bone tired, somehow unwell—something he wanted to know more about—and desperately worried about her father.

It was a testament to just how amazed Devlin was by the experience that, once they left her studio, his psyche forgot the fear that proximity usually caused. For once in his long existence, he felt something that he imagined others might call peace.

Anna's surprise ricocheted through her energy. *What's that?*

Up ahead, shimmery, translucent violet light hung in the sky like a curtain. If the light had been higher in the sky and they'd been in a more northerly latitude, Devlin might've thought they were witnessing a rare purple aurora. They moved closer, closer, and Devlin's gut clenched in realization. The light came from the back yard of Anna's house, which was lit up like a fucking Christmas tree. Just as Chrysander had said.

Because of him. No doubt about it, his energy signature made the Fallston house pretty much the most dangerous place in the world, at least once Eurus became aware of it. Which was absolutely inevitable.

It's the reason you and your father can't stay here, he said, using every bit of strength he possessed to strip the self-loathing from his tone.

Oh.

Yeah, he said.

Her house came fully into view as they flew in over her street. *It's beautiful.*

Anna, it's a death sentence waiting to happen.

I understand the danger, Devlin. I do. But even dangerous things can be beautiful. A cheetah in a full-out run after its prey. The free-fall of an avalanche. Lightning. A pause as Devlin circled around the house, assessing if anyone was awake within. *And it's yours*, Anna added.

Meaning…? Devlin turned the words around in his mind, but couldn't make any sense out of them. She *seemed* to be saying that… that because it was his energy, it was beautiful. But there was no fucking way that was what she actually meant. If she truly understood the danger he'd brought to her doorstep, she'd see him for what he was—the harbinger of misfortune. *Her* misfortune. Just like his father. And damn it all to Hades, there was *nothing* beautiful about that.

Sonofafuckingbitch.

There are two people inside, both asleep, he managed to say.

My father and Evan.

I'll take us inside, then. Where do you want to go?

Devlin brought them in through the chimney, a regular frickin' Santa, except, you know, without the gifts, good cheer, or glad tidings. Inside, he followed her directions to a room at the top of the steps on the second floor. Big, fluffy-looking bed in the center, long dresser topped with jewelry and trinkets, walls covered in paintings and photographs. Anna's bedroom, then. Her most private space.

No big deal.

Except in Devlin's world you didn't let someone into your inner sanctum, well, ever. Because doing so required trust and loyalty, two concepts that were way more theoretical than actual, at least in Devlin's experience. He trusted *no one*. And the only people who had ever been loyal to him were his brothers. One died for it. The other had been tortured and imprisoned.

So damn big deal.

With the maelstrom raging inside his head, *We're here* was all the warning Devlin managed to give before shifting them back into their corporeal forms just inside the door. A second later, he recalled how the experience had impacted Anna the last time, and found in his carelessness with her a whole new reason to hate himself.

She gasped and swayed. Devlin caught her in his arms, even though the emotional tumult he felt had resurrected the fear and anxiety about closeness and being touched that were his old best friends. And *gods*, even though his body was on high alert, Anna's warm curves felt so good in his arms—

"You can let me go," she said. "I know it makes you uncomfortable."

Well, fuck.

For a moment, it felt as though time stopped, and Devlin found himself perched on a cliff's edge. A step forward sent him into the cold, lonely free-fall of solitude, and very likely shut down any future possibility of receiving her touch—because, really, how many times could someone offer affection and have it thrown back in their face before they learned to keep it to themselves…or offer it to someone more worthy?

But a step backward, a step onto the solid safety of hard ground, well, that at least maintained her touch and affection as a potential. Whether Devlin was too emotionally stunted to grasp that potential with both hands and never let go was another matter entirely.

A moment of indecision. And then Devlin did something he almost never did—he took a chance, a risk, a figurative step away from the edge.

He leaned down, planted his hands in her silky hair, and kissed Anna like she was the air he needed to breathe.

And, sweet Zeus, after the slightest moment of surprised hesitation, she melted against him, fisted her hands in his hair, and opened her mouth to his on a high, throaty moan. Her arousal was a living presence all around him, kicking his heart into a sprint and sending blood pounding into his cock.

Devlin's tongue swept into her mouth, tasting and stroking and twining with hers. One of his hands went to her back and pulled her closer, but it wasn't enough. The disparity in their height was part of the problem, so Devlin dropped his hands to her ass and lifted her until her face was closer to his and her legs wrapped around his waist. Gods, but she was a sweet little thing in his arms.

Anna's moan was open and honest and full of need. And gods be damned the tight friction of her heated center over his erection had the room spinning around him until the only thing he knew or saw or felt was her. He stumbled a step until her back encountered the wall next to the door, and the forced collision of her hips into his had both of them crying out.

For so long, Devlin had suppressed and ignored the needs of his body, a penance for the wrongs done to others that lay at his feet. And that part of his brain was pricking at him like a jackhammer against concrete. But when Anna leveraged her back against the wall to grind against his cock, Devlin's body threw his thinking mind into a dark corner and, for just once, let himself have something he wanted with the desperation of a dying man.

And he very well might be that.

With the trip to the Eastern Realm looming on tomorrow's horizon, this could literally be the only time he would ever get with Annalise Fallston. The only chance he'd have to live a life—even if it was but mere moments long—more full and more meaningful than the half-life he'd been forced into for so long. The only opportunity to learn that someone as good as her could want him and that maybe, just maybe, he could deserve her in return.

They kissed and writhed against the wall until Devlin was sure every part of his nervous system had migrated to the outside of his skin—because he'd never felt more deeply, more intensely, or more wholeheartedly in his entire existence.

Anna gasped for air, her fingers digging into his shoulders. He kissed her jaw, her neck, her collarbone, some primal urge demanding that he claim every part of her with his hands, his lips, his tongue. His cock.

He grasped her face in his hand, needing to warn her, needing her to understand where he was. "You only make me uncomfortable because you make me feel so alive," Devlin rasped, shaking his head. "And I want you, Anna. Gods, I want your heat and your touch and your body surrounding mine. But I don't deserve you. And I'm no good for you. I am angry and violent and dangerous. I've been marked by a lifetime of servitude to evil which I must now stand and fight, and that means facing trials I may not survive—"

She kissed him, cutting off his arguments and ratcheting up the tension in his body until he was nearly vibrating. Purple light reflected off her beautiful face and hair when she pulled away to look at him again. "I want this and I want you. Let yourself be loved. Let me love you."

Devlin wasn't deluded enough to think she was saying she loved him, but it was still the first time he could ever remember someone offering him love in any form so freely and without demands for anything in return. *Is this what it's like for other people? Is this what I've been missing while I've fought and raged and struggled for survival and freedom?*

He didn't know the answer to that. All he knew was that her words were both sweet solace and a short-fuse detonator wrapped into one. "You don't understand," he said, leaning his forehead against hers. His hips rolled involuntarily as he ran a too-rough hand from her throat down the valley between her breasts and back again. "I have long abstained, Anna. And now, I want you too fucking bad. If I let myself off this leash, I'm going to come at you like a freight train. I will take you over and over again in ways you can imagine and some you can't. And I'm not going to be able to stop until you've come so often you can't see straight."

Anna's breathing came faster, harder, and she nodded. "Take this off," she said, tugging at his shirt.

Dizziness threatened that his words didn't seem to faze her. And then *her* words sank in. His shirt. His *scars*. Damn, he wished he had something better for her, more worthy of her.

"Hey," she said, pulling him from his thoughts. "Scars are simply proof of survival. They don't bother me, Devlin. I find you so damn sexy that I can hardly think straight." She kissed him, slow and deep. "But leave it on if it makes you more comfortable."

Her compassion, so foreign to him, pushed him to the limits of his comfort zone—not just because it tempted him to expose his flaws to her, but because her words tempted him to believe she didn't see them as flaws at all. He released a long breath and yanked the shirt he'd borrowed from Chrysander over his head. The shift in position put her weight squarely on his groin. His hands went to her hips and pressed her down against his cock.

"You are going to feel so good," he rasped. Something that Devlin couldn't quite make sense of niggled at the back of his mind.

Anna reached for her shirt and lifted it over her head. It caught on her ponytail, and she laughed as they freed it.

Knock, knock. "Anna?"

Eyes wide, she froze and hugged her shirt to her chest. Every muscle in Devlin's body braced for battle, anger flowing through

him—at himself for missing this potential threat before it materialized, and at whoever stood on the other side of that door if they intended Anna even the slightest bit of harm.

"Oh God, I'm sorry. Let me down," she whispered as she dived
back into her shirt. In the darkness of the room, sparks flickered from
Devlin's hands. Anna grasped them before Devlin realized what she
intended to do.

"Anna, no—"

"Shh, it's okay," she said, pressing a kiss to both palms.

It was as if her touch doused the fire of his anger—or at least his
body's expression of it. Suddenly, a whole line of similar instances
flooded Devlin's memory. How he'd been able to calm and clear his
mind after he'd carried her to the couch in her studio, how it was
the sound of her breathing and blood that had allowed him to rein
himself in earlier, how her command that he recall the fire gave him
the strength to actually do it, for the very first time. And then again at
Aeolus's. And now this.

Anna clicked on a small lamp on her dresser and opened the
door. Evan flew through the breach and swept her into his arms.
"Oh, thank God," he said. Given the arousal that still flowed through
Devlin's body, jealousy and possessiveness flashed through his blood,
but the man radiated nothing but concern.

"I'm okay," she said as she returned the hug. "I'm okay."

"I was so worried about you, Anna. And Devlin, too." The man
pulled back and looked over Anna's shoulder at Devlin. "Damn, I
can't believe you're up and around after being struck by lightning. But
I'm so glad," he said, extending a hand toward him.

Devlin returned the shake. "Thanks. Got lucky," he said, nearly
choking on the word.

An awkward pause filled the space between the three of them.

"Well, I didn't mean to interrupt, but when I heard you moving
around up here, I couldn't wait until morning to see that you were
okay with my own eyes." He smiled, his affection for Anna plain on
his face.

"I'm glad you did. How's Dad?" she asked, hugging herself.

"Was a rough afternoon, but by the evening he'd settled down even if he was surlier than usual. Just the stress. And he missed you."

"Me? Or Mom?" Something in the tone of her voice caught Devlin's attention and twisted in his gut.

Evan squeezed Anna's shoulder. "You, baby girl. Don't ever doubt that he loves you. Just shows it in his own way."

"I know," she said on a sigh.

"Well, you look tired, so get your butt in bed," he said, his gaze flickering to Devlin. He winked at Anna and Devlin could feel the heat of the blood that flooded her face. "I cleared my schedule for tomorrow because I wasn't sure what you might need, so no worries in the morning."

"Thank you," she said. "You're a lifesaver."

"Nice to see you, Devlin," Evan said, meeting his eye. There was a bit of assessment there, as though the guy needed to know more about the man Anna had brought to her room.

Devlin nodded. "You, too."

When the door closed behind him, Anna slowly turned to Devlin and gave him a small, uncertain smile. The interruption had sucked all the momentum out of their frenzied, urgent passion. Now, despite the fact that he could almost feel her need and arousal, and the hard state of his body proved how much he wanted her still, there was a distance between them Devlin didn't know how to cross.

That distance allowed him to see some other truths. Like...damn it all to Hades, Evan had been right. Anna *did* look tired. Even though his body cried foul at the idea of not getting to have her, taking care of Anna was all that mattered. Because knowing her, spending time with her, and admiring her had forced Devlin to feel more and more deeply in the short time since they'd met than he'd ever experienced before.

Truth be told, it scared the fuck out of him. But that proved how important and special it was. *She* was. And her needs came first— which meant he needed to understand better what all of her needs included.

Devlin stroked his knuckles over Anna's cheek. "Back at your studio, you said you have a condition that makes you tired."

She hugged herself again. "Yeah. It's called chronic fatigue syndrome, which is sort of a catchall diagnosis for generally having no energy and feeling like crap most of the time."

Soul-deep concern ricocheted through him. "How do they fix it?"

"They don't," she said, dropping her gaze.

He caught her chin with his fingers and lifted her face. Gods, she was beautiful. "And all this is making it worse, isn't it?" She shrugged, but Devlin hadn't really needed her to answer the question. The thought of her hurting was nearly suffocating. "You should get some sleep, then."

"Yeah, I will," she said, giving him a small smile. "But I need a shower first. You're welcome to take one after me, if you want." Pale moonlight lit on the side of her face, making her almost glow in the darkness, like a fairy princess, or an angel. "Make yourself at home. I won't be long."

She grabbed clothing from a dresser, then crossed to a door on the far wall. As she closed it behind her, golden light shone from the gap at the bottom, casting a rectangle of yellow onto the carpet. Blowing out a long breath, Devlin raked his fingers into his hair. He locked and tightened his grip there, letting the burn against his scalp center and focus him. Not in a million years could he have predicted any turn of events that would've led him to the last thirty minutes in this room.

If he never had another moment with Anna in his arms, he still wouldn't forget the way her small frame and feminine curves fit against him, her warmth, or the solace of her words.

The white noise of the shower turned on. Mere feet and a flimsy wooden door were all that separated him from the woman who set his body, mind, and soul on fire, thereby allowing him to rein in the most terrible parts of himself. *She needs rest.* Devlin nodded to himself and paced to the bed.

He sagged against the edge of the mattress and rubbed the heels of his hands against his eyes, trying unsuccessfully to quell the images that sprang to mind every time the tenor and rhythm of the water hitting the shower floor changed.

Half a dozen lesser Anemoi headed your way, Devlin, came Aeolus's voice on the wind.

Thank you. Knowing someone had his back eased some of the tension from Devlin's muscles. Not for his own sake, but because it was that much more protection for Anna and those she loved. Deep down in a quiet part of his soul, Devlin was glad for the help. And it touched him in a totally uncomfortable way to have someone actually think enough of him to offer it and actually follow through.

He dropped his hands into his lap and slowly took stock of Anna's room. She'd acquired more possessions in her human lifetime than Devlin had in his entire centuries-long existence. Books, paintings, photographs, jewelry boxes, a hook overflowing with scarves. It was a space filled with color and brimming with life. He felt privileged to stand in the middle of it.

The whine of the plumbing continued, providing a lulling hum that revealed his own exhaustion. Weariness was as much a part of him as his blood and bones, and had been with him almost as long. But less familiar emotions slunk around the mental playground of his brain, too. Desire. Affection. Protectiveness. And where was his constant companion, loneliness? Sitting here in the mid-night quiet of Anna's space, her scent and energy all around him, Devlin couldn't find that particular emotion anywhere. Because when he was with Anna, she pulled him outside himself and made him engage and see and feel the world. And her, most especially.

Given Devlin's life up until about thirty-six hours ago, that was a gods' honest miracle. And he was not the kind of god to believe in such a thing. Ever.

Which was why it also had him bracing for the blowback he knew was coming. Because Devlin's gut squeezed with the knowledge that it couldn't last—*wouldn't* last—not if his father had anything to say about it. And when hadn't Eurus wanted to control every last, minute detail of Devlin's life? Never. He bore the marks to prove it.

Long minutes passed, and the water still ran. Devlin stared at the bathroom door, unease curling into his gut. She'd said she wouldn't be long, but by any definition, she'd been in there a good while. Was the room somehow accessible from the outside? The question hauled him off the bed and across the room. He paused at the door long enough to listen, assess…and heard a jagged intake of break, then another.

Devlin frowned. "Anna?" he asked, knocking on the door. Nothing. He leaned his head closer. "Anna? Answer me." His fingers clawed into the molding around the door.

"I'm okay," came a strained voice. Strained by fright? Pain?

Dread skittered down his spine and had him pushing through the door. A shower curtain depicting a lily pond separated them. Devlin stepped to the corner where the curtain met the wall, his hands itching to tear it open. "Are you okay?"

"Yeah," she said, her voice reed thin. After a moment, the bottom corner of the curtain tugged back from the inside. Anna pulled the plastic in a way that mostly covered her, though it didn't prevent Devlin from being able to tell that she was sitting in a ball on the floor, her arms curled around her knees. She peered red-eyed up at him, the spray of the shower raining down on her hair and back. "Hey."

Devlin forced his gaze back to the wall in front of him. He didn't want to make her uncomfortable and was acutely aware he was all kinds of invading her privacy. And, gods, as gorgeous and alluring as her nudity was, she looked so small sitting there. Urgent need flooded through Devlin's cells as if it was a part of his very DNA—but it was more an urge to take care of her than anything else. Problem was, he had absolutely no idea what to do, what to say. "Um, what's the matter?"

"Just overwhelmed." In his peripheral vision, he saw her shake her head and wipe a hand over her face. "Stupid."

"No," he said, unable to hear her tear herself down after everything she'd done for him today. He grabbed a towel off a bar and handed it in to her. "Cover yourself. Please."

When she did, Devlin pushed the curtain open wider and crouched at the tub's edge. The towel, now wet where it covered her chest and lap, conformed to and highlighted the beautiful, pale curves of her body. But he fixed his gaze on her face and held it there. "Not stupid at all. You've been nothing but brave," he said, gripping the side of the tub.

Her eyebrows quirked upward as if she questioned his praise, but he meant it from the bottom of his heart. She'd been thrown into the deep end of a pool she hadn't even known existed and managed not only to stay afloat but help others while she was treading water.

And he'd repaid her by putting her in danger. Regret welled up inside of Devlin until it felt like Olympus weighed on his chest. "I'm sorry I crash-landed on your life."

Anna looked at him a long minute. "I'm worried for my father, Devlin, but I'm glad I met you. And that you're here."

The easy acceptance. The freely offered kindness. He'd so rarely encountered either that he had no idea how to respond. All he knew was that her words sent him soaring even as an old angry, knee-jerk response made him want to shake some sense into her.

She gave him a small smile and broke the awkward silence. "I just need to wash my hair and then the shower's all yours."

"I could—" Devlin ate the words, not sure where the impulse had even come from.

Her brow furrowed and then her eyes went wide in apparent understanding of what he'd nearly offered. Truth be told, what he *still* wanted to offer, although she'd probably think it strange. Hell, *he* found it strange, but it was crystal clear she needed comfort after everything the day had thrown at her, and his instincts roared with the need to be there for her. In some way. In *every* way.

She licked stray droplets of water off her lips. "You could…?"

Devlin stared into those gray eyes for a long moment, and then he shoved down the awkwardness that had his hands strangling the tub's edge. "Do it for you," he said with a shrug. An odd flipping sensation in his gut, like free-falling from the very top of the sky, had his instincts roaring to retreat. "Never mind. It's dumb. I didn't—"

A warm, wet hand settled on top of his. "Yes, please."

She couldn't have surprised him more if she'd sprouted a pair of wings. "Oh. Yeah?" As the idea settled into his brain, a low hum of satisfaction spread over his body. He accepted a pink bottle she grabbed from the corner of the tub and squeezed a small handful of creamy shampoo into his palm. Just as he debated the best way to do this, Anna tilted her head back and let the water stream over the silk of her hair. The position bared the tops of her breasts to him, even as she used one arm to hold the towel in place.

Devlin was fucking mesmerized. The curves of her breasts, her throat, her shoulders, captured his gaze and made it impossible to look away. He wanted to trace every one with his fingers. And his tongue.

Squeezing the excess water out of her hair, Anna shifted so her back faced him.

Devlin blinked away the impulse and ignored the aching need between his legs. "Tell me if I'm too rough," he said as he rubbed his palms together. And then he laid his hands on her. Her heat and softness soaked into him, as if there were something magical about touch alone. For him, there was. Since for most of his life he'd never been touched in anything but pain and punishment.

Half afraid of somehow hurting her, Devlin worked the sweet-smelling shampoo into the top and sides of her hair. Stretching over the side of the tub, he focused on taking care of her as if it was the most important job he'd ever done. And maybe that was going too far, but it was certainly the most meaningful. To him.

The throaty moan of satisfaction she unleashed reached into his body and absolutely owned him. He would've done anything to elicit that noise—and others—again and again. "Is this okay?"

"It's perfect, Devlin. Don't stop," she said, all the strain gone from her voice.

As if Zeus himself could pull me away.

He worked more shampoo into the length of her hair, massaging her scalp and rubbing the ends between his hands. Through the thin veil of her hair, his fingers pressed into her neck muscles, using the lather to allow his touch to glide over her skin. She moved her head in response to his touch, tilting this way or that to give him access to one area, then another. And damn it all to Hades and back if the little caught breaths and moaned sighs didn't ratchet up the tension flowing through his body. Because even as he was entirely content to bask in the satisfaction she nearly radiated, he was still a long-abstinent male touching an incredible naked woman. And the most masculine parts of himself envisioned him pinning her up against the shower wall and burying himself deep into her heat from behind.

"Thank you," she whispered, turning her face to glance over her shoulder. The wet shine on her pale pink lips scrambled his brain so hard he could only nod.

"Turn toward the water," he finally managed. He held out thick strands of her hair and let the water stream over until every sud was gone.

"I'll rinse the top," she said, and then she grabbed onto the built-in tile handle on the soap dish and rose.

Devlin had absolutely no idea where to put his gaze, because as she unfurled her petite form, the towel plastered to the front of her and her back bare, everything attracted him at once. Shapely legs, curved hips, the rounded softness of her bottom.

Anna slipped, throwing out an arm to brace against the wall. Devlin was off the ground without a conscious thought and steadied her with one hand on her arm and the other on her waist. His reach into the shower had his arms and upper body nearly as wet as her. Her gaze raked down his bare chest, and Devlin forced himself to let her look her fill. She licked water off her lips and met his gaze. "You're all wet now. Might as well come in." Then she stepped backward once, twice, and tilted her head into the running water.

The invitation pounded blood hot and fast through Devlin's body.

As Devlin watched, she worked at rinsing the soap out of her hair with one hand and held the towel draped to the front of her body with the other. Drawn by the soul-deep need to keep touching her, he toed off his borrowed boots and debated removing his jeans, but knew there was no way he wouldn't be all over her if her gaze caressed his cock the way she'd just looked at his chest. Plus, the fucking cilice. So, yeah, for now they stayed on. He stepped over the edge of the tub, and the water added weight to the denim, but Devlin hardly noticed because Anna stepped closer and then used both hands to wring out her hair. Wet as it was, the towel stuck to her skin, but just one little gust of the East Wind and he could take care of that.

Not that he would do that to her. But it was sure as shit fun to visualize.

She met his eyes and he didn't think he was imagining that hers were filled with scorching heat. Grabbing the open shower curtain, she walked toward him and closed them in. His muscles braced when she came to stand in front of him. "You're still dressed."

"I only meant to check on you," he said, his brain scrambling to resist the urges slowly turning his blood to liquid fire.

She nodded. "I appreciate that very much," she said. "I feel better."

His shoulders sagged in relief. "Good. That's good."

Anna stepped closer and nailed him with a stare. "I'm going to hug you now."

Despite the warning, his muscles still braced. He managed a single tight nod. And then she was on him. Her softness pressed against his hardness and her arms wrapped around his back. She was so much shorter than him that when she laid her head on his chest, he had to lean down to press a reverent kiss against the top of her hair. Slowly, carefully, he wrapped his arms around her slender shoulders and held her to him.

And it was like being found after a lifetime of being lost.

His muscles might've ached from the effort it took not to let himself tremble in her arms, but that didn't change the fact that holding Anna close filled him with a sense of rightness he couldn't ever remember feeling.

Her right arm moved and Devlin sucked in a harsh breath a moment later when she dragged a washcloth down his biceps. Then again. And once more, shifting against him to reach all the way down to his wrist.

"What are you doing?" he asked, his voice raw with emotion.

"Taking care of you," she said simply.

He shivered. "Anna—"

"Shh. Let me." The warm, wet cotton stroked over his shoulder next, the side of his neck, the pad of his pectorals. She pulled away, but Devlin only let her go so far, because he wasn't sure he could handle the tension roaring through his body unless he was holding on to her.

Anna smiled up at him, warm and reassuring. She washed his neck, his chest, his ribs. No matter how tightly he tried to hold himself, he couldn't restrain the occasional flinch. Each time, she'd meet his gaze as if assessing how much he could take, as if she understood that sustained touch like this pushed him way the hell beyond his boundaries. The cloth dragged over his belly, back and forth until her hand brushed the waist of his jeans.

She met his gaze, held it, and put her hand to the top button on his fly. He didn't react fast enough, and she pulled the button free.

His heart was a stampeding herd in his chest. Devlin jerked, accidentally knocking the rag from her hand. She knelt to retrieve it, and the picture of her kneeling at his feet pounded blood through his body and into his cock.

Her gaze lifted upward from the floor. She gasped. "You're bleeding." Her hand fell on his left thigh.

The cilice. Realization slammed into him and embarrassment and shame smothered his arousal. "Fuck. Don't, Anna," he rasped and backed into the cool tile wall behind him.

"But you're—"

"I said *don't*." The trembling was out in full force now.

She knelt frozen on the floor of the shower, one hand outstretched toward his leg. His gaze dropped to where the shower water had caused some of the blood from his ancient wound there to ooze out from underneath the wrapping and onto the skin visible through a tear in the old denim.

She frowned. "There's a bandage. When…is this from today?" He didn't answer. *Couldn't* answer. "Please let me. I won't hurt you," she said, her voice tugging at something raw and exposed in his chest. She crawled closer. Closer. Until she was kneeling at his feet once again, his back up against the wall.

As her fingers separated the gap of denim, Devlin's breath sawed in and out of him, emotion overwhelming him. Soft pressure and an intensifying ache from the metal teeth's bite into his skin told him she was touching the bandage.

If she saw, he'd have to explain, he'd have to give voice to this fundamentally good, true woman what he'd done to deserve paying this penance. His hands fisted. He banged his head against the tile. But in the end nothing he did could restrain the volcano of anxiety and worthlessness welling up inside him.

He grasped her wrist in his hand and yanked it away. She gasped and her eyes went wide as they cut up to meet his.

"Too. Much," he ground out, not wanting to scare her or take her head off, but needing her to understand. Her touch and his discomfort left him feeling so exposed he could barely breathe.

A fast nod, and she scooted backward, but she could only retreat so far because his grip remained firmly planted around her wrist. Finally, she rose to her feet and slowly closed the distance between them again. "Okay, Devlin," she said, looking into his eyes. And while there was a little hurt there that cut into him and made him wish for maybe the millionth time that he wasn't such a fucking misfit, there was also a knowing, an understanding. And that rubbed him raw, too, because it meant she perceived something about the psychosis that made him act this way. "I'm gonna get out now."

Devlin released her wrist and stared at her as she stepped through the gap between the curtain and the wall, turning her bare, uncovered back to him. She tugged the curtain tightly closed again, and though only a thin piece of fabric separated them, the distance allowed him to pull in his first real breath in several minutes.

Small sounds filtered in from the room. The slap of the wet towel against the sink. Cabinet doors opening and closing. The shift of cotton against skin. And then the bathroom door opened and closed, and Devlin could tell from the stillness of the air in the room that she'd gone.

"Welcome to your fucking life," he said to himself. And then he stepped into the stream of water, wrenched the temperature nozzle hard to the right, and braced as ice-cold water rained down over him.

The shock of cold reality was exactly what he needed.

Because the past five minutes had shoved into his face as maybe little else could've why he wasn't good enough for Annalise Fallston and never would be. And if the gods possessed any mercy where he was concerned, she'd come to the same conclusion.

CHAPTER THIRTEEN

Despite it being the middle of the night, Owen and the others materialized in the Hall of the Winds to find Megan, Ella, Laney, and Laney's human friend Seth waiting there. Seth had gotten sucked into their world when he'd arrived at Owen's immediately after the battle and refused to leave Laney's side. Owen hadn't had much time to spend with Seth so far. He spoke little and always stuck close to Laney as though he was watching, protecting, guarding. Truth be told, something about him made Owen a little...not uncomfortable, exactly, but maybe wary. Yeah, there was something about the guy.

"Hey," Owen said, walking up to Megan. "What are you doing up?"

"We all decided we couldn't sleep until you got home," Ella said, pulling Zeph into a hug. "Hi."

Zeph kissed her cheek, and beyond him, Chrys and Laney were reuniting, too. It was clear that every person in the room understood the cloud of danger hanging over their collective heads. For himself, Owen felt it acutely.

"Aeolus," Laney said. "Your friend Tisiphone dropped in after you left. She said she'd return when Devlin did."

Aeolus nodded and something unusually soft passed over his expression. Owen had overheard Chrys and Zeph discussing that something was going on between Aeolus and the Fury who punished crimes of murder and had apparently been helping Aeolus train Devlin. Her particular skill set made Owen glad to have her for an ally, but that didn't mean he was thrilled to have the snake-headed resident of the Underworld hanging out here with Megan when he wasn't around.

"What are those?" Laney asked.

Owen followed her gaze to the grouping of Anna's paintings at Aeolus's feet.

"They're paintings," Chrys said. "Why? Are you seeing something?" Owen's gut clenched. Laney's visions were a double-edged sword, bringing them the advantage of advance knowledge while also forcing them to confront some tragedy yet to happen. Come to think of it, Anna's paintings were the same way.

"Not a vision. They're glowing with light, like the auras I see around you."

"More proof that Devlin's Anna has divine ancestry," Aeolus said.

"Who's Anna?" Ella asked, walking toward the paintings. The others followed to form a small circle around Aeolus, the canvases in the center.

"Anna," Zephyros said, putting his arm around Ella's shoulder, "is apparently Devlin's…" He waved a hand as if he didn't know how to characterize her.

But to Owen, what was between Devlin and Anna seemed pretty damn clear. "She's his girlfriend, or at least they're heading in that direction. She's human. And she's apparently descended from the goddess of the rainbow, Iris." Not to mention someone else none of them could identify, but hopefully Iris could shed some light on that when she and Zeph met. He'd sent a request to her on their way back to the Realm of the Gods.

"Wait. Devlin's interested in a human woman?" Ella asked. "Eurus's son, Devlin? This is good news, right?" She turned to Zeph, who begrudgingly nodded.

"So, Anna's a painter," Megan said, bending over to study the painting of Devlin finding Eurus's key. Painting reminded Owen of Tabitha, their neighbor from the human realm and also an accomplished painter. She, like Seth, had been swept up into this mess during the battle the other night. And thinking of Tabitha led Owen right back to Boreas, because there'd been a spark of interest between them that they'd never had the chance to explore. But honestly, grief was like playing a never-ending game of Six Degrees of Separation, because just about everything could somehow be associated with the one you'd lost. "What is this painting supposed to be?"

"Well, interestingly," Chrys said, taking Laney's hand, "Anna started having visions about a week ago, visions that compelled her to paint these images. They're all of either Devlin or Eurus. When she painted them, they were all of events from the future. This one is of Devlin finding the key to Eurus's lantern—" He pointed toward the stylized *E* on the compass rose tiled into the great mosaic floor. Lantern light spilled from the floor at each point around the compass, the light of the divine energy locked within by the master of each of the directional winds.

"Oh, God, please tell me that's good news, too," Ella said, her gaze meeting each of the men's. "What happens if someone unlocks the lantern?"

Aeolus crossed his arms. "If someone consumes the energy within, they gain mastery over that wind, and the former master dies."

Gasps and wide-eyed smiles emanated from the women. Not that the men weren't as moved by what accessing Eurus's lantern could mean, but they also knew it meant a trip into the Eastern Realm.

Laney frowned. "What are the others? Can someone describe them to me?"

Tension zinged among the men. Owen really didn't want Megan seeing the painting of the moment before Boreas's death, and neither she nor Ella needed to see the one depicting a limp body in Devlin's arms.

Megan glanced up at Owen. After a moment, her expression dropped into concern, then fear. "They show bad stuff happening.

Don't they?"

"Yes," Aeolus said, gently. "We are at war." A sort of communal grief hung over them, as if it was the air they all breathed. Boreas's death was too fresh for any of them to contemplate losing someone else. Yet both Laney's last vision and Anna's painting depicted something happening to at least one of them.

Owen wrapped his arms around Megan and pulled her back against his chest. He kissed her cheek and wished he could make all this go away for her.

Just then Laney touched her fingers to the corner of the top canvas, sucked in a sharp breath, and her blue eyes went glassy, distant. *Aw, Hades. Not again. Not more.*

Chrys was at her side in an instant. Thirty seconds passed. A minute. More. Owen hadn't yet spent that much time with Laney, but in the time he had he'd never seen a vision go on this long. She staggered and Chrys caught her against his chest.

"Are you okay, Laney?" Chrys asked, gold light flaring from behind concerned eyes.

Forehead against Chrys's sternum, she nodded, her shoulders rising and falling in a deep breath. "It was, um, confusing. Like a battle, but in the sky?" She looked up at Chrys and her voice gained strength. "All of you were there and you were fighting...some kind of horrible black creatures." She turned toward Zephyros. "And Devlin threw Zeph through the sky."

"Fucking hell, I *knew* it," Zeph said, gathering Ella into his arms and glaring at Aeolus.

Megan gasped and Owen's gut dropped to the floor. "Put that together with Laney's earlier vision and the, uh, painting and it doesn't look good. But...something's not adding up here." His instincts had been leaning hard in favor of Devlin's trustworthiness. But then what did this vision mean?

Chrys rubbed Laney's shoulders. "Anything else?"

She shook her head. "It was all a jumble."

Arms crossed, scowl on his face, Seth positioned himself next to

Chrys and Laney as if anything that came at them would have to go through him. *What's up with Laney's friend?* Owen asked the other gods.

Chrys met Owen's gaze. *He's always been very protective of Laney, but it's escalated since he arrived in the Realm of the Gods. Aeolus thinks it's because he's got a griffin somewhere way back in his bloodlines and being here is bringing out the protective qualities even more. It's cool.*

Owen hoped he was right, because they so did not need something else to worry about.

Wait. A griffin...as in head of an eagle, body of a lion? That kind of griffin? Zeph asked, exchanging glances with Owen. Chrys gave a single nod, and Zeph scrubbed his hands over his face. *Day just keeps getting weirder and weirder.*

Amen to that, brother, Chrys said.

Why not just take him home at this point? Owen asked. The only reason Tabitha hadn't been sent home was that they'd decided the location, right next to Owen's house where the battle had raged, was way too hot. And they didn't want to put her in the position of having to answer questions from the authorities. None of that was an issue for Seth, however, because he and Laney lived several hours from Owen on the eastern shore of Maryland.

Laney asked if he could stay 'til this was over, Chrys said. *Besides, right now I don't mind having someone else looking out for her, you know?*

Owen gave a subtle nod and pressed a kiss to Megan's hair. He understood that perfectly.

He's nice, Ella added, reminding Owen that her divinity made her able to communicate telepathically, too. He'd first met her as a human, and she'd only been a goddess for six months. Sometimes Owen still forgot. *You just have to get to know him.*

Megan turned in Owen's arms and frowned. "You guys are doing that thing again, aren't you? I really hate being excluded from your conversations. I need to know what's going on with all this"—she waved her hand to indicate the paintings and the group—"as much as all of you. Laney, too." She nodded toward the black-haired woman.

Regret and concern kicked Owen in the butt. "Aw, I'm sorry, angel," he said, rubbing her arms. His gaze dropped to her rounded belly between them. "Just don't want to upset you."

The anger ebbed from her blue eyes. "It's more upsetting to be in the dark. Okay?" Owen nodded. "So, what are the other paintings?"

Aeolus ticked off a description of each of the seven images on his fingers. Sadness filled the room when he mentioned the painting of Boreas's death, and the tension got even heavier when he described that one indicated the injury of one of the dark-haired men among them.

No one spoke for a long moment, and then Laney quietly said, "I'd like to meet Anna if I could. Some of our visions seem to be different pieces of the same picture. Maybe if she and I put our heads together, we could figure out more about what some of my visions and her paintings mean."

"She and Devlin will be here tomorrow," Aeolus said.

"Wait. What?" Ella said, concern furrowing her brow. "Devlin's coming here? When he poses a potential threat to Zeph?"

"Don't worry, love," Zeph said. "Nothing's going to happen while we're all together here. Okay?"

"I don't like it, Zeph. If he is really on his father's side…" Her gaze dropped to the floor.

Aeolus held out a hand demanding silence. He tilted his head as if listening to something they couldn't hear. "We've got company. And maybe a little good news, too. Iris is here. Zephyros," Aeolus said as he nodded for Zeph to join him. They broke from the group and walked toward a dais at the front of the room.

Owen took Megan by the hand and pressed her knuckles to his lips. "I'm sorry, angel."

"It's okay. I didn't mean to overreact."

He laced his fingers between hers and squeezed. "You didn't. At all. You have every right to know what's going on."

The group gathered to the side of the dais while Aeolus and Zephyros waited in front of the steps. Owen sensed the energy enter Aeolus's house one moment, and the next a woman with long pale-blond hair with soft blue highlights appeared in front of them. She wore a shimmery gown that changed colors, and sparkles of light glittered around her when she moved.

She bent in a graceful curtsy to Aeolus. "My lords," she said, her voice almost musical.

"Iris, welcome," Aeolus said.

Iris rose and smiled. "Zephyros," she said. "It's very nice to see you. You look well."

"Iris," Zeph said with a nod, and waved Ella over. "That's because of this woman. I'd like you to meet my wife, Ella. Ella, this is Iris."

Owen braced for awkwardness, but he needn't have. From what Owen knew, Ella was aware of Zeph's prior relationships and, anyway, they were all eons ago. And Iris was all big smiles and warm congratulations on their marriage. Aeolus introduced everyone else, ending with Owen and Megan.

Iris bowed her head. "I congratulate you on ascending to Cardinal Anemoi of the North Wind, Owen, and extend my deepest sympathies for your father's loss."

"Thank you," Owen said, putting his arm around Megan. "This is my wife, Megan."

Smiling, Iris glanced from Megan's face to her belly. "And your newest son or daughter, too. Very pleased to meet you, Megan." Suddenly, Iris frowned and peered around behind her. "I'm sorry, but I keep having the weirdest feeling…"

"That's why I asked if we could meet. Come see," Zephyros said, nodding her in the direction of the stack of paintings. "We seem to have stumbled onto a descendant of yours. A woman."

Iris's breath caught and she slowed as she approached the canvases. Her sky-blue eyes went wide and she reached out a hand. She whirled on Zeph, a shower of colored sparkles flying off in the wake of her movement. "Is she here?"

"No, but she will be tomorrow."

Iris covered her hand with her mouth and her eyes went glassy. She appeared completely overwhelmed by this news. Owen exchanged a glance with Megan and then Chrys, and their expressions reflected the same curiosity and anticipation he felt.

"I've met her, though," Zeph said, waving a hand. "Several of us have. And we watched her paint the one on top. That's how I knew she was yours." Zeph smiled. "She has your energy and she looks like you."

"I want to meet her," she whispered.

"Of course," Aeolus said, stepping closer. "And we were hoping you might be able to tell us who else's divine energy she possesses. There was another present, but none of us recognized it."

It was as if shutters dropped down over her expression. A careful, practiced neutral mask that gave nothing away. Her reticence shot wariness through Owen's blood. What wasn't she telling them? And why?

Iris turned to Aeolus. "When will she arrive tomorrow?"

"In the afternoon," Aeolus said.

"I'll return then." With a bow of her head, she disappeared in a ripple of multicolored light.

"Well, that was...interesting," Chrys said to a round of murmured agreements.

"Who could it be that would make her so leery of telling?" Zeph asked. "And how worried should we be about what powers Anna might possess until we get it out of her?" The question hung in the air. Just one more thing for them to worry about.

Fifteen minutes later, Owen and Megan had checked in on a sleeping Teddy and crawled into bed. Megan laid her head on Owen's shoulder and wrapped her arm across his chest. "Owen?"

"Yeah, angel?" He pressed a kiss to her forehead, loving the way she felt snuggled against him.

Her head shifted, like she was looking up at his face. "What if that painting depicts you?" Her voice cracked. "What if you're the one—"

"Hey, shh. No." He shifted to look her straight in the eye. "I'm not going anywhere. This is going to end soon. And we're going to find a new house for our two beautiful children. Everything will be fine. Okay?"

Tears spilled from the corners of her eyes. "Promise?"

Owen kissed her, a slow, gentle slide of lips. "Yes," he said. "I promise."

And though a niggle of fear planted itself in the back of his brain, Owen refused to believe anything else. Nothing was taking him away from Megan. Ever.

ΩΩ

Devlin had stayed in the shower long enough that when he came out, Anna had already fallen asleep. Light on and book in limp hand, it appeared she'd tried to wait for him, but it was better this way. Because he was walking a very fine line around her—between wanting her and rejecting her out of fear, between claiming her and protecting her from everything, including himself. He felt like a man straddling an ever-widening chasm. Pretty soon he was going to have to pick a side or risk falling down into the pitch-black abyss. But her being asleep gave him a reprieve, some time to get his head on straight where she was concerned. Assuming such a thing was even possible.

Carefully, he eased the book from her grip and laid it on the nightstand, then pulled the blanket up to cover her. Glancing across the bed, he noticed that the covers had been turned down, as if...as if she'd planned to invite him to sleep there. Devlin blinked, and sure enough he wasn't imagining things. They hadn't even gotten as far as talking about sleeping arrangements. But it didn't matter. That wasn't why he was here tonight, anyway.

He was here to protect her, defend her, make sure she stayed safe.

'Bout damn time he remembered that and focused on the job at hand.

Devlin clicked off the lamp, but something made him stay close to her another moment. Gods, he was in so much trouble with this little human, wasn't he? Giving in to the urge, he leaned down and lightly pressed his lips to her forehead. And then he flashed into the elements and went outside to see exactly who Aeolus had sent to guard them.

This should be fun. No doubt these gods were thrilled to be guarding Devlin.

Outside, he immediately sensed six energy signatures forming a periphery around the property. He flew toward the strongest among them, and knew this wouldn't be a walk in the park for a whole host of reasons.

Skiron, he said, addressing the Ordinal Anemoi of the Northwest Wind. The god had reasons to hate the East thrice over. First, because Skiron had been passed over as Zephyros's successor because of Eurus's demand back in the spring that Alastor be so named. Second, because Skiron was Zephyros's most loyal servant. And third, because Skiron had also served the North Wind, whom Devlin's father had just murdered.

Devlin, he replied, his icy tone communicating pretty much what Devlin expected.

Yeah, this was going to be real fun. *Thank you for being here*, Devlin said, trying to make nice.

Just doing what I'm told.

Right. Message received. *Zephyros send you here to keep an eye on me?*

Skiron chuffed out a grudging half laugh. *Pretty much.*

Devlin scanned a 360 around them. Clouds were rolling in, covering the moon and casting the nighttime world in shadows. His survey identified the positions of the Southwest Wind's Livos, the Northeast Wind's Kaikias, and the Southeast Wind's Phoenicias—newly installed several days ago after Apheliotes's death, also Eurus's fault. A little more distant, and throwing off correspondingly weaker energy signatures, were the Inter-Ordinal Anemoi of the South-

Southeast and North-Northeast.

I thank all of you for being here, Devlin projected to the group. *This woman is not only important to me, she's important to defeating my father. I know most of you don't trust me, and I get it. But I'm on your side. I only ask for a chance. If that is not something you can freely give, so be it. I will let my actions speak louder than my words.*

A preternatural wind whipped up all around Anna's house, a physical manifestation of the reaction of the Anemoi.

Your actions…you mean like leading your father to the Rock of Gibraltar and then standing by while he and the Harpies nearly killed Boreas and Chrysander? came Livos's voice.

This *again*. Red-hot rage boiled up within Devlin. Lightning rolled through the sky in a series of connected bolts. As if it wasn't bad enough to have to apologize for the misfortune of being Eurus's son. As if it didn't gut Devlin to have to grovel for the acceptance of a group of gods who were supposed to have cared for and protected him, but hadn't. Now, to have his actions questioned so blatantly. And to have to reveal the shame and humiliation of Eurus's abuse to have the slightest chance of earning their belief.

Hold it together, Devlin. He looked toward Anna's bedroom window, pictured her sleeping so peacefully there, and reined the worst of his anger in. For now.

For the last time, I did not lead him there. And I will say this only once. I did not *stand idly by. I was chained in place by Eurus's will and the standing threat of the death of my brother should I resist. Afterward, he let me go purposely, so that it would color your opinion of my trustworthiness and loyalty.* The wind whipped through the trees. *You all think you know him. You think you know what he's capable of. And I tell you, you do not. Your knowledge is superficial at best. And it doesn't begin to compare to my lifetime of standing witness to it, and being struck down any time—every time—I stood up to him.*

When no one responded, Devlin unleashed a gust of wind strong enough to bend the branches of every tree within sight.

Whatever, he said, turning toward Anna's. Same old, fucking same old.

What he says is true, came another voice. Kaikias? God of the Northeast Wind.

Devlin mentally frowned. Why would a god who'd been such good friends with the murdered Southeast Wind say anything in Devlin's defense? It made Devlin suspicious. Surely there was some trick at play.

Apheliotes and I had many occasions to see Eurus's abuse ourselves. And we, too, were threatened with the death of loved ones if we spoke out or interceded. You'll recall that Apheliotes ascended to the Southeast around the time that Eurus's son Farren died.

Kaikias's unexpected mention of his youngest brother's name was like an ice-cold lance through Devlin's soul.

That was because his predecessor witnessed the murder and intended to report it to Aeolus, the lesser god continued. *But at the edge of the Eastern Realm, he was captured in a trap. Eurus tortured him for forty days and nights before executing him in cold blood. Eurus intended that as an example to me and to Apheliotes, just in case we had any thoughts of resisting his will.*

Minutes passed as Devlin tried to make sense of the words. But no matter how hard he tried, he couldn't get them to sink in. Or maybe it was that he couldn't get his brain to believe that he'd actually heard *these* words in *this* order in the first place. Because if he had, then he seemed to have just heard an Anemoi defend him, vouch for him, and say that, once upon a time, someone had tried to stand up for him and his brothers.

Electricity prickled over Devlin's entire being. Could this be true? *The fallen Southeast Wind…tried to…help us?* he said, trying the idea out in his own brain.

Yes, Kaikias said. *And you should know…every wind associated with the East has been ordered to shun you, Devlin. Eurus threatened retribution toward every one of us should we be seen as befriending, helping, or obeying you in any way.* Pause. *Isn't that right, Euronotos? Olympias?*

The gods of the South-Southeast and North-Northeast winds, respectively. Both called out in the affirmative.

But with the Olympians forcing the Cardinal Anemoi to finally subdue Eurus, it's time to end our silence and reveal Eurus for who he really is, Kaikias said. *I'm only sorry I didn't do it sooner.*

Devlin was well aware that the Olympians had handed down a death warrant on his father's head after he'd killed Zeph's then-human mate, but the sentence mattered little while none of the Anemoi were strong enough to bring Eurus down. And it wasn't as if the Olympians were interested in dirtying their hands with such things. Gods forbid.

Kaikias's words rattled around in Devlin's consciousness. Shell-shocked didn't begin to describe Devlin's reaction. He just…couldn't wrap his head around what he was hearing. A steady rain began to pour, a release of energy that helped expel the pressure building inside Devlin's psyche.

Anger. Sharp and bitter. For the fact that his father had constructed his solitude even more purposely than Devlin already imagined. And for the fact that the lesser Anemoi had allowed themselves to be cowed.

But there was a strange relief born of vindication, too. Because for the first time in Devlin's existence, an Anemoi admitted they'd failed him. And had done it publicly, so that others would know the truth of it, so that others would know that Devlin was not the second coming of his father.

Kaikias's energy neared, lowered to the ground, and then the man appeared in the flesh. He tilted his gaze upward into the rain, his bearded face solemn and serious, toward where Devlin still hovered in his elemental form.

Slowly, Devlin descended, halted the rain, and materialized not far from the back of Anna's house.

The Northeast Wind lowered himself to one knee and bowed his head. "I have wronged you, and for that I ask your forgiveness, Devlin Eston, heir to the East Wind." Suddenly, Euronotos and Olympias appeared behind Kaikias and repeated his actions and his words.

Devlin stepped backward, an instinctive reaction to something he could neither understand nor believe.

Phoenicias materialized next. He stood beside the other three gods' kneeling forms. "As the former master of the East-Southeast Wind, I confirm what Kaikias has said is true. And I, too, ask your forgiveness and promise that, under my command, the Southeast Wind will evermore stand at your side." The young blond-haired god took a knee with the others.

Scrubbing his hands over his face, Devlin realized he was shaking. Emotion surged through his chest. *Not* anger. *Not* bitterness. *Not* grief. For once.

Hope. This feeling was hope. For acceptance, for peace, for a place to belong.

Finally, he nodded. "Thank you," he said. "Uh, forgiven." Another god might've had something more eloquent to say in a moment like this, but Devlin felt lucky to have found the wherewithal to string that many words together at all.

The gods rose to their feet, every one of them looking at him uncertainly, like they weren't sure how *he* would receive *them*. But there was respect there, too. He'd heard some of the errant thoughts about what kind of power would've caused the damage that they now stood in the middle of. One positive outcome of yesterday's fiasco, then.

"Okay, then," he said, feeling like an idiot. "The, uh, plan is to stay long enough to get Anna's father moved out of this location in the morning. Once we do that, we can all return to Aeolus's."

The group of gods murmured in agreement. And it was at that moment that Devlin realized that the two most powerful among them, Skiron and Livos, had not joined their little lovefest. And so be it. It cut, he wasn't gonna lie. But not nearly as much as the other gods' apologies healed.

By Devlin's calculations, the net positive was pretty damn good. For him. And way more than he ever expected.

With a last look toward the gathered Anemoi, Devlin jogged up the back steps of Anna's house, went elemental, and entered through the gap under the door. Inside, he manifested again, sagged back against the door, and crossed his arms over his chest. Damn, he was tired. And the way the past fifteen minutes left his head spinning didn't help. He was also hungry, his stomach squeezing around emptiness despite the fact that he'd eaten an incredible meal yesterday. A meal Anna had made and served with her own two hands. And that made his heart squeeze, too.

Devlin crossed to the fridge and eased open the door. He leaned into the rectangle of light feeling a bit like a kid in a candy store. He wasn't even sure what some of the stuff was, but he knew he could have it if he wanted. A carton of red berries caught his eye. He popped open the plastic, inhaled their sweet scent, and grabbed one of the berries by its green crown.

Sweetness exploded on his tongue and nearly stole his breath. Almost his entire diet in the Eastern Realm consisted of meat, bread, and wine, in small, infrequent portions. He'd always supplemented it when he could, the world's most divine scavenger. But he wasn't sure he'd ever eaten one of these.

The berries were so delicious that he ate another, and another. Before long, the container lay empty in his hands, his fingertips stained pink from the juice. Guilt whipped through him. He hadn't meant to eat them all. He vowed to replace them as he closed the door. Not sure what to do with the packaging, he settled it on the counter while he washed the stickiness from his hands.

Intent on returning to watch over Anna, Devlin wandered into the living room. A gasp drew his gaze to the recliner in the corner. Where Anna's father sat looking at him, wearing an expression of wide-eyed surprise and another emotion Devlin couldn't name.

"Michael? My God, Michael. My son." With great effort, the old man pushed himself out of the chair. Fearing he was going to fall, Devlin set aside his confusion and rushed to help him with a steadying hand on his arm. And the next thing he knew, Anna's father threw his arms around Devlin's waist and held on as if he wanted to make sure he never got away again.

Devlin stood with his arms up, leaning his upper body away from the man's touch, every cell in his body screaming for freedom and bracing for pain.

The man…was weeping. "My son," he said over and over again. "My son."

And Devlin had thought the Anemoi' apologies were the most surprising thing that could ever have happened to him? How could this man possibly confuse Devlin with his son? Devlin recalled Anna saying her father suffered from dementia and he gathered from the brief exchange with Evan earlier that her father must confuse her with her mother. But surely, if Anna was any guide, her brother must've been a good person. Which brought Devlin back to how this man would mistake Devlin for Michael.

Because Devlin was not…good. That message had been drilled in so hard from so many directions that he knew it must be true.

Further proof was in the fact that he really wanted the man—Garrett, Anna had said his name was—to release him. The hold was too tight. The touch too hard. The emotion too strong. But in Garrett's outpouring of grief there was a fragility, too. And Devlin couldn't bring himself to do anything that might add to either.

"Oh, how I missed you," Garrett said through a tear-strained voice. "My boy."

Swallowing hard, Devlin debated, then wrapped his arms around the old man's heaving shoulders. Devlin wasn't sure how long they stood there, but the longer they embraced, the more his chest started to ache.

What would it be like to have a father who loved him the way Garrett must've loved Michael? If Devlin died in the battle undoubtedly coming in the next few days, not a single soul on the entire planet would feel even a sliver of the grief this man felt for his son. And more than that, Devlin identified with the depth of pain pouring from this man's body. He'd lived with it himself for more than a century since Farren's death. It gave Devlin an odd and uncomfortable sense of kinship with Garrett. Made him want to ease Garrett's grief in a way no one had ever tried to ease his own. Left him feeling protective of the old man, even more than he already had just based on the fact that he was important to Anna.

Garrett patted him on the back and pulled away enough to look up at Devlin's face. "Say something, Michael, so I know you're really here."

Devlin wasn't sure what to say. What would make him believe it was Michael to whom he spoke? "Hi, uh, Dad." The last word came out sounding almost like a question, both because he had no idea if that's what Michael had called Garrett, and because Devlin wasn't sure he'd ever voiced the word before in his life.

Clearly, though, he'd done something right, because Garrett's lips lifted in a broad, joyous smile. He reached up and patted Devlin's face. The touch was so unexpected that Devlin flinched, but he forced himself to tolerate it when uncertainty flickered through Garrett's eyes.

"You've gotten taller. And you need a haircut," he said. "But you're still my boy."

"Yes," Devlin said, his throat going tight. How unfair to be looked at with such affection and have it be intended for someone else. Yet Devlin was grateful, too. Because at least now he knew what true paternal love looked like. For whatever that was worth.

"Garrett?" came a voice from the other side of the room. Evan, standing under the arch to the hallway as if he didn't know whether to come or go.

"Ah, Evan," Garrett said, putting his arm around Devlin's back and guiding him across the room. "Meet my son, Michael. He was gone, but now he's back."

Devlin met Evan's eyes and sent him a silent plea to go along with it.

Evan frowned. "Are you sure this is Michael, Garrett?"

The old man scoffed. "Of course I'm sure. I'd recognize my son anywhere."

"Well, nice to meet you, then, Michael," Evan said, extending his hand.

An odd sense of déjà vu settled on Devlin's shoulders as he returned the shake. "Evan."

"Okay, then," Garrett said. "Go about whatever you were doing, Evan. I'm going to visit with Michael awhile." Hand on Devlin's back, he urged him toward the couch.

Devlin threw a glance over his shoulder at Evan and silently asked for some guidance. He settled onto the couch at Garrett's insistence, and the old man sat right beside him.

"So where have you been, son? Tell me everything." Garrett peered up at him like Devlin possessed the answers to the riddles of the world.

He was so out of his depth here, and when he looked at Evan, the guy shrugged like he didn't know what to do, either. So Devlin started talking about all the different places he'd traveled and things he'd seen. These were old memories, ancient even, from back before Eurus had deteriorated into the utter psychopath he was now. When Devlin had had at least a little freedom and occasionally explored the human realm with his brothers. It was a random, almost stream-of-consciousness recounting. When he glanced back to the hallway, Evan had gone. But Garrett hung onto every word as though he didn't want to miss a thing. Twenty minutes. Forty. An hour.

"How has Anna been all these years?" Devlin finally asked.

Garrett blinked as if he was surprised that the rhythm of Devlin's storytelling changed. "Oh," he said, "she's such a good girl. She's going to go far with her painting. I'm so proud of her. And she's missed you every day, too. You know how she always admired her big brother. Still takes care of your motorcycle for you." The smile he'd worn as he spoke slowly faded away, and an uncertainty shadowed Garrett's face. "Tell me more about you," he whispered.

Devlin did. He told stories until the man's eyes went unfocused and his eyelids sagged, until the muscles in his face relaxed and his body went slack against the couch. Staring at him, Devlin debated whether to stay or get away while he could. Maybe if Garrett awoke and Devlin was gone, he would think this nighttime visit just a dream. He pushed off the couch.

"Don't leave me," Garrett said, his voice almost slurred.

"Okay," Devlin said, guilt slinking into his gut because it was a request he'd have to deny sooner or later. But for now, he sat back down next to Anna's father. And though he itched to check in on her, he knew in his gut she was safe.

Garrett fell back to sleep. Devlin sat in the stillness of the night and finally resolved to get some sleep himself. He crossed his arms over his chest and leaned his head against the back of the couch.

But man, there was so much noise playing against the inside of his lids, he was sure he'd never fall asleep. He waded through his rage at his father, his guilt over Farren and Alastor, the mixed reaction of his Anemoi brethren, his interest in Anna. And her apparent interest in him.

He pictured her peaceful, sleeping face and slowly but surely shoved everything else into its own dark corner until there was just her.

And that was when he finally fell asleep.

Chapter Fourteen

Anna woke up with a start, her eyes flashing open and her mind immediately awake. She recognized the light fixture on the ceiling, the paintings on the wall, the furniture. It was her room, but she still felt disoriented. Like not everything was the way it was supposed to be.

She sat up and looked at the other side of the bed…which was empty and hadn't been slept in.

Devlin.

"Devlin?" she said, her voice thick with sleep. She cleared her throat. "Devlin?"

Heart thudding against her breastbone, Anna slipped out of bed and hugged herself against the chill. The gray light of morning was just seeping through the curtains at her windows, and a glance at her alarm clock confirmed it wasn't quite six o'clock yet.

Even though the bathroom was dark, she peeked in and flipped on the light. Empty.

Where had he gone? Standing in the middle of her room, she lifted her face to the ceiling. "Devlin?"

Inside her walk-in closet, she quickly chucked her pajamas to the floor and pulled on a pair of jeans, a T-shirt labeled in the neckline as lavender, and a gray hoodie.

What if Devlin went back to his grandfather's house?

Anna froze with her hand on the closet door, her heart falling to the floor. If he'd gone back to Aeolus's, she would never see him again. She had no way to get there and no way to contact him. Assuming he'd even want her to do so. But would he really have left without saying something? After everything they'd been through together and the importance of her paintings to whatever was going on with his father? After he'd said he would protect her and *her* father?

"No. Don't think the worst, Anna," she murmured to herself.

Which, of course, had her mind conjuring up the image of him in the shower. She hadn't meant to push about his leg, but he'd taken such incredibly tender care of her, and she'd needed that comfort so badly after the day they'd had. All she'd wanted to do was return the favor and show him she cared. But, God, he'd resembled a trapped animal as he'd grabbed her hand, and it was as if they'd taken two steps backward again. He'd pushed her away. He hadn't been mean about it, and he'd made it clear that he felt completely…what? Overwhelmed? Threatened? Panicked? Maybe all of the above.

God, she really hoped she hadn't scared him away.

Because Anna felt more alive around Devlin than she'd felt in many years. It was as if a part of herself she never knew existed came to life when she was with him. Ever since she'd put all her plans and dreams on hold to take care of her father, she'd yearned for a life of her own, adventure, travel, excitement, and passion. And in the several days since she'd first laid eyes on Devlin, she'd found all that and more.

No idea what it actually meant, if anything. He was a *god*, after all. And clearly troubled. And maybe not even interested in anything beyond the impulsive kiss they'd shared up against her wall. But she wanted a chance to find out almost more than she wanted anything.

Forcing herself out of her head, she ignored the aches in her body and dashed into the bathroom to give her hair and teeth a quick brush. When she returned to her room, her gaze landed immediately on the bare expanse of pale-blue wall that had supported her back less than twelve hours before. Devlin's kiss had been so far opposite of her expectations that for a few seconds she'd almost thought she must've been imagining it. He hadn't made any attempt to hide the fact that he didn't like to be touched. And he'd been so angry after their incredible trip through the wind that she'd been certain he wouldn't want to touch her, anyway.

And yet…

He'd kissed her. God, how he'd kissed her. Like a starving man at a feast. Consuming and relentless. And it had been the single most amazing kiss of her entire life. The kind that would haunt her in quiet moments. The kind all others would be measured against—and found lacking. He'd been breathtakingly intense and heartbreakingly gentle and just the memory of the gravel-voiced warnings he'd issued about what he wanted made her core clench with need.

Had Evan not interrupted, Anna had no doubt whatsoever that she and Devlin would've ended up naked in her bed. And no matter if anything else would've ever happened between them or if that would've ended up being a stolen night with a man she could never have, she wouldn't have regretted it one bit. Instead, she regretted that it hadn't happened. Because now, maybe, it never would.

And that made her chest ache with an emptiness that was probably way too pronounced for how short a time she'd known Devlin, but that didn't make it any less real.

"Okay, enough," she said to herself as she left her room and searched the other upstairs rooms for Devlin. They were all empty. Then she tiptoed down the steps so she didn't wake her father, who slept in a bedroom on the main floor, except when he fell asleep in or relocated to his recliner. She skirted the banister at the bottom of the steps and swung down the hall.

Then froze.

She backtracked three steps and peeked around the doorway into the living room.

Her heart flew into her throat and tears immediately filled her eyes. She had to cover her mouth to smother the gasping breath she couldn't hold back.

Devlin hadn't left. Of course he hadn't.

Instead, he was sleeping sitting up on the couch, wedged as tight against the corner as he could get, with his arms crossed over his broad chest. And her father slept leaning against Devlin's arm.

Anna couldn't stop staring at the pair of them.

How in the world had this come about? She couldn't even begin to answer that question.

And though it was crystal clear that Devlin wasn't comfortable with her father sleeping against him—even unconscious, his body moved away from touch—he was allowing it. But…why?

As surprising was the fact that her father had apparently met Devlin, a stranger *and* a man, in the middle of the night, inside their house, and not flipped out. Just the opposite, it seemed, since he was now passed out against Devlin's shoulder.

She stepped into the room, then retreated. Indecision held her there in the doorway for a long moment. Finally, she resolved to let them sleep. No doubt they could both use it.

Almost holding her breath, she crossed to the kitchen. Coffee would make everything a lot less confusing. The first thing she noticed was the plastic carton from the strawberries on the kitchen counter. Her father hated strawberries, so Evan never made anything with them when he handled meals. So who'd eaten them?

Devlin? Her imagination provided a picture of big, dark, hard-edged Devlin eating a strawberry, his lips wrapping around the redness, his tongue swiping at the juice, and her brain absolutely scrambled. Or maybe that was just proof she *really* needed some coffee.

Soon, the pot was brewing and the rich fragrance of the French roast filled the air. Just the smell dispelled some of the fog in her brain, which made her realize that she was starving. With them sleeping in the next room, she didn't want to make a bunch of noise cooking, so she poured herself a bowl of cereal, fixed her coffee, and ate at the table as the morning light finally brightened the room.

As she ate, she couldn't stop shaking her foot. The more she satisfied the physical need for food, the more her mind focused on the other things stressing her out—how to get her father to agree with leaving, where to take him, whether Devlin's father would actually come here, what he would do if he did, and what returning to Aeolus's with Devlin actually meant. Questions popped one after the other into her mind, and she really didn't have the answers for any of them.

When she was done eating, she settled her bowl and mug in the sink and peeked into the living room again. They were still asleep. And she was still mind-boggled.

Her gaze lingered over Devlin—from the way his long black hair fell across his eyes, to the bulge of his biceps under the cotton of the shirt, to the ripped jeans he'd worn the night before. How the heck had he dried them after the shower? She couldn't begin to imagine.

What she did know was that, if she'd thought Devlin could be tender and gentle before, the fact that he was allowing her father to sleep against him like that—a man Devlin didn't even know—proved it. And endeared him to her all the more.

The memory of Devlin calling himself a wretched waste flashed through her mind. As did what he'd said about himself last night— that he didn't deserve her, that he wasn't good for her, that he, himself, wasn't good. Standing there watching him sleep, Anna's heart ached for him. Why did he believe those things about himself when absolutely none of it was true? The possible answers to that question intensified the ache in her chest. She resolved at that very moment that before this day was over, she was going to tell him how wrong he was. About all of it.

As if her thoughts had conjured him into consciousness, Devlin's eyes blinked open and settled on her as though he'd known right where she'd been standing. His gaze slid to her father, then back to her. Emotions she wasn't sure she was correctly identifying slid over his expression in quick succession, but one thing she definitely recognized was discomfort.

Anna crossed the living room to him and knelt by his knee. "I'm sorry," she whispered. "What happened?"

Uncertainty. She recognized that emotion, too. "I didn't mean to wake him," Devlin said, his low voice gravelly and so damn sexy.

"It's okay," she said, shaking her head. "I—"

Her father shifted. Licked his lips. Blinked open his eyes. "Michael!" he called out. Anna barely had time to react to that when her dad looked toward Devlin, grasped his arm, and said, "Oh, thank God, I didn't dream you. My son." He leaned his forehead against Devlin's shoulder.

A roar of confusion and emotion filled Anna's ears as she dragged her gaze from her father's relieved and almost content expression to Devlin's look of mortification. He actually blushed.

"Um, Dad—"

"Can you believe it, Anna? Can you believe our Michael's back?" her father said, such happiness on his face.

She was like a cartoon character being hit over the head with a two-by-four. She was so stunned the world wobbled in front of her eyes. Her dad thought…Devlin was Michael? Yet he was lucid enough to call her by her own name—something that happened less and less these days.

"Uh…" she said, unable to manage a response yet. For a moment, she studied Devlin—not the man, sitting there so visibly uncomfortable she felt bad for him, but his features. His hair and eyes were darker than Michael's had been—she and her brother had always been complete opposites in their coloring, her pale where he'd been dark. And he was a good bit taller. And Michael never wore his hair long. All that meant Anna had never noticed any similarity. But she supposed, in the broadest sense of both men having dark hair and eyes and being tall, she could see how her dad, in his Alzheimer's-riddled brain, had made the leap that Devlin was Michael. Add in a heaping spoonful of grief and missing him and it made even more sense. In a totally crazy way. "Yeah, Dad," she finally managed.

"Um, Dad, if you don't mind," Devlin said, his gaze flickering to Anna's and then away again, as though he wasn't sure he wanted to see her reaction to what he was saying. "I'm going to freshen up, and then Anna and I had something we wanted to talk to you about."

Worry crept into her dad's eyes, but he nodded. "Of course, Mikey," he said, using a nickname Anna hadn't heard in *years*. Her heart squeezed for how much Dad obviously *needed* Devlin to be Michael—and for the fact that when Devlin inevitably went away, Dad would lose his "son" all over again.

Devlin gave her father's hand a squeeze and rose without looking at Anna, and then he crossed to the hallway and headed upstairs.

Anna forced a smile as she looked at her dad. "Want some coffee?"

"Yes, please," he said with a smile. Between the politeness and the eye contact and happy demeanor, it was like having her old dad—her *before* dad—back again. Devlin had done that—through his kindness and tolerance and patience, he'd given her the gift of a moment with the father who knew who she was and, at the same time, her father the gift of a moment without grief for the loss of a child.

"Okay," she said, pushing to her feet. She returned to the kitchen before he had the chance to see the tears filling her eyes. "Want some cereal, too?"

He came through the doorway, and she had to force herself not to gape. When was the last time he'd gotten up from sitting without her having to cajole him into the movement? For that matter, when was the last time he'd sat anywhere besides his recliner? "Sure, honey, that sounds good." He kissed her on the cheek.

Anna dashed away a stray tear. As he crossed to the table, she busied her hands with fixing his coffee and his breakfast. "So, um, when did you see Michael?"

"Last night. Heard him raiding the fridge," he said with a laugh. "Boy always did have a bottomless stomach."

The pressure building up inside Anna's chest made it hard to breathe. "Yeah," she said, hoping he didn't pick up on the way the tightness in her throat strained her voice. "Here you go," she said, sitting his breakfast down in front of him.

"Thanks. You not eating?"

"Oh, uh, I already ate." She returned the milk to the fridge.

"How are the urban gardens paintings going?" he asked, digging into his bowl.

She frowned and met his open, interested gaze, and all the while her brain was trying to figure out— "Oh." *Oh my God.* She'd worked on that series of paintings six years ago. Heart sprinting inside her chest, Anna held back the pain rising within her long enough to squeak out an answer. "Um, really great."

"I'd love to see them, when you're ready."

How long had she yearned for him to take an interest in her work again, as he always used to do? "Of course. Be right back," she said, thumbing toward the doorway. He saluted her with his spoon and took another bite. Anna darted out of the kitchen and almost crashed into Evan in the living room. "Sorry," she said.

"Hey, what's wrong?" he asked.

She shook her head. If she opened her mouth, she was going to lose it. And she really didn't want to do that within earshot of Dad. "You sure?"

She nodded.

"Uh, I need to tell you something."

"About Michael?" she asked.

"Oh. Yeah. Guess you already know." The expression on his face was all sympathetic understanding, and it added to the pressure sitting on her chest and squeezing her throat.

"Yeah. Stay with him, 'kay?" She squeezed Evan's arm and pushed past him, making a beeline for her bedroom. Once inside, she slid down the closed door and buried her face in her knees. Tears fell. And she didn't try to stop them. Between everything that'd happened yesterday and this, it was all too much. Her body felt too small to hold all this emotion inside, as if she might break apart at the seams if she didn't find a way to release it.

She just needed to hide from the world for a minute while she screwed her head back on straight.

"Anna?" came Devlin's voice from the direction of the bathroom.

She lifted her face— The room was pitch black. As in middle of a cloudy, moonless night black. In fact, it was so dark that it even swallowed the light that should've been coming in from the windows. Unease prickled down her spine. "Oh, God. What's happening?"

A hand fell on her knee as if Devlin had knelt in front of her. "This is you, Anna. Somehow, you've shrouded the room in darkness."

"Me?" she whispered. "I…I…"

"Shh, it's okay. It's like before. Concentrate on restoring the light." His thumb stroked reassuringly, the touch warm through the denim.

Like before. Right. *Restore the light.* Nothing. In her mind, she latched onto one of a thousand memories of her bedroom in the early-morning light. *Restore the light, damnit! Throw back this darkness.* She gave a hard mental push that had her fisting her hands against her legs.

The light returned. Not all at once, like the last time when the lightbulbs flashed back on. But incrementally, like a sunrise captured on time-lapse photography. Within just a couple of seconds, the room went from black to gray to light again. And Devlin was right there with her.

"That was me?" she whispered.

"That was you."

Her stomach flip-flopped, making her regret having eaten. "I've never been able to do this stuff before. Or at least, I couldn't command it, and I wasn't aware that I was doing it if I was. Why is it happening now?"

Devlin shook his head. "I don't know." He withdrew his hand from her knee and dropped his gaze to her shins. "Listen, Anna. About your dad. He just assumed, and I didn't know what to say. I didn't mean to deceive him," he said. "I'm sorry."

"Devlin," she said, grasping his hand and pulling it onto her knees again. "You have nothing to apologize for."

His gaze remained lowered.

"Hey, please look at me."

Slowly, he raised his eyes. For the life of her, Anna couldn't understand why his expression resembled that of a kid who knew he'd done something wrong—and gotten caught. It was all the more incongruous for the fact that he was a freaking god. Given the way he'd described his father, though, it seemed pretty likely that he was also a god who'd been ill-treated. Maybe even abused. Between the scars all over his body, his lack of trust, his feelings of being worthless and damaged, and the way he flinched at the possibility of being touched, she wouldn't be surprised to learn that was true.

"You did absolutely nothing wrong. You can't help that he mistook you for my brother. And, frankly, I can't thank you enough for going along with it. He doesn't respond well when his memory and other lapses are corrected. It's very jarring and upsetting to him. So you were incredibly gracious to humor him."

Devlin's gaze dropped somewhere between them again.

"Help me up, please?" She squeezed his hand.

He rose, pulling her to her feet as he did.

"Sit," she said, pointing to the unmade bed. Devlin frowned, but perched on the edge of her mattress. Anna stood between his knees, able to look him in the eyes this way. She debated exactly what to say for a long moment, and then she decided to let him have some input into the decision. "How much truth can you handle?"

Tilting his head, his gaze narrowed, but then his lips twitched. "Depends on the day."

His words tempted a small smile. "How's today looking?"

The left corner of his mouth lifted, just the smallest bit. "I'm not sure yet. Just say what you want to say."

"Okay." She stepped even closer. "Can I hold your hands while I talk?" The debate was clear on his face, but then he slipped both of his big hands into hers. She held onto him tight. "What you did with my dad? You gave him a gift. And you gave me a gift, too. Because whatever joy you brought him by reuniting him with his 'son' has brought my dad back to me, too. It won't last. I know that. But for this morning, he knows who I am. He knows me for me, Devlin. That happens so rarely anymore. *You* made that happen."

His jaw ticked and his struggle to maintain eye contact was clear. It hurt her heart. "I didn't do anything, Anna—"

"Yes, you did. You were kind and generous and compassionate. I know it must not have been easy to deal with him when he first saw you. God, I can only imagine. And to let him sit so close to you. And sleep next to you. I *know* none of that was easy for you, Devlin. But you did it out of the goodness of your heart, and I—"

"No," he said, pulling his hands free and crossing his arms over his chest. "I have no such thing."

Anna threaded her fingers between his forearms and his sternum. "Oh my God, Devlin. Yes, you do. I don't know what's happened to you in your life, but I know it's something bad. And I'm telling you right now, you didn't deserve—"

"Move," he said, pushing off the mattress.

Heart slamming against her breastbone, Anna stepped in front of him. "No. You are a good person, Devlin. Whoever told you otherwise was wrong. And a monster."

He stepped to the other side, a storm rolling in across his expression. "Stop."

She blocked him again. And the fact that he wasn't using his greater strength to force her out of the way when he could've easily done so proved the point yet again. "I won't stop telling you that you're good. And worthy of love. And deserving of good things and good people and good treatment."

Sparks of electricity flickered all around him. "Anna, stop—"

"Why? Why should I stop telling you how glad I am I met you? Or that I like you? Or that I admire the things you said about fighting your father? Or that I regret we were interrupted last night because I wanted—still want—to make love with you? How 'bout that?"

He grabbed her by the shoulders, his grip just shy of painful. "Because you're a fool for thinking any of that," he exploded.

Anna deflected the hurt that threatened at his words and his tone. Her gut told her it was all a defensive measure. And he still hadn't just stormed past her. Hell, couldn't he just disappear if he wanted? She nailed him with a stare.

"No, I'm not. I'm *not*. I'm right."

His expression, the cast of his eyes, the strain in his muscles—she was holding him right on the edge of his tolerance, and she knew it. No doubt no one had ever pushed at him like this, either. If the awkwardness and tension between him and the other gods was any indication, it didn't appear they'd ever sat him down and tried to work through any of this.

"Am I a good person, Devlin?"

Confusion flashed across his face, and he gave a sharp, single nod. "Yes."

"How do you know?" She laid her hands gently on his chest. "How do you know?" she said softly.

"Because…" Under her hands, his heart moved faster than a hummingbird's wings. He licked his lips, confusion and uncertainty flashing across his expression. "Because…you took care of me and worried about me and didn't hurt me even when you were angry." Light flared from behind shiny eyes. "And you fed me. And you were kind. Accepting. Gentle." He shook his head. "I know what you're doing."

She smoothed her hands upward, over his chest and his neck, to hold his square jaw in her hands. Stroking her thumbs over his cheeks, she said, "Last night, you took care of me like no one has since I was a child. I am the one who takes care of others, but I haven't had anyone take care of me in years. And you worried about me. And you got upset, but you didn't hurt me."

"Anna," he whispered.

She smiled, but her heart was absolutely throbbing for the pain Devlin radiated, a pain that someone had clearly spent a long time hammering into him. Maybe even literally, judging by all the scars on his body. "You fed me, Devlin. You were kind to me and my father. Accepting of my magic, like again just now, when no one else in my life would've been, and accepting of my father's misunderstanding, too. And despite the fact that you fear your roughness, you are really so gentle."

He closed his eyes. For a moment, his body became translucent and his skin felt lighter under her touch. The bed was visible through him, and then he was back again. Like he'd fought the urge to run away, and won.

"I can use all the same ways of identifying goodness in you that you used with me. Every last one." When he didn't respond right away, she pushed onto her tiptoes and kissed his cheek.

Devlin sucked in a great breath and threw his arms around her shoulders, crushing her to his chest. He buried his face in her hair and whispered her name over and over. "Anna. Anna."

Relief and affection flowed through her so hard and so much that it took her breath away. She threaded her arms around his neck and held him back. He…was he shaking? "It's okay. I've got you."

She wasn't sure how long they stood there like that, with his tall frame bent down around hers, but she didn't care. Right at that moment, he was the most important person in her life and he needed her more than anyone else. And she intended to be there for him as much as he'd let her.

That thought led her to another. *I'm…oh, man…I'm falling for him.*

She blew out a shaky breath and tried to keep from freaking out. Or over-sharing. She was pretty sure he'd reached his limit on talking about emotions. Fine by her, since she was still trying to wrap her head around the alternate-reality version of her life she seemed to have stepped into.

Finally, he pulled away, just a little—enough to lean his forehead against hers, though his hands were still on her back holding them together. Eyes closed, he said, "I ate all your berries."

"The strawberries?" Anna smiled. "I know. Were they good?"

His lips twitched. "Very. I'll buy you more."

"What's mine is yours, so thank you, but not necessary."

His eyes blinked open. Anna gasped. His irises, normally so dark they appeared black, looked lighter. Still dark, but she would've sworn they now bore an actual color. "Your eyes." He frowned. "Go look at your eyes," she whispered.

Wariness filtered into his expression. "Why?"

"I can't be sure because of my colorblindness, but I think... Go look. Please?"

He grabbed her hand and led them to the bathroom, flicked on the light, and stood in front of the mirror. Deep scowl, free hand fisted, muscles braced, he appeared ready to do battle. But then his expression changed. He leaned in—and his eyes went wide. His reflection met her gaze and his hand tightened around hers. "They're purple," he said around a thick-sounding swallow. "My eyes are dark purple."

Anna smiled, joy she didn't fully understand making her heart swell. "Told you."

Devlin dropped to a knee in front of her and bowed his head against her belly. Words spilled out of him in a language she didn't recognize, but the tone was reverent, solemn, urgent. Her heart recognized the significance of his words even if she couldn't understand their meaning. She laid her hands on his head and stroked his hair.

And realized she was beyond falling. She had fallen all the way for her broken god.

CHAPTER FIFTEEN

Devlin sat at the table in the Fallstons' kitchen, an empty plate in front of him from the huge breakfast Anna had made, just for him, and thought he'd never been more full in his entire life. And he wasn't talking about the four-egg omelet he'd just eaten.

His body felt…it was almost indescribable. Lighter. Buoyant. But filled to the brim at the same time, especially his heart, which felt way too big for his chest. And his head too, which, with his usual rage and grief quieted, left more room for himself. Which didn't even make any sense.

But whatever it was, it felt good. And it was all because of Anna.

Standing in the gray morning light of her bedroom, she'd waged war against his inner demons. And she'd won the battle, hands down. By the gods, his eyes had changed. It wasn't the color itself that was remarkable, but the fact that they bore any color at all. Devlin rarely looked in a mirror, so his memories of his own appearance were few and far between. But as much as he could recall, his eyes had always been black—and that terrified him because it was one more similarity with his father. Well, at least partially—because sometime during the last year, the sclera of Eurus's eye had turned black, too. It was so horrific to see that Eurus hid his eyes most of the time by wearing dark sunglasses. Half of Devlin's resistance to mirrors at this point was fearing the moment his eyes fully blackened, too.

But they were purple. *Not* the same. Just like…Devlin himself was not the same as Eurus.

I am not Eurus, he thought to himself. Going as far as saying he was good? Nope. Devlin wasn't there yet.

Which was why he couldn't quite tell whether Anna had won the war itself.

But just then, Devlin didn't even care, because he was powerless to do anything but bask in the warmth of the caring and belief and acceptance she'd given him. Who knew when he'd feel this way again? Or how long it would last?

"What do you think, Michael?"

A hand fell on his arm. "Michael?" Anna looked at him with pleading eyes.

Devlin shook away the fog of his thoughts and gazed at Anna, Garrett, and Evan, who were all staring at him expectantly. "Sorry, uh, daydreaming, I guess. Think of what?" Realization smacked him in the forehead. "Oh, right. I agree with Anna. Until the building inspector gives the okay on the structural integrity of the house, I think we have to clear out." This was the rationale Anna had come up with before they'd returned downstairs. Smart woman.

Anna smiled at him, then looked at Garrett. "See, Dad? Michael agrees—"

"Mikey, you really think this is necessary? I…I…" Garrett shook his head, a deep frown carved around his mouth. He clasped his hands together tightly in front of him.

"I do…Dad," he said around a lump in his throat. He hated deceiving the man, but it seemed the lesser of two evils compared with breaking his heart. "Hopefully, it'll just be for a few days, and then everything will be back to normal." If the gods were willing.

"But…but…where would I go?" he said, panic rising into his voice like wind filling a sail.

"You can come stay with me," Evan said with a smile. Anna had pulled him aside before they'd gathered around the table to ask him if he'd take Garrett in for a few days. "I have a great guest room and a recliner with your name on it."

"And Evan lives just two streets away, Dad, so we wouldn't even have to get in the car," she said with a hopeful smile. Apparently, Garrett's dementia made him fearful of riding in cars anymore, too. It was a battle Anna said she fought very selectively.

For his part, Evan sat quietly and listened, a concerned expression on his face.

"Hmph," Garrett said, nailing Devlin with a stare. "I don't like this, not one bit. But if you think I should do it, I will."

Such was the belief Garrett had in his son, apparently. A knot lodged in Devlin's throat, so he nodded.

"Anna, if you'll give me some advice, I'll pack a bag for Garrett," Evan said, rising.

"Of course," she said. The two of them left the room.

Garrett stared at him a long moment, then tilted his head as though he was analyzing Devlin. A niggle of unease twisted through his gut. "Whatever happens, take care of Anna. You hear?" Garrett said in an absolutely serious voice.

Devlin schooled his expression even as Garrett's words made his scalp prickle. How had Garrett managed to say something so appropriate to the situation they were actually in, without knowing anything about it? Though did it really matter? "You have my word," Devlin said.

A silent understanding seemed to flow between them after that. Garrett nodded.

Anna returned maybe ten minutes later. "Everything's set," she said. "We'll walk down as soon as you get dressed, Dad."

Only minutes later, they stood at the front door as Garrett attempted to psych himself up to go outside. "What would help you?" Anna finally asked, rubbing her dad's back.

Garrett looked from her to Devlin and back again. "You two." Evan and Devlin each with a bag, they went out the door, down the porch steps, and along the sidewalk to the driveway. When they got to the wider pavement, Garrett wrapped one shaking arm through Anna's, and the other through Devlin's.

The three of them walked in a row. Like they were a family.

And though it was a stolen moment, just then Devlin truly did feel a part of something bigger than himself.

Anna chitchatted with her father and Evan as they walked to the end of the street, crossed the intersection, and then approached the fifth house on the other side. Like the Fallstons' house, this one was an older two-story with lots of what they called character—wide porch, colored fanlight over the front door, lots of carved molding and ornamental details.

A dark-skinned man a little older than Evan stepped out onto the porch just as they started up the steps. Evan's partner, Jake, Devlin assumed. "Good to see you, Mr. Fallston," he called with a big, open smile.

"Jake," Garrett said. "Ravens on tonight?"

"Yes, sir," Jake said, holding open the storm door.

Talk of football continued as Garrett shuffled into the house, the walk clearly having taxed him. Inside, Devlin kept Garrett company as Anna and Evan unpacked his belongings and got him settled in.

Soon, Anna and Devlin were saying good-bye to Garrett and making promises to return quickly. Of course, Garrett thought that meant later today, which they'd purposely left vague with him because Anna thought any effort to explain that they'd be gone for a few days would exacerbate his stress. In reality, Devlin couldn't yet estimate when they'd return and the Fallstons' house would once again be safe. The good-byes were so strained and tense that Devlin couldn't wait to get out of the house, despite the fact that a part of him burned with regret and concern for Garrett. But at least Anna's father was out of harm's way.

Outside, Evan said, "I have to get my car, so I'll walk back with you."

Unlike the walk of a few minutes ago, everyone was quiet as they made the return trip down the quiet street. Evan pointed out his car a short ways from Anna's house, then turned and met Anna's gaze. "Are you sure there's not something else going on here?" Devlin cut his gaze to Anna, but the movement had been a mistake. Evan's expression darkened. "There is, isn't there?"

"No, there's nothing going on." She smiled. "We just gotta deal with the house."

Evan frowned. "I mean this as a total compliment, Annalise, but you have always been a horrible liar."

Concern flashed through Devlin as Anna paled. "I...I..."

"You have devoted your life to Garrett for years." Evan's gaze swung to Devlin. "And *you* come to town, Mr. Tall, Dark, and Bad News, and suddenly things are blowing up and you're leaving Garrett at my house, which, don't get me wrong. I'm happy to help. But, it's so not *you*," he said, staring at Anna.

Heat skittered over Devlin's hands. He did *not* appreciate the man's tone with Anna right now. Not one bit.

She shivered and hugged herself, and Devlin hated seeing that protective posture even more. Hated knowing that something he'd done was the cause of it. "Evan, I just need you to trust me," she said.

Evan swung a ring of keys around his finger. "That would be easier if you'd tell me what's going on."

She planted her hands on her hips. "Asking you to trust me means doing it without needing me to explain. At least, not right now."

"Wow. Okay, then." Without another word, he rounded the car, folded into the driver's seat, and pulled away.

Devlin's presence had caused this deep rift between Anna and her long-time friend. Guilt slunk through his gut, especially as he caught the flash of hurt in Anna's eyes.

Sonofabitch.

Anna whirled on him and pointed. "Don't you dare apologize because none of what just happened was your fault."

Devlin blinked. Hip jutted to the side, eyes nearly blazing silver, a pink flush on her cheeks. Gods, she was sexy when she was telling him what to do. So, even though Devlin *was* sorry, he let it go and decided to take her at her word. "Okay."

She raked her hands into her hair, splaying the light blond in a pale waterfall above her head. The position highlighted her beautiful breasts and revealed a sliver of skin between her shirt and jeans. Anna flung her arms down in a huff and crossed them over her chest. "I'm sorry he talked to you that way." She kicked at a stone on the sidewalk and stepped closer. "I could really use a hug right now."

Forcing himself to move as a human would, Devlin closed the distance between them, his eyes on hers every step of the way, until he folded her in his arms.

Her heat slammed into his chest and her arms wrapped immediately around his back. "Oh, God, Devlin," she rasped. "I was panicking and getting mad and I thought I was going to lose control. There was this pressure building inside me, and I could see the darkness coming, settling over the street and all the houses. If he'd kept asking I don't think I would've been able to hold it back. I don't know how you do it," she rushed on, "how you possess this incredible power and keep it all bottled up inside."

Her words wrapped around him like a warm blanket. "Uh, have you seen your backyard lately?"

A chuckle. Louder. She tilted her head back and let out a full-on laugh. A laugh that *Devlin* had caused. It was the most beautiful sound he'd ever heard in his life. And Anna…she was the most beautiful sight.

"I *am* sorry that happened, especially on top of leaving your father at Evan's house, which I know wasn't easy for you."

She nodded and released a long breath. "Thanks."

Their closeness and her softness and the fact that his touch seemed to ease her fueled arousal through his body. "I want to kiss you," he said in an unusual voicing of his desires.

She smiled up at him. "Well, what are you waiting for?"

Grasping her face, he leaned down. Slowly. Closer. Keeping his eyes open so he could look into hers. Anna shuddered out a breath as her fingers fisted in his shirt, pulling and urging.

Their lips were so close that Anna's breath whispered across his skin. A small whimper spilled from her throat and her gaze went bright with need.

Devlin kissed her.

The minute their lips connected, passion ignited between them, hot and urgent and demanding. Devlin's heart was immediately a jackhammer in his chest. The kiss turned almost rough in its urgency—not just him, but both of them. She sucked on his tongue. He bit her bottom lip. She pulled his hair and urged him closer, deeper.

"Do we have to leave right away?" she whispered.

The implication sank into Devlin's mind. He hardened to the point of painful need. "Told them we'd be back this afternoon," he said, pulling away to look in her eyes. Both of them were breathing hard, chests crashing into each other from how close they stood. "Tell me what you want, Annalise."

"You," she said. "Now."

CHAPTER SIXTEEN

"Hang on tight," Devlin said as he made them invisible.

Anna wanted to whoop in joy and exhilaration as Devlin whisked them to her house, under the gap in her front door, and into her bedroom. When he brought them back into their bodies, they were midair. A moment later, they bounced onto the mattress side by side. Laughter burst out of Anna's chest.

"Like that?" Devlin asked, kissing her throat.

"Yeah," she said, smiling and grabbing onto his shoulders. "Handy."

She scooted down so their faces aligned and found his lips in a breath-stealing kiss. He pushed the hoodie off her shoulders, and together they worked it free. Anna kicked off her sneakers and they thudded on the floor. She yanked at the back of his shirt, needing to feel his skin against hers. When he didn't hesitate to help her remove it, white-hot triumph flooded through her.

"I meant what I said, Anna," Devlin said as he kissed her jaw and throat. "Lift."

She sat up a little, and he made quick work of her T-shirt and bra. When she lay back against the messy covers, he kissed a trail up her stomach to the valley between her breasts.

His hands were huge and warm as they cupped and kneaded her

breasts. "I haven't done this in a long time, so I'm wound tight."

"It's okay." Her hands flew to his hair as he kissed circles around her right nipple. Anticipation of his lips and tongue finally focusing on the sensitive peak had her arching toward him. He flicked her tip once, twice, and she cried out. His mouth covered her completely and sucked and licked and nibbled until she was panting and writhing under him. "Need you," she moaned.

Devlin's fingers worked at the button and zipper on her jeans. A shiver erupted across her skin, fueled by anticipation and adrenaline and pure, unadulterated arousal. He slid off the edge of the bed onto his feet and tugged her jeans off. "Gods, you're beautiful," he said, as he dropped the clothing to the floor. Standing between her legs, he caught one ankle in his rough, calloused hand and lifted it to his mouth. With a groan of appreciation, he kissed and licked up her calf, to the soft, ticklish spot under her knee, and up the inside of her thigh.

And then he hauled her body toward him until her hips were at the edge of the bed. Anna's heart tripped into a full-out sprint.

He leaned over her, his chest falling on hers, his hips providing a maddening friction against her core, and kissed her until she was certain she could live without oxygen or die happy trying.

"Look at me," he whispered, watching her as he kissed her. It was intimate and intense. And, oh, the light flaring behind his now-brighter eyes was so damn beautiful.

Anna saw the question in his gaze. "I'm sure, Devlin."

Another searing kiss, like a reward, or a giving of thanks. As he rose, he dragged his hands down her body to her panties, leaving a trail of fire in his wake. When she lifted her legs, he made quick work of removing them and undoing the fly of his jeans.

Devlin shoved the black denim down over his lean hips, and it was all that separated him from her hungry gaze.

His cock stood straight out from his body, long and thick and heavy. Anna licked her lips and pushed up onto one elbow, then she wrapped her other hand around his length.

He groaned and grabbed her thighs, his hands bracing as if her touch was almost too much to bear. She stroked him once, twice, twisting her wrist on each upward pull. Mouth open and face strained, Devlin groaned again and stilled her wrist in the manacle of his grip.

"Fuck, you're gonna make me come from touching me."

A thrill rippled through her stomach, and she moved her fingers as much as she could with Devlin holding her wrist. "So come."

"Anna," he growled.

"Let go," she whispered, wriggling her hand.

When he did, she smiled and continued stroking him, handling him so his head rubbed against her clit. He gripped her bent knees and watched her hand and trembled against her. His stomach muscles clenched and flinched and his hips started to move. And holy hell was he sexy to watch as his body tightened and shook in pleasure.

"Let yourself go, Devlin," she said, dragging her hand from root to tip.

She felt his cock jerk at the same time he cried out. His hands squeezed her knees and his whole body braced as stripes of his warm release painted lines across her belly.

Anna smiled when his eyes finally focused on hers again. And, man, how she wished she could see what color they were glowing. "That sounded nice," she said.

"Nice doesn't begin to describe it." His gaze dropped to her wet belly. "But, I've—" He frowned, grabbed the corner of the sheet, and gently wiped at her skin. "Soiled you."

Pain squeezed Anna's heart and she pushed into a sitting position. Placing a hand over his heart, she said, "The only thing that just happened is you shared something beautiful and special with me. Understand?" She pulled the sheet out of his hand.

He nodded and met her gaze. His cock jerked against her thigh.

Looking down, Anna smiled. "You're still hard."

"It's been a long time, Annalise."

Biting her lip at the hunger in the way he'd said her name, she glanced toward her nightstand. "Get a condom, please. Gray box in that drawer."

Devlin released her, found the box, and pulled one free. Anna slipped the packet from his fingers. Slowly, much slower than absolutely necessary, she rolled the condom down his considerable length, taking her time to squeeze and drag her fingers over him. Devlin growled.

Butterflies tore through her belly. At the sound. At his size. At the very fact that this was happening.

At getting to share this with him.

He nuzzled her face, kissed her cheek, licked the shell of her ear. With a hand on her chest, he pushed her back and walked his fingers down her belly to her core. "Are you ready for me?" The rough pads of his fingers slipped over her clit to her opening. "Oh, yes you are." He spread her wetness with his touch, making her shudder and sigh and throw her head back. Kissing and nibbling at her neck, he leaned into her and penetrated her with his thick middle finger. "Fuck, Anna. You're so little. I don't want to hurt you."

She kissed him, loving how he had so many rough edges but was also so gentle and considerate. Without breaking the connection, she slowly leaned back until she lay flat, pulling him on top of her and forcing the length of his cock against her clit. Anna moaned at the contact, then again, louder, as he added a second finger. Their kisses grew more urgent and demanding as Devlin fucked her with his fingers and rocked his cock against her clit.

A dizzying pressure congregated low in her belly. Anna whimpered and gasped in raw pleasure.

"Have to have you," Devlin said in a voice full of gravel, pushing his jeans down farther.

"Yes."

She barely had a chance to miss his fingers before he aligned his tip with her center. He met her gaze with his blazing eyes and watched her reaction as he penetrated her inch by maddening inch.

"Oh, God," Anna said as he filled her so deliciously, just slow enough that her body could adjust to the size of his invasion, but not so slow that she lost her ever-loving mind. Looking down at where he entered her, Anna found the fact that he was penetrating her while still wearing his jeans so damn sexy. The extra sensation of the denim against her ass. The impatience it revealed.

Devlin's mouth dropped open on a groan. "Oh, gods, Annalise. I can't...I don't...it's too—"

"There's no wrong or right here," she said. His eyes almost pleaded with her. "Do whatever feels good."

A moment of hesitation. And then Devlin wrapped his hands under her thighs and lifted her bottom off the bed as he drove into her. Again and again and again, each thrust punctuated by a grunt that ripped from his chest.

Anna was completely overwhelmed in the best possible way. She cried out with an answering moan each time his hips slammed into hers. Standing over her, commanding and dominating her body, he looked every inch the god that he was—powerful, beautiful, larger than life.

Without losing his rhythm, he pushed her thighs to her chest so she nearly formed a ball. He rolled his hips as he pounded into her, and each impact ground his public bone against her clit.

"Oh my God, Devlin. Oh my God."

Hooking one arm under her knee and the other hand under her shoulder, he collapsed on top of her, his hips snapping against hers, one amazing stroke after another. Hunched over, he kissed her mouth until her lungs burned for air, and then he worshipped her face, her neck, her ear. "Say my name again," he rasped.

"Devlin," she said as she wrapped her arms around his big shoulders and held on tight.

"Again," he growled.

"*Devlin*." She buried her face in his neck and kissed and licked and breathed his incredible cool autumn spice deep inside her.

He held her tighter as his strokes slowed on a series of mind-numbing punctuated thrusts. "I...can't...get...deep...enough," he ground out. "Anna."

Hot, pulsing sensation spiraled in a tight vortex centered on her clit, and then Anna's body went nuclear as her orgasm detonated. "Devlin!" she wailed, and then the force of her release stole her breath. She clawed her nails into him as wave after wave of ecstasy washed over her, turned her upside down, and landed her back in his arms again.

"Fuuuck," he groaned as he wrapped both arms under her neck and pistoned against her in a series of breath-stealing, bone-melting strokes. "Oh, gods. Anna, I'm…coming." Groans ripped out of him as his cock spasmed inside her. The movement of his body slowed and he worked his hips in maddeningly slow thrusts and circles that had her gasping again.

"Don't stop, Devlin. Just like that. Please," she said, breathless at the possibility of a second orgasm.

"Come on my cock, Anna. Give me everything." He pressed kisses to her cheek and plundered her mouth.

"Faster," she whispered, clenching her eyes in concentration.

"Look at me," he said, resting his forehead on hers. He ground himself against her clit in a series of hard, fast rubs. "Come on. Give it to me."

"Yeah," she rasped, her heart beating so hard she was light-headed. He slid one hand under her ass and tilted her hips upward. His body ground into her clit like a key unlocking a door. Her head wrenched back into the mattress and her whole body bowed as the orgasm crashed into her and rolled endlessly on.

The minute her muscles went slack, Devlin withdrew, removed the condom, and gathered her into his arms. He turned them onto their sides facing each other, her body tucked in against the shelter of his, their legs entangled. Her head lay on the thick pillow of his biceps. Pressing a kiss to her forehead, he stroked her hair back off her face, their labored breathing the only sound in the room.

I don't want this to end, she thought. Realization of the depth of that feeling rolled in close behind. God, the thought of never having him again this way, nevermore being held in his arms so lovingly, made her chest constrict and her throat go tight.

"Today, after we go to your grandfather's, you have to break into your father's house to look for that key?" Anna asked, her voice at a whisper. It was all she could manage just then.

He splayed his big hand over her bare back. "Yes," he murmured against her hair.

"It's gonna be dangerous," she said, not asking, but needing the confirmation all the same. He nodded. "And there's...there's a chance you won't come...back?" Her face and throat filled with the sharp pressure of restrained tears.

Long pause. "Yes."

Emotion welled up inside her until it became hard to breathe. At most, she had a few hours left with him, but she suspected their time alone would significantly decrease once they left the cocoon of her room. And then he'd go confront some kind of evil the likes of which she couldn't even imagine.

And the worst of it? He'd go into battle thinking he wasn't good and he wasn't worthy and he wasn't loved. He could *die* thinking he wasn't loved.

Not if you tell him. Tell him, Anna.

She shifted so she could look at his face. And, oh, God, his irises were lighter yet. What she wouldn't have given to be able to see the color. She brushed the hair off his forehead, his skin still warm with sweat from their lovemaking, and looked him in the eye. "I...Devlin, no one should have to stare down death without knowing that they matter."

Wariness slid into the depths of his eyes and his jaw ticked.

"You matter—"

"Anna," he said, shifting away from her touch and onto his back.

And holy hell, what a sight he was. His shoulders, chest, and abdomen were all formed with lean ropes of muscle. Maybe even too lean. But together with his scars, it gave him a rough, edgy appeal that made her core clench in aftershock. His hair was a sexed-up wreck, his cock lay thick against his lower stomach, and his jeans hung half off. He appeared absolutely ravaged, and it made her want to start all over again.

But not until he knew what she felt for him.

She braced above him with her arms on either side of his head and looked down into his eyes. "Don't run away, Devlin. This is important."

He closed his eyes and swallowed hard. "I…please…" Shaking his head, he threw an arm over his eyes. "I don't like anyone over me," he finally said, reluctance and embarrassment clear in his tone.

Anna flew back from him, her heart thudding inside her chest. "I'm sorry."

"Didn't know," he said, voice thick. "Gods, I'm ruining this…this perfection."

Anger and outrage on his behalf welled up inside her. She ached to hold him, to ease him. "Come here to me, please," she said as she scooted up the bed and settled with her back against the wooden headboard.

Devlin rolled his head to look at her, and finally lifted up off the mattress. He hiked his jeans up over his hips, but didn't zip them, and then he moved toward her.

Patting her chest, she parted her legs and said, "Lean up against me. I need to hold you."

Slowly, Devlin shifted until his back came up against her front. Anna wasn't sure whose sigh was bigger—hers or his. All she knew was the rightness of holding him, of having him in her arms—one arm over one big shoulder and one under the other, her hands coming to rest on his chest.

"Perfection is the absolute right word. And you could never ruin it," she said in a low, calm voice. "Not when it was perfect because of you."

His muscles tensed under her touch. "Anna—"

"Shh. Because of you, Devlin. Because of you," she said, smoothing her hands over him and learning the contours of his muscles, his scars, the thin covering of dark hair on his chest. She kissed his shoulder, then licked the salt from his neck.

He sucked in a breath and in the open fly of his jeans, his cock stirred. Anna smiled, and then her eyes noticed a stretch of off-white gauze under one of the tears in his jeans—the wound she'd questioned him about the previous night.

"No one's ever—" He cut the words off as suddenly as they'd started.

Anna's heart clenched. "What?" She brushed his hair off his face again, sweeping it off his forehead and raking her fingers against his scalp.

Devlin hummed in appreciation and let his head go slack on her shoulder. His ease lit her up inside. "Done this," he finally said.

"Played with your hair?"

"Showed me so much care," he whispered.

The words threatened to break her heart. How and why had anyone treated him so horribly? It made her sad and savagely angry at the same time. "Well, then, we have some making up to do." When he didn't respond, she brushed her fingers through his hair again and again. Looking down his big body, Anna's gaze settled on that bandage visible through the denim again. Somehow, that injury was important, and her heart and gut couldn't let it go. Taking a deep breath, she hugged him in tight and pressed her lips to his ear. "Please tell me about the wound on your leg."

∞〇∞

Dread filled Devlin with ice. He tried to sit up, but Anna grasped his chest with splayed hands and held him tight.

"Please," she said, kissing his cheek.

A war erupted inside him—between the side of his soul that, thanks to her, had never found more pleasure and comfort and solace in his entire life, and the side that didn't want to reveal anything else that might push this amazing woman away. Between his anger and his instability and his scars, he was already a lot for anyone to take on—

not even considering the part about the very high likelihood that he was a dead man walking.

How could he possibly expect her to understand what was going on with his leg? What he was doing to *himself*?

He couldn't.

"Leave it be," he said, as he swung his legs toward the side of the bed. His soul screamed at the separation from her, even as he moved farther away. He slid off the edge until his boots hit the floor. He glanced down at himself and shook his head. Wasn't this the perfect fucking analogy for the difference between the two of them? Anna sat naked and guileless and completely open right behind him, while Devlin hadn't even gotten undressed or taken off his goddamned boots to have sex with this incredible being of light and goodness. He couldn't even be bothered to take off his fucking *boots*.

Still covered up. Still hiding. Still running.

Story of his life.

Anna shifted next to him, still naked and seemingly not self-conscious of that fact. Devlin was glad for it, because petite, soft, and so damn beautiful, she was utter perfection. To him. And her mind and heart were even more stunning. She sat sideways on the edge of the bed, close but not touching him, which made his skin yearn even harder for the touch. "Tell me," she said in a low voice. "It's clearly important to you, so it's important to me—"

"Why?" He swallowed around the knot of self-loathing growing in his throat and threatening to suffocate him. Shame turned his skin hot, adding to the feeling of the room closing in on him. An insidious little voice whispered in his ear. *Too good. Too good. She's too damn good for you.* "Fucking you doesn't make me important," he said, hating the acidic, false taste of the words as they came out of his mouth, especially when her breath caught and halted.

"Don't do that, Devlin," she said, anger clear in her tone. The light in the room slowly but surely dimmed, as if some unseen forced deadened it. "Don't be an asshole to divert me from digging too deep or getting too close. You're better than that."

He shook his head, hair falling over his eyes. "No, I'm not."

"Goddamn it, yes you are!" Dimmer yet.

"No!" He shoved off the bed and turned on her.

She flung out her hands. "Devlin—"

"Why is it so fucking important to you?" he yelled.

"Because I fucking love you," Anna yelled back, her eyes going wide and her cheeks bright red.

The words echoed around the room, silent except for the sounds of their breathing,

Because she...loves me? The words got stuck at the edge of his brain, like it didn't know how to process them. He looked at her beautiful face, pink lips shiny, cheeks a deep scarlet, eyes so bright they were almost silver. That amazingly fearless, gorgeous, generous woman loved...him.

His heart felt like a fist squeezed around it and kept it from beating. The pressure inside ratcheted up until Devlin had to press a hand to his chest. And then the constriction finally broke, and the hard-pounding organ expanded and grew until it totally filled him up. But, gods, what did he know about love? For him, it had only ever meant the drive to protect and defend and provide, which is what he'd tried to do for his brothers in the absence of their father. No, not the absence—Eurus's presence had been so much worse than if he'd just neglected them. Then again, Devlin had failed both Farren and Alastor, so what did he know? That was the problem—because when it came to love, he knew absolutely nothing.

Except...the turmoil inside him needed her soothing touch. And her being in the slightest danger made him a little insane. And this one time with her hadn't nearly been enough. Gods in heaven, he would give up forever in a heartbeat to touch her, hold her, have her for the speck that was a mortal lifespan.

Was that...could that be...love?

And had he just destroyed it with the wrecking ball of his words? After lobbing so many bombs into the space between them, he didn't know what to do or say to try to get back to her again. "Anna," he said, his voice cracking.

He didn't know what she'd heard, but she flew off the bed toward him, the light in the room brightening the minute she crashed into his body.

He caught and embraced her so hard he lifted her off the ground. She wrapped her legs around him, her ankles just crossing against his ass. A profound sense of rightness and belonging settled in him, and it was a revelation after a lifetime of living amid so much that was wrong.

"I didn't mean it," he said. "Making love to you was the single most special thing I've ever done. And it was an honor and a privilege I will always cherish. So fucking sorry."

"I love you, Devlin," she said as if nothing else mattered. And if she truly felt that way for him, nothing else did.

He stroked her hair as he lifted his face to look at her. "I…" Devlin shook his head. "I've never said…those words to anyone. Ever."

"And you don't have to—"

Devlin kissed her, just a soft brush of lips. "Yes, I do. Because, well, I do, Anna. L-love you," he said, the admission of his feelings making him as exposed and vulnerable as he'd ever felt. She pressed her lips to his, and her kiss tasted of acceptance and compassion and forgiveness. He walked her to the bed and sat her down on the edge. And then, before he could second-guess it, he took two steps backward, shoved down his jeans until the ruined denim cleared the bandage around his upper left thigh, and unwound it.

After everything she'd done for him, he owed her the truth—and a man strong enough to tell it, even when it was hard. Especially when it was hard.

He unraveled the last loop of cloth, bloody from being closest to the wound, and dropped it to the floor.

Anna gasped and her hands fisted around the edge of the mattress as she stared at the spiked metal band that surrounded and dug into his leg, which was bloody and swollen. "What is that? And why…?"

"It's a cilice. An instrument of punishment used for paying penance," he said in a low voice, fear and nerves and much older, much darker emotions curling into his gut. "I didn't want you to see it because I didn't think you'd understand. How could you? But I want someone to know who I am, Anna. And I want that someone to be you."

Slowly, she eased off the bed and down onto her knees, her gaze flashing back and forth between his eyes and where the chain-link loop of sharp metal teeth bit into his flesh. Blood oozed from some of the deeper cuts, but in other places his skin tried to heal around the metal. It was why Devlin had chosen this particular device. If he harmed himself, the pain and the wound and the sacrifice would be temporary because he'd heal. An injury had to be inflicted by a stronger god in order to be lasting, which explained the scars covering most of his body. Eurus had been a stronger deity even before he'd stolen Aeolus's Firestone ring, and now that power had increased exponentially. But *this*, this would leave a lasting wound because Devlin never removed it, so the teeth were always chewing at his skin.

"What is it you believe you need to atone for?" she asked, meeting his eyes. Hers were glassy with emotion.

"My errors and arrogance cost my brother Farren his life and ensured that my other brother, Alastor, has lived a life of torture and imprisonment. My actions condemned both of them. So I vowed to make certain sacrifices until I made it right. Or at least, as right as I can—by saving Alastor and avenging Farren." His heart beat in his throat and nervous energy prickled down his spine. Devlin dropped his gaze to the floor.

She moved into his line of sight, still on her knees before him. "So, the long abstinence?" He nodded. "And this…cilice?" Nodded again. "But if you hurt yourself like this," Anna said, swallowing thickly, "how can you be as strong as you need to save Alastor and destroy your father, too?"

It was a fair point, which made it particularly uncomfortable. "The pain focuses me," he said, grasping at an old rationalization.

"It hurts you, Devlin." Her gaze dropped to his thigh, where his skin in between the teeth was an angry, puffy red. "It takes from you. Your intention to honor them is admirable, but when will it be enough? How much and for how long will you have to deny yourself the right to life and happiness? And how can you do the things you need to do to truly free yourself and Alastor from that past if you don't give yourself every advantage? If you don't stop hurting yourself?"

Anna crawled closer until her heat seared his calf, his knee, his thigh. Sitting at his feet, she softly wrapped her arms around his injured thigh and laid her cheek against the metal.

Devlin absolutely loathed the sight of her skin touching that *thing*.

And then, eyes closed, she turned her head and pressed a kiss against it, her lips just brushing his ruined skin through a round link. Again and again, she repeated the torturously beautiful gesture until Devlin wasn't sure he could speak.

But he could act.

Reaching to the inside of his thigh, he found the leather tie that determined the cilice's tightness. He untied it, then released the metallic clasp. Anna leaned back, but of course the device was buried too deep in Devlin's skin and muscle for it to fall loose.

He was going to have to tear it out tooth by tooth.

"Oh, God, you have to pull it out, don't you?" she asked, coming to the same conclusion.

"Yes," he managed, his stomach threatening to rebel. "But this wound will heal." He leaned down, caressed Anna's cheek, and pressed a kiss to her lips. "You're right." Resolved, he stepped out of the immediate circle of her embrace and yanked the end that wrapped around the front of his leg free. Brilliant pain flashed from his leg through his entire body. He grunted and blinked back the white spots flickering at the edge of his vision. A quarter of the way out. Another yank. A roar of pain. Then another and another. He screamed. Or maybe that was her? And then it was free.

Metal clanked against the floor.

Devlin staggered. But Anna was up and had caught him before he'd even seen her move. "No more, Devlin. Please tell me you'll never use that again."

He heaved a rasping breath and tried not to lean all his body weight against her. "No," he said, feeling oddly lighter despite the pain. "No more. I need...to be strong...for you."

She helped him to the bed and he fell heavily onto its edge.

"And for you, Devlin. So you can do what you have to do and come back to me."

He nodded. "For both of us, then." He licked at dry lips, unconsciousness luring him under. "Lie with me for a while? It won't take my body long to undo this damage."

"Thank God for that," Anna said. "But I should tend to this first. Just stay here."

He caught her hand. "Don't worry about it. It'll heal." He tugged his jeans over the wound and patted the bed beside him.

"You sure?" He nodded as she crawled over his legs and settled in against his injured side toward the bed's middle. "I wouldn't mind taking care of you, you know?"

"I know," he mumbled. He tugged the blanket behind her so he could wrap it over her body. "I want...take care...you, too," he said, sleep nearly claiming him. Her heat settled into the crook of his neck and her arm crossed his chest. And despite the major emotional and physical ass-kicking he'd just undergone, it was the closest to heaven that he'd ever been.

CHAPTER SEVENTEEN

They were almost back to Aeolus's compound—her, Devlin, and four gods Anna had seen but not formally met. A storm had been whipping up as they'd prepared to leave, and Devlin's expression had darkened as he'd studied the sky and then ordered two gods off to stand guard over her father at Evan's house—just to be on the safe side, he'd said. Then he'd insisted they hurry. The introductions would have to wait until some other time when the world wasn't maybe ending.

As they soared through the storm-darkened sky, Anna felt like she'd lived an entire month since she'd gotten out of bed that morning, panicked that Devlin had left. And, oh, what highs and lows. The joy and pain of her father's semi-return to himself. The fight with Evan. The heart-pounding ecstasy of making love with Devlin. The horror and sadness of seeing how he tortured himself. God, the pain he carried, it was almost unimaginable.

Devlin had been very quiet since they'd gotten out of bed after their nap, though the little touches and presses of kisses against her hair as they'd prepared to leave made it clear his silence wasn't based in anger. And so Anna gave him her touch and her silent support and held on to him with all her heart and soul as they flew through the sky. She didn't think she was imagining the deep satisfaction flowing out of his elemental form and into hers.

After all that they'd shared this morning, that satisfaction meant everything. He deserved it and so much more. Her chest still ached for him. But at least when they'd awakened after two hours' sleep, the horrible wound on his leg from the cilice was significantly better. All the open cuts had closed, and the jagged, ripped skin had knit itself back together again. Even the swelling had gone down. At this rate, Anna wouldn't be surprised if all traces of the injury disappeared by tomorrow. It couldn't happen soon enough.

When he'd peeled away the last layer of the bandage, Anna's heart had felt like a glass figurine that had been smashed into a million pieces. It boggled the mind that a *god* could've been so badly abused that he blamed himself for the consequences of his father's horrible actions. Who would've thought that the divine could be guilty of the same failures toward their children as some human parents were?

And it made Anna realize how lucky she'd been. For everything she'd had to give up as an adult, she'd had possibly the best father ever while growing up. Devlin's experience reminded her of how much she had to be grateful for. And that resurrected her worry for her father. God, she hoped he'd be okay while she was gone. The one saving grace was she knew Evan would take great care of him just like he always had.

Aeolus's compound came into view, rising out of the clouds like a verdant oasis in the middle of great nothingness. Lush greenery surrounded a series of interconnected buildings in an architectural style she might've associated with an Italian villa. It was beautiful, alluring scenery. It was paradise.

And Anna could see it in color. Again.

Their divine escort remained at the perimeter of the compound, and then she and Devlin were inside a great ornamental hall decorated with enormous and *colorful* floor-to-ceiling murals. Tiles of all colors made up a massive compass face on the floor. The next thing she knew, her feet were standing just outside of the circle.

"I've got you," Devlin said, his arms around her shoulders. Anna melted into the comfort of his body even though the adjustment to becoming corporeal seemed much easier this time than the last. She glanced up…and gasped. Just as she'd suspected, his eyes were the most beautiful violet—

"You're late," came a voice from behind her.

"I know," Devlin said, not moving. Anna startled and lifted her head. "Don't rush. Just take your time."

"I'm okay," she said. And then the splendor of the space chased away every other thought. "What is this place? It's the most beautiful thing I've ever seen." The murals depicted the four seasons in glorious bold colors, and everywhere she looked she found amazing details in the art that she yearned to examine closer. Holding his hand, she turned in a circle, scanning the—

A huge group of people stood maybe ten feet away, every single one of them looking at her.

"Oh," she said. "Uh. Hi." Several women, including one who was very pregnant, stood among the group of gods she'd already met.

Devlin squeezed her hand and stepped beside her. "My lords," he said, bowing his head toward his grandfather and the three big Anemoi.

"Devlin. It's good you're here," Aeolus said.

Next to Aeolus, a tall, thin woman wearing some sort of a black scarf over her hair gave Devlin a small smile. "Good to see you," she said with a bit of an accent.

"Tisiphone," he said with a nod.

But they were the only ones to offer a greeting. The awkwardness that hung thick in the air made it clear the others didn't share Aeolus's sentiment. Anna looked between Devlin's reserved and uncertain expression and the faces of the others. She didn't think she imagined the hostility radiating from Zeph and the pretty brown-haired woman standing next to him, or from a dark-haired man she hadn't yet met.

"Has something happened?" Devlin finally asked, obviously sensing the tension, too.

"No," Aeolus said. "Everything—"

"Yeah, dude," Chrysander said. "Laney had a vision." Aeolus frowned as the blond god nodded toward a black-haired woman with striking blue eyes standing next to him. Anna's brain latched onto the word *vision*. There was someone else like her here?

"And?" Devlin asked, his thumb stroking over Anna's knuckles.

The brown-haired woman stepped forward, pulling out of Zeph's grip when he tried to restrain her. "And she saw you attacking Zephyros," the woman said, bronze light flaring from behind her dark eyes. So, a goddess, then?

Anna's stomach dropped as she realized…holy hell…*They don't trust Devlin.* He was here to risk his life, and they didn't trust him. Did he have no one on his side? Besides her, of course, but how useful was she against a wall of gods?

"I don't know what your Laney saw, but I have no fight with Zephyros," Devlin said in a low voice. "I'm here to put an end to our troubles, not add to them." He stepped forward, and Anna hated it when Zeph came to Ella's side in a clearly defensive posture. "Is your name…are you Ella?" he asked, making Anna wonder why he didn't already know. Had they never before met? But weren't these gods his family? The woman nodded. "Well, then, is there anything I could do to put your mind at ease, Ella?"

Uncertainty crept over her stern expression, and she and Zeph traded glances.

Laney whispered something to Chrys. For a moment, they went back and forth. Finally, she said, "His aura is purple. It's pure, bright purple. Eurus's is a black so dark it deadens the light around him. I think…he's not like his father."

Aeolus whirled on the group. "Of course he's not! I'll not hear this debate any longer. For the thousandth time, he is not his father. At great personal risk, he has trained to help us. At additional great risk, he plans to travel into the Eastern Realm to retrieve Eurus's key. I expect better of every one of you. If the father is the best and only way to judge the son, then that doesn't say much for you two, does it?" He stared pointedly at Zephyros, then Chrysander. "Because as you've both pointed out—and correctly, I'll admit—this whole situation, from the way I treated Eurus to his long history of retribution to hiding the loss of the Firestone ring, is my fault. I've been an arrogant, conceited god for most of my existence, reveling in my power over others as a means of grappling with the losses I've suffered. Should the world hold you responsible for all that because of your association with me?"

The woman beside him rubbed Aeolus's back, and the gesture left Anna with the impression they were together.

Chrys's and Zeph's mouths both hung open, as if they'd never heard Aeolus say such things before. And though some part of Anna resented whatever role Aeolus had played in the bad things that'd happened to Devlin, another part was cheering the older god's defense of him. Anna looked to see Devlin's reaction, and was heartsick to find him head down, shoulders hunched, fists clenched. Clearly uncomfortable and defensive and bowing under the open debate on his character.

"Children bearing the sins of the parents. It's a timely question, my lord," said a woman's voice from behind the group of Anemoi. The group parted, and a strikingly beautiful woman walked regally between them. She wore a long, shimmering dress that appeared to be different colors as she moved and shifted, and her almost-white hair included strands of sky-blue highlights. Anna gasped. In the woman's hand, she carried a tall, winged staff that glittered and threw off prisms of light, and around her waist, a small silver flask attached to a braided silken belt.

"Iris, welcome back," Aeolus said, as she sank into a graceful curtsy.

Wait, Iris? As in…goddess of the rainbow and my ancient ancestor Iris? Anna gaped at the woman as butterflies whipped through her belly. Translucent colors trailed behind her every movement like a train on a gown. A living embodiment of the rainbow.

The woman rose and her blue-eyed gaze settled on Anna. Iris's magic shimmered all around her, and Anna found it stunningly beautiful. Grief suddenly gripped Iris's expression.

"Iris, may I introduce you to Annalise Fallston? Anna, this is your forebear, Iris, goddess of the rainbow and messenger of the gods," Aeolus said, beckoning them together.

Anna's heart was trying to run away it was beating so hard. "Hello," she said, feeling the strong urge to curtsy herself but fearing she'd look ridiculous. Devlin's hand fell on the small of her back, and she could've kissed him for the silent support because she was shaking so bad she was sure everyone could tell.

Iris approached Anna with an avid curiosity on her face. "Are you well, child?" she asked.

"Uh, yes. Yes, I'm fine."

"You are beautiful," she said.

Heat flooded into Anna's face, especially since she was a very pale reproduction of the Technicolor goddess standing in front of her. "Thank you," she managed.

"May I embrace you?" Iris asked, her hands fluttering at her chest.

"Of course," she said.

Iris smiled and then the goddess's arms surrounded her. She was little, just like Anna, and warm, and she smelled of rain on roses, clean and sweet. Emotion clogged Anna's throat, and the moment felt so significant she forgot all about their audience. Finally, Iris withdrew, but she clasped Anna's hands in hers and stared at her.

Something flashed behind her blue eyes, and she pressed her lips into a thin line. "How old are you, Anna?" she finally asked.

"Twenty-nine."

Iris's jaw dropped open and her cheeks paled. "And when is your birthday?"

"September thirtieth," she said.

Impossibly, Iris paled further. She put her hand to her forehead. "No," she said pleadingly.

Anna glanced over her shoulder at Devlin and found on his face the same dread that was crawling into her belly. "What?" Anna asked her.

"You turn thirty in two weeks?" she asked, incredulity and outrage straining her voice. She turned to Aeolus. "You must keep her here. Do not let her return to the human world."

Aeolus exchanged concerned glances with the men. "Why?"

"She cannot go there anymore."

The storm god frowned. "Iris—"

"She's my daughter," Iris said, "and she will die if she goes back."

Goosebumps rippled over Anna's skin. Her...*what*? She didn't know what to believe, what to think. Anna pressed her hands to her face as tears pricked the back of her eyes—tears for the distress pouring off this woman. "I don't understand," Anna whispered.

Iris grasped her hand again, though the goddess's grip had gone ice cold. "I mean exactly what I say, Annalise. You are of my flesh and blood. And you are cursed—we both were. In the human world, where your powers are suppressed, you are destined to die on your thirtieth birthday. Truth be told, I'm surprised you seem so well."

Anna shook her head. "My mother died years ago. Her name was Tessa—"

"No, child," Iris said, her expression so sad. "She was but a vessel for the life I brought forth thousands of years ago. A baby I was forced to give up because my race of gods, the Titans, fought to wrest control from your father's race. As punishment for the forbidden affair, the Titan elders commanded that I never see your father again and that I place you in the human realm immediately after birth. Now things are different, but then, the war between the gods made the world so volatile that the Titans feared the power you would grow to possess. They couldn't destroy you, because you were stronger, even then, so they cursed you twice over to limit your power—first by imposing death in each lifetime on your thirtieth birthday, and second by only allowing each new reincarnation a certain, small proportion of your true power."

"I'm, um, I'm not all the way well." Instinctively, she reached back for Devlin's hand, which gripped hers immediately.

Iris frowned. "What do you mean?"

Anna shook her head, trying to gather her thoughts. "Six months ago I was diagnosed with an incurable syndrome because I'm exhausted and in pain almost all of the time."

"The curse," Iris gasped.

"This can't be," Anna said, hearing her own voice as if through a long tunnel.

"But it is. You are my daughter, and I am your mother. And you are a goddess."

A…a goddess? Anna shuddered out a breath. "And I'm going to die in fourteen days?"

"They never expected you to make your way back to the Realm of the Gods, or even to learn what you really are. The curses don't apply here, Anna. Here, you will live and in time, you will come into your full powers. Which is why you must not leave. Oh, gods, I cannot believe we are actually here together." She clasped her hands in front of her chest, waves of pink light trailing her movements.

Anna wished she shared Iris's joy. But she couldn't just take off living some new life and leave her old one behind. She had friends, family, responsibilities… "I can't just stay here. I have a father at home who needs me."

Devlin gently squeezed her shoulders and stood right behind her. Anna sagged against his strength and warmth. "Iris, if I may," Devlin said in a tight voice. "Who is her divine father?"

Iris wrung her hands and paced a few steps away. Anna didn't want the answer to this question. As it was, her world was being dismantled brick by brick until she barely recognized her own life. To be told her father wasn't really her father? No. Anna didn't want that at all. And then Iris returned again. "Though he never knew about you," she said, "your father is the primordial god, Erebus."

Gasps rang out from around the group, followed by whispers that grew in volume. But it was all white noise against the roar in her head. Not because she recognized the god's name, but because she was seriously engaged in a conversation wherein the parents she'd known her whole life weren't truly her parents.

Needing a break from the intensity of the beautiful goddess who might possibly be her biological mother, Anna turned in Devlin's arms and buried her head against his chest. His hands went to her hair, stroking, soothing. Finally, she lifted her gaze to his. "Is it true?"

He searched her gaze for a long moment. "She has no reason to lie," he said. "In fact, as the messenger of the gods, she's not capable of it."

"That's right, rain god," Iris said from behind Anna. "By Zeus's decree am I unable to perjure myself."

"But that…that means…"

"I fell for a goddess?" He shrugged with one shoulder. "Already knew that."

A sad chuckle bubbled up from within the massive wave of confusion building inside of Anna. "But my father, Devlin…"

"Is still your father." He looked over Anna's shoulder to Iris. "She has two weeks?"

"You love her, Devlin Eston?" Iris asked, tone suddenly no-nonsense. He gave a solemn nod that made Anna's heart squeeze. "Then you cannot chance it. If she dies in the human realm, she would be lost to you forever. She would be lost to both of us."

Feeling like the walls of the cavernous room were closing in on her, Anna shook her head. "But—"

"Hey," he said, "look at me." Anna brought her gaze back to his concerned face. "We will work this out somehow."

"Somehow?" He nodded. "Are we still lying in my bed? Maybe I'm dreaming." He twisted his lips in regret, and it told her everything she didn't really want to know. "Okay. Okay," she said to herself. She heaved a long breath and turned to Iris. "So, uh, who is this Erebus?"

"One of the oldest deities in the universe," Aeolus said in a reverent voice. "The god of darkness. Son of Chaos, the being from which all life sprang forth." Aeolus lowered to a knee. The woman wearing the scarf followed suit.

"The god of darkness?" She spun to Devlin. "Is that why I can make the light come and go?"

He brushed his knuckles along her cheekbone and tucked her hair behind her ear. "Very likely." Anna felt like the amazing colors of the room spun around her until they turned into a multicolored blur. The daughter of the rainbow and the god of darkness? Her? And if it was true, did that explain why she was both color-blind and able to see and manipulate color while she painted? And did Iris's belief that her powers would strengthen in the Realm of the Gods explain why she was seeing in full color now?

Just considering these things as real stole her breath.

And then the surreal nature of the moment escalated as, one by one, the other gods and goddesses in the room followed suit. Chrysander. Zephyros. Ella. Owen.

Smiling, Iris sank into a curtsy so deep, her head almost touched the floor.

Beside her, Devlin grasped her hand, pressed a kiss to her knuckles, and knelt. He laid his forehead against her fingers.

Anna's heartbeat tripped into a sprint. "What...uh...please get up," she whispered. "I don't...I'm not..."

"Annalise," Devlin said, looking up at her with abject awe. "You are the ranking deity in this room. By a long shot."

CHAPTER EIGHTEEN

And Devlin had thought he wasn't good enough for Anna *before*.

By Zeus and all the Olympians, her lineage as Erebus's daughter was so rarefied that just the thought of it ran a shiver of wonder over Devlin's skin.

"Um, thank you, but please," she said, tugging on his hand, urging him up.

But as far as he was concerned, she deserved every bit of the honor being bestowed upon her in this moment. And he was damn glad to see that the others obviously thought so, too, because no one moved a muscle.

Finally, Iris and Aeolus rose, and the others followed suit. Awkwardness washed over Devlin's skin when he stood, knowing without a shadow of a doubt that every god in the room was silently thinking he had no business being with the daughter of one of the primordials. He withdrew his hand from Anna's and crossed his arms over his chest, pretending not to see the question in her eyes when he did.

"Iris," Zeph said. "There's something we were hoping you could help us with."

Standing next to her daughter, Iris arched a brow. "My darling sisters?" That made them sound way the hell too nice. Her sisters were the Harpies, a group of vicious, cruel, screeching bird-women known for abducting and torturing for the sheer fun of it. And as of a few days ago, they'd seemed happy to turn their treachery on Eurus's enemies. How his father had gotten the Harpies as allies, Devlin had no clue, though from what he understood the bird-bitches were pretty cheap and easy.

"They're working with Devlin's father," Zeph said, and hell if it hadn't felt like a purposeful jab. "And they nearly killed Chrysander and Boreas a few days ago when they caught us unawares. Would you consider putting a leash on them until we get Eurus under control?"

Iris sighed and said to Anna, "Your aunts. I'm forever chasing and cleaning up after them. I'd like to say they're harmless, but I can't lie." She scanned her gaze over the group of gods. "Keep Anna safe. Keep her *here*. And you can consider it done."

Anna gaped and her expression filled with displeasure. Devlin had to resist the urge to comfort her.

"Thank you, Iris," Zeph said, nodding.

"Your helping level the playing field will not be forgotten," Aeolus said with a small bow.

"Bringing Eurus down has been a long time coming. I'm only too glad to see it finally done." Iris's gaze turned toward Anna, then to Devlin standing beside her. "You are fighting against your father, then?" she directed at him.

"I'm fighting against evil," he said, feeling the weight of the coming battle on his shoulders. "They happen to be the same thing."

Zeph coughed, a forced, skeptical sound.

Devlin's gaze swung to the Western god. Same story, different fucking century. No way they could be successful in battle together with this bullshit creating a debris field between them. "Gods be damned, what do you want from me, Zephyros Martius? What will it take to put this behind us so we can spend our time strategizing the fight ahead rather than refighting the conflicts of the past?"

Fists clenched, Zephyros nodded at Iris. "Pass the messenger's test on every question I have."

Confusion had Devlin frowning. What test? But before he'd

opened his mouth, Aeolus shook his head and said, "Absolutely not."

Which didn't help Devlin's confusion at all. "What test?" he asked. Without touching him, Anna stepped beside him as if lending her silent support. And damn if he didn't need it, no matter how sure he was he didn't deserve it. Not from her.

Clasping the flask at her waist, Iris stepped into the middle of the three-way standoff. "This is easily enough done." She tilted her head as if evaluating Devlin.

"It's too dangerous," Aeolus said. "He already has the Styx flowing through him."

Surprise widened Iris's eyes and mouth, and colors rippled on the air as she turned to Aeolus. "How did this come to be?"

Aeolus held up his hand, the one still bandaged around his amputation. "Eurus stole the ring that holds ultimate power over the winds, the weather, and the seasons. I needed to regain some advantage against him, and Devlin agreed to let me turn him into the tool most capable of bringing his father down. He drank a potion made of the Styx and the Phlegethon."

Iris gasped and cut her concerned gaze to Devlin. Her expression was almost disbelieving. "How did you survive it? Drinking those together is a bit like swallowing a nuclear bomb."

"It was a rough few days at first," Devlin said in what might've been the biggest understatement of his life. For the better part of a week, he'd thought he was going insane as uncontrollable fire had spilled from his pores and licked over his skin day and night, elevating the feelings of rage and hate inside him until he was no longer anything *but* rage and hate. Then, suddenly, the fire had seeped inside his skin and over the course of the two days that followed he regained his consciousness and sense of self.

"Indeed," Iris said. "Aeolus is correct, then." She turned and addressed Zeph and the other Anemoi gathered behind him. "Normally, a drink of enchanted water from the River Styx," she said, unhooking the flask from her belt, "will merely put a liar to sleep. But in Devlin's case, because the river flows through him already, I fear the reaction would be volatile. And I cannot predict what that might mean."

Anna sucked in a sharp breath.

Devlin nailed Zeph with a stare, and before he even allowed the other god to react to Iris's assessment of the situation, Devlin said, "I'll do it. Ask me your questions." Otherwise, this shit was never going to be put to rest.

"Devlin, no," Anna said, putting her arm across his stomach like she was holding him back. Or shielding him. "Why doesn't what Aeolus said matter to you all? I realize I know very little of what's gone on between you, but you have to admit in the days that I have been here, Devlin's been nothing but committed to this goal you all have in common."

"But for what reason?" Zeph said. "That's what we've never known."

Anger and resentment clawed up Devlin's spine. Why was it necessary for him to throw light on every humiliating, dark corner of his soul to earn some basic fucking respect? Fine. Let him ask his questions. This was it, though. Last time. If Devlin didn't walk away from this test with their belief in his motives, he wasn't ever trying again. "So ask me. I *said* I'll do it."

Anna turned and clutched his sides, her grip on him warm and commanding. "You've been hurt enough."

"I need to do this," he said, nodding toward the other gods. "We need for me to do this. But you should step back."

Instead, Anna came closer, her chest against his. So close she had to tilt her head way back to hold his gaze. "No, Devlin—"

Zeph laid his hand on Anna's arm. "Anna, you should—"

The light in the room dimmed in direct proportion to her head turning to glare at him. "Back off. Please," she gritted out, the room sinking into darkness. Tension buzzed through the air. As quick as it had gone dark, the light returned. Anna was looking at him again, and Zeph had in fact backed off. Devlin got perhaps a perverse amount of pleasure from that fact. Damn if Anna's power wasn't sexy as fuck—and clearly getting stronger, just as Iris had said. "I'm not going anywhere. If you're doing this, I'm staying by your side. Just like the firestorm, Devlin. Watch me. Focus on me. Whatever this is, we'll deal with it together."

He slid his hand around her neck and leaned down. "You are everything that is good and right and true in the world, Annalise." Then he forced his gaze to Iris. "Now let's do this."

"As you wish." She unscrewed the flask. "You will take a drink. I will ask you a question. Answer it truthfully and there should be no consequence. Answer it falsely, and…" Iris shook her head, sparkles of color twinkling from her pale hair. So like Anna's. "With you, I'm not sure what will happen, but the Styx will exact some consequence." Iris stepped closer and offered the flask, but she pulled it back just as Devlin reached for it. "Since we don't know what the consequence will be, I'm going to have to ask you to lie on purpose to a question that doesn't matter so we can know what a lie will look like on the questions that do."

Joy. "I have some breaking and entering to do yet today, so let's get to it." Looking deep into Anna's eyes, Devlin accepted the flask and took a swig. Sour bitterness filled his mouth and burned a trail down his throat to his gut. He wiped a drop off his lip with the back of his hand.

Iris gave a nod. "What color is your hair?"

"Black."

Another nod. "Is Eurus your father?"

He chuffed out a disgusted halflaugh as an itching, cloying heat slithered along his nervous system and invaded every part of his body. "Yes."

"Where did you and Annalise meet?" Iris asked.

"Her studio," he said, his muscles going rigid and tight from the additional infernal water inside him. His heart pounded out a thunderous boom in his chest.

"Drink again," Iris said. He did, sending his body temperature up another couple good notches. "Do you want Anna to die? Lie this time, please."

Rage at the question, the thought, the very idea. "No, I do *not* want her to die. And I will not lie about that. Ever. Next question." Anna's hands rubbed his sides as if she was trying to soothe and calm him.

"Very well," Iris said. "Did you conspire with Aeolus to drink of the Styx and Phlegethon and defeat Eurus? Now, *lie*."

Devlin released a deep breath, bracing for...he didn't even know what. "No, we didn't—"

Snap, snap. Breath-stealing, inescapable pain. Devlin dropped to one knee and wrapped his arms around the right side of his rib cage as Iris's magic cracked his ribs.

"Oh, God. Look at me, look at me, Devlin." Kneeling beside him, Anna's hands cupped his jaw and her thumbs stroked his cheek. He met her gaze, and it was only the love shining from her eyes that kept him from lashing out. Whether or not Devlin deserved that love was not a question that mattered in the heat of this moment. "I'm here," she said.

"Next," he said, his voice like sandpaper.

"Zephyros?" Iris asked.

Zeph planted his hands on his hips. At least his broken ribs had earned Devlin something, because the smug self-righteousness of moments before was gone from the Western god's face. "Did he double-cross Aeolus and purposely lead Eurus to Gibraltar the other day?"

Iris repeated the question, and Devlin answered, "No." No bones snapped. True.

"If he's on our side, why didn't he help when the Harpies attacked at Gibraltar?" Zeph asked.

Devlin swallowed against the acid rising up the back of his throat. "I told you. Eurus had chained me to the rock with his will. He wanted all of you to doubt my loyalty." All of Devlin's bones remained intact again.

"Why did you agree to work with Aeolus?" Zeph asked, his tone a lot less aggressive than it had been moments before.

"Because I wanted help putting an end to Eurus and freeing myself and my brother." True.

"I think that's enough," Owen said, his mismatched eyes flashing with silvery light. "He's done more than enough to prove himself."

Devlin shook his head and nailed Zephyros with a hard stare. "Get it out of your system now, my lord, because I'm never giving you free rein like this again. That's for goddamned sure." The broken ribs made it burn like a bitch to breathe normally.

"Drink again, Devlin," Iris said. He did, anger humming inside his body now.

"Did you obstruct Chrysander this summer in his efforts to find and apprehend Eurus?" Zephyros asked. Iris repeated.

A single nod. "Yes," Devlin said.

"Why?" they asked in succession.

Uncontrollable tremors racked Devlin's body from the buildup of anger and preternatural power inside him. "Because Eurus commanded it of me. He expected it of me. He used a variety of ways of getting me to do what he wanted."

"Like?" Zeph asked.

Sonofabitch. He really didn't want to get into the specifics. Aeolus and the Anemoi had seen him shirtless, for gods' sakes. They could use their damn imagination. "You don't need to know all the gory details." *Snap.* "Aw, fuck," he gasped as a rib on the left side fractured. "Whippings, beatings, brandings with a hot poker, solitary imprisonment without food or water, marking me as his slave," he said, thrusting out his wrists and grimacing when the movement rattled his broken ribs. His hands visibly shook.

Anna grasped them and brought them to her face, then kissed his knuckles over and over.

Devlin met and held her gaze, the only thing in the world that could get him through these words. "Killing my brother in front of my eyes as punishment for disobedience, and imprisoning and torturing my other brother to guarantee it didn't happen again." Devlin panted, sweat making his hair stick to his forehead. The warmth of Anna's touch surrounded him as she slipped her arm around his back and tucked herself gently against his left side. He couldn't help leaning against her, just a little. "How's that for some examples?"

"Is it your plan or intention to harm anyone in this room?" Zeph asked, his voice low and tone regretful.

"Unequivocally, *no*," Devlin ground out, holding Zeph's intense blue gaze. "Any. More?"

"No, I'm done," Zephyros said, his expression serious. "And it's obvious I owe you a huge apology."

"Whatever," Devlin said, struggling to his feet and hugging his ribs as he tried to take in a deep breath. It was like getting shanked every time he tried to fill his lungs. "You'll forgive me if I'm not particularly in a make-nice sorta mood right now."

Zeph sank to a knee in front of him and bowed his head. Devlin would've been less surprised if the god had smacked him for dishing out the attitude. Before the lesser Anemoi had done it the night before, no one had *ever* bowed to Devlin—and now the strongest of the Anemoi was down on his knees before him. "I have grievously wronged you, Devlin Eston, and I humbly apologize and ask your forgiveness. The West Wind pledges to stand as your friend and ally evermore."

"I'm sorry, too, Devlin," Ella said. She went to kneel next to Zeph, and Devlin caught her hand and pulled her up. Pain lanced down his sides.

"Not necessary," he said, his voice suddenly tight, not from the pain of his ribs but from the significance of their gestures. "Please."

Zephyros rose, dark-blue light flaring from behind his eyes. "I'm sorry I let my issues with your father color my opinion of you," he said. "And I'm sorry I—we," he said, gesturing to the whole group, "did nothing to intercede in your situation."

Heat surged into Devlin's cheeks and he dropped his gaze to the floor. "Okay," he managed.

Awkwardness invaded the space between them, and then Zeph said, "I'd like to heal those ribs if you'd let me."

Devlin shook his head. The last few minutes had already put him under the spotlight almost more than he could tolerate. "I'm fine," he said, pretending not to notice the exchanges of concerned glances.

Zeph stepped closer, his voice gentle when he spoke. "We need you in the best possible fighting shape if you're going to survive whatever the Eastern Realm throws at you." When Devlin opened his mouth to turn him down again, Zeph cut him off. "If you won't do it for yourself, do it for Anna. Give her one less thing to worry about while you're gone."

Devlin cut his gaze to Anna, standing beside him, and managed to catch how her expression almost melted in relief before she schooled her reaction. "Do you want me to do this?" he asked her, a weird sensation squeezing his chest.

"Remember what we talked about earlier today? Give yourself the advantage." She shrugged like it was totally cool with her either way, but Devlin didn't think he was imagining the fear in her eyes. And he hated that, for her.

"Fine," he said. If it would give everyone one less thing to worry about today, he'd give in even though he hated all this attention.

"Just, uh, lift your shirt," Zeph said, light already shimmering from his palms. "This won't take long."

When Devlin hesitated, everyone got busy talking to one another and saying good-byes. Off to one side, Laney unfastened a necklace and held it out to Owen, who shook his head, but eventually relented. Farther back, Ella walked up to Seth, and then they joined the other group. Off to the other side, Aeolus and Tisiphone stood together and made no effort to look away. Of course, they'd been with him from the beginning of all this—Aeolus suggesting the partnership and Tisiphone making it possible by bringing them the water from the infernal rivers. The head of snakes hidden under her scarf aside, Devlin had actually grown to like the Fury in the weeks he'd trained with Aeolus. She had the driest and most cutting wit he'd ever known, but was loyal and had accepted him without question. Aeolus gave Devlin a nod.

Devlin lifted his shirt and fought back the urge to squirm and cover himself. Most of them had seen his scars anyway. What was one more time? The moment Zeph projected that glowing light on the right side of his rib cage, Devlin nearly groaned in relief and forgot all about his bitching. Why in the world had he rejected this again? "Aw, Hades, that feels better," Devlin said to Zeph when he finished a minute later. "Thank you."

"Least I could do. The very least. We are all here for each other," he said, his words quieting the room. "And you are one of us. You need something? Anna needs something? Just ask. Always."

A knot formed in Devlin's throat, and he had to swallow twice to clear it. He nodded and ducked his chin to hide whatever his face might be doing.

"I'm afraid I'm the one who most failed you, Devlin," Aeolus said from behind Zephyros. "I know I've apologized to you before, but I want to say again, here, in front of everyone, that I'm sorry for letting you and your brothers down, for being so self-absorbed that I ignored Eurus both as an impressionable young god and later, when he had children of his own. My neglect of him—and of you—are sins that break my heart and pierce my soul."

Devlin nodded, afraid his voice would fail him if he tried to speak. But their words, their emotions, their efforts to gain *his* forgiveness were so surreal that his head actually hurt.

"Devlin?" Laney said, coming closer with Chrysander right behind her. Her bright-blue eyes didn't exactly track on his face when she looked at him. "I want to apologize to you, too. I think what happened here today is all my fault." Her expression was earnest and sad.

"I'm sure it's not," he said, overwhelmed by the pain and the remorse flowing off of everyone. For him. It made it even harder to breathe.

"The visions I have…it's all new. And what I see isn't always clear."

"Speaking of visions," he said, hoping to deflect all this attention away from himself, "this is Anna. She's pretty new to getting visions, too."

"Hi, Anna," Laney said, a bit of shyness in her voice. She held out her hand and waited, and something about the way she moved and where her eyes landed cemented Devlin's suspicion that the woman's vision was off.

"Hi," Anna said, shaking Laney's hand. "I'd love to talk to you about your visions."

Laney agreed with a smile.

"What did you mean about my aura being purple?" he asked.

"Oh, well, I have a degenerative eye disease and very little regular vision left. But for some reason I perceive a glowing light around each of the gods. Yours is purple." She looked in Anna's direction. "And yours is really interesting, Anna. It changes color and intensity. And then, when it got dark in here before, it disappeared altogether. I could still see all the other gods' auras in the dark, but you were just a…blank, I guess is the best way to describe it. You're pink right now," she said. "Isn't that the strangest thing?"

Anna smiled. "Very, but it's pretty cool, too."

Devlin nodded. "And how do you know Eurus's is black?" he asked, dread slipping into his already-sour belly.

"Because a few days ago he attacked me and Chrys at my house." She shrugged, as if it were no big deal. Standing behind her, Chrysander squeezed her shoulders and pressed a kiss to the top of her head.

Of course, that's what his father had done. "I'm sorry," Devlin said.

"Thank you, but it wasn't your fault."

"Okay," Devlin said, way less comfortable with everyone's eyes on him than he'd been ten minutes before.

"For what it's worth, I'm sorry I doubted you, too," Chrysander said. "I meant what I said at Anna's studio. I'm ready to fight by your side."

Devlin nodded. Was it hot in here or was it just him?

Owen brought a cute, very pregnant blonde forward next. "Devlin, I would like to introduce my wife, Megan," Owen said.

"Hello," Devlin said, feeling like an idiot. But he appreciated Owen's gesture down deep—both that the guy *hadn't* apologized and that he'd stood up for him while the interrogation had been underway.

"Hi," she said with a smile. "Oh." Her hands flew to her belly, and she laughed. "I think the kid wants to say hi, too."

Devlin's gaze dropped to her belly. "Congratulations on the baby," he murmured as he wondered how it must feel to know that your daughter or son grew in the belly of the woman you loved. His imagination offered up the fantasy of Anna's belly, round with *his* child— Devlin squashed that one like the insidious little bug it was. "You're a lucky man," he said to Owen unthinkingly.

"I am," Owen said.

Another awkward silence descended for a moment, and then Anna said, "And you are?" Devlin followed her gaze to a human man standing back from the group.

"Seth," the man called out.

"Oh, Seth's my friend," Laney said, waving him forward. "After the battle the other night, the Anemoi brought me, Seth, and Owen's friend Tabitha here to safety." Laney put her hand to her mouth and leaned close. "Apparently, that's not really allowed," she whispered. The gods chuckled.

"Hey," the man said quietly, his expression serious and also a bit bewildered. "Nice to meet you." He offered his hand to Devlin, and they shook, and then to Anna.

"Oh," she said as her hand touched Seth's. Anna's gaze flew to Seth's face, then went distant.

"What is it?" Devlin asked, dread stirring up the heat inside him. He came closer and stroked his palm down her hair.

Laney grasped her hand. "Are you okay, Anna? Oh my God. I can see what you're seeing."

The men traded glances at her declaration, and everyone moved in closer.

For a moment that seemed to go on forever, the vision held both women in its thrall. And then they both blinked, looked at each other, and started talking animatedly at the same time. What the hell could it be now?

"He's some kind of creature," Anna said.

"Yes, it's called a griffin, but I've never seen it that clearly in my visions before," Laney said excitedly.

"Like a lion, but with wings," Anna said, looking from Seth to Devlin and back again.

Laney nodded. "With an eagle's head. But what was going on? Could you tell?"

"No, it seemed that he was defending someone, but I couldn't tell who or why."

"What were those black things?" Laney asked.

"I didn't see that. What did they look like?"

Shoulders slumping, Laney said, "It was hard to tell, but they were everywhere. You didn't see that part, though?"

"Wow. No. Does that mean we saw different parts of the same thing?"

"I don't know," Laney said. "We'll have to try it again the next time it happens to one of us."

"Definitely." Anna nodded and turned to Devlin. "That was so wild. I don't feel like I have to paint it this time."

Devlin thought about what the women had said. "You're a griffin?" he asked Seth.

The man crossed his arms and frowned. "So I've been told, but I'm way the heck out of my depth here, to be honest. I don't know what I believe."

Well, Devlin could sure as hell relate to that.

"I shall go find my sisters, then," Iris said to Aeolus. "But afterward, if it's okay with you, my lord, I'd like to come back and spend some time with Anna?"

"Of course," Aeolus said. "My door is always open to you, Iris. And we thank you for your help."

"Well, it's the least I could do after you found my daughter. After all this time."

Aeolus smiled but shook his head. "You have to thank Devlin for that."

"Yes, I do," she said, moving in front of him. "You, Devlin Eston, are brave and true, and I'm moved beyond words that you found her. Not just for me, but for her, too. You are a good match. Thank you."

The words made Devlin a little dizzy, or maybe that was just his inability to take a deep breath. *Good? Me? And true?* "You're welcome," he whispered, no idea how to respond to the rest but cherishing the sentiments from the bottom of his heart.

Iris bowed her head to him, to Anna, and then to Aeolus, and disappeared in a small shower of colored light.

Devlin scrubbed a hand through his hair. "I should go, too," he said.

Anna put her hands on his chest and peered up at him. "Already?"

"The clouds and rain at your house this morning were the outer bands of Eurus's storm, and it's already escalated to a hurricane," he said. "I've delayed longer than I should've as it is."

"I'm coming, too," Zephyros said. "You shouldn't face this on your own."

The warmth of belonging settled over Devlin's shoulders. Between Anna's love and the Anemois' apologies, Devlin felt a part of something—a part of a *family*—in a way he never had before. And despite the emotional roller coaster, it left him feeling stronger and more resilient than he'd ever felt in his life. He nodded to Zeph.

Owen whispered something to Megan, then kissed her cheek. "Me, too."

"I've got your back, man," Chrys said.

"Then it's settled," Aeolus said. "We'll all go. The entire cadre of lesser Anemoi have arrived now, and Tisiphone said she'd stay, so we've got plenty of coverage here."

"We should leave right away, then," Devlin said. "The sooner I find that key, the sooner we put an end to this once and for all."

CHAPTER NINETEEN

They were almost to the Eastern Realm. Home.

No, not anymore. At least, not for a long time. Though he supposed if they were successful at defeating Eurus and Devlin succeeded to his Cardinal Anemoi position, Devlin would have to return. Rebuild. Restore.

Be ready for anything, Devlin said as they crossed over the border into his father's realm. What before had been calm, peaceful skies now left him with a feeling of dreadful anticipation. It was *too* quiet, *too* peaceful, *too*…easy. Yeah. *You all should hang back. Let me take it from here.*

We're coming, Devlin. Aeolus. *As far as we can.*

Hailed pelted down from the skies, rocks of ice the size of Devlin's fist. He flinched as the first chunks of ice made impact. Had the gods been corporeal, each hailstone would've caused savage bruises and broken bones. But even in an elemental form, hail this size could send shockwaves of phantom pain through them with each impact against the core of their preternatural being.

Hang back. I got this, Chrysander said. He shot up, up above them, and then unleashed a blast of heat in a circle around him. As the hailstones passed through Chrys's shield, they melted so they turned into small shards of ice or into rain altogether. *Everybody okay?* he called.

Affirmatives rang out from the group.

And then came the clouds. So thick, dense, and black that it became quickly disorienting. And there was no flying above or around them, either. The gods agreed to slow their forward progress lest they run smack into some trap or foe they'd have no time to see.

The very fact that Devlin was experiencing these defenses the same as the others proved he'd lost his father's favor—not that he'd truly ever had it. But only when Eurus wanted to make a point or exact punishment did he set his enchantments to inhibit Devlin's return to the realm.

Quick flashes of orange and gold electricity jagged through the clouds.

Grunts and shouts echoed through the blind nothingness as they dodged the seeking bolts. One good hit with electricity of this magnitude could easily force them out of their elemental state—or at least make it a helluva lot harder to hold. Forced into their physical form and *then* hit? Bye-bye heart rhythm.

Damnit all to Hades, Devlin shouldn't have to face this bullshit in his own realm.

He banked right, then left, narrowly missing a twin set of bolts chasing him, wanting him. Then two more, in quick succession. On and on it went like that until their collective evasive maneuvers had whipped up a windstorm all around them.

Someone cried out in agony. He couldn't tell who, just that it came from behind.

Finally, they cleared the cloud bank—and came out right in the middle of three monster tornadoes. Spinning, bending, roaring, the rotating storms pulled inexorably at the Anemoi as they attempted to navigate between them. The funnels seemed to possess some unholy awareness, as they lurched in front of the gods and forced them back or sideways.

I'll try to call them to the north. All of you, dart around them, Aeolus said. As the storm god, his powers normally gave him the ability to control and manifest all manner of storm elements. It was how he'd been the one to spawn the Anemoi winds long ago. But without the ring, his powers weren't as extensive.

Aeolus shot hard to the north. Slowly, very slowly, the leftmost of the tornadoes lumbered in that direction. All the while, Devlin and the others struggled not to get sucked into the remaining massive vortexes. Their sound was unbelievable, so loud and turbulent, Devlin felt like he might vibrate into pieces.

Finally, the middle tornado began to move, too, following the first one northward as if against its will—and that was probably true, as Aeolus was fighting Eurus's magical command, not Mother Nature. That left the final tornado standing between them and the approach to Eurus's mountaintop compound.

I can't hold them! Aeolus shouted.

I have an idea, Devlin said to the others. *The three of you, take turns at skirting south around that last funnel. It will track your movements and block you. I'll shoot north around it. Just distract it however you can. And hurry.*

The three took off to the south.

With Aeolus luring the first two to the north and the Anemoi tricking the third one to veer southward, that left Devlin a needle to thread right up the middle.

Devlin shot like an arrow, straight and true between the storms. And, of course, they noticed. The two tornados Aeolus had been holding broke free, slingshotting across the sky toward him. The southern tornado had noticed his movement, too, and reversed its course back in his direction. Ahead of him, the two were closing in, converging—oh, damn it all to Hades, he wasn't going to make it.

Come on, you bitch, came Zeph's voice as he feigned breaking south again—really damn close to the heart of the funnel.

Watch out, Z! Chrys shouted.

As if torn by who posed the bigger threat, the more southerly tornado faltered.

Mentally cringing against the probable impact, Devlin darted through a gap so small he was surprised he'd made it without being sucked into one vortex or the other. A sharp cry sounded out from behind him. Zephyros? But Devlin couldn't stop to check, because the storms chased him, bearing down like their existence depended on halting his progress. Until they suddenly stopped as if they'd crashed into a glass wall and could come no farther. Triumph shot through him at the realization he'd crossed some invisible boundary beyond which they couldn't travel. Eurus couldn't have them tearing up the compound itself, after all.

Safe from the tornadoes, Devlin turned. Dread whipped through his psyche. The three existing storms had spawned two others, and now the Anemoi and Aeolus were trapped in between, unable to find a way forward to him, and blocked from returning into the roiling black clouds behind.

Go on, Devlin! Go! Aeolus called. *If we can't get through we'll backtrack to the boundary of the realm and wait for you there.*

Hating to leave them in such a precarious position, Devlin knew the best thing he could do was hurry his ass up.

Up ahead, the craggy mountain came into view with the dark, forbidding hulk of a castle rising up at the top. The flora of the mountain itself was mostly brown and gray and dead, a perpetual state of decay resulting from Eurus holding the place in stasis as if every day was the last day of autumn. "Bleak" and "uninviting" were generous ways of describing the home in which he'd grown up.

Devlin bypassed all the obvious points of entry into the fortress, as well as the ones that seemed more subtle but which he knew were in fact well defended. He flew around to the back of the curtain wall where the cliffs were steepest and most deadly and searched until he found a tiny rough-hewn hole he'd once as a very young god spent two months hand-drilling through the thick stone. He had half a dozen of these scattered throughout the castle walls, emergency points of ingress and egress about which Eurus didn't know and therefore couldn't magically seal off.

He whizzed through the opening and inside a dank, dim hallway.

Up ahead, a single burning torch threw off the only light. There shouldn't be anyone here—the lesser Anemoi of the East had all deserted Eurus and fought alongside the Cardinal Anemoi. But Eurus's dark magic would more than make up for their absence. And he had no idea what kinds of spells and enchantments Eurus had added recently.

Still in his elemental form, Devlin surveyed his surroundings to get his bearings. Eurus had cast spells over the building to confuse and entrap anyone who acted against him, so the hallways and stairs shifted and disappeared, especially when the dwelling felt threatened. Therefore, things never looked exactly the same—which was why Devlin had long ago devised a faint system of markings on the stone walls to help him identify his location. You'd see them only if you knew to look for them, but the various symbols he'd chalked low on the walls indicated what part of the castle he was in and where a particular door or passage led. The markings he was most interested in were the forbidding X's, because those were paths that led to Eurus's private suites, something Devlin generally tried to avoid, not seek out.

Hovering just above the stone floor, Devlin kept his eyes peeled searching for the X's and his ears trained for the sound of any movement. The place was quiet as a tomb—a fitting analogy given the lack of life that had ever taken place here. He passed a circle with a hash mark through it, indicating a dead end if he continued that way, two lines pointing upward indicating that the passageway led to stairs going to the upper floor. And then finally he came to the two lines next to an X. Bingo. The stairs here would go to the upper floors that housed his father's suite. Devlin was almost to the top when the staircase filled with stone in an effort to trap him within the wall.

Devlin bolted, just squeaking through the crack before the last of the space became blocked off. At the next marking of two lines and an X, Devlin wasn't so lucky: the stairs swung sideways fast, dumping him into a dead-end hallway and trying to strand him there. Backtracking, it took him two more tries to make it up another floor. Now he was close.

And now he could go no farther in his elemental form. As a security precaution, Eurus's magic would force anyone who tried to approach his apartments in the more stealthy elemental form into their physical form, and the magic by which he did it wasn't averse to breaking some bones in the transformation. He'd had enough bones broken today, fuck you very much.

Especially with no Zephyros here to fix him this time. Even though, holy Hades, letting the god be that close to him and touch him had made him feel a whole lot like he might crawl out of his skin. At least the massive wave of relief that washed over him immediately afterward helped beat back the worst of his anxiety.

Forcing his mind to the task at hand, Devlin skirted away from the anteroom into which the stairs had dumped him and toward the ceremonial center of the compound. A door there would provide the most direct route to Eurus's office, so he was gonna make a play for the time-saving front door since the Anemoi were out in the open waiting on him.

However, that door meant going into the Hall of the East Wind, something that Devlin absolutely loathed doing. It was where Devlin had most often been punished—and, more horrifically, where Farren had been murdered.

Screams, from up ahead. Back against the wall, Devlin froze. Real or a trap? And if real, who the hell was screaming and why? He crept along the wall, glancing behind him every so often just to be sure his senses hadn't failed him. You never knew, here. But everything was drab, foreboding, gray, stone walls and preternatural firelight. No decoration, no creature comforts, no natural light. And luckily no company, that he could see.

Closer still. The screams became more desperate. Then: "Devlin! Devlin, help!"

Devlin's whole body went ice cold. He recognized that voice. Farren.

Instinct had him taking off at a dead run, even as his rational mind caught up and questioned the logic of what was happening. Farren had been dead for well over a century. Devlin could not possibly be hearing him. And yet, a voice Devlin would know anywhere was screaming out for him to help.

By the time he stood with his back to the wall outside the arched entrance to the ceremonial hall, Devlin's heart hammered out a fast, shattering beat against his breastbone and he'd broken out in a cold sweat. Absolutely no idea what he was about to walk in on, Devlin counted to three, peered over his shoulder, and, finding it clear, plunged forward.

Empty. The great circular, domed Hall of the East Wind was empty except for him.

Yet the screams echoed around the cavernous space. The sound slithered into his brain and set him on edge, like nails on an emotional chalkboard. He crossed the room, doing a couple of 360s to make sure the room remained empty, until he came to a large black *E* tiled into the floor at the head of an inlaid compass rose. Blood spread in an oozing puddle at the bottom of the *E*, pushing up from the floor as if it was a living, breathing thing.

He stared at the bright red, so stark against the white and black tiles. The exact spot where Farren had died.

Nausea washed through Devlin's gut as rage and anger heated his own blood.

But if this was supposed to scare him? Not even close. Farren had idolized Devlin—which had made his death and Devlin's inability to prevent it so much fucking worse. So if Farren's spirit still roamed this place, it would mean him no harm. In fact, it would mean his little brother had been a silent witness to everything that had transpired since his death. No doubt Farren's ghost self would be up for a little ass-kicking itself.

The thought almost made Devlin smile even as Farren's screams played on an unending loop of misery from somewhere behind him.

I miss you, brother, Devlin thought as he pressed his fingers to the floor and allowed the spreading crimson to kiss his fingertips.

He smeared the blood in stripes over his cheeks, a *fuck you* to Eurus in the form of fraternal war paint. And then he crossed to the door behind Eurus's thankfully empty throne—but the *X* wasn't there. Crouching, he searched again, but…there was no mark at this door at all.

And then, as he sat there, the room spun—the dome in one direction, the floor-level wall of doors the other, and the floor itself rotated counterclockwise like the dome but at a much faster speed. So, this was new. Not sure what to expect, Devlin stayed low until the movement finished, grimacing against the screeching grind.

Finally, everything came to a stop—and the room had been totally reconfigured. The throne now sat at the bottom of the compass rose rather than the top, and no door existed where Devlin crouched.

He was going to have to go door by door. To all eight.

Round and round the circle he went without finding the one he'd marked as the direct route to his father's office. Dread and anger blossomed in equal proportion inside his chest.

There! He'd almost passed the door by when his gaze caught the *X* carved into the rock. Devlin reached for the handle…and the room started its presto-change-o routine again. *No!*

Devlin dashed after it. But running one direction on a floor moving the other and all different from the wall right next to you felt pretty much like a one-way ticket to vomiting. The floor sped up, as if the room were aware of Devlin's effort and was equally intent on thwarting him.

He lunged and grabbed the doorknob. When the walls stopped moving, Devlin used the forward motion he already had to crash his shoulder against the corner of the door. It exploded open, making Devlin glad there was no one here to hear it.

He hoped.

Bolting up the stairs, Devlin pushed hard for the top, but beneath his feet the steps grew higher and higher. No matter how many stairs he climbed or how fast, he never got any farther. *Not real, not real, not real*, he said with his eyes clenched tight. *Not real!* When he opened his eyes, he was nearing the top of the staircase and an ornate black door stood in front of him. He was half surprised it'd worked, but it was one of the things he'd learned as a child trying to cope with living in a place that terrified him.

Devlin burst through the door before it disappeared. He nearly fell into a stark rectangular room with two wooden chairs—the waiting area for Eurus's study. The desire to celebrate the victory of getting this far tempted him, but so much could yet go wrong that it would be a mistake. He could never get complacent in this place. Ever.

He gripped the interior door's handle. Locked.

He ran at it, shoulder braced for the impact. And ricocheted to the floor after an unsuccessful, bone-bending impact.

When his eyes stopped rolling around in his head, he found himself gazing at the ceiling—where a movie of sorts played clip after clip after clip from his life. The happy pictures of him and Farren and Alastor stole Devlin's breath. Gods, had they really ever laughed so freely? For long moments, Devlin lay there, mesmerized. The remembered happiness was such a balm, he never wanted it to end. He could just stay here forever, couldn't he? What did he have in his life that would make him feel any better than this?

Nothing.

Nothing at all.

So he could totally just stay right here.

Anna, a tiny voice whispered.

Devlin blinked.

Anna is real.

Devlin narrowed his gaze at the ceiling, where the happy memories played on and on. "This is a trap," he said, loudly. "Get up."

Crawling to his feet, Devlin's back screamed in achiness from not having moved for a while. How the hell long had he lain there? No way to tell, but Devlin would bet his ass it wasn't the five minutes it felt like.

Sonofabitch.

He couldn't open the door, break it down, or unlock it, since he didn't have the key. What did that leave?

Fire. He could burn it down. Assuming he could control the fire inside him.

He needed rage. One more image pulled from his mind more than did it: Eurus stabbing Farren in the back over and over as his brother attempted to crawl away on his stomach. Sparks flew off Devlin's hand at the memory of Farren's screams calling out to Devlin, who'd been blocked just outside the open door to the ceremonial hall by some unseen force. Flames flickered over Devlin's palms at the recollection of the soul-shattering frustration of being unable to help a brother he'd promised to protect. The handheld blazes grew and the flames rippled up Devlin's arms.

Shaking from the heat and the gathering energy of his new powers, he extended both arms toward the door and focused all his concentration and will upon it. He projected the fire outward, trying to find a balance between something that would be strong enough to be effective and not torching the whole place.

Damnit, work!

Trembling now, Devlin struggled to hold his focus and not go nuclear. His teeth clenched, bones rattled, and head throbbed at the effort. Fire licked outward, forming a ball around him he wasn't going to be able to control.

Watch me. Focus on me. Anna. Her words from before he'd submitted to Iris's test. The image of her beautiful pale face, so fragile and delicate in appearance, filled his mind's eye. She'd believed in his ability to rein in the fire in her backyard. If she were here now, she'd believe in him still. He could do this. He mentally tugged and pulled and wrestled the fire back into himself and concentrated it in the palms of his hands.

A giant ball of fire formed in front of him. With a yell, he threw it and it exploded against the door. Shards of wood and jagged bits of rock rained down around him, but the door still stood. *Again!* More heat, a bigger fireball, a harder projection.

This impact was so big that part of the wall crumbled in an

avalanche of stone. When the smoke cleared, the door was half gone, the rest engulfed in slowly consuming flames.

That would have to do. Devlin kicked a thick, broken board inward, and then carefully climbed through the tight opening, silently thanking Anna for helping him keep it together.

Eurus's office. Behind a massive carved wooden desk stood an equally massive floor-to-ceiling bookshelf filled with chests and boxes and trunks. Hundreds of them. Maybe even thousands.

How the hell am I going to decide which one?

CHAPTER TWENTY

Devlin hadn't been in this room for years. Bad memories of verbal tirades and painful punishments for a variety of mostly imagined slights and infractions echoed between the stone walls and filled Devlin with remembered dread.

The fire popped.

He turned and watched as the flames climbed up the molding around the doorjamb. Just one more reason to hurry the hell up.

Crossing the room, Devlin studied the massive bookshelf, his gaze jumping from a golden chest on a pedestal to a carved mahogany chest to a little silver keepsake box. It was just as Anna had painted it. And the only thing that kept Devlin from freaking out at the impossibility of this task was the fact that her painting had depicted him with Eurus's key in hand.

Question was, did how he was positioned in the painting tell him anything about which box?

Standing immediately in front of the bookshelf impressed him with just how hard this would be. Shelves stretched way above his head, so high he couldn't even see all the boxes and chests they held. He grabbed the heavy, ornate desk chair from behind him, swung it toward the shelf, and climbed up. Then he counted.

Ten shelves in all, each eight feet wide. All packed with boxes.

What Devlin most hated in this moment was the need to put himself in his father's shoes and mind. Eurus's ego would argue for the most ornate of the boxes, but he wouldn't want to be that obvious. And his father's quest to always be clever meant there would be some irony or twisted joke about his choice of box. The irreplaceable nature of the key and its life-and-death value argued for a box that locked in some way. Beyond those considerations, the size of the key in Anna's painting seemed to rule out the smallest of the boxes.

So where did that leave him?

A silver box with a compass rose inlaid with jewels caught his eye—not because of its ornate nature, but because the compass rose oriented the East at the top of the rose. Certainly represented Eurus's belief in the way the world *should* be. A small lock hung off the front, meeting that criterion, too. Reaching behind two smaller boxes on the fifth shelf, Devlin grasped the silver rectangle so he could examine it closer.

He turned it around in his hands and shook it, but the box made no noise and had no mechanisms on the outside that might release the lock. *Here goes nothing.* He grasped the little lock, melted it into a puddle of molten silver with his fire, and flicked the clasp upward. Muscles braced for anything, Devlin took a deep breath and opened the lid.

Nothing. Nothing inside and nothing happened.

Unsure what to make of the lack of consequences, Devlin frowned and dropped the box to the floor. It hit the stone with a clank as he turned back to the shelves. Next he chose a shiny, lacquered wooden box with a golden crown carved in the top. Understated and subtle, with something within that rattled when Devlin shook it. He melted the little lock and opened the top.

Cockroaches poured over his hand and up his arm. Devlin heaved the box across the room. It exploded in a shower of splinters against the stone wall. He beat and swiped at his arm and chest to knock the bugs off, and then stomped on them. Even when he thought they were all gone, his flesh crawled at the imagined sensation of their movement on his skin.

"Sonofabitch," he muttered. Just his father's kind of humor.

Blowing out a breath and scowling, Devlin reached for a long, thin hammered-bronze box that had the words "The Sun Rises in the East" etched in the top. Devlin shook his head. *Tell us what you really think of yourself, Eurus.* This lock was so dainty that Devlin was able to break it off.

Brilliant, blinding sunlight poured out of the box and burned Devlin's retinas. The intensity was so stunning, Devlin dropped the box, sending the light in a spin to the floor that created a dizzying strobe-light effect. Grasping the back of the chair for support, Devlin stepped down and then dropped to his knees. He used one hand to shield his eyes from the overpowering solar rays radiating from inside the bronze and the other to feel across the floor. Everywhere the light touched bare skin stung as if he'd been sunburned. His eyes wouldn't stop watering. Finally, he found the box and slammed the lid closed.

Nausea swamped Devlin as sunspots swam over his vision. He looked up at the boxes but his eyes' ability to focus was completely shot, and the effort to do so intensified their burning and gave him a bad case of vertigo.

He didn't have time to sit here until the effects wore off. Forcing himself up again, he selected a navy-blue box painted with the sun and stars. The lock on this one was woven out of some sort of thick twine. He couldn't break it with his hands no matter how hard he pulled, so he finally burned through the tangled heap of it and yanked it free.

Boom!

The sound was the first thing to hit him. Then the explosive's blast wave. Then he was flying across the room and slamming against the stone floor on the other side of the office.

Devlin coughed and rolled to his side, momentarily unsure what the hell had just happened. Dazed and half blind, he pushed himself into a sitting position. Damn it all to Hades, how much more of this could he take?

You find the key, you find the key, he repeated to himself. *So get up and do it.*

He staggered across the room, head and back screaming, and was surprised to find that the chair, the desk, even the bookshelf were exactly as they'd been. Apparently the box's explosion had affected only its opener. With a groan, he climbed back on the chair. The next box was another dud. The one after that spewed vines that tried to bind his hands. And the one after that unleashed a bright-red poisonous snake that divided into two when he chopped it in half with a piece of the broken silver box. He'd fried them with his powers, accidentally setting the desk on fire. Devlin gleefully unleashed the rain to douse it, not caring about the damage.

Choking on the smoke, Devlin set his sights on a heavy iron box on the third shelf up.

The dark color made him wonder if it could be made out of infernal iron, which would be ironic since infernal iron could kill a god, yet the key protected the life of his energy in the lantern. That had his father written all over it. He melted the lock and pushed its molten remains free. Sweat poured off his face, and he wiped it away with the back of his arm as he braced for the next blow.

He lifted the lid.

The golden key sat nestled in a fold of golden velvet. Devlin blinked and squinted, half convinced his blurry vision was playing tricks on him. He pulled the key free. The metal was cool and heavy in his fingers, and totally real.

Time to fly.

Across the study, down the stairs, and into the ceremonial hall.

Farren's screams and blood remained, and Devlin stopped long enough to offer a last promise of vengeance. *Snick, snick, bang.* Something smacked Devlin on the shoulder. He looked up and found the ceiling vibrating and pieces of the stone and tile raining down.

Devlin bolted across the compass rose as bigger and more deadly pieces started to fall. And then the ceremonial hall itself started spinning like a top. It was as if the building was mad at Devlin's success at finding the key. The movement stirred up wind that blew Devlin's sweaty hair into his eyes. The gravitational force turned the debris into projectiles that Devlin couldn't always successfully dodge. With the walls and floor spinning in opposite directions, Devlin lost sight of the exit.

Between his stinging eyes and the speed of the room's movement, Devlin didn't have a prayer of finding a way out. He had one recourse—he shifted into his elemental form and took his chances with his father's enchantments. He shot toward the exit and had just cleared the doorway into the wide foyer beyond when something with the power of a hammer crashed against his skull and forced him into his corporeal form. When Devlin looked over his shoulder, nothing was there.

He slammed to the floor, cradling his head. *The key!* His hand flew to his pocket…and relief flooded through him to find it still there.

Ignoring the pain and disorientation, Devlin got his ass off the floor and ran. And it was a good thing, because the ceilings caved in above him as he went. He dodged right and left, shifted in and out of the wind, and backtracked again and again as walls shifted and staircases collapsed right in front of him.

He had to get out of here before the whole place came down.

Regret flashed through him as he thought of Alastor, but Devlin didn't have a prayer of rescuing him until he put this key to use and became master of the East. Still, while he was so close, he had to let his brother know he'd be back.

Alastor? Alastor, can you hear me?

Devlin backtracked through the building, heading for one of his escape hatches.

Dev…?

Soul-deep relief pushed every other sensation away. *Oh, thank gods. I'm here—*

Don't, Alastor said, the word so faint Devlin was certain he'd heard incorrectly. *It's…a trap…and I…bait.*

Just like he'd thought. *I hate to leave you, brother, but I'll be back.*

Devlin felt the vow to the depths of his soul. Once he'd taken their father down, he'd free Alastor or die trying.

Nothing.

Alastor?

When there was no response again, Devlin tried like hell not to let his imagination run away with what that could mean. Sadness and anger washed through Devlin, but the building didn't give him the chance to wallow. Massive bolts of lightning exploded across the hallways in front of him. Devlin reared back at the last second, putting him in the path of the collapsing ceiling. He just whipped between the falling rock before it closed him in.

Doing a double take, he realized the building's destructiveness had forced him near one of his emergency holes. Devlin made a break for it, shooting down a long hall, and whooshing through just as the ceiling collapsed above him.

He flew outside into a massive lightning storm. The sky had gone pitch black. Bolts of electricity speared down at him. He weaved through them, feeling their searing heat against his essence, until he arrived back at the monstrous tornadoes.

The Anemoi weren't there, and Devlin hoped they'd gotten away safely. But that also meant he was going to have to figure out how to deal with these storms on his own.

He really only had one resource at his disposal.

Hearing Anna's encouragements in his head, he called on his infernal powers and built a massive fireball. Feeling as if he were shaking apart with the effort, he shot it into the center of the closest tornado. A massive explosion, and then a blast wave sent him head over ass. But when he looked back again, the funnel was breaking apart, the debris that had been whipped around inside it falling from the sky and raining down to the ground.

Again and again, he projected the preternatural bombs across the sky and took the tornadoes down one by one.

By comparison, making it through the electrical cloud again was a piece of cake.

Victory surged through him as he met clear sky again, the boundary to the Eastern Realm coming closer and closer.

And then his hope smashed to pieces.

There, ahead of him, just this side of freedom, were his Anemoi brethren. Except they weren't alone. Black figures tore this way and that through the sky as the Anemoi attempted to defend themselves and pick off their enemies one by one. He surged forward into the fray, ready to fight, ready to die.

ಬೋಡ್

Keres. Female daimons who fed on the blood of the dying and weren't averse to helping a warrior along the path to death to get what they wanted. With gnashing teeth and vicious claws, the black-cloaked wraiths whipped through the air, attacking, slashing, and grasping for the deaths of the Anemoi.

Devlin flew into the chaos and called on his powers to take them out. As he projected balls of fire toward them, they exploded in a horrific spray of blood and gore. Devlin flew and dodged and maneuvered for good firing positions to pick them off as he could, but there were so fucking many of them his kills didn't seem to make an appreciable difference. And his power was getting hard and harder to call forth.

Where the hell did they come from? Devlin shouted to whoever could answer.

Someone else is commanding them! Zephyros responded as he whizzed by, two daimons on his tail. *There's another presence here, but we sensed it too late, and then the Keres were on us.*

The fight went on and on, with Devlin's fire, Aeolus's lightning, and Chrysander's infernal dagger making the most impact against the Keres. Since Owen apparently wore Laney's amulet made of protective infernal iron, that left Zephyros as the most vulnerable to Keres' attacks.

Working together, they picked the Keres off slowly but surely, the sky dark with their blood and alive with the wind the great battle whipped up. Owen and Zephyros would lure a Keres into an open bit of sky and allow one of the three of them to swoop in behind and take the daimon out. But Devlin wasn't sure how many more swipes of claws or splashes of acidic daimonic blood Zephyros could take. Already he flew slower, banked less gracefully, and dodged as if his instincts had become dulled.

But they were making progress. A strong chance existed that they could defeat the Keres. A great hulking shape flew past Devlin, divine energy pouring off of it. *Whatever you felt before is here!* Devlin yelled.

Christ, what is that? Chrysander asked as he sliced into another Keres with the dagger.

A scream pierced through the chaos of the embattled sky.

Devlin whipped around to find a huge black-cloaked being holding Aeolus aloft in his physical form. A wide hood covered the being's face and he held a long staff with a curved blade on one end.

Across the wide blue sky, Devlin's gaze locked with Aeolus's. His grandfather looked at him with kindness, affection, and resolution, then he said, "Thanatos."

One beat of confusion, then another, before realization set in. Thanatos. The god of death was said to revel in the taking of life, both among men and gods. One of the sons of Erebus—which made him… gods be damned…Anna's half brother.

The death god reared back with his scythe and buried the blade in Aeolus's chest. Devlin was so shocked he felt a sympathetic echo of pain in his own heart. Blood spilled from the storm god's mouth. And then Thanatos discarded Aeolus as if he were so much garbage, and the god's body dropped into a free fall.

No! Zephyros yelled, charging across the space.

Grief splintered Devlin's soul, but he didn't have time to give in to the emotion. Devlin charged forward and intercepted Zeph, crashing into him so hard that thunder exploded across the sky. *Get Aeolus before a daimon does. You are his most obvious successor. You must receive his essence before he is gone for good.* Without waiting for a response, Devlin threw the Western god in the direction of Aeolus's falling body. *Chrys, Owen, help Zephyros recover Aeolus!*

The gods took off in pursuit, fighting Keres where they had to. The wind moaned with their collective grief.

Devlin shot across the sky at Thanatos. If he survived—if they all survived—it was going to be thanks to Annalise. Of all people. The death god raised his scythe, ready to attack again.

Devlin hoped his gamble paid off. He needed to act fearless to sell what he was about to say—as if he really were allied with the primordial god of darkness. *Do you make it a practice to attack those allied with your own father, Thanatos? Do not even Erebus and his other offspring warrant your respect?*

Thanatos's grip on the staff faltered and he lowered it just enough that Devlin knew the words had hit home. *What is this nonsense you say?* His words echoed across the space between them.

I am betrothed to a daughter of Erebus, begotten upon the rainbow goddess and messenger of the gods, Iris. Now he and Anna were even for telling that little lie. But if Devlin survived this madness, maybe, just maybe she would let him make both of their declarations honest. *She is ancient and powerful, Thanatos, and only until recently was lost among the humans. Now she is found. And she is mine. And you are attacking her brethren—for what purpose?*

As Devlin whipped around him, Thanatos followed the trajectory of his flight. *I was hired by the Supreme God of the East Wind to guard his realm,* he called.

At what price? Devlin asked. Silence. *At what price?* he roared, throwing a great ball of fire at the death god.

Thanatos's robe burst into flames, revealing a being made entirely of bones beneath. And then the robe regenerated, as if nothing had happened. *My reward was to be the spirits of all the Anemoi, but I...I knew not of any association between my family and the gods of the Anemoi.* His tone was less haughty, more subdued now.

Shoving down his grief, Devlin circled around to stand in front of Thanatos and returned to corporeality—a show of fearlessness and confidence he needed to convince the death god that what he said was true. "Of course not. Eurus kept that from you, didn't he? As ancient as you yourself are, you must know my father's reputation. Did you really think he'd make good on his promises?"

Hope rose up within Devlin that Thanatos would worry just enough to back off. Had the Anemoi rescued Aeolus yet? How much more time did he need to buy them?

"Your lack of answer speaks for you. Now call off the Keres. If you cooperate from here, I will consider not reporting your trespass against us to your primordial father."

Thanatos raised and lifted his staff twice as if banging the bottom of it on the ground, though only sky surrounded him. But the movement apparently made some noise that Devlin didn't hear, because a half dozen or more Keres whipped passed them in retreat. *I will verify what you say, Devlin of the East. If you have lied to me, you will be the first I consume.*

"Then I have nothing to worry about," Devlin said.

Thanatos turned, then asked over his shoulder. *Where is this goddess-sister now? I should like to meet her.*

Devlin debated, but it would only take the tap of his staff to recall the Keres and renew the battle. With Aeolus injured—or worse—and Zephyros badly drained from the fight, Devlin wasn't sure how much more they could take. So he went with the truth. "She is at Aeolus's compound."

Thanatos whirled around in a great cloud of black. *Aeolus's? By the gods, we must go now! I must call them off!*

Icy dread slithered through Devlin's psyche as the Anemoi approached in their physical forms with Zephyros carrying Aeolus's limp body. "Call who off?" Devlin bit out.

The rest of the Keres. Knowing all of you were here, I sent half of them there. They are attacking the storm god's realm as we speak.

ଅଧ୍ୟ

Sitting on the couch in this beautiful, full-color living room, Anna was slowly going crazy. Hours had passed since Devlin and the other Anemoi had left for the Eastern Realm and they still hadn't returned. What if Devlin had been hurt? Having just found him, her heart would never recover if she lost him so soon. Because the time they'd so far had together in no way equated to the depth of feeling she had for him. Anna loved him so deeply he'd become a part of her.

"Let's get a snack," Ella said out of nowhere as she rose from the couch.

"I'm not really hungry," Megan said, holding a sleeping toddler in her arms.

"You should still eat, though," Megan's friend Tabitha said. Probably in her late thirties or early forties, Tabitha had dark-blond curls and a warm, full laugh, and it was clear from the way she fussed over them how much she cared for Megan and her son.

Laney stood up. "I'm not hungry either, but it would give us something to do. Let's go make a big dinner for when the guys get home."

"Yeah," Ella said, rounding the back of the couch. "I like that idea even better."

Anna smiled as she got up, too, appreciating the opportunity to think of something beside her worry. "Devlin is always hungry, so I know he'll want to eat."

"Oh my God," Laney said, laughing. "I bet his appetite isn't as big as Chrys's."

"Help me with Teddy?" Megan asked Tabitha. She handed the boy off and heaved herself to her feet. "Laney, honey. *No one* eats as much as Chrysander. Trust me. He'd come visit for the weekend and there wouldn't be a speck of food left in the house that wasn't frozen. And that was only because it was too cold for him to eat."

Everyone laughed, and Anna loved this feeling of being a part of a group of friends, of a family, of something bigger than just herself. She had her dad, of course, and she never discounted that, but most of the time he didn't know who she was or what was going on in her life. These women knew *exactly* what Anna felt in this moment, because they felt it, too.

Suppressed fear. Guarded hope. Constant longing.

Seth stepped into the doorway, blocking them. "Wherever we go, we go as a group and we stay together," he said. When everyone agreed, he nodded to Tisiphone.

"I'll take up the rear," she said in that clipped, quiet way she had. Laney had told Anna that Tisiphone was supposed to have snakes living under the scarf she wore, but she'd never seen them for herself. Anna wasn't sure whether to be horrified or curious. Either way, she bet *that* would be cool to paint.

As a group, they ambled down the hall, guided by the pace at which Megan could walk. Chatter and laughter bounded between the marble floors and beautiful murals on the ceiling. If she spent the rest of her life here, Anna wouldn't be able to study all the artwork that decorated Aeolus's home.

The thought resurrected what Iris had said about the curse and the only way to beat it. To stay here. To never go home again. Just considering that sent her mind immediately into chaos. Over the idea of never seeing her father. Over the possibility of never returning to her life and her world. Over the realization that her deteriorating illness had absolutely nothing to do with chronic fatigue syndrome but with a thousands-of-years-old curse.

And the longer she was in the Realm of the Gods, the more she believed in everything she'd learned, because she didn't have a headache, her joints and muscles didn't throb, and she actually felt that she had the energy to hang out with these women 'til the wee hours of the night. She couldn't remember the last time she'd felt this good.

Not that the realization settled her mind at all. If Anna *did* stay here, would she live at this place? Or with Devlin? Would he want her to live with him? And where would Devlin live? In the East? How far away was that? Anna heaved a breath. The more she learned, the more she didn't know.

But she and Devlin could figure it all out, she just knew it.

"How are you doing?" Ella said, slipping in beside her.

Anna smiled. "It's been kind of a crazy day."

Ella chuckled. "I've been sorta where you are. I understand completely."

Anna opened her mouth to reply when a dark, blurry image slammed into her brain. She gasped and froze.

"Oh," Laney said from behind her. "Oh, no."

Commotion erupted around her as the image sharpened. Something black and grotesque, with horrible teeth and razor-sharp claws. "I have to get this out," Anna rasped, and then she stepped around Ella to the wall of the hallway, raised her hand, and pictured the colors she needed.

Gasps rang out around her as Anna "painted" the image in her mind's eye onto the wall with the movement of her hand spreading shape and color as if she held a brush. Except, the image wasn't *on* the wall so much as hovering just over its surface, giving the horrific image a lifelike, three-dimensional quality.

"Oh, God," Laney said, stepping beside her. "I just saw us running through the halls," she said. "Because something was chasing us."

Anna continued bringing her painting to life as icy dread shivered down her spine. God, she wished Devlin were here to see this and to help her figure out what it meant.

"*That*," Tisiphone said, coming closer, "is a Keres, a death daimon that feeds on the blood of the dying and dead. Is this what we were running from?"

"I…I'm not sure," Laney said, panic slipping into her voice.

As soon as Anna had the whole image out of her head, she stepped back and surveyed what she'd painted, horror filling her belly.

"Your powers are definitely getting stronger," Ella whispered.

"Where are my other paintings?" Anna asked, whirling on the

group as prickles ran over his scalp. "There's one I need to see. Now."

"Still in the Hall of the Winds," Seth said. "Let's move."

Anna gave her newest painting one last look as they left, not as amazed as she would've thought she'd be at the fact that she'd just painted with nothing more than her hand and her mind. It had just felt so...natural while she'd been doing it.

Within several minutes' time, they arrived at the hall. Anna sprinted across the space to where her paintings leaned in a stack against a wall. The others came up behind her as she sorted through them, finally finding the one she'd thought of in front of the small portrait of Eurus. She lifted the painting and words of fear rose up from the group.

It was the one with the damaged ceiling, and through it, the sky was streaked with black.

Those death daimons Tisiphone had described and she had just painted. Anna knew that now for sure.

"What is it?" Laney asked, reaching out her hand. Anna turned toward her, and the moment Laney's fingers connected with the canvas, her eyes went wide. "That's what chased us. They're coming!" she rasped.

"Now?" Seth asked, moving right in front of Laney.

"I think...yes. Now," she said, grasping his hand.

"We go to Aeolus's chambers. They're the most secure. That way. Now," he said, herding them toward the door.

They were halfway down the long hallway that crossed in front of the ceremonial hall when a horrible shrieking noise echoed from outside the building.

"Faster, ladies," Seth said. "Keep your eyes peeled, Tisiphone."

Outside the windows, flashes of light exploded here and there, highlighting the streaks of black against the brightness. The other Anemoi gods? They must be fighting the Keres.

Part of Anna wished Devlin were here because she knew his touch would comfort her, while part was glad he wasn't—because then he'd probably be outside fighting those horrible creatures, too.

Boom! The building shook as something made impact.

One heartbeat passed, then another. And then the shrieking noise sounded out from inside the building.

"Oh my God," someone said as Teddy started wailing.

Another explosion, more vibrations, more shrieking, this time coming from another direction.

"Oh, no," Megan moaned. "I think my water just broke."

Anna peered over her shoulder and her stomach fell. Deep red was bleeding through the front of Megan's stretchy pants. "That's not your water. Seth, Megan's bleeding," she called.

The shrieking got closer and closer.

"Oh my God," Megan was saying over and over again.

Seth led them around a corner…and the hallway up ahead was dark with the flying, roiling bodies of long, gauzy black wraiths. The Keres.

"Go back, go back," Seth said, pushed them around the corner again. The lights over their head wavered, and Anna immediately sensed it was her doing it.

"Don't make it dark," Megan cried.

The light returned. Just like that. "Let's get hidden somewhere and then I can shield us in darkness." She looked over her shoulder at Megan, who was moving mostly because Ella and Seth were half carrying her. Blood had leached into her pants down to her knees and a trail of it followed her on the floor.

"The blood is attracting them," Tisiphone called. "You need to hide them somewhere now."

At the next door, Seth urged them in. Ella and Megan first, then Laney, then Anna.

The shrieking closed in, followed immediately by a scream that quickly turned into a deep, screeching call. Anna whirled in time to see Seth's body burst into another form, one made of fur and feathers. One moment he'd been Seth, the next, a beast. At the same time, Tisiphone shed her scarf and unleashed a headful of snapping, hissing serpents. Jagged red light shot from Tisiphone's eyes and took out one

Keres, then another.

"Come on, come on," Tisiphone hollered, waving at something off to the side.

"He won't let go!" a voice called. Tabitha.

Oh, God, Tabitha and Teddy were still out there.

"Teddy?" Megan called, apparently just realizing the same thing. She lunged for the door. Anna rushed after her.

They got to the door in time to see Tabitha forcefully prying a crying Teddy's arms from around one of Seth's furry griffin legs. On hands and knees, she crawled with him to the door, using her body to cover his. She pushed Teddy into Megan and Anna's arms, then scrabbled to her feet.

Tabitha was wrenched backward as if something had grabbed her hair.

"No!" Megan screamed, pushing Teddy behind her with one arm and reaching out with the other.

Seth roared and Tisiphone flung more of that horrible red light at the Keres—now three of them—grasping and pulling at Tabitha. And, oh, God, what their claws were doing to her arms, her face.

And every time Tisiphone and Seth tried to get her, other Keres darted for the door. They were using Tabitha as bait.

"Get back!" Tisiphone shouted. When they cleared the doorway, she backed in. "There's nothing we can do for her, Seth. She's already dead. Trust me."

He roared and lunged one more time. Anna could see him rising up on his huge rear paws and his massive wings unfurling.

"If you go after her, you leave the rest of them unguarded," Tisiphone yelled. "Griffin, *now!*"

With an angry, mournful roar, he folded his wings and backed into the room, bowing his head low to clear the doorway. Oh, God, he was bleeding everywhere. His face, arms, back, and wings had been clawed open. With a swing of his great head, he urged them back.

"Dizzy," Megan said, tears streaming down her face. "Need to lie down."

"Her bedroom's that first doorway," Ella said.

Seth swung his great eagle-like head up and down.

Everyone followed Megan in, and Tisiphone ran to the far wall. "Help me," she called, the snakes agitated atop her head.

None of them paid the serpents the least mind. Laney held Teddy while the Fury, Anna, and Ella shoved a giant armoire in front of the window, almost blocking the whole thing.

Banging and crashing and shrieking sounded out all around them, as if the bowels of hell itself had erupted. And from the looks of those things, Anna thought that might be true.

"If you can make it dark, Anna," Tisiphone said, "do it now."

Scared out of her mind, it took Anna no effort at all to comply. She called the darkness, and everything went completely, totally, uncomprehendingly black.

CHAPTER TWENTY-ONE

Owen had never been more terrified in his life. Not two years ago in Megan's cabin when he thought he'd been dying. Not when he'd feared she could never love him. Not even, may his father forgive him, when Boreas was struck dead several days before. Then, he hadn't had time to be afraid.

Now, it was the *only* thing he could be.

Because he'd left Megan and Teddy, and now they were being attacked.

Heart already breaking, his only hope was that the cadre of lesser Anemoi they'd left behind had been able to fend off the daimons.

Flying through the sky in their physical forms, Aeolus hung on to the tiniest thread of life provided by Zeph's healing power. He would not survive—that much was certain. But Zeph had stanched the bleeding just enough to bring the storm god home. Badly drained, Zeph had finally allowed Devlin to carry Aeolus's body.

Between fighting the Keres and being absolutely stunned at the imminent loss of the god who'd always been the strongest among them, the Anemoi hadn't even had time to react to what had happened. But the constant rumble of thunder in their wake and the mournful moan of the colliding winds all around spoke of the shattering grief they all felt.

First Boreas. Now Aeolus. Owen's heart lay in pieces in his chest. How were they going to come back from these losses? Because Aeolus's death changed *everything*.

Once Zeph ascended to Aeolus's position of power, the West Wind would be left without a guardian until Devlin's brother could be installed. Because of a deal Zephyros had made with Ella's Olympic ancestor to save her life, only Alastor could succeed Zeph as his heir. With the East Wind gone rogue and the counterbalancing West Wind unmanned, the human realm was in grave danger of catastrophic weather extremes that would play right into Eurus's hands.

Which meant they didn't have much time.

"How is he?" Zeph called weakly to Devlin.

"Holding on," Devlin said, response full of bitter grief. "Just."

Owen's grief surged for Zephyros and Chrysander, who were just beginning to make amends with their father. For Devlin, whom Aeolus had believed in when no one else did. And for himself, who as a freshly anointed Anemoi had found in Aeolus a new father figure. The death of the storm god was almost too much to bear. Owen could hear it in all of their thoughts, feel it in their wind, and see in it their mournful countenances.

And then Aeolus's realm came into view. The sky was in absolute chaos. Keres and Anemoi battled in the air above the compound, screams and screeches echoing across the distance. Smoke poured upward from one of the buildings.

"Call them off," Devlin growled to the death god who hovered just far enough away to be respectful of their familial mourning. "Now."

With two beats of Thanatos's scythe upon the air, the Keres fled, rising up like a great dark halo before disappearing altogether.

Dropping back to make sure the Keres did indeed leave, Owen noticed that, with his back hunched over the limp form of a dark-haired god, Devlin had brought Anna's painting to life.

Would you like my help? Thanatos asked.

"For now, wait here," Devlin said.

Anticipation filled Owen as they entered the compound through a collapsed piece of ceiling outside the ceremonial hall—the result of a lightning strike if he'd read the charred ruins right.

The inside of the mansion was an inky, unnatural black that dampened his usual ability to see in the dark.

"Megan!" Owen yelled just as Chrys shouted, "Laney!" Their voices thundered through the space. Zephyros didn't have the energy to yell, so he communicated telepathically with Ella.

We're at Owen's, Ella replied at the same time Laney's voice called distantly, "Chrys? We're in Owen's apartment."

Why were they all there? And why hadn't Megan called out, too?

"Go," Devlin said, pulling Owen from the questions. "I'll take Zephyros and Aeolus into the hall." His voice softened at the end, as if he didn't want to say the words. Holding Aeolus's lifeless body between them, Devlin grabbed Owen's arm, his grip like death itself. "This darkness is Anna. I can feel it. Find her for me."

"I will," Owen said, grasping Aeolus's hand. He didn't want to say good-bye, but he wasn't sure what else to say. So he squeezed the limp hand in his grip, fighting back the sting in his eyes and the knot in his throat. And then they parted ways.

Nearly choking on fear, Owen shifted back into his elemental form so he could move faster through the pitch black. Chrys was right beside him as they tore through the halls and finally through the keyhole of the barricaded door to his apartment.

Crying. The first thing Owen heard was Teddy crying.

"Megan?" Owen said as he shifted into corporeality.

A screeching roar sounded right in front of them, but Owen couldn't make out what it was. Gods, had one of the Keres gotten in here?

"What the hell was that, bro?" Chrys said from beside him.

"Owen? Chrys? Is that you?" came a feminine voice. Laney's? Both gods answered at the same time. "Anna, it's them, you can turn back on the lights," she called. Then, "It's okay, Seth. Let them pass."

Light flooded the apartment. And a huge golden creature

crouched between Owen and the door to his bedroom. Head and wings of an eagle. Body and tail of a lion. A griffin. Laney stroked her hand over the fur of its shoulder, which was about as high as she could reach.

"Uh, Laney. Step away…" Chrys said, arms raising as if placating the giant beast, so tall it hunched to avoid hitting its head on the ceiling.

"It's Seth," she said, face streaked with tears. "Those…*things* chased us but he changed into this and protected us. He's hurt."

Great open gashes marred the griffin's head, paws, and back. But right now, all Owen cared about was that the creature stood between him and his angel.

With a mournful *caw*, the griffin lay down, opening a path to the bedroom.

Owen darted through the door.

Relief poured over him in a great waterfall. Ella, Teddy, and Anna surrounded Megan on the bed. Tisiphone leaned against the wall across from the foot of the bed, her gaze shifting from Owen to Chrys to the doorway.

And then Owen registered their panicked expressions. Saw the blood covering Anna's hands and the sheets between Megan's legs. Megan's face was so pale that even her lips held little of their usual pink.

"Oh, gods, what happened?" Owen said, flying around to the side of the bed. He could barely breathe.

"Dada! Mama!" Teddy wailed, turning and throwing his arms out toward Owen. Ella patted his back and cooed in his ear.

"Baby's trying to come," Megan said, licking her lips. "Something's wrong."

"She started bleeding during the attack and those black creatures came after her," Anna said.

Megan grasped Owen's hands and her face crumpled. "They got Tabitha. I couldn't get to her…"

The news was like a punch to the gut. "Shh, angel." He wrapped his hands around Megan's too-cool fingers and kissed her knuckles.

"She was Boreas's…" Megan said, tears dripping down her cheeks.

Owen swallowed around the huge lump in his throat, feeling like he'd failed his father. "I know. Gods, I'm so sorry I wasn't here."

"You're here now," she whispered. And then she grimaced and grunted in pain, her whole body seizing up. Red-faced and inconsolable, Teddy screamed.

"Take him out?" Owen asked. "I don't want him to…" *see his mother…* Owen couldn't bring himself to finish the thought.

Ella squeezed Megan's hand. "We'll be right outside," she said. Ella slipped by Chrys and Laney in the doorway, but the sounds of Teddy's crying told him she hadn't gone far.

Anna shoved the sheets over Megan's knees and leaned in. "I know nothing about labor, but the baby's not coming. Maybe it's turned around?" She looked at Owen with pleading eyes just shy of panicked.

This can't be happening. There has to be a way. There has to be something I can do. Gods, if we were home, she'd be in a hospital and she'd be safe.

The contraction eased off, and Megan squeezed his hand. And, aw, gods, it was a pitiful little squeeze. "He can't come by himself," she said, her gaze so sad it stomped the broken pieces of Owen's heart into dust. "You're going to have to…take him out, Owen."

Take him? Owen frowned. "Megan, I don't—"

"Cut him out," she whispered, her voice breaking.

Horror washed hot as the sun over Owen, making him break out in a sweat and pant for breath. Aching from the center of his soul, he shook his head, his mouth open but no words coming out.

"You have to," Megan said.

"No, angel, no. I…no."

Megan paled impossibly more as another contraction gripped her body. She screamed and arched, her hand threatening to crush his now, but Owen didn't care. He would bear every bit of this experience if he could. Gods, he remembered his terror during her first delivery. But even though Teddy had been a larger-than-usual baby, Megan had come through it like a champ, leaving him even more awed at her strength and bravery. And Boreas had teased Owen mercilessly for his pacing and worrying.

"Oh, oh God, Megan. Don't push. Try not to push," Anna said. The shaking hand she laid on Megan's knee was shiny with bright-red blood. "I don't know what to do, but I think she's right."

Owen couldn't imagine doing as Megan asked. Bad enough that the attack had stressed her body into an early labor, but to kill her with his own hands? No. Never. He might as well bury the blade in his own chest.

His brain scrambling for a solution, Owen looked across the room where he found Chrys and Laney standing in the door. Chrysander wore possibly the most serious expression Owen had ever seen on his face, and it was like a steel knife in his windpipe, a suffocating agony. "Get Zeph," Owen said. "Please, get Zeph."

Chrys nodded and disappeared.

"Just hang on, angel. Help is on the way," Owen said, stroking her sweaty blond curls back from her forehead. "Okay?"

Megan blinked lazily. "No time." Her eyes struggled to focus on his face. "If you don't get…baby out…both die." Her eyebrows raised in a plea. "Save our son."

Owen shook his head. "Megan, you are my life, I can't—"

She raised her hand, and it swayed as though it took a mountain of effort to lift it to his face. As she pressed three fingers to his lips, tears dripped from the corners of her eyes. "And you are my true north, Owen Winters. My…true north. Always." Her hand dropped lifelessly to the bed.

"Megan!" Owen said, grasping her face in his hands. Her eyes rolled back. Grasping her shoulders, he shook her as gently as he could. "Megan, don't you leave me!"

"Oh, God, there's so much blood," Anna cried.

"No, no, no." He tilted his head to the ceiling and screamed,

"Zephyros!"

Two fast heartbeats later, Chrysander returned to the room looking stricken. And alone.

"Where's Zeph?" Owen rasped, his hope crashing to the floor.

"In the middle of ascending to the god of storms and keeper of the winds," Chrys said, his voice like gravel.

"What?" Ella said, leaning around the doorjamb but keeping a quieter Teddy out of the line of sight. Tisiphone lurched from her position against the wall.

"Oh, uh, Aeolus...during the battle..." Chrys shook his head. Gasps rose up from the women at the news. Tisiphone disappeared.

Owen's gaze drifted back to Megan. He was going to lose her, too? Grief and rage and despair welled up inside him until Owen was sure his skin would burst.

Ella blanched. "Zephyros—"

"Is drained, but fine. He'll be restored after the ascension, but it'll take a while." Owen stared, his brain almost refusing to process the news. For a moment, Chrys stared at the ground, almost defeated. And then the god of the South Wind raised his gaze and held out a knife. "From the kitchen. I, uh, sterilized it," he said, his voice so full of pained sympathy that Owen felt as if he were drowning.

And Owen had thought his heart beat fast and hard before. Now he was almost dizzy. "Chrysander, no."

Chrys walked around the bottom of the bed to Owen and knelt. Hand on his shoulder, Chrys said, "Save one of them before it's too late."

Tears falling now, Owen shook his head. "I can't."

"Owen—"

"Could you do it?" Owen yelled.

"I would hate it, but if it was Laney's dying wish..."

Owen dropped his head in his hands, the losses of the past few days swamping him in a maelstrom of inescapable grief. Boreas. Aeolus. Tabitha. Megan.

"Okay, Owen," Chrys said, and then he rose, ordered Anna to

pull Megan's feet downward, and pushed the blankets aside to bare Megan's belly. The blade was against her skin before Owen's brain had caught up with what he intended to do.

"Wait!" he said. "Just in case…I can…let me numb her." Chrys gave a tight nod. Leaning over the love of his life, Owen blew the North Wind across her belly until the skin turned ice cold. Well, colder. Choking on a sob, Owen sat back, grasped Megan's hand, and pulled it to his lips.

Chrys slowly sliced the blade across the lowest part of her stomach. Owen moaned as a ribbon of bright red bloomed over her skin, which Chrys probed with his fingers and the blade until he made an opening through which the baby's bottom was just visible.

"Oh my God, Chrys, you're doing it," Anna said from between Megan's legs, her breath shuddering. In the doorway, Laney and Ella cried silently. Teddy had blessedly fallen asleep against Ella's chest.

Owen watched all this as if floating outside his body. Sound came to him as if through a long tunnel. Looking down at the slender hand he held, Owen turned it over and pressed two fingers to the veins at the top of her wrist.

For long moments, the only sound he heard was his own pulse whooshing behind his ears. No matter how he moved his fingers, he couldn't find a pulse.

Megan was gone.

His angel. The one who had brought him back to life. Who had given him a reason to live. Gone.

Slowly, Chrys pulled the baby through the cut in Megan's abdomen with Anna's help. The child was almost purple in color. Chrys unlooped the umbilical cord from around Owen's son's neck, and that's when Owen snapped back into his body.

Panicked, grief-stricken words filled the room in a second wave as Chrys cleared the baby's mouth and tried to restart his heart—first by patting him, then by massaging his tiny chest over his heart, and then by pouring the healing warmth of the South Wind into the baby's body. Owen might've objected to the latter, given that the boy was a child of the North, but it was so obviously, heartbreakingly clear that the baby was gone that Owen thought it couldn't possibly hurt to try.

"Come on, *come on*," Chrys said, nearly panting.

"There's no… Chrys, there's no aura," Laney said, her voice so filled with grief and apology that it made Owen a little insane.

Gone.

In one night. Aeolus. Megan. And their son—Athan. Short for Athanasius, which Megan had picked because it meant "eternal life."

What a horrible cruel joke that was now, when Athan would never live at all.

∞∞∞

Devlin watched in horrified wonder as Aeolus transferred his power to Zephyros. At Aeolus's rasping instruction, the pair lay side by side on the floor in the center of the compass rose, facing each other, with Devlin kneeling by their heads. Aeolus was so close to death that Zeph, weak as he was, had to hold Aeolus's hand to his chest, while Devlin held the other hand to Zeph's forehead.

As Aeolus telepathically recited an oath, Zephyros repeated a few lines at a time in the ancient language, out loud. Light and color and whirls of power slowly lifted up out of Aeolus and settled into Zeph, the latter's body arching and seizing as one by one the transferred powers took hold and sank into Zeph's chest.

"I accept the power, the privileges, and the duties of Ruler of Storms and Master of the Winds," Zeph continued in the ancient language. "I will be a fair and faithful master and will never favor one wind over another. I will seek balance in all things and protect all which has been entrusted unto me to the best of my ability. From this moment until I am no more."

Aeolus's eyes blinked open, a dull, lifeless green. When his hands slipped to the floor, a skeleton key much like the one in Devlin's pocket appeared in one of Aeolus's palms. "Your lantern," he rasped to Zeph, eyes momentarily angling toward the ceiling. "Always know…you…are worthy." And then he was gone.

The ache. The surprise. The inability to draw breath. It was like being punched in the heart. The first to ever believe in him. And one of the only. Devlin felt Aeolus's loss as acutely as if the god had been his father and raised him from birth. Certainly, he'd shown Devlin more care in the short months they'd been working together than Eurus ever had. And now he was gone.

Zephyros reached out a shaking hand and gently pushed Aeolus's eyelids closed, then he grasped the key in his fist. Suddenly, his eyes flared a brilliant royal blue. Wind whipped around his body in a translucent and preternaturally lit whirl, lifting Zeph off the floor until he was fully upright over the center of the compass rose.

On his knees, Devlin watched as the swirling funnel lifted Zephyros higher and higher, until he was almost to the ceiling. And then a dark lantern descended from the ornate ceiling. Bright light lit the whole room for a moment, and then Zeph deposited it inside the golden container, which now glowed with his divine energy—the energy of the new storm god and ruler of the winds. Devlin longed for Anna's strength here beside him.

Now that their transition was complete, various matters demanded Zephyros's immediate attention. For he was now master of them all. Several of the lesser Anemoi had been badly injured and Chrys's quick visit had revealed that Owen's wife was in some kind of grave distress. And now that the West Wind had no master, freeing Alastor became all the more important.

As the lantern settled back in its vault in the ceiling, the preternatural storm lowered Zeph to the floor. When his boots hit the tile, the light and wind disappeared.

Devlin rose to a single knee and bowed his head. "My lord."

Zeph crossed the room, a sad, harsh expression on his face, but rejuvenated and stronger than before. "Thank you, Devlin," he said, voice gritty with grief. In his hand, he manifested a blanket, and together they gently covered Aeolus's still body.

"Wait. Let me…"

Devlin tracked the voice to find Tisiphone standing near the doorway. Sadness washed through him in another crushing wave. He exchanged glances with Zephyros, who nodded.

Tisiphone was beside them in an instant. "I will take him home," she whispered. "And see him off on the ferry to the Elysian Fields."

Zeph squeezed her shoulder. "I know he would like that."

Folding the blanket back, Tisiphone leaned over Aeolus's body and stroked his face. While they watched, the pair disappeared. And the sharp tearing sensation in Devlin's chest told him they'd taken a piece of his heart with them.

"You have the key to the East Wind?" he asked, voice cracking. Devlin nodded. "Then it's your turn next."

A sharp, masculine scream cut through the stillness.

With one meeting of their gazes, the gods reached an understanding, dematerialized, and went in search of the source of the sound. It led inside Owen's apartment—

Where an enormous griffin lay guarding an interior door. The eagle head lifted and tilted when they entered. After everything that'd happened today, Devlin was amazed something could surprise him, but seeing this magnificent creature did. Was this what Laney and Anna had described before? *Seth?* Devlin asked, his gaze taking in the multiple wounds the griffin had clearly taken in battle.

Yes, the man replied at the same time that the creature gave a small, agonized cry, its feathered head settling back on its paws.

"Thank you for watching out for them," Devlin said.

The griffin gave a single nod of its great head.

In the bedroom, the scent of metallic blood was sharp on the air. And, oh, gods, Devlin was not even a little prepared for the sight that greeted him.

Megan, pale and still as death, pooled blood visible around and through the covers. On the floor beside her, Owen knelt rocking a baby in his arms, a baby who wasn't crying, wasn't moving, and definitely wasn't pink with life.

Devlin's gaze jumped to Anna, sitting at the foot of the bed, hands stained red. Heart in his throat, Devlin was next to her in an instant, pleading with his gaze for a sign that she was okay. Looking up, she nodded and lost the battle against her tears. Devlin pulled her to her feet and embraced her against his chest, beyond glad to have her in his arms again. He stroked her hair and beat back the guilt he felt over his relief that Annalise was safe when Megan lay dead before him.

Zephyros gasped as he pulled Ella into his arms, careful not to wake a black-haired little boy she held whom Devlin had never seen before. "Gods in heaven," he said, hand to his mouth.

The weight of Aeolus's death on his shoulders left Devlin absolutely stunned as he tried to process these new losses. He hadn't known Megan well, but above the other Anemoi, Owen had most given Devlin the benefit of the doubt. And, oh, gods, losing his wife and child just days after he'd lost his father? Devlin's heart broke for Owen, particularly as the god's expression was stricken with a pained grief so intense that it was honestly hard to look at.

Sympathy and red-hot vengeance welled up inside Devlin's chest. More losses at the hands of his father. Again. He gripped the key in his pocket—it ended *today*.

Devlin didn't know what to do, what to say, or how really even to act. So he gave Anna a last squeeze, settled onto a knee, and bowed his head in respect. She knelt next to him, her hand tangling tightly with his. And for once in his life, *touch* was the thing that held him together, that made it possible to weather this horrible moment.

Amid cries and whimpers and shuddered breaths, the others all followed their lead until seven of the world's most powerful beings knelt to pay their respects to the two weakest among them.

A rattle. There again. Devlin's gaze whipped up, searching for the source of the odd tinkling noise. He traded glances with Zeph and Chrys on either side of him, and their expressions said they'd also heard it, but Devlin couldn't figure it out.

Tink, tink, tink.

Devlin cut his gaze to the dresser. But what—

Tink, tink, tinktinktink.

Inside an ornate lidded jar, something started to move, to spin, to throw off a silvery white light. It grew brighter and brighter as the objects inside the jar spun faster and faster. The jar vibrated and danced on the wooden surface as if there were an earthquake, but everything else was still.

What now? Devlin thought, suspicion and wonder filling him in equal parts.

"Owen, buddy," Chrys said, tapping the god of the North Wind on the shoulder. He'd been so far into himself, he was the only one in the room who hadn't heard the noise and wasn't staring slack-jawed at the spinning lights. "Owen?" Chrys squeezed his shoulder.

Slowly, Owen lifted his face, his expression beyond gutted, his eyes lifeless and dull. For a long minute, he didn't seem to know why Chrys had called his name. And then he finally checked back in and noticed what everyone else was looking at.

It was like someone had turned a light switch on. Owen's eyes snapped to attention, his expression morphed into something skeptical and disbelieving, color returned in slow degrees to his cheeks. "You're seeing that, too?" he said in a reed-thin voice.

"Yeah, man," Chrys said. "We see it. We all see it."

Staring at the jar, Zeph said, "Isn't that…aren't those —"

"Boreas's snowflakes," Owen said. "The ones from his lantern."

Prickles ran over Devlin's scalp. As if the snowflakes possessed some conscious awareness, speaking about them made them spin faster and faster until they gave off a high-pitched hum against the side of the glass.

I cannot change everything that I wrought, came Thanatos's voice from somewhere above them. *But I'm holding two souls in my hands right now and I hear the call of another who would like to give you a last gift.*

Zeph, Chrys, and Devlin all shifted toward Owen as he rose to his feet, still cradling his son in his arms.

He licked his lips and shook his head. "This isn't possible," he said.

"I don't…I couldn't stand—"

Believe. The single word made the breath catch in more than one throat. The voice was deep and formal, but affectionate, too. Devlin's throat went tight as Owen's expression shifted to something resembling soul-deep awe.

Owen tilted his face toward the ceiling. "Boreas?" After a moment, Owen's gaze dropped to the jar and he darted around to the far side of the bed, everyone rising and making way for him. Gently resting the baby on the bed, Owen grasped the jar in shaking hands and lifted it until the lights flashed across his face. Devlin squinted against the intensity as Owen removed the lid.

Three blurs of twinkling silver light shot out of the glass and spun around the ceiling of the room. The temperature plummeted and the air smelled cold and crisp, like a winter day after a fresh snowfall. It had been many years since Devlin had had more than a passing interaction with the former Supreme God of the North Wind, but even he recognized the god's presence in the form of his scent, his cold, his silvery light. Which explained why Zephyros and Chrysander, shivering next to Devlin in the whirling cold, wore expressions of pure, joyous awe.

Lay your son with his mother, Owen. I do not have much time.

Kneeling on the bed, Owen moved the baby into the crook of Megan's arm. He caressed Megan's pale cheek with the knuckles of his shaking hand, and the three of them made such a heartbreaking sight that Devlin pulled Anna into his arms. He couldn't imagine the crushing grief losing her would bring, and he hadn't been with Anna anywhere near as long as Owen was with Megan nor shared the bonds that parenthood created. But, gods, did he hope—for the first time in his life—he might have the chance.

Owen slid off the bed onto his knees and clasped his hands in front of him in silent prayer. The snowflakes circled the room in tight loops, three points of light spiraling lower and lower over Megan and her child. Anticipation filled the air and connected them all in a circle of love and hope and family—family in which a father's love was so strong that it crossed over the divide separating the Underworld from the realms of the living to offer comfort and solace and strength one last time.

Snow began to fall from the circle of lights, soft, floating flurries at first, and then heavier, until the falling snow formed a curtain that surrounded mother and child.

"Oh my God," Anna whispered. "What's happening? It's so beautiful."

The curtain stretched from the mattress to the ceiling, a tunnel of glowing snow anchored by the three pinpoints of light made by the snowflakes. Suddenly, shadows moved inside the curtain. Devlin's racing heart echoed the gasps and murmurings of surprise all around him. He wasn't sure what he was witnessing right now, but it was beyond spectacular, and Devlin hoped like hell that it left Owen a whole god again.

The shadows floated downward until they merged at the bottom of the tunnel that lay flush with the bed.

Then, in a great spray of light, one of Boreas's snowflakes detached from the inside of the curtain and fluttered to the bottom. Devlin traded glances with Zephyros, who appeared as bewildered as Devlin. Next to him, Ella wore an expression of hope. In her arms, the little boy had awakened, and he was mesmerized by the display in front of him. His eyes shone brightly, one brown and one blue. Owen's eldest son, then. Teddy, Devlin thought his name was.

Anna gasped and Devlin looked just in time to see a second snowflake fall inside the glowing tunnel. And then another, the last.

Teddy thrust out his hands toward the whirling snow. "Gampa, Gampa!"

A spray of snowflakes shot out from the side of the tunnel and sprinkled down on Teddy's head. He laughed and caught them in his little fingers. Smiling, Ella burst into tears. Zeph caught one of the snowflakes and touched it to Teddy's nose, then the new storm god looked down and wiped at something on his eye. Chrys didn't flinch as a few of the snowflakes glided onto his arm, his expression absolutely rapt.

Anna reached out and caught several of the fluttering snow-flakes. Every trace of Megan's blood disappeared from her skin. Anna gasped.

With all the love in my heart, I give you the last of me. Boreas's voice, though much more distant and thinner now. The swirling snow over the bed sucked in on itself and then exploded in a burst of snowflakes that rained down over the room.

The air cleared to reveal Megan and the baby lying still uncon-scious on a bed of crisp, clean snow—but looking brand new and ab-solutely radiant. Devlin almost wanted to hold his breath lest he do anything to interrupt the incredible miracle unfolding in front of him.

Owen scrabbled up beside her and grasped her hand in his. "Oh, gods, it's warm. Her skin is warm." With a low cry of relief, he stroked his palm over the baby's fine hair and pressed Megan's knuckles to his face. "Oh, thank God. Thank you, Boreas. You saved their lives and mine."

"She…she has an aura," Laney said from beside Chrys. "White and strong, just like Owen's. The baby, too."

Chrys frowned. "But I thought you only saw auras around—" His eyes went wide and his mouth dropped open.

Gods. Laney had told Devlin she saw auras around all the gods. He looked from Laney's and Chrys's amazed faces to Megan, who was not only the picture of health, but absolutely beautiful—her skin flawless, her lips deep pink, her blond curls shiny and bright. Against her side, the baby was a pudgy little bundle with a shock of black hair on his head.

Slowly, Owen turned his face toward Laney. "Are you saying they both appear to you as I do? *Exactly* as I do?"

Laney nodded, her tears turning into a huge, joyful smile. "Exact-ly."

"If this works like it did with Ella, you might have to wait a few days, maybe even a week, for them to awaken into their godhoods," Zephyros said.

Silvery light flared from behind Owen's eyes and he turned back to his wife and new son. "I'd wait forever if it meant they came back to me," he said, and then he bowed his head and launched into a long speech of thanksgiving in the ancient language.

Devlin ached with a foreign happiness for Owen and his family, and his heart clenched at the idea of a father having so much love for his son. Devlin would never have that kind of father, but maybe he could *be* that kind of father. Someday. Because now he knew what it looked like, now he knew it was possible, now he knew that kind of loving bond existed in the world.

Anna turned in his arms and ran her gaze over his face, which still stung from the sun in the one box. She pushed up on tiptoe to kiss him, and Devlin fell into the kiss like a man dying of thirst. When they broke apart, she wrapped her arms around his neck and pulled him down for a hug that felt like finally coming home. "I'm so glad you're all right," she said. "I don't know what I would've done if..." She shook her head against his chest.

The words filled Devlin up and made him feel ten feet tall. Emotion gripped his throat. "I'm here, Annalise. I'm here." And though Devlin's deepest feelings yearned to spill out, what he had to say weren't things he wanted to say in front of his entire family, and certainly not while they were celebrating the miracle that had unfurled here.

Because that's exactly what the moment had turned into. As Megan and the baby slept, laughter, hugs, and words of love rose up from every corner of the room. And Devlin was entirely positive he'd never been surrounded by so much happiness in his life.

Suddenly, Chrysander froze. His gaze cut to Devlin and Zephyros beside him.

"What is it?" Zeph asked in a low voice as he moved in front of Chrys.

"I just sensed..." Chrys placed a hand on Zeph's arm. "Eurus's storm is arriving way ahead of schedule. And it's worse—much worse—than we ever expected."

CHAPTER TWENTY-TWO

Ice filled Devlin's gut. Since they'd returned from the East, the lesser Anemoi announced that the storm had upgraded to a hurricane. Now it was worse than expected? Devlin didn't let himself ask how much worse, because knowing his father, the sky was the limit. Fear for Anna's father and all the Anemoi who would have to confront Eurus in the coming fight flooded through him, replacing the amazing happiness he'd felt just moments before at finding Anna safe *and* at the miracle of Megan and her baby coming back to life.

"To the Hall of the Winds," Zephyros said, and then he turned to Devlin. "You must ascend to the East Wind. Now."

A shiver of anticipation ran over Devlin's skin. He'd been all but certain this day would never arrive.

"May I come?" Anna asked. "I want to be there for you."

"Yes" sat on the tip of Devlin's tongue, but he'd never been to a ceremony like this before and had no idea what the rules were. He glanced at Zeph, who gave a tight nod.

"I mean no disrespect, Zeph, Devlin, but I'm not leaving here until Megan and Athan can leave with me," Owen said.

"None taken, Owen. I wouldn't let them out of my sight, either," Devlin said, taking Anna's hand. And the warmth that flowed into him at getting to touch her this way, at her wanting to be there for him, beat back some of the stress clawing up his spine.

Zeph rounded the bed and came up behind Owen. He clasped a hand to the god's shoulder. "Anything you need, just ask."

Owen nodded, then reached for something under the neck of his shirt. "Here. You should have this," he said, grasping an iron amulet on a cord.

Shaking his head, Zeph said, "No, Owen. You keep it. This situation isn't over yet, and I refuse to chance something happening to you after what you and your family went through here."

"Zeph—"

"No, I'm pulling my new rank on you. Keep it. That's an order." Zeph winked.

Humor passed over Owen's expression, and it was a miraculous change from the devastation of only moments before. "Okay, boss," he said. Zeph smiled. "Ella, I'll take Teddy. I just want us all together right now," Owen said. She passed the boy off with a smile, and the father-son resemblance was even more obvious.

With that, Zephyros directed everyone to leave, but they halted again just outside the closed bedroom door. Seth lay in a naked heap, his back, arms, and face flayed open and bruising. Laney gasped and went to her knees beside him. "You all go on, I'll take care of him."

"I'll help," Ella said, kissing Zeph on the cheek.

Zeph grasped Ella's hands. "After all he did to keep you safe, let me." Devlin agreed with the sentiment to the bottom of his soul. Who knew what might've happened to the women without Seth's presence? Zeph knelt with his hands over Seth's back. Brilliant golden light shot out of Zeph's palms and healed the wounds almost instantly. Much quicker than when he'd healed Devlin's ribs or Anna's hand—a benefit of his elevated status, Devlin guessed. Zephyros repeated the action on all the other injuries until Seth blinked up at him, surprise and relief in his gaze. "Jesus, thank you."

Chrys handed the man a blanket that he wrapped around himself as he sat up.

"Laney said you protected everyone, so the thanks are all mine," ction, me, too. Without him, what use is my long life?”ction, me, too. Without him, what use is my long life?”ction, me, too. Without him, what use is my long life?”ction, me, too. Without him, what use is my long life?” action, me, too. Without him, what use is my long life?”action, me, too. Without him, what use is my long life?”

Zeph dropped his gaze to the floor and shook his head. “But I—”

“I’ll be here,” Seth said, appearing strong and healthy again. “Now that the whole…griffin thing has happened once, I can feel it inside me. It will come again if I need it—if anyone here needs it.”

After another moment of hesitation, Zeph looked to Chrys, who nodded. Zephyros pushed the iron band onto his pinkie finger with a sigh. It wouldn’t go all the way down, but from what Devlin understood, it just had to be worn against the skin to protect the wearer from evil magic.

Laney threw her arms around Zeph’s neck. “Thank you. Oh!” She reared back. “I guess I shouldn’t do that anymore.”

Zeph gave a small smile and Chrys chuckled. “I’m the one who should be thanking you. Besides, I may be a different god, but I am not a different man. Not everything has to change." He squeezed her hand as he rose to his feet. Crazy as he might've thought the idea of it a few days ago, respect welled up inside Devlin for Zeph, who didn't seem to be letting his new position as the master of all of them go to his head.

Chrys bent and kissed Laney on the head. "Promise me you'll be okay." His voice was filled with a worry Devlin totally understood. Every woman here had powers of her own, Anna foremost among them, though hers weren't fully developed, but that didn't lessen Devlin's fear for her even a little.

She nodded. "I will. Now go do what you need to to end this once and for all."

Zephyros led the way as they wound through the halls to the ceremonial center of the compound. The closer they got to the ceremonial hall, the faster Devlin's heart raced in his chest. As if sensing his anxiety, Anna squeezed his hand, and he was so glad—*lucky*, even, and who ever thought he'd use *that* word to describe himself—to have her by his side.

"Zeph?" Devlin asked. The storm god looked over his shoulder. "What do you think is going to happen when I ascend? To Eurus?"

"I hope when you consume his power, it ends him once and for all. But we're so far off the grid with this situation, I just don't know."

Devlin nodded as lesser Anemoi joined the procession, some badly injured but there all the same. An end to his father? It felt like a fucking dream, and that wasn't something he'd ever done much of in his life.

And then they were in the hall, and all the Anemoi took their places around the great compass rose. Though they all wore the weariness of battle like a second skin, anticipation zinged around the circle nonetheless. Notable openings stood not just at the North and East, but at the Northeast and Southeast, too, as Kaikias and Phoenicias had remained in the human realm to watch over Anna's father. Most problematically, the Western point on the rose currently stood unguarded, and that would change only when Alastor, the officially agreed-upon heir, was free and well enough to do his duty.

Alastor. *Free.* It was another dream that felt almost too good to be true.

But, *damn*, was Devlin ready for some happy endings. Just once.

And the sooner they replaced the god of the East Wind, the sooner they could confront Eurus and take him down once and for all. Devlin hoped the strength of righteousness and the power of justice turned out on their side today, because if Eurus's storm had progressed as severely as Chrysander sensed, they were going to need every ally they could get.

Devlin kissed the back of Anna's hand and then let her go so he could take his place just outside the large blue *E* tiled into the floor. His heart lodged in his throat. He couldn't believe this moment was about to happen, but he was filled with so much hope for a better life that he could barely stand still. He shifted feet, shoved his hair out of his face, clenched and unclenched his fists.

And then Zephyros stepped to the center of the circle. "I stand before you today with great humility and an even greater sense of duty. I promise to you what I promised upon ascending to this godhood—that I will be a faithful servant to the winds and the storms, that I will rule fairly and without favoring one wind over any other. We need all of you. Humanity needs all of you. And each of you is equally important." He walked toward Devlin. "I also say this day that we have all done this god"—eyes flaring with royal-blue light, he pointed toward Devlin—"a grave injustice in painting him with the same brush as his father. Devlin Eston has proven himself to me personally, and to my father before me. We will be honored and strengthened to have him join our ranks." Zeph bowed toward Devlin.

Stunned by such a public and explicit rejection of the legion of rumors about him, Devlin mechanically returned the bow. "My lord," he managed.

Zephyros gestured toward the large *E*. "Devlin, son of Eurus, son of Aeolus, step forward to claim your godhood and your rightful and just place as Supreme God of the East Wind and Guardian of Autumn."

Feeling a little like he was floating above his body, Devlin stared at the tiles for a long moment, and then stepped into place as the master of the East Wind. As Zeph recited the oath, Devlin repeated after him, "I accept the power, the privileges, and the duties of the East Wind. I will be a fair and faithful master and a true and conscientious guardian. From this moment until I am no more."

Zephyros lifted the circular glass lantern out of the floor. "The key?"

Devlin pulled the golden skeleton key from his pocket and glanced from Zeph's face to the lantern, then over his shoulder to Anna, who stood against the wall with her hands clasped over her heart. Her expression radiated so much pride that Devlin could barely process it. She gave a small nod, and he focused back on the lantern and inserted the key. With a deep breath, he turned it to the right until a loud *click* rang out. The glass and iron door eased open, exposing the dancing reddish-orange ball of Eurus's divine energy.

"Hold out your hand," Zephyros said. As Devlin did, Zeph raised his hands toward the sky. "As master of storms and ruler of the winds, I command the great, cooling winds of the East to bow to the new master now before them. It is not the vessel of the god, but the wind and the season that must be honored and protected. This, the current master has not done, and the new master must and will do. So I command the East Wind, with all of its powers, privileges, and duties, into Devlin of the East and commend him as the next Supreme God of the East Wind and Guardian of Autumn."

For a moment, nothing happened, and Devlin's heart dropped to the floor at the thought that even the wind he was destined to command might reject him. But then slowly, a cool, crisp breeze stirred within the great hall. The wind picked up more and more until it was a fast, strong current that swirled immediately over Devin's head. Leaves of orange and gold and red floated in the whirling ring above him, reminding Devlin of the beauty that his season possessed.

It wasn't something he'd thought of—or that had been well protected or cherished—in eons.

Devlin would change that. Devlin would restore the grandeur of the East.

As if the thought beckoned it, Eurus's divine energy levitated out of the lantern and hovered in front of Devlin. Without any warning, it divided in half and shot straight at Devlin's forehead and chest. At first, Devlin flinched, the reaction so well ingrained. But then he held firm against the pressure, refusing to have his first moment as Cardinal Anemoi of the East Wind marred by fear. For Devlin did not fear this new mantle of responsibility so much as he yearned to begin the task of rebuilding and restoration.

A terrible scream rocked through Devlin's head so loud that he put his hands to his ears. Eurus. Howling in agony and absolute outrage. For a long moment, a battle for the East played out inside him, a push and pull that felt like getting punched from the inside out. And then his father's presence inside his mind was gone.

The lights crashed into Devlin's psyche, tearing him apart and remaking him as a new and stronger god. He hummed with a new energy now—one that combined the rage and fire of the infernal rivers with the strong flow of the East Wind.

A moaning, angry gust of wind burst through the hall, causing all the Anemoi to brace and crouch against its force. But not Devlin. As far as he was concerned, the whipping gusts simply represented Eurus's fear and desperation about their proceedings. He took a perverse amount of satisfaction out of his *father* being the one to be afraid. For once.

Zeph yelled out over the roar of the wind, "Now it is time for *your* light to guide and lead the East Wind, Devlin. Place it within so all will know you as its master."

His hair whipping around his face, Devlin nodded. The ball of translucent fire flickered from his hand the instant he raised it. With a small mental push, Devlin braced his muscles against the savage gusts and willed the flaming orb inside the lantern. Zephyros secured the lock with the key and lifted the lantern high. "Long live the East Wind."

The preternatural wind slowed, then ceased altogether. He could feel the wind in his blood, in his mind, ready to be called forth. Soul-deep gratification roared through Devlin.

"Long live the East Wind," everyone answered, the collective voices echoing against the tall ceiling.

"Now we put an end to what has for so long divided us!" Zephyros shouted to great cries of support and applause. "Chrysander!" Zeph waved him over as the ceremony broke up, and the Southern god offered Devlin a handshake and quick words of congratulations. "Are you sensing any difference?" Zeph asked.

Devlin stepped closer, hope and curiosity mingling inside him. Had the transfer of the East Wind and the loss of his divine energy been enough to take Eurus down?

Chrys's expression blanked for a moment, and then he frowned. "That screaming wind was E, so it definitely had an impact. For a moment the storm sputtered, but then it picked up again."

"Exactly what are we talking about, Chrys?" Zeph asked, crossing his arms.

"I'm sensing this storm along almost the whole U.S. eastern coast. The lesser Anemoi report sustained wind speeds of one hundred sixty miles per hour right now and getting stronger."

"Damnit! And the loss of his wind didn't change anything?" Zeph braced his hands on his hips.

Chrys's frown deepened. "It had been at two-ten."

Zeph's eyes went wide.

Fuck. Then it hadn't done as much as they'd hoped. Two hundred and ten miles an hour? Nothing on earth could stand up to those kinds of winds.

"Straight up, this hurricane has all the makings to be the biggest ever to hit the Atlantic coast," Chrys said, dragging his hand through his hair. "There are two things contributing to this. The lack of an Anemoi of the West Wind is throwing everything out of balance, and

Eurus is using that to his favor right now."

"Yes," Devlin said, itching to free his brother now that he'd become master of the East.

"And the second—"

"Is the fucking Firestone ring," Zeph said through gritted teeth. "Which means it's time to get back what's rightfully mine."

"It's clear the loss of the East has weakened him some," Chrys said. "But yeah, I think it all comes down to the ring."

Zeph nodded, his royal-blue eyes flaring. "While he has it, he has all of us. So say your good-byes. Quick. We fly in fifteen minutes."

ଔଔ

Anna had never felt prouder of someone in her life. How she wished for his sake that his ceremony hadn't had to be done with so much danger and uncertainty hanging over his head—over all of their heads. Still, to hear Zephyros stand up for Devlin that way and see him be embraced by a family it seemed he'd long been estranged from made her so happy that she was aching to hug him.

But she'd have to wait a few more minutes. Devlin was deep in conversation with Chrys and Zeph, and it was clear from their expressions and tension in their bodies that something bad had happened. Was it about the storm? Anna shivered in dread thinking about what her father and friends back in Jarrettsville might be going through.

Suddenly, Devlin broke from the group and made right for her.

He seemed to walk taller, more forcefully, and radiate a power that drew her in. God, how she wanted him.

An arm's reach away, Devlin halted. A series of expressions shifted over his darkly handsome face—concern, determination, desire. "Anna, I—" He blew out a breath and tugged his hair out of his eyes.

Anna couldn't stand the distance anymore. She threw her arms around his waist and laid her head on his chest. "Congratulations," she said. And, God, his lean hardness felt so good against her.

His arms came around her on a groan. And the need in that single sound reached into Anna's chest and gripped her heart. She wasn't sure she'd ever met another person more in need of love and acceptance and a place to belong than Devlin Eston, which made her just perfect for him. Because her heart overflowed with love for this god who could be fierce and gentle, strong and vulnerable, giving while refusing anything for himself.

And she was so thankful he was safe. He'd faced whatever hell awaited him in his father's realm, those horrible black creatures, and Eurus's displeasure during the ceremony. And he'd come back to her again. Which made it all the harder to know he was going to have to leave her one more time.

Finally, Devlin pulled back. "I need to say something."

She smiled. "Okay."

Violet eyes flared with the most mesmerizing light. "I don't have a lot of time, so I have to lay this out more directly than I otherwise would." Anna nodded, curiosity rolling through her. "I want you, Anna. I want you like I've never wanted anything. But even with who I am now, I'm still nowhere near your stature."

He glanced away to where Zephyros and Ella were embracing by the door. "You're a primordial, Anna." He met her gaze again. "That means something here."

"I'm the only one who gets to decide who's right for me, Devlin. And if you want me like you say you do, I pick you."

Gently, he clasped her hands in his. "Be sure, Annalise," he said, his voice a raw scrape.

"Oh, Devlin," she said, pulling his hands close so she could kiss his knuckles. There were a lot of things she didn't have a good grasp on yet. If it weren't for her Technicolor vision, the way she'd darkened the compound on command during the attack, and having seen her resemblance to Iris with her own eyes, she'd be sticking with common sense and…you know, *reality*, and saying the very idea that she was a goddess was ridiculous. But she couldn't, because all those things *had* happened. And somehow, in just a few days' time, her reality had taken a hard left turn into the unimaginable…and led her to this beautiful, broken god—whom she had no doubts about whatsoever. She stepped closer, so close she had to tilt her head way back to see him. "A primordial god might be *what* I am, but it's not *who* I am. And who I am is a woman in love with a man. With you. So I'm sure."

Red-hot desire darkened his eyes and sharpened the angles of his face. Like he couldn't hold back anymore, he clutched her in his arms and pulled her into the elements.

Surprised laughter bubbled up inside her soul. And then they were back in their bodies and up against a wall in a quiet, dim hallway—Anna didn't know exactly where and couldn't have cared less. Because Devlin was kissing her as if she were the air he breathed, the water he drank, the source of all his power in the world. Even as Anna's body flashed hot at the fervor of his touch and his tongue and his lips, tears pricked at the backs of her eyes for the intensity of his surrender, for the battle of wills he'd played out inside his own mind. And won.

"I don't have long."

Icy dread skittered down Anna's spine. "You have to confront Eurus," she said, not knowing exactly what that entailed but knowing it couldn't be good. Anna had known this battle was coming all along. She just didn't realize how much all these people were going to mean to her when it happened. How much *Devlin* would mean to her.

He nodded as he grasped her face to control the kiss, and kissed and sucked and nibbled at her lips until her pulse pounded, and her panties grew damp, and his muscles were all that held her up against the wall.

Her breath caught at the competing floods of desire and worry rushing through her. "I don't want to lose y—"

Devlin kissed her, silencing the words. "The only thing I can control for sure are these next minutes. I have so few left. And I just want…" He rested his forehead against hers and shuddered out a breath.

"What? I'd give you anything," she said, caressing his hair.

Blazing purple eyes bored into hers, and then his hands unfastened the button and zipper of her jeans. "I want to give you pleasure. I want to feel you fall apart in my arms. Because of me. Just in case…" He swallowed hard as he slipped his big hand under her panties. "I want to experience your ecstasy one last time." His fingers rubbed soft circles over the bundle of nerves at the top of her sex.

"Devlin," Anna whispered, the arousing movement of his fingers and the urgency of his words making it hard to know what else to say. "Oh, God."

He devoured her on a breath-stealing, bone-melting kiss Anna felt everywhere. He kicked at the inside of her foot, forcing her stance open and allowing his hand to slip down until his fingers found her opening. "Mmm, Annalise, is this because of me?" he asked, spreading the evidence of her arousal around.

"Yes. All you," she murmured. "All you, Devlin." Anna gasped and clutched at his shoulders as he pushed a finger inside her and ground the heel of his hand against her clit.

Kissing her cheek, her ear, her neck, Devlin fingered her while he held her pinned against the wall. "I wish I could be inside you right now," he rasped, slipping a second finger inside her.

"So do I," she said, and then the need for him overwhelmed her. She pulled his hand away, shoved her jeans down to her knees, and turned against the wall. "Do it, Devlin. I need you." Heart racing and nearly panting in anticipation, Anna peered over her shoulder.

"Good gods," he rasped, tearing at the fly to his jeans and shoving them down. And then his hardness was right there, pushing into her, filling her. They both groaned when he was fully seated inside her. "Fuck," he whispered in her ear.

And then he started to move. Slowly at first and then faster, harder. Anna rocked her hips backward into his thrusts as Devlin's big body enveloped hers against the wall. In that moment, Devlin was her whole world. His cool, crisp scent filled her nose, his hard muscles bunched all around her, and his little groans and rough breaths were music to her ears. And, holy hell, his cock was a delicious, driving fullness inside her. A tingling pressure stirred low in Anna's belly, building and tightening until she nearly whined in need.

He sucked at a maddening spot just behind her ear and alternated fucking her with quick strokes and slower, punctuated thrusts that made her moan his name. Anna was pure physical sensation as her body barreled toward what promised to be an explosive release.

"You feel so fucking good," he growled.

The words, the tone, his breath in her ear all shoved her a giant step closer to the ecstasy they both craved. Anna ground her hips as his fingers came between her legs and found her clit. He stroked his fingers over her harder, faster, more urgently. Suddenly, she was right there, an amazing tension holding her on the edge of shattering to pieces. "Oh, I'm—" The orgasm stole her words, her breath, her mind. She cried out as her release detonated, sending her soaring. Again and again, her body milked at his cock inside her.

"Anna," Devlin groaned, and then he was pulsing inside her over and over. He moved through the orgasm, setting off small aftershocks that made her gasp. When his body calmed, he wrapped his arms around her and hugged her to him. He remained deep inside her, and Anna was in no hurry for him to go. Ever.

In the stillness of the moment, Anna's brain just caught up with what they'd done. No protection. Just as quickly, Anna decided she didn't care. If the gods gave her his child, she would want and love it no matter what. *And if he doesn't make it—* Anna refused to finish the thought.

"That was beautiful. Perfect," he said against the shell of her ear. Anna nodded. Gently, he pulled away. Fabric rustled behind her and then something soft pressed between her legs, cleaning her. His shirt.

When he was done, she turned and put herself together as he did, too. "You didn't have to—"

"I'll get another." Wide eyes peered down at her. "We didn't use anything. I'm so—"

She pressed her fingers to his lips and shook her head. "I'm not sorry."

His eyes went wider, and slowly the hint of a smile played around his lips. "Thank you," he whispered, pressing a kiss against her fingertips.

"No, thank you, Devlin." She kissed him in a warm expression of appreciation and love. "Do we have to leave now?"

The question seemed to pull him out of a haze and his eyes narrowed and head tilted. "Not we."

"But my father—"

"Will be fine. If you're there while this is going down I'm going to be distracted with worry. And you know how you feel in the human realm because of the curse. But if you want, I'll take you home or"—he shrugged, discomfort plain on his face—"someone else will afterward. You'd have a day, max, to make any arrangements and say good-bye. But you can't stay, Anna."

Anna's brain scrambled for a response.

"Promise me. No matter what, promise me you'll live." His gaze filled with such sad pleading that Anna couldn't help but nod. Plus, the last thing she wanted was to argue with him.

Besides, he'd be back in a few hours or a day and then they could work out the details. As challenging as figuring everything out would be, they could put it off until he returned. Because Anna refused to accept any other outcome. "Okay. Promise."

"Good," he said, pressing a kiss to her hair. "Now I have to go. Zeph is bitching at me." He winked and pulled away, and it was like he'd reached into her chest and forcibly removed a piece of her.

Anna crossed her arms against the pain. "Well, we don't want that, do we?" He shook his head, and Anna stared as his face like she was trying to imprint the memory of it to her soul. "Go kick some ass and hurry back to me." Tears clogged her throat, but she wanted to be strong for him.

One corner of his lips quirking up just the littlest bit, he winked. "That's the plan." He reached out a hand. "I'll take you back to the others."

Shaking her head, Anna blinked against the pressure building up in her eyes. "That's okay." Glancing at the hall that led to the huge kitchen, she swallowed, hard. "I know where I am. I'll find them," she said.

Devlin leaned in, planted a kiss on her cheek, and met her gaze. "I...I love you, too," he said, more easily this time. And then he disappeared.

The words hit Anna like a ton of bricks, lifting her up in sheer joy and crashing her back down again—because the man who loved her, and whom she loved, was going off to fight an unimaginable supernatural war. Her mind resurrected the memory of those awful black demons darting through the air with their grotesque, gnashing teeth and long yellow claws, and the kind of thing he might be facing wasn't so unimaginable anymore. And that fact did nothing to dispel her fear.

Tears brimmed over and dripped down her cheeks, and Anna just needed a minute to hide and be alone with this awful wave of dread and panic. She slid down the wall into a tight ball and buried her face against her knees.

Darkness, come.

Anna didn't even have to open her eyes to know her command had worked and the hallway all around her had turned pitch black. Somehow, she could feel its inkiness settling around her like a cool, thin blanket. And as always, she found the darkness reassuring.

"Please, please, please keep him safe," she whispered to whatever god might be listening. "I don't know what I'll do without him." And it was true, because everything inside her said Devlin was her future.

Devlin was the one who had revealed her powers, exposed her to this world, and introduced her to her mother. Had she never met him, she never would've known this world existed, never would've known who and what she really was, never would've known what true love felt like. And given the nature of the curse, she would've left her father one way or the other within the next two weeks. The thought of leaving her dad, of never seeing him again, or not being there to take care of him, opened up a jagged hole in her heart. Guilt and grief threatened to swamp her, so if she had to do that one way or the other, she wanted it to be *for* something, to mean something. For her, that something was love. It was Devlin.

More tears dampened her jeans.

If he died, what would she do?

Sitting there in the darkness, Anna wasn't sure she had an answer to that question.

"Okay, enough," she said to herself. She wasn't doing anyone any good sitting here wallowing. On a long sigh, she lifted her face and scrubbed her cheeks dry.

In the quiet of the darkness, Anna suddenly felt she wasn't alone. Once the idea planted itself in her consciousness, she was absolutely sure it was true.

"Who's there?" she asked, prickles running over her scalp and down her neck. Nothing. But the sensation of another presence grew stronger. *Restore the light.*

Darkness remained.

Restore the light. She gave the command an extra mental push. "Restore the light, damnit," she said, uneasiness spilling into her voice. Still, nothing happened. She rose to her feet, muscles tense, instincts jangling, heart pounding out a thunderous beat against her breastbone.

"Do not be afraid" came a deep voice out of the darkness.

Anna's gaze darted right and left, seeking out some shape or movement, but she couldn't see anything nor tell from which direction the words had come. Her mouth went dry. "Who are you?" she finally managed.

"I think you know."

Anna licked her lips, her brain racing. "Uh, no."

"But you called on me. Twice today, as a matter of fact."

"I don't…" She shook her head. Who had she called for? Playing back her thoughts of the past few minutes, she couldn't think of anyone. And then the words *Darkness, come* flickered through her mind. Anna's entire body erupted in goosebumps. "Darkness," she whispered.

"Yes," he said.

Anna had no idea what to say. The only thing that came to mind was the way the Anemoi had reacted at learning who her father was. And now, it seemed, he was actually *here*. Slowly, she sank to a knee and bowed her head.

Warmth wrapped around her hand and urged her up again. "Not necessary, my child."

Heart sprinting inside her chest, Anna sensed the presence congregating immediately in front of her. "Can I see you?"

A long pause that made her wonder if she'd offended him. One of the most powerful and ancient gods in existence. Him, as in her biological father. Erebus. "If you wish."

She nodded, and the dimmest light filtered through the pitch black. The light didn't come from any fixture, but rather seemed to come from the retreat of the darkness into a figure standing a few feet in front of her. Even when most of the hall—including where she stood—possessed the gray light of the day just before sunrise, dark shadows surrounded the god's physical form.

Anna's gaze lifted up over the polished leather shoes, finely tailored black suit, black shirt, and black tie, to his face and eyes, which remained shrouded in clinging shadow. Impressively tall, even taller than Devlin, he wore his black hair short and parted on one side, and except for the obviously abnormal shadows that clung to his body and covered the floor all around him, he was so stylish and debonair he could've appeared on the cover of *GQ*.

"You look just like your mother," he said. "It's uncanny. How are you called?"

"My name is Annalise, though most people call me Anna. And you're Erebus?" Did her voice sound as shaky as she felt? Not from fear, though his power hummed in the space between them as if it was part of the very air, but from the desire to please him, and her amazement that this was happening at all.

"Indeed." He stepped closer, close enough that his shadows fell over the front of her. Inside the circle of that darkness, his face became clear. With his strong brow and shadowed, dark eyes and swarthy skin, he might've been Italian or Greek, but whatever he was, he was unquestionably handsome and moved with a grace born of confidence and power. "I didn't know about you," he said, gaze running over her face. "Until today."

"I didn't know about me, either," she said. "I mean, about all this." When he didn't respond right away, she felt compelled to fill the silence. "I guess it's a good thing I did, though, or else I would've been dead pretty soon." Her stomach flip-flopped.

Erebus went absolutely still and darkness shrouded his face again. "What do you mean?"

Oh. Anna had assumed since he knew about her that Iris must've been the one to tell him and that she would've told him everything. "Uh, Iris didn't tell you about the curse?"

His voice went quietly lethal. "I haven't seen Iris yet. I learned of you from one of my sons, Thanatos. Who by the way also tells me I am allied with you and these gods here in some sort of battle."

Anna could've sworn one of his eyebrows lifted in a questioning, disapproving scowl. But more disconcerting than that was the fact that she didn't know what he was talking about. How had this Thanatos learned of her? And, she had a *brother*? That news rocked through her. Somehow she'd gone from a girl who'd lost—or would soon lose—everyone in her family to a goddess with a family tree that would make her head spin. "Oh," she managed. "Um, I don't know about any alliance, though if it were true it would be amazing."

"The curse, Annalise," he said.

Her heart beat faster. "All I know is that to punish Iris for being with you and having me, I was taken away from her and put in the human world with limited powers, and to keep me from getting powerful, I was cursed to die on my thirtieth birthday before being reincarnated again with a new set of limited powers. Because they couldn't just kill me. But apparently the curse doesn't work in this world. Or something." That totally didn't sound crazy. Right?

His hands fisted and the darkness around him grew. "I should have known something—" He shook his head. "I will talk to Iris and learn more about this curse."

"Okay," she said, hugging herself as she dropped her chin to her chest. And she'd thought she couldn't get any more overwhelmed by this day. Had the battle started yet? Was Devlin still safe? The others? She heaved a breath that failed to calm.

"What troubles you, child?" The shadows retreated again and he moved closer. Fingers on her chin, he tilted her head upward until their gazes met.

"Someone I love is in great danger. I might never see him again." *Actually, two someones—Devlin and Dad.*

"Might this be the young god whose energy surrounds you?"

Anna's cheeks went immediately hot. She didn't exactly know what her, uh, father was sensing, but her gut told her it probably had something to do with their making love not long before. "Yes. Devlin, the Cardinal Anemoi of the East Wind."

"Ah, yes. This is the god who revealed your existence to Thanatos. I owe him words of thanks for that."

"If you were at all open to the idea, your help would be appreciated, too." The words were out of her mouth before she'd even considered whether saying something like that to him would be appropriate. But what did she know? Not much. She'd been dumped into a world in which she didn't really know the rules. Yet another reason she needed Devlin.

Erebus chuckled, a low, dark sound that was part amusement, part incredulity. "Fearless, aren't you?"

She shook her head. "No, I'm actually pretty terrified right now, if you want to know the truth. But I'm willing to take a risk for the people I care about. And they don't have a lot of time."

Rubbing his fingers over his lips, Erebus stared at her as if trying to unlock some puzzle. "Hmm" was all he said.

A long silence made Anna about half crazy, and then she shook her head. "Look, I would like to get to know you more, if you'd like that, too. But right now, I need to do something to help here." She took slow sideways steps in the direction that led back to the living quarters, thinking she might find the other women with Seth, Owen, and Megan. Erebus's gaze tracked her movement. "I'm sorry I asked you. I'm sure I violated about ten things-you-don't-ever-say-to-a-primordial-god rules just now, and I'm sorry. I don't mean any offense."

Still he didn't answer, just watched her with this stern expression on his face.

Walking backward, Anna gave a little wave and felt ridiculous. "Okay, well, then—"

"Ever since the war with the Titans, I have worked to remain free from the fights of others and entangling alliances."

Anna nodded. "Sure, I get it. Again, don't—"

"Annalise?" He turned toward her.

"—feel like you have to—"

"*Annalise*." His volume echoed through the darkening air around her, as if it came from the darkness itself.

She froze. "What?"

"I've just learned I have a daughter and she's asked me for help. How could I say no?"

CHAPTER TWENTY-THREE

This storm was a fucking monster.

Devlin flew in between Chrysander and Zephyros, and only four things gave them a fighting chance. First, that Iris had neutralized the Harpies, and Thanatos, the Keres. Second, that Eurus had lost the East Wind. Third, that Chrys and Zeph were each protected by infernal iron. And finally, that Devlin possessed and had significantly honed his infernal powers. Thanks to Anna. So now it was the three of them with a little infernal assistance versus an extremely pissed-off, powerful god without a conscience and with a magical ring that controlled them all.

And an escalating storm that nearly spanned the length of a continent.

Approaching the U.S. East Coast over the Atlantic was a lot like flying at a brick wall. At least, that's the way it appeared. The hurricane was a roiling mass of clouds that extended from the sea to the top of the sky. Jagged bolts of lightning flashed yellow and orange and purple through the clouds and over the water. Here and there, waterspouts coiled like ancient sea serpents reaching up from the depths to drag them down.

They needed to get on the other side of it so they could halt its progress over land. No one and nothing could survive a storm as catastrophic as this. And they had to do it fast, not just for those immediately affected, but for the world as a whole. Now that Devlin possessed the power of a Cardinal Anemoi, he could sense the East Wind and the season of autumn unlike anything he'd ever experienced before, almost like another presence in his mind or a shadowy second set of senses. Either way, the East Wind was telling him that the scale of this storm was already causing coastal flooding and interfering with wind and water currents through the entire Western Hemisphere. Chrys and Zeph were getting the same messages from their winds.

Left unchecked, this storm would be a world-killer.

Which meant Eurus must be totally out of his fucking mind. Not even he benefited from a scenario where he ended absolutely everything.

Going around the storm's northern edge would be too cold and therefore dangerous for Chrys. Going around the much-larger southern edge would take too long. Flying close to the water surface and going under the storm was sure to beat them to Hades and back and leave them in no condition to fight. So that left going over the top.

Up, up, up they went, the wind shear coming off the massive clouds sucking at them and making it difficult to fly the closer they got. The screaming of the abused winds under Eurus's control was so loud that Devlin couldn't hear much of the other gods' telepathic communication in his own head.

And Holy Zeus and all the Olympians, the storm was way bigger up close than it appeared from a distance. They flew a good six miles upward. So high that the air pressure threatened implosion even in their elemental forms and they could make out the stars through the top of the daytime sky. When they finally made it to the top and began to cross, it was like flying over the pits of Tartarus itself. The winds wailed and reached up to them in desperate pleas and angry grasps, trying to pull the three of them down into the churning air. They flew hundreds of miles, maybe even a thousand, before they finally cleared the far side of the storm a good hundred miles inland.

Which meant the outer edge of the hurricane had already made landfall and now approached Anna's hometown.

They banked hard to the right to face the storm.

And it was the most horrifying thing Devlin had ever seen. The entire side of the lowest-hanging clouds was in the grotesque shape of a face. Eurus's face. Twisted in anger and hate. Eyes flashing with lightning. Mouth open as if he literally intended to devour the world. In the form and color and shading of the clouds, Devlin could even make out the scar that slashed down his face from the fight with Aeolus when he'd stolen the ring.

Holy. Fucking. Hades, Chrysander said.

I don't even have the words, Zeph replied, his thought-voice like sandpaper.

Time to take my new powers for a spin, Devlin said. In his mind's eye, he saw the ferocious tornadoes in the Eastern Realm exploding when he'd launched balls of infernal fire into them. *Same tactic as before. You two fly hard north, and I'll come at him from the east.* From Devlin's position of power—one that Eurus didn't possess in the same way he had before. Whether or not that would play out in their favor now, though, Devlin couldn't say.

He could only hope. Which wasn't something he had a whole lotta experience doing.

Then again, he'd never had so much on the line before. For him. For Anna. For his family.

For the world.

You got it, Chrys said, banking away.

Expect anything, Zeph said. *And watch your back.*

With Eurus, always. Devlin cut around to look for the best attack position. He needed to get closer, close enough that his fire would cut far inside the storm. A hit against the exterior walls of clouds wouldn't do enough, and having never tested it at this level before, Devlin wasn't sure how much juice he had in him before he'd drain.

He had to make every hit count.

In the distance, Chrys cried out.

Fall back, fall back! came Zephyros's gritty voice.

Devlin focused and saw a frosty white wind roar through the sky. The North Wind. Chrys was going to be most vulnerable to Eurus's control over the North, but as long as Eurus controlled *all* the winds he could project any of them anywhere. As the more temperate seasons, Devlin and Zeph had more tolerance, but the far extremes could harm them, too. Hesitating, Devlin debated going to their aid.

We're good over here, Devlin. Do what you're doing, Zeph said, reading Devlin's thoughts—a new side effect of Zeph's status as the ruler of the winds, apparently.

Right, then. Devlin flew around until he only saw the cloud-face in profile, but couldn't find any openings or weaknesses in the cloud structure. Flying lower, he fought against the g-force created by the storm and his own velocity through the air. It pressed on him so intensely, Devlin felt like he might explode apart. But he pressed on, examining the bottom of the roiling storm for the best place to attack.

For a split second, Devlin's gaze dropped downward. And saw utter devastation.

At the edge of the storm, twisters tore across the ground. The flooding was so significant already that Devlin could see water standing on the streets and fields below. Whole neighborhoods of buildings were gone, leaving only shapes of the foundations to prove anything had ever stood there. Debris careened through the sky like a hailstorm of bullets in battle.

Appropriate, since that's exactly what this was.

He had to hurry.

Flying back around toward the face, Devlin kept waiting for the moment Eurus struck out at him. Why hadn't he done so already? He could tell from Chrys and Zeph's running commentary that they were dealing with a shitstorm. Devlin didn't trust the good fortune, even as he came close to the front of the face.

The mouth.

A shiver of hopeful triumph roared through Devlin's being.

If he could fly into the mouth of the clouds and attack from within, he might have a chance.

Without giving it a second thought, Devlin rocketed through the sky, shifted into his physical form, and called forth his infernal powers. Fire and electricity rippled into his hands and grew and grew.

There you are, you backstabbing little shit, Eurus said, his voice echoing through the sky and setting off massive cracks of thunder. *I figured you were sniveling in a corner somewhere letting others do your dirty work.*

Devlin ignored his father's berating words, because he'd heard them many times before and had pretty much become immune. What was more interesting was the fact that Eurus apparently hadn't sensed Devlin at all.

He poured on another burst of speed and drew more force into the fireballs in his hands. But when Devlin was maybe an eighth of a mile from the jagged, gaping hole of the mouth, it began to close.

Now or never.

Devlin hurled the fireballs. Then two more right behind them, and the release of so much energy at once felt a lot like someone tearing his arms right off his body. The pain didn't matter, though, especially when the first two entered the clouds moments before the mouth closed, and the second two immediately after. A massive explosion erupted from inside the cyclone, taking out the whole bottom half of the face and sucking all the power out of the surface clouds anywhere near the explosion.

Devlin pulled back hard, but still got caught up in the blast wave that rolled him uncontrollably through the sky until he didn't know which way was up.

Lances of lightning barreled past him, but he didn't have enough control to avoid them. One caught the edge of his energy and Devlin howled.

Got ya! Chrys said a moment before Devlin slammed into the Southern god's energy. *Thanks for the heat, D. I'm ready to kick some more ass now.*

You got him? Zephyros said. He was a few hundred feet in front of them, using his powers as storm god to deflect the lightning bolts away from them.

You good? Chrys asked.

Yeah. Thanks, Devlin said. And he was, especially once he noted that the explosions had taken out a whole swath of the storm. The clouds were gone, twisters had fallen apart, and rain had stopped in one whole sector of the sky.

We're good, Chrys called.

I'm going in for round two, Devlin said, already looking for another in.

Stay behind my shield and I'll get you closer, Zephyros said.

The hit to the mouth had been devastating because Devlin had gotten the bombs inside the storm. His gaze rose to the eyes, roiling and flashing black holes sparking with lightning.

Bingo.

Head upward, Devlin called. Zeph guided them within range of the eyes as Devlin drew forth his power again. *Get out of here now*.

Zeph and Chrys fell back, banking off to the side in a coordinated attack on another part of the storm wall.

You are a miserable disappointment as a son, Eurus thundered. *You are* nothing *compared to me.*

That's probably the nicest thing you've ever said to me. And it was true given Eurus's evil points of comparison. For once, Devlin was *proud* not to have lived up to his father's expectations. Without giving a second thought to the vitriol continuing to spew into the sky, Devlin hurled another set of four bombs directly at Eurus's eyes.

Each discharge of power siphoned off more of Devlin's energy, draining his ability to pour on the speed. Which explained why he'd barely gotten away when the blast wave hit him again.

The force of it drove him backward through space as surely as if a giant hand had plastered itself against his body and pushed. For a moment, he had a fantastic view of the sky blazing with fire and lightning, and then his elemental form slammed into something so hard the impact forced him into his corporeal form.

And, fucking Hades, his body *hurt* as if someone had stomped on every one of his bones.

But above him, the whole top of the storm disintegrated, removing the most unstable part of the upper atmosphere from the storm's fuel. Somewhere in the back of his mind, the East Wind whispered that the easternmost fringes of the storm were weakening under the assault.

Devlin had to get up. He had to go at it one more time. He had to find a way to force Eurus into his corporeal form.

Attempting to move felt a lot like that hammer had come in for a second round of bone-breaking, but Devlin pushed through it until he was on hands and knees in a grassy puddle shaped by his body, panting and grinding his teeth through the pain. Gritting it out, he forced himself back into the wind and took off, and while the elemental form shielded him from some of the physical pain, in this form he felt the depletion of his infernal powers more acutely.

Devlin wasn't sure how much more he had.

Back in the sky, he found Chrys and Zeph running one coordinated attack of countering wind and lightning after another. Occasionally, the lightning hit home and destroyed the fringes of the storm, but just as often, Eurus pushed them back and sent them reeling.

Devlin wasn't sure how much *they* had left, either. Which meant he had to act, no matter the consequences.

How's it feel knowing your miserable son is the master of the East Wind? he called. *And that I* stole *it right out from under your nose?*

The baiting worked just as Devlin thought it would. What was left of the face—mostly the bottom of the eyes through the top of the lip, turned toward Devlin as easily as if it had been real. *I feel nothing, because I will shortly have it back*, he boomed as thunder cracked loudly enough to shake the air itself.

Not if I have anything to say about it. Devlin called forth every bit of his remaining power and shot it at his father from his elemental form. He'd gone for another four bombs, and only gotten three—but they hit squarely and true on the flat expanse of the cloudy cheek, exploding apart the middle of the hurricane's wall and causing it to crumble in on itself.

Devlin didn't even try to get out of the way this time. What would've been the point? He barely had the strength left to stay in flight.

The last thing he heard before the wave of heat and explosive force hit him were the cries and panicked voices of Zeph and Chrys.

Please let it have been enough.

BAM!

The concussive blast crashed into him and hurled him into the ground a second time. He hit the blacktop of a street so hard, the road caved in around him.

Pain rushed through and over him so purely he *was* the pain.

There was no pretense of getting up or fighting again. This was it. The only thing he had left, he realized, was his voice. And while he had any resource at his disposal, he had to use it.

"See," he called as loudly as he could—and even that much movement was a sharp agony that went all the way down to his cells. "I'm still the master of the East Wind! And you're still an abusive, psychotic son of a bitch."

And you're just as pathetic as you've always been. What a fucking waste of air you are. And you've always been. The voice echoed through the thunder, but got closer and closer by the end.

"I...am more...than you have ever...been, or could ever...be," Devlin managed, his jaw screaming at the effort to speak, his head in an inescapable vise of pain.

A sudden pressure alighted on his chest, and Devlin had to force the haze away from his vision and focus his eyes. Eurus stood above him—literally, since he had one foot planted on Devlin's sternum. The only thing that wasn't black on his father was the blood streaming from his mouth, eyes, and ears, and the pale white of his skin. His usual sunglasses were long gone, revealing the pitch black of his sclera. It was like looking into the eyes of death itself. Worse, actually, since even Thanatos wasn't anywhere near as evil as the warped god standing on him.

Devlin narrowed his gaze and gestured with a small nod of his head. "Looks like you might be bleeding a little there," he said. Eurus's mangled face twisted into a furious scowl. And Devlin burst out laughing. The laughter was *excruciating*, but he couldn't stop, because it felt so fucking good to just say what he thought to his father, to not hold back, *and* to throw some of his own bullshit back in his face.

Eurus stomped on Devlin's chest so hard that he couldn't breathe. For a moment, he was sure that, if he'd been able to lift his head and look, Eurus's foot would've pounded a hole right through Devlin's ribcage.

Hovering on the edge of consciousness, Devlin couldn't quite make out Chrys's and Zeph's calls and commands. And he couldn't quite comprehend the odd sense of new energies in the sky above them. But what he could understand—about the only thing he could understand—was what the giant, blazing lance of lightning in Eurus's hand meant.

Devlin's time was up.

Annalise, he thought, picturing her porcelain face, pale blond hair, and gray eyes. *This*. This was the only thing he wanted to think about in his final moments. And even though every one of his pains multiplied at the thought of never getting to spend his life with her— because he knew for sure that's what he wanted, ranks or rules be damned—at least he'd known what it felt like to be valued, to be accepted, to be loved.

Because of her.

"You…can't…hurt…me…" Devlin managed. Thinking of Anna, he smiled.

"Think again," Eurus growled, and then he stepped off Devlin's chest and raised the lance.

めめ

Flying through the air, Anna was buoyed by two gods. On the one side was Erebus, who had agreed to throw his might on the side of the Anemoi. On the other was Owen, who'd determined to helped his brothers after Erebus had used his primordial powers to call forth the full strength of Megan's and baby Athan's godhoods so they would awaken immediately. And if Anna hadn't realized the full meaning of power before seeing Erebus use his bare hands to restore Owen's little family back to consciousness, now she did.

And apparently, that power ran through her, too. It was scary and thrilling and still a little unbelievable.

As they neared the edge of a horrendous storm—one that looked a whole lot like that massive supercell storm she'd painted—Anna's attention was pulled in multiple directions. To the devastation of everything on the ground—white-hot terror ripped through at the thought of what her father had gone through. Chrys's and Zeph's efforts to attack Eurus also captured her attention, except some impenetrable force seemed to surround the god and—Anna gasped as her gaze settled on the thing that grabbed and *held* her attention. Devlin. Lying broken on the ground, Eurus's long spear of lightning poised to strike.

No! she cried.

Owen shot forward, throwing a frigid blast of air and ice directly at Eurus. All around the evil god, a frosty dome appeared separating Eurus from the other gods.

He is just as powerful as you said, Erebus said. *But still no match for me. This is going to be a bit rocky. I've got you.*

She barely had time to process that, what with her soul crying out for Devlin, when they crashed into the earth so hard, a shock wave rolled through the ground, lifting it up right under Eurus's feet, causing him to stumble, and, more importantly, causing the bubble of rigid air all around him and Devlin to splinter and crack…and finally burst in a sharp, screaming gust that sent Chrys and Zeph reeling. Owen shouted something Anna couldn't hear.

Back in their physical forms, Erebus roared, "Eclipse the light!"

And everything went suddenly, totally black as an instant and preternatural eclipse of the sun settled over the world.

The only light Anna could perceive was the lightning of Eurus's lance.

And then it started to move on a downward strike.

"Nooo!" she screamed.

Every inch of movement was like a knife cutting into Anna's heart. She couldn't believe they'd come all this way only to watch Devlin die before their very eyes.

"Nooo!" came a mighty scream, followed closely by a wall of cold unlike anything Anna had ever felt.

Back in the human world, Anna couldn't see color anymore, but she still had her excellent night vision. And in the blackness she could just make out the form of a blast of whitish energy swooping in on Eurus and striking at him with something that glinted in the brightness of the lightning.

There was a terrible, ear-splitting howl of agony and anger. And then the lance of lightning sagged awkwardly and fell to the ground. Had Eurus dropped it?

The dark gray of the stormy day returned by slow degrees, enough to reveal Owen standing over Eurus's crumpled body, a bloody knife in his hand, and Chrys and Zeph slowly picking themselves up off the ground in the distance.

Anna made to run, but Erebus restrained her by the shoulders. "Let me, first."

Fisting her hands so tightly her knuckles hurt, Anna watched as Erebus crossed the ruined ground toward Devlin and Eurus. Zephyros scrambled across the debris until he lunged for something on the ground near Eurus. Oh, God, was that a hand? With a shout of victory, Zeph held up a glowing red object. The ring she'd heard so much about? Zephyros slipped it on his finger, and beyond him, clouds began to scatter as if the storm was moving in reverse.

With a glance at the evil god, then at Devlin, then Zephyros, Erebus turned to her and gave her a nod.

Anna tore into a run and came crashing onto her knees next to Devlin. "Oh my God," she said as tears came unbidden to her eyes. "Devlin? Devlin, I'm here." But he couldn't hear her. Because there wasn't a part of him that wasn't bloody, bruised, or swollen. The only thing that gave her the slightest ray of hope was that his eyelids fluttered when she spoke, although only the whites of his eyes were visible. "Oh my God, help him," she said, looking up to the group of gods surrounding her.

But they weren't looking at Devlin. Everyone's eyes were on Eurus.

Anna cut her gaze toward him. She gasped and reared back.

She'd never seen Eurus before, of course, so she didn't know what he'd once looked like. All she knew was that Devlin had said they'd resembled each other. But the god before her looked nothing like Devlin now, because he was aging before her very eyes.

Kneeling at his son's feet and cradling the bloody stump of his arm, Eurus had the salt-and-pepper hair and leathery skin of a seventy-year-old. Now the white hair and gaunt face of a ninety-year-old. Now...*God*...Anna couldn't even guess.

As they all watched, Eurus's skin shrank and his hair thinned and fell out and his bones seemed to cave in. Yet he was still alive. Chrys and Zeph both knelt to watch the process unfold, relief and grief both present on their faces. Eurus groaned and cried and whined as the aging progressed, and inside deep eye sockets, his black eyes begged his brothers for some ease. When it was over, he almost appeared petrified.

All around her, the tension melted out of the other gods' bodies, as if they no longer perceived any danger from the evil god behind so much pain and destruction.

At her side, Owen stood still gripping an iron knife in his shaking hand. "I didn't know *this* would happen," he whispered. "But I'm not sorry."

Zephyros shook his head. "Nor should you be. Besides, losing the ring was just the last straw in his demise. We'd already assured his death when he lost the East Wind." He looked up at the Northern god. "Why are you here, anyway? I mean, thank you, because Chrys and I were about fried, but—"

"Because of Erebus," Owen said, gesturing to the god standing back from the group. "He woke Megan and Athan up so I could be here."

Chrys and Zeph had already taken a knee as Eurus deteriorated, so now they bowed their heads. "My lord," they both called, absolute awe obvious in both their voices.

"Thank you," Zephyros said. "Just being in your presence is an honor. Receiving your assistance is a debt I will forever try to repay."

Erebus slowly walked forward, as if he were on a casual Sunday stroll, not sidestepping trash and roofing and downed tree limbs. "Your gratitude is appreciated but I count no debt. I was merely helping my daughter." Crouching beside Anna, Erebus brushed her tears away with his knuckles and grasped her hand. He pressed a kiss to the back of it and then said, "Is this the god you love?" He nodded to Devlin.

Anna nodded. "Yes," she said around the knot of tears in her throat. "With all my heart."

"Then I will help him," he said. Holding his hands over Devlin's broken body, Erebus's gaze went unfocused as he concentrated. A thin, translucent light dropped down from his palms to cover Devlin and she heard a soft bubbling noise. The sound got louder and louder until water seeped from the ground below Devlin's body and slowly but surely covered him.

Anna lunged, her mind filled with the image of Devlin drowning before her.

Someone caught her by the shoulders. "It's okay," Owen said, holding her back. "This is a good thing." His mismatched gaze cut from her to Zephyros and Chrys. "It's the Acheron. He's called forth the Acheron…*here*." Awe was plain in his voice.

Zeph nodded. "I recognize the smell of it," he said, wonder and respect filling his expression.

"What's the Acheron?" Anna asked, not understanding why the other gods were acting that way.

"One of the infernal rivers of the Underworld," Owen said, giving her a reassuring smile. "And one of the strongest healing powers that exists in the entire world. Trust me."

Anna's gaze tore back to Devlin, now surrounded in a pool of water that covered every part of him except a small ring of his face.

"How long does it take?" she whispered.

But no one answered.

Anna was absolutely dying to touch Devlin, but she didn't want to mess up whatever Erebus was trying to do.

Five minutes passed. Ten. Maybe an hour. And all that time, Erebus called forth the magical waters, and all the gods kept vigil around the one who, not long ago, none of them had accepted. And that made Anna realize that Devlin's life had changed every bit as much as hers over the past few days.

"You have to live, Devlin," she said. Because she loved him so much she thought her chest might crack open at the force of it.

Long minutes later—Anna didn't know how long because she was silently praying for Devlin's life—his hand twitched. A small splash of water, and then nothing.

"Devlin?" she called, hovering as close to him and the odd light emanating from Erebus's hands as she could. "Devlin, it's Anna. It's Annalise. I'm here. Come back." His hand twitched again. A small cry spilled from her throat. "Devlin," she whispered.

His lips moved as if he were trying to speak, but no sound came out. And then his eyelids eased open. "Anna," he said so quietly it almost didn't make a sound. But that was all she needed. Anna started laughing and crying and the others joined her, clasping hands and clapping one another on the back. A small celebration of the thwarted tragedy that might've been Devlin's death.

Anna turned to Erebus as he lowered his hands and sat back on his heels. "Thank you so much." And she threw herself at him and hugged him tight.

Erebus caught her with an *oomph*, which made Anna laugh again because he was like the most powerful god ever and yet she'd tackled him so hard and unexpectedly that she'd knocked the air out of him. Erebus chuckled and embraced her back. "Your happiness is its own reward, my daughter," he said, a shadow surrounding him in the growing daylight.

Slowly, the water receded, leaving not only Devlin's skin rejuvenated, but his clothing, too, as if the waters had left him a wholly new man. The moment the water was gone, Devlin's entire body dried instantly. Finally, slowly, Devlin sat up in the middle of a huge, deep, body-shaped crater in the asphalt.

Without a word or a glance anywhere else, his arms came around Anna. He hauled her into his lap and crushed her body to his. "I thought I was going to have to leave you," he said against her neck.

"Me too," she said, crying on his brand-new gray shirt. "I love you." She lifted her gaze to his.

"I love you, too, Annalise. You are my forever and always. Would you be mine?"

"Yes." The word wasn't even fully formed when Devlin's lips crashed down on hers. The kiss was a celebration, a reunion, a coming together of souls. When they finally broke apart, Devlin crushed her to him again, like he didn't want to let her go.

And Anna couldn't have been more content.

Against her, Devlin went rigid. "What…" He shook his head. "Is that…"

Anna pulled away and followed his gaze to the petrified shell of his father's body. "Your father. He nearly killed you, but they stopped him," she said, looking at the gods standing in a ring around them.

Devlin helped Anna to her feet and then rose himself, coming face-to-face with Erebus. His skin paled and he dropped to a knee. "My lord," he said, his voice tight.

Erebus cocked his head to the side. "Devlin. How do you know me?"

Anna wondered that, too.

Head still bowed, Devlin said, "Anna's energy signature resembles yours."

"Indeed," Erebus said, staring down at him. "Look at me." Slowly, Devlin raised his face. "Did you tell my son Thanatos you and I were in an alliance?"

Anna's gaze glanced between them. In the midst of everything else, she'd nearly forgotten Erebus mentioning this earlier.

Devlin grimaced, but nodded. "Yes, to save my family. I take responsibility for the lie. Are you taking me to Thanatos now?"

Anna gasped. "Ereb—"

The primordial god raised a hand that had her swallowing her words. Erebus tilted his head and narrowed his gaze. An eternity passed while Anna waited for his reply. He couldn't have brought Devlin back to life just to see him punished, could he? Finally, Erebus said, "No. Because the lie saved not only your family, but mine. And without you finding her, I would never have known Annalise existed."

Relief rushed through Anna so hard she felt a little dizzy, and the look on Devlin's face told her he felt the same way.

Erebus extended a hand. "Rise, son."

Devlin's gaze went wide as he accepted the older god's hand and rose.

"Do you promise to take care of her?"

Devlin's reply was instant and strong. "On my life."

Erebus nodded. Then he extended Devlin a hand.

Eyes going wide, Devlin stared at Erebus's offering, and then he grasped it and rose to his feet. Erebus tugged him in and said, "You *are* worthy."

Tears pricked at the backs of Anna's eyes, but they were born of happiness, especially given the look on Devlin's face. Like the satisfaction of a man finally given a morsel to eat after years of starvation.

For a moment, Devlin gathered himself, and then he turned to the husk of a god still kneeling on the ground before them. Crouching right in front of Eurus, Devlin stared at the god for a long time, and then he released a sigh. "Be free of this life you have so hated. I hope you find some peace."

No one would've blamed Devlin, least of all Anna, had his parting words been filled with vengeance and accusation. But her god had a good heart and a kind soul, and it made Anna fall in love with him even more.

And then Devlin tilted his head back and heaved a deep breath. When he released it, a strong, cool breeze surged from behind them. Slowly, bits of Eurus floated away on the wind. Zephyros joined him, and the breeze strengthened. Chrys fell in line next, then Owen. And together, the four gods joined their winds and scattered Eurus to the corners of the world.

Amazed, Anna glanced at Erebus, who gave her a nod and pulled her in against his side.

By the time they were done, most of the clouds of the hurricane had scattered, leaving the hesitant light of the sun just peeking through after a storm.

"It's finally over," Zephyros said, his voice tight.

As Devlin rose and nodded, Zeph threw an arm around him.

The Anemoi stood there together for a long time, as if they could still see the remains of their fallen brother drifting off on the wind.

When she couldn't stand the distance any longer, she came up behind Devlin, laid her head on his back, and wrapped her arms around his stomach.

He turned in her arms and kissed her forehead. "None of this would've been possible without you. You saved me, and I don't just mean here," he said, nodding at the crater in the road behind her. "I love you, Annalise Fallston."

Her heart couldn't have been any fuller, even as an old, familiar ache settled into her back and chest. Proving that what Iris had said about the curse was true. "I love you, too."

"Annalise?" Erebus said.

She turned to him, surprised to see such a sad expression on his shadowy face. "Yes?"

"We should return to the Realm of the Gods now."

"I know, but first I need to find—"

He shook his head. "He's waiting for you."

She frowned. "What?"

"He's waiting to say good-bye."

೫✿೮

It was the only time Anna had ever flown in the wind that she hadn't enjoyed the experience. Because it was taking too long, yet at the same time, it was going by too fast. Her father being in the Realm of the Gods waiting for her could only mean one thing.

And her heart was shattered.

How could this have happened? How could they have defeated Eurus, saved Devlin, and lost her father? Where was the justice in that?

Finally, Aeolus's compound—or Zephyros's, now—came into view, but the restoration of her colored vision held no joy for her, because it only meant she was that much closer to having to say good-bye to her father for the very last time.

They entered the Hall of the Winds and found a group of people awaiting their return, just like before. Except this time, everyone was happy. Because a tall man with brown hair was talking a mile a minute and telling stories that had everyone laughing out loud.

Anna came back into her body—there was no adjustment time at all anymore—and saw the splendorous room in full color. It took her ears less than ten seconds to realize the voice telling the story of how Anna had once caused a blackout in a hotel when she was six and having a temper tantrum was her father.

"Daddy?" she asked, stepping closer, but not believing what she was seeing or hearing.

He turned around, and Anna gasped. The father of her youth stood before her. Twenty years younger, happy, talkative, and fully in his right mind. "There she is," he said, holding out his arms.

Anna ran into his embrace. "I'm so sorry," she said, trying and failing to hold back a sob.

"There, there," he said, stroking her hair. "You have nothing to be sorry for."

She pulled back and looked into his kind eyes. "If I had been there—"

"Then you might've been lost, too."

Another thought crashed into Anna's brain, stealing her breath. "Evan and Jake—"

"Are both fine. Injured, but they'll be good as new. They worked so hard to save me. Those god fellas, too." Her dad shrugged. "But I was ready to go." He held out his arms and grinned that old grin she remembered so well. "And look at me now."

"Daddy," she said, torn between sadness at his loss and happiness at how he was now. Just the way he used to be.

"You're gonna be just fine, Annalise. You have this big family here who will take care of you." He smiled and squeezed her hands.

"You're my family."

"Of course I am. But so are they." He nodded to the group around them.

Amazement at his easy acceptance of all this flashed through her. "You know, then? About all this, I mean?"

"Your mother and I always knew something was different about you, Annalise. No one else in our family has your pale blond hair, or gray eyes, or is color-blind. You know I'm hard-pressed to even draw a stick figure, let alone create the amazing art that has always come so naturally to you. Your mother used to joke that she would've thought the angels had dropped you in a basket on our doorstep if she hadn't given birth to you herself. Miss Iris over here filled me in," he said, smiling at the pale-haired goddess Anna so much resembled. "So now I know."

The moment he spoke the words, Anna recalled the sound of her mother's voice saying that jokingly but with such affection. "You're still my dad."

He leaned down and kissed her forehead. "You better believe it. Nothing could ever change that. Now, introduce me to all these fine folks," he said in his old, jovial style.

She went around the room making introductions, her heart so, so happy to have this moment with him, but absolutely dreading saying good-bye. Why couldn't she have *this* forever? Couldn't he be saved the way Devlin and Megan and the baby had been?

Finally, she came around to Erebus and Devlin, whom she'd saved for last. She stepped in front of her biological father, and seeing the two men face off was like seeing two worlds collide. Except, the meeting wasn't a collision, it was gentle, friendly, respectful. "Daddy," Anna said, "This is Erebus. My, uh—"

"Your biological father," he said, extending his hand. "Pleasure to meet you, sir. And might I say it's been an honor to be in Anna's life."

Anna simply couldn't hold back the tears anymore.

Erebus returned the shake with a warm smile. "You've raised a beautiful, accomplished woman. I'm honored to know you, Mr. Fallston."

"And thank you for making this possible," Dad said, waving at the room around them.

Anna blinked. "Wait. What?"

"Oh, you didn't know?" her father said. "After I passed, Erebus guided my soul back here."

Anna's gaze cut between her fathers, and in that moment she couldn't decide which one she loved more. And the best thing about it—she didn't have to decide. She could love them both, and she did. "Thank you," she managed.

Erebus bowed. "My pleasure, Annalise."

"And who's this young man, then? Not Michael," Dad said with a wink.

Devlin blanched. "No sir. And I apologize for—"

"For what? Making an old, confused man feel better?" He shook his head. "It was a great kindness."

"Daddy, this is Devlin. My…uh…" Anna looked among the three men as her tongue got tangled on the words.

"Groom-to-be, sirs," Devlin said, glancing at Dad, then Erebus. "That is, if I have your blessing."

Anna's face went hot. *Groom-to-be?* He was going to…he was asking for… Anna put her hand to her forehead.

"Hot damn, Devlin," Dad said, extending his hand and pulling Devlin into a hug once he held it. "Now I really know my girl is cared for."

Devlin pulled back wearing something close to a smile. "Our girl, sir."

"Ha!" her father laughed. "I like you, kid. You take good care of her, treat her right, make her laugh plenty, and say 'yes' to everything she wants. I was married a lot of years, and I'm telling you that's the formula to success." Dad clapped him on the shoulder, and Anna couldn't help but chuckle.

"Yes, sir," Devlin said, his smile growing. And, oh, *God*, the happiness shining from his eyes made Devlin almost too gorgeous to look at. And he was all hers. He turned all that happiness on her, causing Anna's heart to skip in her chest. Then he took her hands and knelt in front of her. "Annalise Fallston, you are my savior, my heart, and my light. I love you more than I ever thought possible, and I cherish you as much as any god has ever cherished any goddess. Would you do me the greatest honor of my very long life and become my wife?"

Anna's heart beat so hard and so fast she was almost light-headed. Or maybe that was the incredible joy flowing through her and lifting her up. She looked from Devlin's expectant face to her father, who was absolutely beaming with pride and joy, to Erebus's, who gave her a nod and a smile. In that moment, Anna felt so surrounded by love and support that every bit of sadness and guilt fled, leaving only a woman who didn't know how she'd gotten so lucky, but who was beyond grateful.

"Um. Anna?" Devlin said.

"Oh my God," she said, squeezing his hand to her chest. "I'm sorry. I'm just so happy, I blissed out for a minute." Everyone chuckled, including Devlin. "It would make me the happiest woman ever. Yes."

And that was the first time Anna ever saw Devlin truly, freely, joyously smile.

In a fast motion, he rose to his feet, lifted her in his arms, and kissed her right there in front of two fathers, a mother, and a bunch of…well, in-laws, she supposed. Not that she was paying them any mind. Because just then, she was lost in the ecstasy of her eastern god and the deep satisfaction at bringing him the same joy he brought her.

The best part? For her and Devlin, happily ever after was going to last for all eternity.

Epilogue

If Annalise Fallston thought rough, tough Devlin Eston was hot, that guy was nothing compared with the god at the height of his seasonal power standing at an altar waiting for *her* to be his forever and wearing an all-black tux. Holy hell, Anna could barely stand it in all the best ways.

Standing at the end of the aisle, Anna smiled up at Erebus, her dashing divine father who gave Devlin a run for his money in the handsome department. Almost.

"Garrett would be so proud of you," he said with a smile. "In fact, I know he is."

Anna blinked back tears and managed a "thank you." The only thing that could've made this day anymore perfect was if her human dad had been able to be there, too. But his soul had moved on to peaceful rest after they'd said their good-byes that day in the Hall of the Winds. She'd been so lucky to have that chance that she couldn't bring herself to regret anything about the way that had worked out—the way Erebus had *made* it work out.

"Before we make this little trip, I have a present for you," he said.

Anna grinned and glanced at Devlin. "Now?"

"Yes," he said. "I want you to know that Iris and I had your curse repealed."

Gasping, Anna's hands flew to her chest. Not that she wanted to *live* in the human realm, but if this was true she and Devlin could see the world together. It gave them options that her restriction to the Realm of the Gods did not. "What? How?"

"We paid Iris's elders a visit. The fears that drove the curse no longer exist, at least not for most. And I was"—he gestured with his hand—"persuasive."

Anna pressed her hand to her mouth and blinked back tears. "Thank you," she whispered. "Oh my God, I have to tell Devlin."

Erebus leaned down and kissed her cheek. "He knows."

Anna's mouth dropped open and she cut a disbelieving glance toward her groom, who wore the most adoring smile. She laughed.

"Ready?" Erebus asked, smiling broadly.

She nodded. "A hundred percent yes."

To the side of the altar, a harpist began to play. Anna wasn't sure where the waiflike musician had come from, only that Iris had told Anna not to worry about a thing and made all the arrangements like the loving mother she was.

Taking a deep breath, Anna started down the outdoor aisle covered with big, jewel-toned leaves that matched the reds, golds, coppers, and bronzes in the sash on her otherwise white gown. The towering trees around them absolutely blazed with fall color, just like in Anna's painting, and it made her so completely happy. Not just because it was so gorgeous she would never forget it, but also because Devlin's ascension to the East Wind had brought his entire realm back to life.

Apparently, everything here in the Eastern Realm had once been gray and brown and in a state of perpetual decay. But when Devlin had returned to the East to rescue his brother Alastor from Eurus's dungeon, he'd found that Eurus's evil enchantments had died with him. So the trees danced with the colors of his season and all the old dark magic of his childhood home had disappeared—including the traps preventing Alastor's escape.

Anna's gaze cut to the front row, where the god who looked so much like Devlin sat, quiet and shy. Alastor didn't speak very much, he was jumpy in that same way that Devlin used to be, but much worse, and he'd spent much of the past month recuperating, even after Erebus had taken him personally to soak in the waters of the Acheron. But he was alive and healthy and could be very sweet when he opened up. Anna had loved him from the first moment he'd returned to Zephyros's compound. Because the sheer joy and relief on Devlin's face had told her how very important Alastor was to the man she planned to love for all time.

Next to Alastor sat Zephyros and Ella, which pleased Anna to no end. In the past month's time, Zephyros had taken Alastor under his wing, helping him master the West Wind and regain his confidence. Ella had helped every step of the way and was able to draw Alastor into conversation almost more than Devlin. Devlin and Zeph's relationship had improved by whole worlds before Alastor's rescue, but the way Zeph had cared for Alastor these past weeks had bonded the three men in an amazing way no one could've ever seen. Anna couldn't have been happier for all of them.

Breathing in the incredible, crisp air on this beautiful fall day, Anna smiled at Megan, Owen, and the boys. Seeing them now, it was almost hard to believe what had nearly happened a month ago, but she was so happy to see the little family together and thriving. She waved at Teddy as he called out her name at a volume that made everybody laugh.

In the row ahead of them sat Laney and Chrysander, who waggled his eyebrows at her when she glanced his way, making her laugh. The more she got to know him, the more she realized what a huge goofball—and sweetheart—the god was. Laney remained the only human among them, but because of the immortality she'd won and her unique powers of prophecy, Zephyros had negotiated with the Olympians for a special dispensation that allowed her to live in the Realm of the Gods if she wanted. She and Chrys hadn't decided exactly what to do yet, because Laney had a beautiful horse farm back home that she absolutely loved. The place needed a lot of work after the hurricane, which Seth was overseeing, so right now they were taking it day by day.

Laney had confided in Anna that, in part, she was worried about choosing to leave her home because that would leave Seth alone. But his status as a griffin meant he could visit the Realm of the Gods. And given the way Anna sometimes caught her mother and Seth staring at each other, Anna wasn't sure Seth was going to be single for that much longer.

Everywhere Anna looked, she found the most incredible happiness shining back at her. As she reached the altar, it was a moment of such pure and perfect joy that she turned and stared at the small gathering so she could memorize every detail of it for all time. Once she had it imprinted on her mind's eye, she turned to the most handsome groom any bride had ever had.

As she and Devlin grasped hands and faced one another, Iris took up a position behind Anna and Erebus stood up for Devlin. And there in front of their large family, they exchanged words of love and honor and commitment.

And all the hearts of the Anemoi were finally, totally in love and at peace.

ACKNOWLEDGMENTS

If you are reading this, you have followed me on an amazing journey that has taken me to the end of my very first romantic series. But it's been so much more than that, too. It's been a labor of love between me and my wonderful editor Heather Howland, who believed in the Hearts of the Anemoi from the very first moment I described it to her in a blog's comment section (and who gave me these fantastic covers!). It's been a wonderful partnership between me and amazing author friends Christi Barth, Lea Nolan, and Stephanie Dray, who brainstormed and plotted and held my hand along the way. The series would never have been anything like it is without Christi's expert comments on books two through four. And it's also been a wonderfully fun experience I've shared with readers like you, who were always what it was all about.

Because of you, I got to bring Owen and Zephyros and Chrysander and Devlin to life. You cheered with me when Owen returned and Ella lived and Laney met Hephaestus and got to make her choice. And you cried with me (and some of you yelled, too, and that's okay because I understood why!) when we had to say good-bye to Boreas. Along the way, you voted for these books in contests and told me how much you loved them and how much you wanted more.

And you made it one of the most amazing experiences of my

career.

I also must give thanks to my amazing family for always supporting me and cheering me on, even when the workdays grew long and Mom got a little deadline-crazed. I couldn't do any of this without you.

So, for one last time, I say thank you. And long live the Anemoi!

~LK

Discover Laura Kaye's
Heart of the Anemoi *Series*

NORTH OF NEED

Her tears called a powerful snow god to life, but only her love can grant the humanity he craves...

Hoping to escape the memories of her late husband, Megan Snow builds a snow family—and collapses in tears at the sight of what she'll never have. Called to life by the power of those tears, snow god Owen Winters appears unconscious on her doorstep. As she nurses him to health, Megan is drawn to Owen, believing he's a Christmas miracle. But this miracle comes with an expiration date, and Megan must let go of her grief or lose Owen forever.

WEST OF WANT

Betrayal is all he's ever known, but in her, he'll find a love strong enough to be trusted...

Zephyros Martius is the Supreme God of the West Wind and Spring, but being the strongest Anemoi hasn't protected him from betrayal and loss. When Zeph's heartbreak whips up a storm that shipwrecks human Marcella Raines, his guilt forces him to save her. Ella's honesty, empathy, and unique, calming influence leave Zeph wanting... *everything*. When Eurus threatens her, she and Zeph struggle to let go of the past, defend their future, and embrace what they most want—a love that can be trusted.

SOUTH OF SURRENDER

*She's the only one who can see through his golden boy façade to
the broken god within...*

Chrysander Notos, Supreme God of the South Wind and Summer, is
on a mission to save his brother from a death sentence. But when he's
injured in a fight that triggers vicious summer storms that threaten
the mortal realm, Chrys finds himself at the mercy of mortal Laney
Summerlyn. As they surrender to the passion flaring between them,
immortal enemies close in, forcing Chrys to choose between his
brother and the only woman who's ever loved the real him.

Other Entangled books by Laura Kaye

HER FORBIDDEN HERO
a Heroes novel

Former Army Special Forces Sgt. Marco Vieri has never thought of
Alyssa Scott as more than his best friend's little sister, but her return
home changes that. Now that she's back in his life, healing wounds
he never thought would heal, will he succumb to the forbidden
temptation she presents one touch at a time?

ONE NIGHT WITH A HERO
a Heroes novel

After growing up with an abusive, alcoholic father, Army Special
Forces Sgt. Brady Scott vowed never to have a family of his own.
But when a one-night stand with new neighbor Joss Daniels leads to
an unexpected pregnancy, can he let go of his past and create a new
future with Joss?

Introducing a new series by romantic suspense author Tonya Burrows

"A super sexy thrill ride guaranteed to make you swoon!"
- *New York Times* Bestselling Author Laura Kaye

SEAL OF HONOR
a HORNET novel

When Navy Seal Gabe Bristow's prestigious career comes to a crashing halt, he's offered the chance to command a private hostage rescue team. . It seems like a good deal—until he meets his new team: a drunk Cajun linguist, a boy-genius CIA threat analyst, an FBI negotiator with mob ties, a cowboy medic, and an EOD expert as volatile as the bombs he defuses. And then there's the sexy, frustratingly impulsive Audrey Van Amee. She's determined to help rescue her brother—or drive Gabe crazy. God help him if he can't bring her brother back alive, because Gabe's finally found something worth living for.

HONOR RECLAIMED
a HORNET novel

An interview with a runaway Afghani child bride leads photojournalist Phoebe Leighton to an arms deal involving a powerful bomb. Forming an unlikely alliance with a team of military and government delinquents called HORNET, she meets Seth, a former Marine sniper with PTSD, who ignites passions within her she thought long dead. Racing against the clock, Seth, Phoebe, and the rest of HORNET struggle to stop the bomb before it reaches its final destination: The United States.

Explore more of Entangled's titles...

TOUCH OF THE ANGEL
a Demons of Infernum novel by Rosalie Lario

Interdimensional bounty hunter Ronin Meyers is on the trail of an incubus who's using succubi as murder weapons. Failure means a one-way ticket back to the hellish Infernum, so when he captures Amara, the beautiful succubus who stole his heart—and nearly his life—during the most mind-blowing hour of his existence, he knows he's screwed. To find salvation, they must bring down the madman hell-bent on destroying everything—and everyone—they love. If he doesn't kill Ronin and Amara first. a Demons of Infernum novel by Rosalie Lario

TANGLED HEARTS
a Highland Hearts novel by Heather McCollum

Pandora Wyatt knows trying to rescue her surrogate father before he's executed will be difficult, but she doesn't expect to have her life saved by the sexy Highland warrior Ewan Brody. After tricking him in to playing her husband at King Henry's court, Ewan learns Pandora is not only a witch, but also a pirate—and possibly a traitor's daughter. When dark secrets lead them to the real traitor of the Tudor court, Ewan and Pandora may lose more than just their hearts.

SUNROPER
a Goddesses Rising novel by Natalie J. Damschroder

Marley Canton possess the ability to nullify power in those who aren't supposed to have it. Gage Samargo wants to cut off his younger brother's dangerous power source. As they track down a goddess who's gone insane with power from the sun, Gage falls for Marley's sharp wit and intense desire to right wrongs. But once he discovers that every time she nullifies someone she takes on some of the goddess's insanity, is it too late to back away?

FIGHTING LOVE
by Abby Niles

Tommy "Lightning" Sparks is a former Middleweight champion and confirmed bachelor. His best friend Julie Rogers is a veterinarian who has secretly been in love with him since she was ten. A devastating fire brings them together, but will his playboy ways and her time spent with another fighter tear them a part? Can two childhood friends make a relationship work, or will they lose everything because they stopped FIGHTING LOVE.

DYED AND GONE
by Beth Yarnall

Hairstylist Azalea March is looking forward to a wild weekend in Las Vegas. But fun turns to drama when Dhane, the biggest celeb of the hair-styling world, is found dead and her friend Vivian confesses to the murder. Azalea knows Viviandidn't do it. Now she has to convince Alex, the sexy detective from her past, to help her comb through clues more twisted than a spiral perm. But proving Vivian's innocence turns out to be more difficult than transforming a brunette into a blonde.

BLACK WIDOW DEMON
a Demon Outlaws novel by Paula Altenburg

Half-demon Raven is nearly executed on the orders of her fundamentalist stepfather. She escapes the burning stake using her otherworldly gifts with the help of a mortal stranger—retired assassin Blade. But while she's set on revenge, Blade wants redemption. To get it, he must deliver her into the hands of loved ones. But as Blade's sense of duty becomes something more, and threats—both mortal and immortal—stalk the woman he can't abandon, he could very well fall back into the life he's trying so hard to escape.